MURDER AND A MISSING MANUSCRIPT

RICHARD TYLER JORDAN

OLIVERHEBERBOOKS

PUBLISHER'S NOTE: This is a work of fiction. Names, characters, places, and incidents either are the product of the author's imagination or are used fictitiously. Any resemblance to actual persons, living or dead, business establishments, events, or locales is entirely coincidental.

Murder and a Missing Manuscript Copyright 2025 © Richard Tyler Jordan

Cover art by Dar Albert at Wicked Smart Designs

Published by Oliver-Heber Books

0 9 8 7 6 5 4 3 2 1

For Neil and Merrill Crabtree-Livesey
(With gratitude for your unwavering support and cherished friendship.)

1

TWO MONTHS AGO ...

The village library in Abbots Clover, England, was supposed to be a haven of tranquility. For over two centuries, the Georgian building, with its ivy-covered stone walls and large, multipaned windows, welcomed readers to escape into the embrace of books.

Rose Harding was the librarian. She looked the way you might picture a librarian—if you had a simplistic and narrow-minded view of how librarians should look. She had a no-nonsense backbone, a strict sense of duty, and a by-the-book (literally) attitude toward her career. Her silver-white hair was neatly pulled back, knotted into a tight bun, and tied with a pink ribbon. Fake-tortoiseshell-frame glasses, which she frequently adjusted with an unconscious touch, were perched on the bridge of her nose. She wore high-collared blouses fastened at the top by a family heirloom cameo pin. Her demeanor was almost always composed (except if she found a wad of chewing gum stuck under a chair or reading table—then look out because that would make her go bat**** ballistic!). Rose exuded an air of intimidation and commanded, if not respect, at least guarded manners from those around her.

She hadn't planned on becoming a librarian. Rose had dreamed of being a famous writer like Emily Brontë (but without the tuberculosis). However, the Fickle Finger of Fate had led her down a less *primrosy* path. It had begun with a scathing critique from her college creative writing instructor—a woman who wielded red ink like a broadsword. Her verdict on one of Rose's short stories had struck with surgical cruelty: "Merely a collection of words, devoid of meaning or cumulative value." It wasn't a critique; it was a complete evisceration. Rose's fragile confidence had crumbled under the weight of those unyielding words. Decades later, she could still recite them—verbatim. Their power to crush her was undiminished by time.

What followed were years of quiet resignation, days that blurred into one another in a haze of uneventful tedium. Until, somehow, Rose found herself with no loftier ambition than to collect enough stamps on her Whisker Whackers Rodent Exterminators loyalty card to earn a complimentary vermin inspection for her cottage. Pathetic. It was hardly the life she'd dreamed of.

Occasionally, when the library was quiet—before opening or after closing—Rose would stand before the shelves, glaring at titles by Colleen Hoover, Stephen King, and Ben Tyler. She'd rant under her breath: "You think you're so special, don't you? You're immortalized in print while I linger here like a literary zombie with nothing but unpublished dreams. I pictured my books on these shelves. Now I'm dusting *your* covers, straightening *your* spines, and shelving *your* stories instead of writing my own."

Then, with a sigh, she'd admit the truth: "Yeah, I know ... that's all on me."

Still, the Abbots Clover Library was her sanctuary—a bibliophile's paradise where she could drown her unfulfilled ambitions in an endless sea of other people's words. *If you could have been, you would have been,* she often told herself, parroting her mother's blunt wisdom. Some cosmic committee had clearly vetoed her dreams, and Rose had grudgingly accepted the verdict. On the bright side, at least she wasn't inspecting sewers or stunning animals in a slaughterhouse for a living. That small silver lining made shelving romance novels and tolerating the occasional gum-popping teenager almost feel like destiny's consolation prize.

The clock was ticking toward six p.m., and Rose quietly announced to the reading room: "Attention, please. The library will be closing in fifteen minutes. Bring any items you wish to borrow to the lending desk. Thank you." How many times had she said the same thing over the past twenty-five-plus years? She once calculated 6,522 (including six leap years and minus holidays). As the last visitor of the day left the library, Rose locked the heavy, solid oak door and glanced at the antique clock on the wall. She relished these last moments of solitude each evening. The day's bustle had faded, and she was alone in the literary domain she ruled. The familiar scent of aged paper and leather-bound volumes created a soothing atmosphere that made all her cares, and the outside world feel distant.

She really didn't want to go home to her cottage on the outskirts of the village. It was a humdrum little place. Sure, the love of her life, Danny, was waiting for her. But Danny was a cat. She'd named him after her secret romantic movie-star crush, Dan Stevens. *Shhh!* Rose adored everything about Dan Stevens, especially his audiobook narrations. She melted into a puddle of hormonal chaos whenever his velvety voice breathed life into the *Frankenstein* audiobook. In her imagination, his piercing blue eyes locked onto hers as he read, every word steeped in gothic intensity, as if he were channeling all his smoldering passion directly at her—and into her. (And no, never in a million trillion years, even under severe torture, would she ever admit to the wildly inappropriate fantasies these moments inspired. Let's say she'd given *"It's alive!"* an entirely new—and erotic—meaning.)

As Rose moved about the silent reading room, tidying up, she thought of Abbots Clover's upcoming literary festival—always a highlight of her year—and only days away. Colorful banners publicizing the event were strung across the village square, fluttering in the springtime breeze. A vacant cow pasture would soon be transformed into a literary marketplace occupied by tents and vendors' stalls selling rare and second-hand books, literary-themed T-shirts and coffee mugs, and gourmet street food. Self-published authors, as well as renowned writers from all over England, would intermingle with readers.

Of course, the library—and the Bound to Read bookstore and coffee shop across the street—would be the festival's heart, hosting readings, book signings, discussions with authors, and storytelling for children.

Deeply involved in the festival's planning and execution, Rose loved the clout she held—coordinating with authors, organizing their schedules, and ensuring the library and bookshop were ready to welcome the influx of book lovers.

This year, the event would be especially momentous and unlike any other in Abbots Clover's history because Rose had the honor of overseeing the unveiling of the literary find of the century: *Vanity and Virtue,* the handwritten, unpublished book manuscript by Abigail Townsend, an obscure but admired nineteenth-century novelist who had lived in the area.

This extraordinary treasure had been discovered almost by accident, hidden in the attic at nearby Thistlethorne Lodge, the castle inherited by iconic American comedienne and TV star Polly Pepper. The manuscript, unseen for over two centuries, promised to shed new light on Townsend's enigmatic life and work, potentially revolutionizing the study of English literature altogether. Its discovery was nothing short of a literary miracle —comparable to finding a lost diary by Emily Dickinson—and would draw scholars of classic literature from around the world, eager to immerse themselves in Townsend's previously unknown words.

However, not everyone shared the excitement. Controversy had already shrouded the event, fueled by the simmering rage of Arthur Townsend, Abigail's twenty-first-century descendant. He believed the manuscript rightfully belonged to him and his family—not to Polly *Hollywood-TV-star* Pepper. Arthur Townsend argued it was a family heirloom, an unjustly appropriated piece of their history. A feud had ignited, adding a layer of tension to the otherwise celebratory festival atmosphere, casting Polly and the library in a contentious role against him. Some of the villagers, torn between praise for Polly's discovery and sympathy for Abigail Townsend's descendant, couldn't help but feel the tension of the unfolding drama.

But Rose didn't want to think about that now as she gathered up stray books left on tables and chairs. She straightened misaligned rows on shelves, switched off the reading lamps, and at her lending desk, she sorted and cataloged the day's harvest of returned books.

An hour later, as she turned off the lights in the main reading room, Rose was brought to a sudden standstill by an unexpected sound that broke through the otherwise silent library. It sounded like a soft thud coming from the storage room down the hallway. "Don't tell me that darn badger's gotten in again." She remembered the mess the animal had made only a few weeks earlier. "I've told the girls to keep the window shut!"

Setting her handbag on the lending desk, she moved toward the source of the sound. On high alert, Rose stopped before the storage room door and listened.

Silence.

Rose didn't want to startle the animal—they could be vicious if frightened or cornered. She cautiously turned the doorknob and pushed open the door. She flipped the light switch on the wall and saw a discouraging sight. *Oh, phooey!*

The room, which she always kept orderly despite the array of miscellaneous supplies, audio-visual equipment, and plastic bins filled with old magazines and newspapers, was a mess. "Darn you," she huffed and automatically glanced at the window. But the window was closed. Her eyes instantly darted to the back door, which was ajar. *That's how you got in!*

But as she started toward the door, her eyes were drawn to a shattering sight: the antique safe—a hulking, black behemoth of solid iron with a formidable combination lock—was wide open.

Once a guardian of fortunes in the Trust & Savings bank, its imposing presence dominated the room. Despite its age, it still exuded unyielding strength, daring anyone to challenge its security. Yet, to her disbelief, the seemingly impenetrable strongbox stood wide open, revealing a dark, empty interior.

"The manuscript!" Rose cried, her hands covering her mouth in shock and confusion as she raced to the safe. Abigail Townsend's long-lost and only recently rediscovered *Vanity and Virtue* manuscript—was gone.

Rose was enveloped in a wave of panic that nearly knocked her off balance. *Vanity and Virtue* was more than an important piece of literary history, it was a priceless artifact, and she was responsible for its security. Her heart pounded as the magnitude of the catastrophe set in. *This isn't possible!*

What she saw next was another sucker punch to the gut, leaving her momentarily paralyzed with terror. In a shadowy corner of the room, beside a box of used books to be sold at the festival, lay an even more harrowing sight: Dr. Jonathan Fieldstone—the eminent manuscript expert from the British Library in London—was lying still on the floor, his lifeless eyes wide open, staring at—nothing. He'd spent the past few weeks in this room, diligently studying and authenticating the work of Abigail Townsend.

Rose's mind raced in a torrent of disbelief and horror. Desperation clawed at her as her eyes darted from Dr. Fieldstone's still form to the safe and back again. She had to call for help! But at that moment, the two losses weighed so heavily on her that she was immobilized. The room seemed to close in around her. Every shape and shadow grew more menacing. Rose remembered Dr. Fieldstone's voice and the pedantic, scholarly discussions they'd had. His presence had brought a sense of gravitas to the library. Now, his inert body brought an overwhelming sense of doom.

Rose felt the weight of the calamity pressing down on her. Her pulse raced, and her body trembled as she reached out for the doorframe for support. Her legs felt like lead as she staggered backward to the main reading room, each step a battle against the paralyzing terror that gripped her.

Finally reaching the lending desk, she ransacked her handbag to find her phone. Her fingers quivered as she tapped the emergency services number: 999.

"Help ...!
"The library ...!
"A body ...!
"A dead body ...!
"Maybe ... murdered ...!"

2

ONE MONTH EARLIER …

Polly Pepper, American television comedy legend and faded Hollywood star now living in England, was in a *mood*.

Not a moping-around-because-she-didn't-have-anybody-to-play-with *mood*. Nor a steam-shooting-from-her-ears-because-a-critic-trashed-one-of-her-performances *mood*. Today's grumpiness was more subtle.

But her adult-and-still-living-at-home son, Tim, knew this particular air of long-faced misery. As did Tiara, Polly's personal maid and best chum/confidante. It was the same disposition she had when she had to fake cooing noises while looking at pictures of someone's grandchildren (gaping yawn). Or when she was required to sit through awards ceremonies, smiling and clapping for winners who weren't her. In other words, her *mood* was complete boredom.

It was her own fault.

Polly's overactive imagination—or greed, if she was honest—had led them to the cluttered attic of Thistlethorne Lodge, the ancient castle in the Southwest of England she'd unexpectedly inherited from an obsessed fan. Convinced (without a shred of evidence) the castle hid untold riches, she was determined to uncover a treasure, even if it meant dismantling the place stone by bloody stone. Surely, in the thousand years since Thistlethorne was built, its succession of rich occupants had found clever cubbyholes to stash the rent and taxes squeezed from impoverished tenant farmers. But where? The lack of answers was driving Polly absolutely cuckoo.

In the months after moving into Thistlethorne, Polly, and her troupe had searched the place high and low. A secret passageway that led from Tim's bedroom to the castle's dungeon had yielded nothing more than mouse/rat droppings and blackened candle stubs—probably left over from others throughout the ages who had been on the same treasure hunt. And when they opened a concealed panel in the library wall and peeped inside, all that slipped out was a dead body.*

Now, accompanied by Mr. Boots—the castle's resident cat and rodent ranger—Polly and her posse embarked on a hunt through the attic.

"Dust is so ... *dusty!*" Polly complained as she warily scanned the space, her hands stiff by her sides, reluctant to touch anything that might rub off on her. "Where does it all come from?"

"Flakes of dead skin. Disintegrating spider legs. Crumbling moth wings." Tiara delighted in teasing her boss and seeing the grimace of revulsion.

"Spider legs?"

"Probably some pulverized rat bones and decayed bat poo, too."

The attic at Thistlethorne Lodge was a world filled with forgotten reminders of centuries past. Cobwebs hung from the

---

* You can read all about that in *Shadows at Midnight,* available wherever fine cozy murder mysteries are sold.

beams like shredded curtains. A gilt mirror was propped against a wall, its once-reflective glass now clouded and dim. A table held a tray with a crystal decanter. Its stopper was in place, and inside, a small amount of amber liquid remained—perhaps a fine brandy enjoyed by the perpetually (so the legend went) drunk-as-a-skunk Duke of Droitwich, the inbred, psychologically loopy nobleman with delusions of grandeur who'd built this house inside the ancient castle's fortified walls in the 1700s.

Propped against another wall, a large, framed portrait of a corpulent, stern-looking lady with an unusually prominent schnoz and an elaborate satiny gown gazed at them condescendingly. Her crossed, judgmental eyes seemed to follow their movements, adding an eerie touch to the attic's already unsettling atmosphere.

Tiara looked at the nameplate at the bottom of the frame: *Catrina, Duchess of Droitwich, 1754.* "The duke was supposed to have been an arrogant little wanker. Imagine the desperation it must've taken to voluntarily become Mrs. Little Wanker," she mused, tilting her head at the portrait. "Then again, maybe she figured a higher standard of living was worth putting up with his ego and self-aggrandizement." She stepped closer, narrowing her eyes at the duchess's pained expression. "Though judging by her tight smile, I'd say she was either constipated—or regretted the marriage somewhere around day three."

"Love may be blind, but it can still spot a fat wallet." Tim chuckled.

Polly, already weary with tedium, glanced around at the array of grimy artifacts. She'd been in the attic all of ten minutes and was already disappointed at not finding the crown jewels or at least an original copy of the Magna Carta. "Junk!" she declared. "Those dudes on *Antiques Road Trip* would take one look at this stuff and drive off in reverse!"

Tiara brushed cobwebs from the hair of an old porcelain

doll with a hand-painted face. "A thrift store would be thrilled to have donations like this. An adorable dolly is always a fun toy for a little girl. Or little boy. No judgment here."

As the trio continued to wander around, they were lured deeper into the dusty maw by Mr. Boots, who seemed eager to show them his favorite nooks and crannies. *About time someone appreciated my skills as a tour guide.* He flicked his tail, wandered to the farthest reaches of the vast space, and rubbed his head on the side of an old wooden chest. *See what's inside. Dibs on any mice you find.*

As if reading Mr. Boots's thoughts, Tiara lifted the creaky lid.

"Moth-eaten rags," Polly scoffed, peering over her shoulder. "Just more stuff to toss out."

Tiara, however, was intrigued by the garments and marveled at their hand-sewn craftsmanship. "Check out these stitches. They don't make clothes like this anymore."

Rummaging deeper, she withdrew a tarnished silver hand mirror, a matching comb and hairbrush set, and an ornately decorated paper fan with brittle and fragile pleats. Then she withdrew a velvet jewelry box.

"Bingo!" Polly cried and instantly swiped it from Tiara's hands with the speed of a hawk swooping down on a field mouse. "My 'riches radar' has pinpoint accuracy!" She opened the box and instantly made a face. She turned it upside down, shaking out all of the nothing inside. "I've been robbed!"

"Hey, look at this," Tiara said, withdrawing a stack of old papers bound together with a nearly disintegrated ribbon. "*Vanity and Virtue*," she read from the top page. "Abigail Townsend. Eighteen twenty. Maybe someone's diary?"

Polly scoffed. "Some lonely young girl whining about suitors, proposals, and the pressure to marry well." She instantly transformed into Petunia Fluffington, a comedy character she'd recently created after bingeing two seasons of *Bridgerton* (which she spoofed as *Blabberton*). Petunia would have been comedy gold and a fan favorite if she'd ever graced the screen on *The Polly Pepper Playhouse*, Polly's old TV variety show. Though academically dim, Petunia was the darling of high society in Regency-era England, with a penchant for saying things like, "Oh, my stars! I shall simply faint if Mr. Fancy Pants doesn't propose soon!"

Polly began to improvise, narrating a fictional diary entry. She adopted an exaggeratedly demure posture, fluttered her eyelashes, and griped, "Today, Mother and I visited Lady Willoughby for tea. She has the most charming garden. We discussed the latest fashions from London. Mr. Harrison was there, too. He paid me a great deal of attention. Mother says he is a good match, but I find him rather dull." Polly rolled her eyes. Her voice dripped with mockery. "Mr. Harrison looked at you for a full five seconds, Girly. How will you ever survive the excitement? Gag me with a crumpet!"

Tiara let out a chuckle but remained focused. "Let's see what the diary really says," she sassed, reaching for the ribbon tied neatly around the bundle. But the moment she tugged, the string crumbled, and the pages began to slide free.

"Whoa!" Tim exclaimed, diving to catch the fragile sheets before they hit the floor. Holding the rescued stack, he squinted at the top page. "Look at this handwriting. It's beautiful." He tilted the page toward the window, where sunlight illuminated the delicate strokes and intricate loops of penmanship. "I don't think it's a diary. I think maybe it's a book." His eyes scanned the text, and he began to read aloud:

"*Vanity and Virtue*. By Abigail Townsend. Chapter One. The sun rose over Whitemarsh Hall with a brilliance that seemed to promise a day of delightful tranquility. However, as is true with much of my life, tranquility proved to be more of an illusion than reality. My uncompromising father, Everett Slocum, was quite beside himself when I openly rejected his choice of a suitable husband for me. That he also misplaced his valuable gold oak leaf brooch—a small but treasured token representing the power and prestige of his bloodline—escalated his distress. This is a poignant reminder of the delicate threads that often bind a family together. Yet an undercurrent of something darker, a sense of unease, pervaded the morning air."

"Oh, brother!" Polly frowned. "I was right. Insipid observations about life and love from a virgin. Purple prose at its *purpliest*."

"Is that even a word?" Tim scowled, then continued to read:

"Later, as I prayed at St. Clematis, reflecting upon this upsetting domestic disturbance, it occurred to me I must find sanctuary from the vexations of the world—a place where my soul may find solace and my mind peace. Yet even in that holy refuge, I could not shake the ominous feeling that the absence of the gold brooch was more than mere carelessness."

Polly interrupted with a wry edge, parodying the author's tone. "I must find sanctuary from the vexations of the world. Me too!"

Tim ignored his mother and kept his focus on the text:

"Alas, I am filled with a sense of trepidation, for I harbor a great secret. I know the truth about where Father's gold oak leaf brooch lies. I don't consider myself clever, but I do believe I have been clever to know this secret. Alas, it is a fragment of a much larger scheme, a puzzle piece in a sinister game that will surely unravel our lives. Sin is upon me, yet I am compelled to preserve the secret—at all costs."

"Ooh, I love secrets! But where's the gold brooch? She can't have lost it!" Polly complained, dismissing the writing as anything more than nonsense.

"If you'd listen and not talk so much, maybe you'd find out," Tim said.

Tiara raised an eyebrow and reminded them of the date on the first page. "Hold on a second. This manuscript is old—like, seriously old. If the date on it is real, it's from around the time of the Industrial Revolution! And I vaguely recognize the name Abigail Townsend from an English lit class I had in college— Scandalous Quills. I think she's only known for one book. But she was famous in her time. Or maybe infamous is a better word. As I recall, she got into a lot of hot water because of her writing. I seem to recall she lived somewhere close to Jane Austen. What if ... judging by the name and the date ..."

Polly's eyes widened, her excitement bubbling over as $$$ signs flashed before her eyes. "Are you saying this could be something written by a famous author who died hundreds of years ago?" Her voice trembled with a mix of awe and eager speculation. "Maybe it's worth ..." She could barely contain her excitement as images of fit construction workers in hard hats and high-visibility vests over bare chests laboring to make much-needed and costly repairs at the castle danced in her head.

Tiara nodded. "We shouldn't risk damaging the pages by handling it too much. Just in case. Each touch could affect its condition—and value."

Tim was already moving toward the attic door with the pages cradled like a baby in his arms. With a renewed sense of purpose and temporarily setting aside Polly's original quest for attic riches, the trio carefully descended the creaky stairs and made their way down to the main reception room. Tim placed the manuscript gently on the oak coffee table in front of the

Chesterfield settee beside the fireplace. The weight of history was palpable, and they felt a surge of excitement as they stared at the stack of pages for a long moment. Polly tried to imagine who the person was who had scrawled on these pages more than two hundred years ago and marveled that the work had survived over such a long time.

"Be careful with it," Tiara reminded, her voice steady and authoritative.

Polly nodded, her fingers lightly tracing the edges of the stack of pages. Though yellowed with age, the graceful, looping penmanship had been preserved. With bated breath, she began slowly and carefully turning the sheets, pausing long enough for the others to read the text along with her. As they scanned the words, a story began to unfold:

The main character seemed to be Lady Cathryn Slocum, a young woman of the eighteenth century living in a manor house called Whitemarsh Hall. Cathryn's life was filled with the societal pressures of courtship and marriage. But it quickly became evident her story was far more interesting than the average privileged young woman of her time. And the misplaced gold brooch referenced earlier was not any ordinary piece of jewelry. It almost seemed to be a character in the story—a symbol of family power and a clandestine romance with a man named Rupert Lancaster.

The trio leaned in, completely absorbed, their breaths synchronized as they pieced together the intrigue.

And then it happened ...

With the stealth of a ninja and the chaos of a tornado, Mr. Boots launched himself onto the coffee table like a ballistic missile. Time seemed to slow as his paws landed squarely on the fragile stack of pages. The air exploded with a flurry of parchment, each sheet spiraling upward in a chaotic dance. Polly shrieked, clutching her chest as if she'd been mortally wounded.

"MR. BOOTS!" she bellowed and dropped to her knees, scrambling to collect the scattered pages. Her glare could have melted steel, but the cat sat imperiously in the middle of the table, licking his paw as if the whole ordeal were beneath him. "Please sit still. I promise you won't miss a word. I'll read the whole thing. Just ... no more acrobatics, okay?"

Mr. Boots flicked his tail, giving her a look that clearly said, *I was merely editing. You're welcome.*

As Polly carefully sorted the scattered pages back into order, something caught her eye—a folded piece of paper dislodged by Mr. Boots's antics. Her annoyance gave way to curiosity. The delicate sheet was as brittle as an autumn leaf. Slowly, she unfolded it, her breath hitching as she took in handwriting starkly different from the manuscript's—less decorative, more hurried, almost panicked.

> *My Dearest Abigail,*
> *Time is running short, and I fear for your safety—and mine. The gold brooch must remain hidden, as it represents your legacy. However, should you ever need to retrieve it, remember: the oak that stands alone guards its resting place. That is our eternal secret. Trust no one but your one true love.*
> *Yours in devotion,*
> *RL*

Polly's eyes widened as she repeated, "'The oak that stands alone ...' What the heck does that mean? A riddle? A clue to a puzzle? And it mentions a gold brooch, like in *Vanity and Virtue*."

Tim's head bobbed in agreement, and his eyes took on a distant gaze as he contemplated what appeared to be a romantic message. "Yours in devotion," he repeated. "The initials RL.

That's gotta be Rupert Lancaster in the story. I'll bet he was dashing and handsome. Like a movie star. Did people know they looked like movie stars if there was no such thing as movies back then?"

Oh, the depths of this boy's philosophical questions, Tiara thought, with a roll of her eyes. "'Yours in devotion.' It sounds like he was in love with Abigail Townsend," she said. "I'm picturing Cathy and Heathcliff from *Wuthering Heights*."

"Or Ennis and Jack from *Brokeback Mountain*." Tim smiled. "Although they were dudes in cowboy hats. 'Trust no one but your one true love,'" Tim quoted the letter again. "That's so passionate. Maybe the gold brooch was their symbol of love, like the pocket watch Jane Seymour gave to Christopher Reeve in *Somewhere in Time*."

"These people were rich, so they were probably more like Jay Gatsby and Daisy Buchanan," Tiara countered, her own amorous thoughts evident in her eyes.

As Polly resumed reading the text aloud, she realized this wouldn't be some Regency-era chronicle of manners and etiquette with a bunch of sulking dukes, viscounts, dowagers, and other misunderstood toffs of the realm. It was soon revealed that, upon Cathryn Slocum's marriage, she would take with her a large dowry. This attracted numerous suitors, one of whom, Rupert Lancaster, was revealed to be more interested in her wealth than in passionate love.

Cathryn had apparently fallen deeply for Rupert. There were intense moments between them, followed by confusion and, eventually, betrayal. The manuscript, although missing at least one page—it seemed to skip a couple of paragraphs—revealed Rupert was not just a secret lover but someone who'd insinuated himself into the Slocum family with a hidden agenda. He had manipulated Cathryn's emotions, making her believe in their divinely orchestrated fate while he secretly plotted to abandon her and abscond with her dowry.

The plot thickened as Cathryn discovered the full extent of Rupert's deceit—in collaboration with her father. Her heartbreak was palpable on the page as she grappled with the realization that the man she thought she loved was using her to further his social ambitions. She transformed from a naïve young fiancée into a resolute and vengeful woman who devised a clever plan to turn the tables on Rupert and her father. *Vanity and Virtue* was turning out to be a tale of betrayal and a young woman's quest for revenge, all set against the backdrop of the elegant yet superficial British aristocracy.

Several hours passed as Polly continued reading aloud to Tim and Tiara (and a surprisingly attentive Mr. Boots), her eyes and voice growing tired but riveted by the unfolding drama. By the time she reached the final page, the room was filled with the dimming light of late afternoon.

Despite their fatigue, the trio (quartet, if you counted Mr. Boots—and the family certainly did) was gripped by a mixture of awe, sadness, and triumph from Cathryn's heroic story. She'd battled against the repression of her father and society—and won.

Polly felt deep empathy for Cathryn as she reflected on her own past with disloyal husbands who had taken advantage of her wealth and celebrity status and broken her heart. Like Cathryn, she'd faced betrayals but emerged victorious, reshaping her destiny on her own terms.

As the family sat in silence, the gravity of their discovery began to sink in.

"How the heck are we going to find out if this thing is authentic and written by a famous writer?" Tiara asked. "I don't suppose we could Google 'how to tell if I've found a long-lost Jane Austen novel in my attic.'"

"This has to be our secret," Polly said firmly. "You know how it is in this weird village. If one person finds out, the entire population instantly knows about it, too. They're all wired like a genetically connected 5G network." She sighed, feeling the weight of responsibility. "It's like we found a winning lottery ticket and can't tell a soul. I'm getting paranoid already!"

"We need to be smart. But who can we trust?" Tiara agreed and went down a mental list of ethical and reliable friends who might be able to guide them. *Ethical? Reliable? Friends in Hollywood? Not a chance!*

"Constable Jenkins!" Tim suggested, referring to his *affaire de coeur* and the sole officer of the law in Abbots Clover. "He's legally required to be honest. Or at least that's always the expectation," Tim said, clearly eager to impress Gray with a secret that could be as monumental to the literary world as the discovery of King Tut's tomb was to archaeologists. "I'd definitely score brownie points."

Polly shook her head. "He might be required to file an official report or something. Maybe I could talk to Terrence. He's honest and reliable."

"Terrence?" Tim dismissed the idea. "He may be your beau, but he owns the village newspaper, for crying out loud. A reporter, no less! That's a worse idea than me telling Gray."

Just then, the newly hired maid, Elara, glided almost silently into the reception room, her footsteps barely making a sound on the polished wooden floor. "What about Rose Harding, the librarian?" she suggested.

Tim exchanged a frown with Tiara, and Polly wondered how much of their conversation Elara had overheard. Elara always seemed to appear unexpectedly and at inopportune moments.

Polly forced a smile, trying to mask her irritation with the maid. "Rose Harding? That dowdy, stern-looking thing who auditioned here a couple of months ago for a role in the village musical?"

Elara nodded, her expression earnest and eager to please. "Rose knows a lot about the history of Abbots Clover, Thistlethorne Lodge, and the whole region. She has a particular interest in eighteenth-century events in the village. She once came to my school and lectured."

"A librarian. That's not a bad idea," Tim agreed.

"How well do you know Rose?" Polly asked, still annoyed by the sudden intrusion but intrigued by Elara's recommendation. "Is she trustworthy? Is she a gossip? Can she keep a secret?"

Elara shrugged. "Who's she gonna tell? She lives alone with her cat. Plus, I think librarians are honor bound to respect the privacy and confidentiality of library users and their information-seeking activities. How else do you think I got away with borrowing *Lady Chatterley's Lover, Fanny Hill,* and *The Well of Loneliness*—without my mother ever finding out?"

The Well of Loneliness? Tim thought. Is Elara keeping a secret from Mommy?

Polly pondered the idea, twisting her mouth in contemplation. "How would we approach Rose without letting on about what we've found?"

Elara lowered her voice conspiratorially. "Abbots Clover's annual literary festival is coming up. There's always an antiquarian bookseller or two there. You could ask Rose to introduce you. Or you could tell her you want advice on a personal research project. That's actually true."

Polly nodded slowly, her intrigue growing. "And if someone sees us—or telegraphs our plans?"

Elara shrugged. "It's no one's business. But if anyone asks, you could tell them you're donating some rare books from Thistlethorne's collection. You'll be seen as a generous benefactor. Which would be a nice change because most people in the village think you pretty much stole the castle."

"Thistlethorne was an inheritance, for crying out loud!" Polly complained.

Tiara said, "If Rose is into local history, she'd probably jump at the chance to see something as amazing as this old manuscript."

Tim agreed. "If she's as knowledgeable as Elara says, she might even know more about Abigail Townsend the writer."

"All right let's do it," Polly said triumphantly. "But Elara, you are forbidden from breathing a single word about this to anyone! On your mother's grave! So help you God! Not even if you're kidnapped by Charles and Camilla and lashed to the rack in the Tower of London and stretched like a rubber band until you snap! Understand? Not even an entry in your journal. Apologies to your mother. I know she's still with us."

Elara nodded. "Scout's honor. If I utter a single word, may Loki, your stinky ghost dog, follow me around forever—nauseating intestinal fumes and all."

3

_____

The morning dawned with typically gray English skies, and a fine mist shrouded Thistlethorne Lodge. It seemed a perfect day for making literary history—at least, that was the way Polly saw it. The yucky weather certainly seemed an ideal backdrop for a melancholy eighteenth-century novel like *Vanity and Virtue.*

The atmosphere in the breakfast room was decidedly warmer. Soft light filtered from the chandelier, highlighting the three co-conspirators seated around the table. Polly sipped her Bloody Mary, relishing the spicy tang of the drink. Tim clutched a can of Red Bull, seeking a jolt of energy to slap him into the new day. Tiara stirred her cup of Earl Grey with lackadaisical disinterest. Each was lost in thoughts about visiting Rose Harding at the Abbots Clover Library.

Lowering their voices to evade Elara's eavesdropping from the kitchen, they discussed their plan. Polly took the lead. "We can't come right out and tell her what we've found. It's potentially priceless. We need her advice for getting the manuscript authenticated, but we can't risk her running up and down the village green like a town crier."

"Hear ye, hear ye, good citizens of Abbots Clover!" Tim teased. "Polly Pepper found the lost Ark of the Covenant in her castle attic!"

"I've thought about this and have an idea," Tiara said cautiously. "Elara mentioned the upcoming literary festival. Tell Rose you want to volunteer to help. Sure! Offer your theatrical services. Maybe say you'll perform a scene from a classic play: 'To be, or not to be ...' Or maybe you could read an excerpt from a famous novel: 'It was the best of times, it was the worst of times ...' Or maybe recite a poem: 'I wandered lonely as a cloud ...' Something to ingratiate yourself and win her support."

Tim nodded, a spark of intrigue lighting his eyes. "That could work," he said, leaning back in his chair. "Freebie public events usually need all the volunteer staff they can get. Once she's warmed to you, you can casually mention our little discovery."

Tiara smirked, raising her teacup in mock salute. "Subterfuge suits you, Polly. It always has. Just remember the three C's: cunning, charisma, and confidence. We need her to think we're helping her. At least until we can trust her and draw her into our scheme."

Polly grinned, a gleam of determination in her eyes. "Theatrics is my specialty. By the time I'm done, Rose will be so beguiled she'll be begging to help us authenticate the manuscript!"

The main reading room of the Abbots Clover Library exuded timeless elegance. A relic of the Georgian era, except for electricity and indoor plumbing, it remained largely untouched by modernity. As Polly and her team stepped inside from the rain, they were met with the comforting scent of old leather and aged paper. The high ceilings were adorned with intricate plaster-work molding, and a grand (dusty) multiarmed brass chandelier hung in the center like a literary angel watching over. Two tall, multipaned sash windows were framed by velvet drapes, and the spacious room somehow seemed cozy.

As the trio walked farther into the room, Polly paused beside one of the tables and steadied herself. "Librarians intimidate me," she whispered. "It's that whole intellectual-superiority thing. Plus, Rose wasn't exactly a docile pussycat when she auditioned for *Cats on a Hot Tin Roof* last month. What if she's still mad about not getting the role?" Polly took a deep breath and looked over at the lending desk. "I don't remember which one she is."

Like a tribunal of stern judges, three older women sat behind the long, raised-platform lending desk with an air of formidable authority. Each wore the same no-nonsense expression, their eyes fixed on the room like prison guards in a tower overseeing inmates in the exercise yard. Together, they exuded a quiet but undeniable power, silently commanding respect from anyone who crossed their path.

Polly hesitated, her mind racing to remember which of these women was the Bernadette Peters wannabe from the village musical audition. She pictured the woman she'd met wearing a 1920s flapper dress, a black bobbed wig, belting out "Time Heals Everything." But beyond that image, the details were frustratingly fuzzy. Taking a deep breath, Polly tried to connect the memory of Rose's performance to the faces before her. She stepped forward, hoping recognition would come as she spoke. "Good morning," she cooed, offering a tentative smile. "We're here to see Rose Harding?"

The three women exchanged glances. Then the librarian in a floral blouse said, "You obviously don't recognize me. When I auditioned for your show, you said I was unforgettable."

That wasn't a compliment, lady. Polly's mind raced as she recalled Rose's performance, an off-key rendition of one of composer Jerry Herman's greatest torch songs. Polly smiled warmly, determined to navigate the situation with grace. "Everyone looks different when they're out of context. I've often thought about that audition and the brave spirit you brought to it. If casting had been up to me ..."

Rose wasn't buying it.

Polly was desperate to figure out how to escape this uncomfortable moment. She cleared her throat. "We've heard about the upcoming literary festival and want to help. I've always loved the smell of books! It's like ... aromatherapy, but dustier. And hey, who wouldn't want to spend time with literary icons like Harper Lee, Maya Angelou, and Agatha Christie? Plus, it would be a great way to meet new people from the village. We want to help make it a grand success."

"The festival is already guaranteed to be a success. It always is," Rose said dryly. "The committee has been planning everything for months. We have all the help we need, thank you. Check with me next year." She was curt, her lips stretching into a tight, fake smile.

Panic flickered in Polly's eyes as she realized she'd failed. Desperate to find another way in, she pivoted. "What about a staged dramatic reading? I could perform a scene from a classic novel or play. *Pride and Prejudice* or *Romeo and Juliet*? Audiences would love it. I am a professional, you know. I'm even world famous—at least in America."

Rose raised an eyebrow. "You can save the press release and bio. I know who you are, Polly Pepper. I have Google, like you do in America. But a dramatic reading? Hmm. That could be ... interesting." An evil grin played at the corner of Rose's mouth as she hatched a plot. "I'd have to see what you can do. Quality control, you know."

Quality control? I'll bet! Polly's heart sank, her bravado slipping as she processed Rose's proposal. She knew exactly what was going on here. "You mean ... audition?"

Rose's reply was a tight, saccharine smile. Her delight in Polly's discomfort was plainly evident.

Polly swallowed hard, a sense of horror settling in her stomach. Tit for tat. Rose wanted Polly to squirm the way she had at the *Cats on a Hot Tin Roof* audition. The irony was not lost on her, but she managed a shaky laugh. "Sure. Why not. I'm a pro."

Rose gestured toward a small stage usually reserved for children's story time at the back of the reading nook. "The floor is all yours," she said, settling into a chair with a look of smug satisfaction, arms crossed as if daring Polly to impress her.

As Tim and Tiara sat in chairs near Rose, Polly stepped onto the small stage and took a deep breath. She could feel the weight of Rose's gaze and judgment. *I haven't had to audition for anything since I landed the starring role in* Bacteria: The Typhoid Mary Story. Summoning all her theatrical experience, Polly masked the anxiety churning in her stomach and the rapid thud of her heartbeat. She decided to go with a monologue from *Hamlet*—or at least a satire of *Hamlet* titled *Shamlet*. She'd performed this once before on her legendary TV comedy show. Closing her eyes momentarily, Polly transported herself back twenty years to her television soundstage and the world of Shakespeare's Denmark. With a determined exhale, she began to speak, her voice filling the quiet room:

"To nap or not to nap—that is the question: Whether 'tis better for the brain to power through the drowsy haze of midafternoon meetings, or to sneak off, perchance to snooze— ay, there's the rub!" Polly emphasized a laid-back, postmodern take on Hamlet's indecision and existential crisis. As the words left her lips, Polly focused on the layers of emotion in Hamlet's contemplation of life and death, the weight of the soliloquy settling over her. She infused each line with flair, hoping to convey the character's inner turmoil—and her own. She tried to block out the sensation of being judged by Rose, concentrating instead on the power of the words Shakespeare—and her in-house team of staff writers—had created. She let her voice rise and fall, each syllable carefully measured, attempting to lose herself in the cadence of the monologue and forget her imperious audience entirely.

As she delivered the closing words, Polly took a steadying breath, her heart slowing now that the performance drew to a close. She felt a sense of accomplishment in the face of Rose's scrutiny. When she finished, a soft silence filled the air, the room seeming to hold its breath momentarily before several appreciative library patrons who'd been watching began to clap politely. Polly offered a dramatic curtsy.

"That's not how it goes," Rose said, dismissing Polly's parody. "But your voice projection was commendable."

Polly managed a smile. "So, do I get the job?"

Rose chuckled softly. "We're fully booked for entertainment. But I'll discuss your proposal for a reading with the events committee for next year."

Next year? Polly's heart sank. Taking a deep breath, she glanced at Tim and Tiara for support and stepped closer to the librarian. "Rose, I'll be honest. We're here because ... well, we need your help. I ... we ... found something in the attic at Thistlethorne Lodge that might be historically important. It's an old handwritten manuscript. Looks like it might be a book. Maybe a novel. It has the name Abigail Townsend written on it. I need someone with your literary expertise to help authenticate it."

Rose's eyes widened; her interest was visibly piqued at the mention of Abigail Townsend's name. The librarian's expression shifted to guarded curiosity.

Polly could almost see the cogs turning in Rose's head as she connected the dots.

"Abigail Townsend?" Rose repeated, her voice tinged with intrigue. "That's a name I haven't heard in years. She was a brilliant writer who lived around here in the eighteenth and nineteenth centuries."

Polly was relieved she'd managed to spark Rose's interest. "The manuscript. It looks like it could be from that time period."

Rose masked her excitement, but Polly watched as her expression shifted from curiosity to skepticism, her initial intrigue tempered by practicality. "Claims of lost manuscripts surface all the time. Hemmingway. Joyce. Hardy. They usually turn out to be nothing more than wishful thinking or forgeries."

Polly nodded. "Sure. But this thing looks real. It's old. It was tucked away at Thistlethorne Lodge for God knows how long. Maybe two hundred years. There's a date on it that says eighteen twenty."

Rose pursed her lips, clearly trying to temper her interest. "The idea of a lost work suddenly appearing is romantic, but as I said, these things are rarely as they seem, and I wouldn't want to get anyone's hopes up." She paused, staring at Polly with a hint of challenge in her eyes. "You must understand Abigail Townsend was known for only one novel. She never published another. Scholars have speculated for two hundred years about her unfinished works. But nothing other than letters and diaries seems to have survived."

Polly understood Rose's skepticism but was determined to win her over. "That's exactly why I thought of you, Rose. Your knowledge could help determine if it's real. It might be legit. It might not. We need you to help us find out. You're the only one we can turn to."

Rose fell silent, her thoughts tangling as she processed Polly's proposition. The idea of uncovering something written centuries ago by an obscure female author from this quiet corner of England seemed almost fantastical. Yet, a flicker of memory surfaced—a conversation she'd had a few years ago with a visiting scholar. He'd claimed an intense interest in local literary history, particularly the works of women writers from the Regency period. At the time, she'd dismissed it as little more than academic curiosity, but now the recollection tugged at her, persistent and nagging. Against her better judgment, a faint spark of interest took hold. "I suppose it wouldn't hurt to take a look," she said, her tone cautious. "But I'm no expert, Polly. You'll need to manage your expectations."

Polly nodded eagerly, relieved to have made progress. "I completely understand. Come to the castle for dinner. We can show you the manuscript, and you can see for yourself. Friday night. Seven o'clock. Just bring your lovely self—and if Daniel gets a bit clingy, tell him you're off for a moonlit rendezvous with his namesake. That should keep him positively purring with envy. Ta!"

4

The next two days flew by in a hypersonic blur of preparations for Friday's dinner. The castle buzzed with activity as Polly and Tiara busied themselves in the kitchen, surrounded by stacks of cookbooks and scattered recipe cards. Polly's eagerness to impress Rose went beyond mere hospitality. Sure, she wanted the librarian to have a tummy full of tastiness but food was just the beginning. Polly wanted to dazzle Rose because she was the gatekeeper of knowledge who could authenticate *Vanity and Virtue* as a lost novel by Abigail Townsend. If Rose validated the manuscript, it would elevate it from a dusty attic relic to a historical treasure. A treasure, Polly hoped, that would bring the funds needed to repair her crumbling castle.

As was often the case, Polly's imagination ran wild with possibilities. If Rose declared the manuscript genuine, Polly envisioned a fierce bidding war, collectors battling to own the pages, fortunes tossed at her feet like rose petals. The media would swoop in—interviews, news articles, maybe even a Netflix documentary. She pictured herself sipping champagne at some exclusive auction house, nodding politely while anonymous bidders drove the price higher and higher.

The idea of elevating Abigail Townsend from relative obscurity to posthumous literary darling? Sure, that would be nice, Polly supposed. But that was a side effect—a quaint little footnote in the story of her own financial windfall.

As Polly and Tiara searched for the perfect menu to tantalize their guest, Polly suddenly paused and looked up with a curious expression. "What do librarians eat?" she asked.

"What do librarians eat?" Tiara repeated, bracing herself for a dippy explanation. "They're a unique species, I'll give you that. But ..."

"They're smart. Maybe they have, like, special brain food that keeps them sharp. Something that nourishes their minds as much as their bodies."

"Like alphabet soup?" Tiara said dryly. "Essential letters for building strong vocabularies twelve ways? Or maybe you mean they eat *Gutenburgers* or *Dewey decimal dumplings*. That sort of thing? Or maybe they have *Sherlock scones* with their tea." She arched an eyebrow. "Polly, librarians are regular people. They eat regular people food. Unless they're allergic to nuts—in which case the surgeon general recommends avoiding contact with you!"

"Don't exaggerate. I'm just making sure. We've never hosted a librarian before," Polly said, thinking of the grand dinner parties she'd had over the years in Hollywood. Her mind drifted to those glittering nights, where conversations flowed as freely as the champagne, and guests always included a lively mix of movie stars, directors, and writers. She knew the secret to a successful dinner lay not just in the food but in the blend of personalities around the table. "Having a few additional people might help create a more dynamic atmosphere and spark interesting conversations. Plus, if we choose the right personalities, they might contribute valuable insights about the manuscript."

"Who in this tiny village fits the bill?" Tiara asked suspiciously. "I mean, these people are lovely, but they're not the most sophisticated inhabitants of the planet—bless their Blighty souls."

"Sarah, Terrence, and Gray," Polly said decisively, naming the only people in Abbots Clover she knew personally. "We enjoy their company. Each would bring added value to the evening. Sarah owns the village bookstore and is a voracious reader, so she'd have that in common with Rose. Terrence is the owner of the *Abbots Clover Overview* freebie newspaper, so he's into words, too. Plus, he's a reporter so he's good at asking interview-type questions. He could talk to Rose about the manuscript's origins."

"What about Gray?" Tiara asked. "He's a policeman. You said you didn't want him to know about us finding the manuscript in case he might be required to file an official report about it."

Polly tapped her chin thoughtfully. "True, we don't want professional snoops poking around. But Gray's skills could prove invaluable for finding out how the manuscript ended up in our attic. His investigator training might uncover details we'd miss. We'll make sure Tim emphasizes the evening is strictly off the record. Gray is putty in Tim's hands—and wherever else he wants him." She smirked, her eyes sparkling with amusement.

Tiara agreed, and with their plan in place, they threw themselves into preparations for the dinner, eager to set the perfect stage for their scheme.

～

Friday arrived sooner than it was supposed to. Tim busied himself with the décor, lighting candles to create a warm, inviting glow throughout the entryway, reception room, and dining room. He selected music that evoked a sense of timeless elegance, mixing classics from Sinatra to Streisand to set a tone of sophistication. He also took the time to arrange fresh store-bought flowers in vases, placing them strategically to add splashes of color and a subtle floral fragrance to the air.

Tiara double-checked the wine pairings, ensuring the chosen selections complemented each meal course. With an eye for detail, she supervised Elara, making sure the glassware gleamed, and carefully set out the flutes for champagne and wine. Adjusting the seating arrangements, she fussed over chairs and cushions to guarantee their guests' comfort. Normally, she wasn't this jittery—not even when George and Amal came to dinner. But Polly had made it clear: this was a potentially life-and-death (or at least financially dire) situation.

Tim and Tiara shared a quick, satisfied glance as the final touches were made, confident they'd thought of everything to ensure an elegant evening. The atmosphere of Thistlethorne Lodge was now a perfect blend of sophistication and hospitality.

Of course, Polly Pepper focused on ... *Polly Pepper*. Her Lady-ship's preparation for the evening revolved solely around herself. She selected an ensemble that screamed, *"Yes! I'm a star!"* —a shimmering silver cocktail dress adorned with enough intri-cate beading to rival a disco ball. The dress boasted a plunging neckline aimed specifically at her new maybe/hopefully/ fingers-crossed beau, Terrence Marks. She complemented the dress with diamond earrings and a matching bracelet. Bold red lipstick and a pair of strappy heels completed her outfit.

With each detail attended to, Polly felt ready to make her grand entrance—when the timing was right. Surely, her sparkle and charm would secure the evening's success, strengthening her budding relationship with Terrence and winning over Rose. As she took a final glance in the mirror, she reminded herself that dazzling her guests was only part of the plan; the real coup would be convincing Rose the manuscript was genuine. Polly flashed a confident smile, knowing full well with the right persuasion, she'd end the evening with more than compliments on her outfit. "Mirror, mirror on the wall, who's the most dazzling of them all?" she quipped with a wink. "Tonight, it's clearly me, sweetums— diamonds and all."

At seven o'clock sharp, the iron knocker on the front entryway door thumped three times, and Tim moved to welcome their first guest. As suspected, it was Rose Harding. Punctual to the second. No doubt she'd arrived early and had been watching the hands of time sweep to the designated hour.

"Ms. Harding." Tim smiled warmly as he opened the door. "Any problem finding the place?"

Rose's lips tightened ever so slightly, deflecting Tim's attempt at levity. "There aren't too many crumbling Norman castles in Abbots Clover."

She stepped inside, her modest velvet dress, with its high neckline and long sleeves, lending her an air of quiet elegance. The embroidery along the cuffs and hem, complemented the delicate silver chain around her neck, from which hung the antique watch she had worn during Polly's visit to the library. Her hair was styled in its usual neat bun, polished and sophisticated, as always.

As Tim ushered Rose into the foyer and hung her coat and umbrella on the hall tree, Rose's eyes momentarily betrayed her. She stole glances at the high ceilings, the intricate crown molding, and the wide staircase, all while doing her best to appear disinterested. *It's just another old house*, she told herself as she drifted over to a portrait of an aristocratic lady in a blue satin gown. She studied the delicate brushstrokes, the richness of the fabric, and the haughty tilt of the woman's chin. "Hmm," she murmured, with nonchalance, as though she encountered art of this caliber every day.

But Tim could tell the place made an impression. "Thistlethorne isn't just a house; it's practically a museum. Some of these antiques have witnessed more history than I ever will," he said, with a touch of pride, offering trivia about the house and its furnishings. "Each piece has a story."

Rose paused, her expression shifting to one of mild irritation. "I'm quite familiar with Thistlethorne's history, thank you," she replied, her voice dripping with condescension. "Having lived in Abbots Clover all my life, I dare say I know more about this place than someone from California. You'll find I'm something of an expert."

Tim instantly felt as though he'd been dismissed by a snooty sommelier. *Excuse me for trying to make small talk,* he thought, resisting the urge to roll his eyes. *And what's with the dig about California? It's not like I'm trying to sell you a surfboard, for crying out loud.* He shifted awkwardly, trying to mask his discomfort.

An awkward silence filled the room, and Tim realized the one thing he hadn't prepared for was an arrogant guest. He cleared his throat, searching for a way to recover. "Of course, Rose ... may I call you Rose? Your knowledge of the village—and our castle—would naturally be far greater than mine. I'm sure there's a lot I can learn from you."

Rose's expression softened slightly. She gave a curt nod, accepting his attempt at diplomacy but leaving the atmosphere palpably uneasy.

"Let's move through to the reception room, shall we?" Tim said, gesturing toward the arched hallway, eager to escape the weight of Rose's disapproval. "Mom, er, Polly ... is still putting on finishing touches. You know she's gotta make a show stopping entrance once everyone is here."

"Everyone? I thought you insisted on keeping the news of

your discovery to yourselves." Her tone dripped with disapproval. "Unless you're boasting—which, in my opinion, is never—"

Great, now she thinks we're throwing a manuscript-bragging party. Tim forced a smile, determined to steer the conversation back to safer waters. "Only three others," he countered smoothly. "They're discreet. You probably know Sarah Rogers from the Bound to Read book and coffee shop, Terrence Marks from the *Abbots Clover Overview*, and our brilliant man in blue, Constable Grayson Jenkins."

"Brilliant?" Rose sniggered, the derision in her tone unmistakable. As though Grayson's policing skills were some village joke.

Tim winced. "Grayson's a clever man."

Rose offered a tight smile, and Tim could almost feel the frost of her judgment. To Rose, Polly Pepper's fame likely embodied everything tacky and unserious about the civilized world. Intellectuals like her thrived on the weight of old books, obscure knowledge, and reputations built on academia. Tim, by contrast, had grown up surrounded by glitzy parties, shallow admiration, and a mother who cared more about entertaining her audiences than impressing high-brow critics.

The judgment hung in the air, sharp and unspoken, and it stung. He guided Rose toward the reception room, hoping the fire's glow and a glass of champagne might thaw the chill that seemed to cling to her like a winter coat.

They stepped inside, where dark wood-paneled walls, adorned with somber portraits of distinguished ancestors, enveloped the room in an air of quiet gravitas. The carved stone fireplace commanded attention, its roaring flames casting flickering light and long shadows danced across the polished wooden floor. An Oriental rug, rich with intricate patterns, lent the space a sense of warmth and luxury. In one corner stood a grand piano, its glossy black surface mirroring the firelight. Above the mantel loomed an antique oil portrait, the subject's face locked in a sneer. His drooping jowls framed a thin, petulant mouth, while his bulging, bloodshot eyes hinted at years of self-indulgence. The pallor of his complexion was as if he'd spent a lifetime avoiding both sunlight and good humor. He seemed to glare down at the room with a disdain that transcended the centuries.

"The Duke of Droitwich," Rose sneered, correctly identifying the portrait and casting a withering glance at the dour, self-satisfied face on the canvas. "Why would anyone hang a painting of such an irredeemable prat? According to my research, the man was a boil on the backside of the village. He built Thistlethorne inside these castle walls in the 1700s, to shield himself from the rising tide of people who loathed him."

Her voice rose as she warmed to the topic. "Even his dog, Loki, objected to him. That poor creature apparently took to wandering the halls, letting the most noxious tailwinds rip to express his disdain for his odious master. Granny Grumbles— the castle witch—called the duke 'a pustule of entitlement.' In her diary, she wrote, 'Were he not so bloated with self-importance, he'd drift off like a fart caught in a gale. Even maggots, with their undiscerning appetites, would turn up their writhing noses at the sight of him.'"

Tim had heard it all before. The duke's reputation as a nincompoop had survived four hundred years. "Believe it or not, Loki, is a ghost dog now and still haunts this place," he said. "We've seen ... and smelled him. Pretty rank. Like meat rotting in the sun." Tim pinched his nose and waved his hand in front of his face. "Never mind. Please make yourself comfortable." He pointed to the Chesterfield. "A glass of champagne?"

Rose shrugged with indifference.

Jeez, lady! It's not like I'm twisting your arm. A moment later, in the nick of time before Tim might have said something sarcastic and spoiled the evening before it began, the sound of the iron knocker on the front door drew him away from Rose.

"Perfect timing," Tim said when he opened the door to Sarah. "I'm about to strangle someone."

"Dinner-party jitters?" she asked, displaying her trademark radiant smile and handing him her jacket and a bottle of wine.

"High-handed librarians with long noses to look down on their inferiors," he grimaced.

Sarah chuckled. "Rose Harding must be here. We go way back to when I was a girl. She's a pussycat—maybe not the domesticated type—but she'll chill ... once she knows you're not looking down on *her*. It's a control-issue thing. A protection mechanism. She can't allow herself to show any vulnerability. Pretty common with people who have low self-esteem."

Tim grinned, remembering Sarah held a degree in philosophy and feeling his mood lift with her positive attitude. "Follow me," he said, leading the way to the reception room.

"Rose!" Sarah exclaimed as she entered the elegant room. "I haven't seen you since ... was it Mary Radcliff's book signing in the store a few months ago? What a fiasco that was, right?" She laughed and watched Rose's lips curl into a smile of recollection. "And I see you've made friends with Mr. Boots. Smart cat. He knows who gives the best belly rubs!"

Rose glanced down at the cat grazing her ankles. Her expression softened measurably as she stroked the feline's head, marking her as a cat lover. "Mr. Boots does seem to know the best people," she joked, momentarily distracted from her irritations.

Sarah's charm was working its magic. She shot Tim a look that said, "You owe me," then accepted a flute of champagne and scanned the room. "I never tire of being invited here. Such a lovely setting. You've been here before, haven't you?" she asked Rose, her tone light.

Tim suppressed a grin. Sarah already knew the answer but was subtly acknowledging Rose's importance without making her feel like a newcomer.

Rose hesitated, as if weighing whether to admit her unfamiliarity. "First time," she said with quiet pride. "It's impressive."

Sarah smiled, and sensed Rose's defenses easing. "The atmosphere here is always as rich as the conversation." She smoothly steered Rose into a chat about the village and its history, drawing a hint of interest from the aloof librarian.

Tim exhaled, silently grateful for Sarah's skillful diplomacy. Rose, once an antagonist, was slowly becoming a willing participant in the evening's unfolding drama.

The door knocker echoed again, and soon Terrence and Grayson swept into the room, bringing a fresh spark to the evening. Terrence, all charismatic charm, worked the room with firm handshakes and easy laughter, while Grayson, effortlessly composed in his open-collared shirt and dark blue trousers, exuded understated style.

As champagne flutes were passed around, Tiara breezed in, her smile bright and a tea towel slung over her shoulder. "Madam will join us shortly," she announced, eyes twinkling. "She's performing emergency triage on her face."

Then, as if on cue, Barbra Streisand's inimitable voice poured through the speakers, crooning "My Heart Belongs to Me," and the pocket doors between the reception and dining rooms slid open with a theatrical whoosh. There she stood—Polly Pepper—her gown shimmering under the chandelier's glow. "Darlings," she announced, her glittered eyelids sparkling and arms outstretched as if expecting applause, "your patience has been rewarded! The star has arrived—and no, I'm not talking about Tiara's roast beef."

Polly didn't enter; she glided, with the effortless grace of a queen who knew she was stealing the spotlight. "Welcome, sweetums!" she trilled, her voice a playful symphony of charm and mischief. Her eyes shimmered—part Hollywood star, part hostess extraordinaire—as she surveyed her guests. "I'm absolutely thrilled to have all of you here. Let's make this an evening to remember—or at the least, one that'll take *ages* to forget!"

As the guests drained their second flutes of bubbly, Tiara announced dinner would be served presently. Rose was the only one who had not previously experienced this welcome-to-the-dining room show but tried her best to act blasé. The room was dominated by a long, polished mahogany table that reflected the soft glow of the Waterford crystal chandelier. The Royal Doulton rose-pattern dinner plates sat on sheer lace embroidered placemats, accompanied by heavy cut-crystal glasses and antique silverware. Tim gallantly withdrew Rose's chair so she could be seated to Polly's right, then assisted Tiara with serving the starter: Caprese salad. Soon, everyone was settled in for the evening.

Ever the gracious hostess, Polly guided the conversation. The room buzzed with laughter and anecdotes as they enjoyed the meal. Sarah recounted humorous tales from her bookstore and coffee shop. Terrence shared amusing stories from the *Overview's* one-man newsroom.

Eventually, as the main course was ending, Polly turned the conversation toward their special guest. "Rose, I understand you're an expert on Abigail Townsend. Tell us who she was? What was her life like?"

Rose set down her cutlery, her eyes alight from being the center of attention. "Not an expert. But certainly, an ardent admirer. From all I've gleaned, Abigail Townsend was a remarkable woman—for any era. She was born into a wealthy family in the late eighteenth century. She was one of seven children. Only four of them—all girls—survived. She was known for her literary talents, her keen intellect, progressive ideas, and her religious devotion. She went to church every day."

The guests listened intently, drawn in by Rose's storytelling flair—honed over decades of facilitating readings at the library.

"Abigail published her only novel, *The Chains of Conscience*, when she was only twenty-two," Rose continued, her voice filled with admiration. "I won't go into specifics, but like many of her contemporaries, her writing explored societal norms and the constraints imposed on women. The novel follows the life of Patricia Elizabeth Girard, a young woman celebrated for her beauty and virtuous nature. But her intellect is not only overlooked, it's outright dismissed—especially by her domineering father.

"As the story progresses, Patricia becomes entangled in a series of relationships that challenge her understanding of herself and the world around her. She's promised to a wealthy suitor chosen by her father, but she finds herself irresistibly drawn to a charismatic but poor laborer. Their intimate clandestine meetings ignite an internal conflict in Patricia. She struggles with her desires versus the constraints placed upon her by her father and society."

Terrence leaned forward, intrigued by the complexity of the characters. "And this laborer she falls for, is he a positive influence on her?"

"In many ways, yes," Rose replied. "But perhaps more influential is her friendship with Muriel Bright, an aunt who defies traditional societal expectations. Muriel encourages Patricia to question the patriarchal structures they live under, inspiring her to seek to move beyond the confines of her expected role."

Sarah, intrigued by the depth of the characters, leaned in. "What kinds of themes does the novel explore?"

"*The Chains of Conscience* delves into themes of love, morality, and self-discovery," Rose explained. "It examines the tension between what family and society expect and one's personal desires. As in every era, it takes courage to swim against the contemporary current and pursue one's own goals. As a novelist, Abigail critiqued the limitations placed on women, advocating for their self-empowerment."

The guests listened intently, clearly captivated by the story's complexities. "Abigail Townsend's characters grapple with the choices between conformity and authenticity, offering readers a glimpse into the struggles and triumphs of women striving for self-actualization," Rose continued. "Much like Margaret Atwood does today. Abigail's ability to weave intricate plots and thought-provoking themes earned her comparisons to Jane Austen and Mary Shelley."

"What eventually happened to Abigail?" Tim asked. "Why didn't we study her in school?"

Rose paused, a note of sadness creeping into her voice. "Abigail's life was a short one. She died in 1820. Age twenty-four. She fell from her horse. That's pretty much all we know."

The guests exchanged sympathetic glances, sensing the profound loss of a talented writer at a young age.

"According to a diary and a few letters I've seen, she was on the verge of publishing her second novel."

"Why wasn't it published posthumously?" Sarah asked.

Rose shrugged. "That's a mystery. We know her family didn't approve of her first book. In fact, they were apparently enraged by it. Or at least her father was. He forbade any of them to even read it. That might have had something to do with the second one not being published. A lot of her writing disappeared. Although some letters and diaries survived and ended up in various library collections."

"It sounds like a terrible injustice," Terrence said, shaking his head. "Imagine having such brilliance in your family, only to stifle it out of shame or ignorance."

"The world was robbed of her voice simply because her family couldn't see beyond their narrow-mindedness," Sarah added. "It makes you wonder how many other creative minds have been silenced by similar circumstances, and maybe how many other great works are still out there waiting to be uncovered—or worse, lost to history. The thought of all that brilliance being dismissed and discarded, it's ... it's sad."

Rose nodded. "Abigail's death and the loss of her next novel meant her legacy faded over time. Without a body of published work to sustain her memory, she became a relatively forgotten figure in literary history. But for some reason, I've always been fascinated by her."

"Imagine what might have been," Grayson added, his voice reflective. He leaned back in his chair, the weight of his thoughts evident in his posture. "If the manuscript Polly found is authentic, it's not just a piece of history—it's a second chance for Abigail to speak to the world."

Rose agreed. "Abigail had the potential to influence generations of writers and readers, much like her more famous contemporaries. If the manuscript is Abigail's, it could reignite interest in her work and restore her rightful place in literary history."

The room fell silent as the guests absorbed the weight of Rose's words. The idea of uncovering a lost manuscript added an air of excitement and urgency to the evening.

As the meal concluded, Polly rose to her feet, her voice calm but tinged with anticipation. "My lovelies," she began, her gaze sweeping across the room, "a piece of the past has found its way into the present, and it's waiting for us. So, let's move through to the library and take a step into history together. It's showtime!"

5

The walls of the library at Thistlethorne Lodge paid homage to Hollywood's Golden Age, adorned with a dazzling collection of movie star memorabilia. This collage of celebrity artifacts was the life's work of Alistair Drake, the home's former owner, whose fanatical obsession with the silver screen culminated in his ultimate gesture: bequeathing his entire castle to his favorite living star, Polly Pepper. Over his lifetime, Alistair had amassed an eclectic trove of treasures tied to the icons he idolized. The most bizarre among them? A Maxwell House coffee can he'd gleefully shake at guests, daring them to guess its contents. The answer—*cremains of Joan Crawford's German shepherd, Prince*—was invariably met with a mix of nervous laughter and uneasy silence.

Now, taking center stage, Polly opened her arms as if to embrace her guests. "Ladies and gentlemen," she began, "I am delighted—no, intoxicated—to share with you something truly extraordinary." She paused, savoring the expectant looks on their faces. "You already know the backstory. There I was, playing Cinderella to Tiara's wicked stepmother, forced to sweep the attic floor amidst the dust, spiders, bats, and rats. Suddenly, I was overcome by some powerful magnetic force and drawn deep into the farthest, darkest corner of the attic, where I found an antique wooden chest."

Polly's eyes widened as she launched into her wildly exaggerated tale, her voice rising with each dramatic twist. "The chest didn't vibrate—it *shuddered!* It practically screamed: *Pol-ly Pep-per!* I lifted the lid, and the hinges let out a tortured screech, the kind you hear in haunted houses—or from opera singers. And then, I kid you not, moth-eaten underwear started *flying out* —hurtling through the air like they were trying to escape! Then I saw it! Tangled in a whirlwind of bloomers, I uncovered the literary find of the millennium. A priceless—please, sweet merciful heavens, let that be true—manuscript destined to rewrite the course of literary history. And with any luck, rescue my poor, tragically anaemic bank account from its current state of depression."

Tim raised an eyebrow.

Tiara stifled a roll of her eyes.

They exchanged a bemused glance. This was Polly at her most dramatically imaginative. Her theatrical flair on full display.

Polly's gaze fell on Tim. That was his cue to join her act. He seized the moment and moved to the fireplace at the other end of the room, where he paused and faced a bookcase to the right of the hearth. Even without a drumroll fanfare, the room became silent with expectation. The excitement in the air was palpable as the guests watched him trace his fingers over an ornate rose carved into the bookshelf. He felt the smooth curves and petals, and with a knowing smile hinted he knew a big fat secret. He pushed the rose with his thumb. A soft click echoed in the room as a hidden latch was released. A panel slowly opened, revealing a small, concealed room that exhaled a musty scent as if it were exhaling a breath held for centuries.

"A priest hole!" Rose declared with astonishment, correctly identifying the space that would have been created to hide clergy when it was illegal to be Catholic in England during the reign of King Henry the Eighth. "I've always wanted to see one in real life. I shouldn't be surprised a house this old would hold such a marvelous secret."

With the flair of a magician unveiling an empty box where his pretty assistant had been handcuffed only moments ago, Tim opened the panel wider. The guests leaned forward, their curiosity piqued as they peered into the dark recess. He reached into the space, withdrew something wrapped in a white bath towel, and handed it to his mother.

Savoring the spotlight, Polly accepted the package with a gleam in her eyes. The guests' gazes were locked on her as she glided across the room and set the bundle on the desktop. She paused, drawing out the moment. The room seemed to hold its breath. Her fingers fluttered over the cloth before she teased a corner, relishing the rising curiosity in the room. Then she slowly pulled back the fabric, her every move a master class in creating suspense. When she fully revealed the manuscript, nonverbal sounds of awe rippled among the guests.

Rose leaned in to get a closer look, her heart racing as her professional demeanor fought to contain her thrill. Her breath hitched when she noticed the first page: in the upper right-hand corner was a delicate sketch of an oak leaf: the Townsend family crest. Instinctively, her fingers hovered near the page, drawn by the allure of history in her grasp. She froze mid-motion, protocol snapping her back to reality.

"I brought cotton gloves," she murmured, reaching into her dress pocket. "The oils in our hands could damage the paper."

A faint, musty scent of old paper wafted as she gently lifted the first page. It was yellowed with time and inscribed with elegant, flowing script. "*Vanity and Virtue*, by Abigail Townsend," she read, her eyes almost misty with fascination and reverence. Her mind raced with the possibility of its authenticity. This could indeed be one of the writer's long-lost works. The precision of the handwriting ... the watermark on the paper ...

Rose carefully turned another page and noted annotations in the margins. *Perhaps Abigail's revisions to the text,* she considered. *A glimpse into her thoughts as an author.* Rose imagined Abigail, quill in hand, crafting the words before her. "This is extraordinary," she murmured. "The script is consistent with the eighteenth century. If this is genuine, you may well be right that you've uncovered one of the great literary finds of our time."

Polly gave a triumphant smile as the guests leaned in, captivated by Rose's analysis.

As Rose continued her inspection, she voiced her observations aloud, like a medical examiner conducting an autopsy on a TV police procedural drama: "I'd say it measures roughly eight and a half by thirteen inches and is approximately six inches thick." She turned a page, allowing the guests to glimpse its aged and textured surface. "It's surprisingly well preserved." She carefully lifted another page, holding it to the chandelier's light. "Watermarks were a common feature in paper produced during this period. They served as both a mark of quality and a way to identify the paper mill where it was produced."

Rose paused, allowing the guests to observe the elegant script that filled the page. "The handwriting is exquisite— flowing and precise. It's indicative of someone who was well educated—as Abigail was. The ink would have been soot-based and a rich black. But as you can see, it's faded to brown or sepia over time. That's consistent with what you would expect from the eighteenth or nineteenth century."

Rose pointed to the margins of the pages where annotations could be seen. "These are particularly interesting. They suggest this was a working document, perhaps a draft Abigail was revising. The presence of these notes might add an invaluable layer of insight into her creative process."

As Rose concluded her examination of the manuscript, the guests' imaginations were clearly ablaze with the possibility they were the first people on the planet to lay eyes on a previously lost book by a talented writer.

Polly, her eyes wide, was barely able to contain her enthusiasm. "If this is one of Abigail Townsend's lost works, what do you think it's worth?"

Rose shrugged. *Typical self-serving question from a rich American*, she thought, but held her tongue. "The value is impossible to determine without a full professional authentication," she said, choosing her words carefully. "If it's verified as genuine, it could be considered priceless in terms of literary and historical significance. It's true value lies not in the monetary aspect, but in what the manuscript represents: a chance to uncover and celebrate a forgotten voice from literary history."

Yeah, yeah. Don't preach to me about academics and bookworms. I want to know how I can turn this relic into cold, hard cash. Polly nodded, her face a mask of polite interest. "Yes, of course, preserving its integrity is paramount," she said, feigning concern for the manuscript's historical importance.

Terrence asked the question on everyone's mind. "Rose, it's amazing to imagine this manuscript was hidden in a chest for centuries, but how do you suppose it ended up at Thistlethorne in the first place?"

Rose took a moment to gather her thoughts, her expression thoughtful as she pieced together the fragments of what she knew from her years researching the history of Abbots Clover. "From what I know, there's a fascinating connection between Thistlethorne and literary circles of the eighteenth and nineteenth centuries. After the Duke of Droitwich went mad—he accused King George the Third of insulting his dog, Loki, and was summarily locked away in a dungeon, where he should have been placed years before—the Langley family purchased the castle. Walter Langley became a friend and mentor to Abigail Townsend. He was known for hosting salons where writers and intellectuals gathered to exchange ideas and critique each other's work. Jane Austen, Percy Shelley, and Lord Byron, they were all here from time to time."

"Was Abigail Townsend part of that crowd?" Sarah interjected, her eyes wide with awe and wonder. The idea that those legendary figures, writers whom she'd read and admired all her life, might have once walked the halls of Thistlethorne Lodge, perhaps even sat in this room, sent a thrill through her. The thought of being in this place that had nurtured some of the greatest literary minds in history was almost too much to take in and filled her with deep reverence.

"I believe she was part of that crowd," Rose confirmed. "At least she mentioned them in her diaries. She often visited Walter Langley here during summers. They were rumored to be intimates, and she likely brought her manuscripts here to discuss and share with him or others."

"If they were lovers, she likely trusted Walter with her work," Sarah said. "Given her time in the area and their relationship, it's plausible she shared her manuscript with him for feedback. Writers often exchange works in progress and critique each other's drafts. Or perhaps she left it with him for safekeeping—and then she died."

Rose hesitated, a flicker of intrigue sparking in her eyes. "Yes, over the years, I've come across a rumor that suggests Abigail entrusted some of her work to Langley because she feared her family would destroy her writings if they were found. Walter was someone she knew would appreciate the true value of what she'd written." She paused, her gaze momentarily distant. "A few years ago, a scholar—an English linguistics professor, I believe

—visited Abbots Clover. He said he was tracing Abigail's life and mentioned her rumored manuscript. At the time, I thought it was another academic chasing shadows, but perhaps he was searching for this very work."

Tim's brow furrowed as he considered this new piece of the puzzle. "Abigail's relationship with Walter explains her presence here, but it raises even more questions. Like, how did the manuscript end up hidden away in a chest and potentially forgotten for all time?"

Rose nodded. "That's a true mystery, isn't it? Who hid the book, and why? We'll probably never know for sure," she said, her expression taking on a more serious and contemplative tone. "It's possible Walter held onto Abigail's manuscript to safeguard it after her death, until he determined the right moment to publish it. Given the discord within Abigail's family, he might have felt a moral obligation to protect her work, fearing her father—who was furious about her first book—would destroy it."

She paused, letting the weight of her words sink in before continuing, "But then Walter himself vanished under mysterious circumstances, and many of his possessions simply disappeared—including, perhaps, this manuscript."

Polly raised an eyebrow, her curiosity fully piqued. "Disappeared? You mean Walter just went ... *poof?*"

"Precisely," Rose confirmed, leaning in slightly as if to share a long-guarded secret. "He was last seen on his way to a literary conference in London in 1820. But he never arrived."

Grayson, not long out of police academy training, said, "Way back in those days, they didn't do complex investigations into missing persons like we do today. Constables and watchmen were only responsible for dealing with petty crime and ensuring public order."

Rose gave him a nod of approval and glanced around the

room. Lowering her voice, she said, "Some believe he vanished willingly, seeking a new life in anonymity. Others suspect something darker—an accident or even foul play. Whatever the truth, he was never heard from again. His disappearance remains one of the great unsolved mysteries of our village."

The room fell into silence, the air heavy with the implications of what Rose had revealed. The guests exchanged glances, each one wondering if Walter's fate was somehow intertwined with the manuscript being hidden away for two centuries.

Polly drifted into a reverie, her thoughts piecing together the fragments of history they'd learned. "Abigail and Walter had a thing going on. She died suddenly ... He put the manuscript away, maybe for safekeeping ... then he mysteriously disappeared. Over the generations, the ownership of the house changed. The manuscript has been here all this time, waiting for me to rediscover it. I think the house waited for me to come along. I've felt that ever since we first set foot in the place."

Mr. Boots meowed as if to say, *"Who led you to the chest in the first place, lady!"*

A contemplative silence settled over the room as the guests absorbed the weight of the manuscript's strange history. Then Polly interrupted everyone's stupor. "I'm absolutely sure the manuscript was written by Abigail Townsend! No fancy-pants historian with an academic degree can refute what I know in my gut." She stood straighter, her hands gesturing with an enthusiasm that couldn't be contained. "I'll sell it to a collector or a museum." Her eyes sparkled, as if she could already see a packed auction room at Sotheby's and the final, jaw-dropping sale price as the gavel cracked down on the block. "Now, how can I unload it?"

Rose smiled, recognizing Polly's avarice. "It's not as simple as uploading a photo to eBay and waiting for bids. Authenticating an old manuscript is a meticulous, scientific process. First, we need to establish its provenance—tracing its ownership history. We need to confirm it could have come from Abigail Townsend. Then there's material analysis. Someone has to examine the paper and ink to ensure they match what was used in Abigail's time."

Rose continued, her tone patient but firm, "Handwriting examination is another crucial step. Experts have to compare the script to known samples of Abigail's writing to ensure consistency. And then there's the content itself. Literary experts need to analyze the style and references within the text to confirm it aligns with her known works." She paused, letting the weight of the process sink in. "I have a friend at the British Library in London, Dr. Jonathan Fieldstone. This is precisely his area of expertise. He'd be the best person to guide you through the process. But these things take time. You'll have to have patience."

"Good luck with that!" Tiara controlled a laugh. "Patience is not one of madam's virtues. She once took up knitting, and after about five rows ... let's just say the scarf she started is now an uneven potholder."

Rose nodded. "I'd be happy to help connect you with Dr. Fieldstone, but there are a few things we need to consider first." She glanced at the manuscript. "For one, Dr. Fieldstone is incredibly busy. He's undoubtedly on one major project or another for the library. Getting his attention might take longer than you'd like. He's also particular about the outside cases he takes on—he'll need solid evidence this manuscript is worth his time. And he's expensive."

Polly frowned, the obstacles beginning to mount. "What evidence? How expensive? Since you're friends maybe he'll give us mate's rates."

"We'll need to gather as much information as we can about

the manuscript," Rose explained. "That means doing some preliminary research ourselves."

Polly's shoulders slumped at the thought of the time involved.

But Rose seemed optimistic. "I know you want this done yesterday, Polly, but we need to be methodical. I'll reach out to Dr. Fieldstone tomorrow. With a bit of luck, he'll agree to take a look at this."

6
―――――

Throughout a restless night, Polly tossed and turned, her mind racing with schemes for soliciting Dr. Fieldstone's coveted seal of approval on *Vanity and Virtue*. Rose had warned Fieldstone was a busy academic, and piquing his interest in the manuscript might be challenging. But where $$$ were the reward, Polly Pepper wasn't one to back down from a challenge.

Polly stared into the darkness of her bedroom, contemplating ways to lure Fieldstone to examine the manuscript sooner than later. It can't be hard to seduce a stuffy academic whose nose is buried in dusty old documents, she mused, picturing him—tweed jacket with elbow patches, wire-frame spectacles, shuffling around a dimly lit library that smelled like decaying parchment and mothballs. She imagined him a man more inclined to caressing beloved first editions and dreaming about fictional characters than associating with real, live, flesh-and-blood people.

Her first thought for persuading him to take on the project was to flaunt the name "Polly Pepper." Back in the good ol' turn-of-the-'oo-century fun days, that name was pure gold—guaranteed to turn heads and open doors. Surely, even now, the most bookish academics would leap at the chance to meet a legendary Hollywood icon and inspect her treasures. But then, this was England—darn it all—where Polly's name didn't mean squat. The Brits were more likely to confuse "Polly Pepper" with a brand of fizzy drink than recognize her as the darling of the American small screen.

Okay, plan B, Polly thought, her mind spinning like a roulette wheel as she considered other ideas. Maybe a generous donation to Antiquarian Angels, a charity that rescues old books from the clutches of dust and decay. That should catch Fieldstone's attention. Polly imagined herself a benevolent benefactor, pen poised like a magic wand above a blank check. "Just a small token," she'd purr. "There's more where that came from— if you do me one teensy, weensy, insignificant authentication favor!"

But that idea lacked the sizzle Polly was envisioning. She needed something that would grab Fieldstone by his academic lapels and shake sense into him. Suddenly, inspiration struck. "Aha!" she said, her excitement rousing Mr. Boots from his cozy slumber on the pillow beside hers. She'd tell Fieldstone one of his long-forgotten ancestors was mentioned in the manuscript. Lots of scandal! A juicy little lie would have him hooked faster than he could say *Ancestry-dot-com*.

Polly could already picture it: Fieldstone's eyes growing wide, his mouth agape, as she innocently dropped tantalizing hints about shocking family secrets buried within the pages of *Vanity and Virtue*. The thought of him poring over the manuscript, desperately searching for any mention of his forebears, filled Polly with a giddy sense of triumph. This was it— the perfect bait for her academic fish.

~

At the same time, Rose Harding found herself under her warm comforter, pondering how best to coax Dr. Fieldstone into their literary web. She lay awake in her quiet cottage, Danny purring by her side, and the ticking of an antique clock providing a steady rhythm to her thoughts. Rose knew Dr. Fieldstone well enough to understand dropping flashy celebrity names like Polly Pepper would not be enough to interest him—he was a man of academic substance. He valued the weight of history and the thrill of uncovering truths long hidden in dusty archives.

She would send him a carefully worded email that played to his cerebral vanity. She would suggest a recently discovered manuscript contained references to obscure historical events and figures—things only a scholar of his caliber could decipher. She would say the manuscript might challenge some long-held assumptions about nineteenth-century British literature that would spark a scholarly debate and further elevate his name in academic circles.

But then Rose paused, a small smile curling at the edges of her lips. Dr. Fieldstone was known for his obsession with medieval manuscripts and their mysterious marginalia—those little drawings and notes scribbled in the margins by monks and scribes. What if she were to hint that *Vanity and Virtue* might contain similar Easter-eggs? Perhaps she could include a tantalizing line in her message about enigmatic symbols and notes that defy translation, waiting for a mind like his to unravel them. That was partly true. There was a small sketch of oak leaves on the first page.

"Hello, my lovely daffodils!" Polly sang out as she buoyantly entered the breakfast room the next morning. "Why looking so wilted?"

Tim sat glumly, guzzling a Red Bull, while Tiara scrolled through BBC News on her phone with the expression of someone reading a particularly grim headline. Polly might have been in a sunny mood, but the atmosphere, inside and out, was the exact opposite. Yes, it was technically spring, but someone had taken a damp cloth and wiped away all the color. A steady drizzle clung to the air, and the trees, still bare from winter, looked like skeletal fingers clawing at the sky, their buds reluctant to bloom under such dismal conditions. This was England, after all, where spring was more a fantasy than reality.

Tim harrumphed a begrudging good morning at his mother. "I'm in a deep existential crisis," he declared dramatically. "Rose was supposed to tell us the manuscript was authentic, and I had big plans for the money we'd make—sunny beach, fruity drinks, Gray in a swimsuit. Now all we've got is some random guy named Fieldstone, who may or may not even care about our dusty attic treasure. Honestly, what am I supposed to do with this level of disappointment?"

Polly grinned, her optimism unwavering. "Not to worry, sweetums. Mummy has a plan." She opened the Contacts folder on her phone and tapped on Rose's number. After three rings she gushed, "Rosie, my precious! It's your *Peppery* Polly. Just calling to say it was fun seeing you last night, and I have the perfect plan for getting Dr. Fieldstone to look at the manuscript. Send me his contact info, and off we go."

There was a brief pause on the other end as Rose likely ensured she wasn't disturbing anyone in the quiet sanctuary of the library. "Way ahead of you. I've already sent an email." Rose's tone was measured as if she were speaking to an excitable child. "I explained the situation in detail. He hasn't responded yet, but it's early. We need to be patient."

Polly frowned, her foot tapping against the floor. "Patient? Rose, you know that word mysteriously vanished from my vocabulary sometime between learning to spell it and realizing I could get what I wanted without it. I'll contact him. He'll drop everything."

Rose's voice remained steady, though Polly could sense the librarian was probably shaking her head on the other end of the call. "Polly, Dr. Fieldstone is a busy man. He's likely buried under a mountain of other manuscripts and academic papers. He'll take his time before responding, even for something as potentially significant as this. We can't rush the process."

Sensing an opportunity to channel Polly's energy into something productive while she awaited Fieldstone's response, Rose seized the moment. "Polly, you previously offered to help with the literary festival. We're in the crucial stage of selecting potential speakers, and we've got a handful of self-published authors lined up who need to be pre-interviewed before we make our final decisions about including one of them. How about lending a hand in the vetting process?"

Polly's smile froze, the corners twitching slightly as her inner critic sharpened its claws. "Self-published? Isn't what people do after every agent on the planet sends them a letter that starts with, 'While we found much to admire ...'?" Her imagination wandered to visions of amateur authors with covers featuring shirtless werewolves and titles like *Passion at the Petting Zoo*. She caught herself—barely. *Now, Polly, be gracious. Everyone deserves their moment. Even if their moment includes a self-written glowing review attributed to "Avid Reader."*

"Self-publishing has come a long way," Rose insisted. "A lot of authors purposely choose to self-publish because it gives them creative control. Some have built impressive followings. In fact, some bestsellers started out as self-published books. *Fifty Shades of Grey, Legally Blonde, Still Alice.*"

Polly blinked, slightly taken aback by the conviction in Rose's defense of authors. "Well, I suppose if someone's got a good story to tell, that's what matters," Polly conceded, her tone softening as she reconsidered her stance.

"These authors may have taken a non-traditional path, but their work deserves as much respect and consideration as Amy Tan or Laura Levine," Rose added.

Doubt it! Polly sneered inwardly. "Sure, I suppose I could help out. As long as I don't have to read their books. The last novel I read cover-to-cover was a Reader's Digest Condensed Book. Honestly, they had the right idea—cutting out all the extra words nobody needed in the first place. I mean, why describe a character's dress for three pages when 'pink' will do?"

Rose wondered why Polly Pepper was considered sophisticated. But she was relieved she'd found a way to keep the star occupied. "We're looking for writers with something compelling to say and who can engage and inspire an audience. You'll need to assess their charisma, ability to think on their feet, and whether they can tell a story that captivates a crowd."

Polly nodded, already picturing herself as the gatekeeper to literary fame. "I'm practically a human lie detector—I'll know within five minutes if they're interesting or a bore with a thesaurus."

"I'll send names and contact details. I want you to look for authenticity, passion, and a spark that makes a good writer an even better speaker. It's not all about what they've written—it's about how they connect with readers."

Polly and Rose exchanged goodbyes, and as the line went silent, Polly started to feel a renewed sense of purpose. Her task might be behind the scenes, but she could picture herself in the center of the literary world.

Already into his second Red Bull, Tim looked up. "You, interviewing literary types?" he said with a smirk. "What's your first question going to be? 'Which chapter will I fall asleep reading?'"

Tiara, who had been dividing her attention between Polly's

conversation with Rose and scrolling through her news feed, set her phone down and looked at her boss with amusement and concern. "Remember, not everyone thrives under the spotlight like you do. These are writers ... some might be more comfortable hiding behind their laptops than being in front of an audience."

Polly waved her hand dismissively. "If they want to be part of this festival they have to step up to the plate and 'sparkle, Neely, sparkle'—if you get my drift. And who better to bring out their inner *celebutante* than *moi*? Trust me. By the time I'm done, we'll have a lineup of speakers to rival a TED Talk conference."

It was noon-*ish*, and the crackling fire in the reception room cast a golden warmth over the rich, dark wood-paneled walls. April drizzle coated the windowpanes, but despite the bite of lingering winter outside, the room exuded an inviting charm.

Polly sat comfortably on the Chesterfield settee, her phone in hand, when a soft ping announced the arrival of an email. Her eyes eagerly scanned the screen, and within moments, she'd summoned Tim and Tiara. "Rose sent the list of authors for pre-interviewing. Listen to this—"

After mocking the descriptions of a Depression-era recipe book, a private investigator thriller, and a paranormal romance, Polly landed on a title that immediately caught her attention. "This sounds intriguing. *Full-Service Provider.* Author: Elliot Davies. Synopsis: In the glittering world of contemporary London high society, Lady Vivienne Worthington is the epitome of grace and poise. But beneath her refined exterior lies a body desperate to be touched by calloused hands. When her internet suddenly crashes, Vivienne gets her wires crossed with the engineer sent to fix her faulty connection. Sparks fly as he repairs her router, pulling her into a web of temptation and carnal desire. Torn between the luxuries of her gilded life and the electric charge of forbidden love, Vivienne discovers she can't live with being hardwired."

"Oh, brother! That's nauseating. But definitely one I'd read," Tiara laughed, fake fanning her face with her hand. "Stories about service technicians making house calls and messing it up with the customer is right up my fantasy alley." She leaned over to look at Polly's phone screen. "And the author's picture is smokin'! What's his bio say?"

Polly tapped on a link that said Stats for Elliot Davies. She scrolled down and enlarged his publicity photo. The image filled the screen, and Tiara, who'd been casually sipping her tea, nearly choked on her next sip.

Elliot Davies was seated in a leather armchair, fingers casually touching his temple in a thoughtful pose. His narrow shoulders and slim frame gave him a lean, understated presence, while soft, dark brown curls fell across his forehead, lending a casually disheveled charm. Behind wire-rimmed glasses, his brown eyes looked out with a quiet intensity, hinting at emotional depth and sharp intellect. His face was narrow, accentuated by high cheekbones, full lips, and a light stubble tracing his jawline. A bright-white smile, paired with his slightly scruffy look, reflected the introspective and complex nature of the writer. His charisma leaped off the screen.

"Hands off this one, Polly!" Tiara playfully declared, utterly smitten by the photo. Her tone was half-joking but her intent crystal clear. "That goes for you too, Tim! I'm staking my claim. Oh, but who am I kidding ..."

"Don't even think about looking for sympathy and playing the age card," Tim said, mocking Tiara's self-deprecation. "He looks smart. You might be exactly the woman who could catch his eye. You're sophisticated. Worldly. You've aged gracefully—and you know it."

Tiara gave a mock sigh, though her smile betrayed her pleasure at Tim's words. "But let's be realistic. A man who looks like that—"

Tim waved her concerns away. "I don't see a wedding ring in the picture. Besides, what's the harm in exploring possibilities?" He looked at his mother. "Here's an idea. You have to interview the dude. Don't do it by phone. Invite him here for tea. Nothing fancy. Tiara can get a better look at him, and he'll see Tiara's more than your right-hand man. No law says the interview has to only be about his book. You can surreptitiously delve into his love life."

Tiara's eyes sparkled with curiosity and amusement. "You think that's a good idea?" she asked, tilting her head as she considered the possibility.

"I know so," Tim replied. "Right, Mom?"

"I suppose," Polly agreed. "Open a new window! as the saying goes. Life's too short for what-ifs. Besides, it's about time you had your motor checked."

7

"For crying out loud, it's only been a few hours!" Rose snapped, her patience fraying after Polly's fourth call that day. Each call was a variation on the same relentless question: "Any news?" Rose could practically feel Polly's anxiety buzzing through the phone as if sheer persistence could force a response from Dr. Fieldstone. "I swear, the moment I hear anything, even a smoke signal or message in a bottle, you'll be the first to know. Give it—and me—a rest!"

Rose sighed, imagining Polly walking around, clutching the phone like a lifeline, ready to pounce the moment it rang. The thought of the famous Polly Pepper, who was usually composed (at least in public), teetering on the edge of a meltdown was almost enough to make Rose laugh—if she weren't so exasperated. "You've got to give the man some time! I doubt he's staring at his inbox, waiting for mail."

Polly let out a dramatic huff. "But this is *Vanity and Virtue*, for crying out loud—a masterpiece that could rewrite literary history." *And give me financial security in my dotage!* "What on earth could possibly be more important! He could at least send a quick note. 'Got your message. Sounds cool. Hit you back soon.' Don't they teach manners at Oxford or Cambridge?"

Rose matched Polly's intensity, her tone firm. "Listen. Fieldstone is known for his precision. I think it's a good sign he's taking his time. A quick response might mean a quick rejection. This maybe means he's seriously considering it."

Polly pressed her lips together, the logic of Rose's argument slowly sinking in. "All right. Fine. But if he hasn't responded by the end of the day ..."

Rose cut her off sharply. "No news is better than a door-slam-in-our-faces rejection. So please, for the love of God, let him do what he needs to do."

Polly exhaled slowly, her tone tight. "Okay. But this had better be worth the wait." The uncertainty gnawed at her, leaving her feeling suspended in torturous limbo.

Rose sensed Polly was on the brink of a meltdown. Thanks to the diva's impatience, she wasn't far from the edge herself. "You need to take a deep breath and find a distraction. Where are you with the authors interviews? That's where your energies should be focused."

A long pause followed, and Rose could almost feel Polly's internal struggle. She imagined her pacing, torn between her obsession with the manuscript and the need to do something—anything—to stave off her mounting anxiety.

Finally, Polly sighed with resignation. "I get it. You win. I'm driving myself cuckoo. And yes, I've already got calls in to several of the authors. They haven't called back. But keep me posted about Fieldstone. I need to know what's going on."

"I promise," Rose replied, her voice softening. "But let's not lose our heads."

Polly reluctantly agreed and hung up. But her thoughts were racing. If she couldn't control Dr. Fieldstone's timeline, at least she could throw herself into the interviews.

With her phone practically glued to her hand, Polly plopped down in a huff beside Tiara at the kitchen table. "Everyone's ignoring me! Rose. Fieldstone. And those self-published nobodies who should be leaping at the chance to interview for a speaker's spot at the festival."

Tiara didn't even look up from the trashy Ben Tyler novel she was reading. "Maybe they're doing what a lot of people do when faced with a big opportunity—panicking," she said absently. "Maybe they're Googling to find out who this American Polly Pepper diva is."

Polly rolled her eyes and threw her hands up in mock disbelief. "Or maybe they're busy consulting their astrologer to see if Mercury's in retrograde! They should be groveling with gratitude! How are they supposed to take my mind off Fieldstone if they don't communicate with me?"

Tiara finally looked up, a knowing smirk on her lips. "Ah, there it is. This isn't about the authors or the festival, right? You're using them as a distraction. They're your entertainment." She shook her head with a chuckle. "Polly, you don't care if they're speaker material or not—you want them to keep you from obsessing over Dr. Fieldstone."

Polly's impatience simmered beneath the surface, manifesting in her fingers drumming on the tabletop. She checked her phone's Recents folder again—empty. But then, as she was about to make another disparaging fuss, her phone *did* ring! Polly's heart skipped a beat as she glanced at the screen. A number she didn't recognize. Without hesitation, she tapped the Accept icon and pressed Speaker. In her most affected voice, she cooed, "*Hell-ew*. This is *Polly Pep-pah*. How may I assist?"

"Ms. Pepper, this is Elliot Davies." It was the deep, velvety voice of the author of *Full-Service Provider* and immediately caught Tiara's attention. The richness of his baritone sent a thrill through her navel. It was the voice that could seduce radio listeners into buying whatever product he was pitching. Each word he spoke seemed to coil around Tiara, sending heat through her.

"I just found your message—it must have gone straight to voice mail—and I'm honored by the invitation to interview for the Abbots Clover Literary Festival. Being a self-published author has big challenges when it comes to publicity and marketing, so this would be amazing. It's difficult to break through the noise and get your work in front of the right audience. The festival is pretty important down here in the Southwest, and the chance to speak there—if I'm selected—would mean the world to me. It's not just about sharing my books; it's about connecting with readers."

Polly's smile broadened, her excitement bubbling over. "Mr. Davies, I'm happy you see it that way. I believe our festival could be the perfect platform for the right author, and I'd love to discuss your potential participation. Could we meet in person? Would it be an imposition for you to come to Abbots Clover? I don't have a UK driver's license."

"Yes. Absolutely. I mean, no, it's not any imposition at all." His tongue was tied with excitement. "I live in Shepperton Foal. That's over the hill and a wee stretch."

They agreed to meet at noon the next day, and after Polly placed the phone down, her eyes were alight with triumph. She smiled at Tiara. "Tea with Elliot *Full-Service Provider* Davies! Make your famous lemon drizzle cake!"

Over the next few hours, Polly finally received callbacks from the other three authors she'd called. She'd settled onto the Chesterfield in the main reception room, expecting brilliance from them, but as the conversations dragged on, her excitement fizzled. The first author, a well-meaning but excruciatingly dull man who had penned a book about the history of stained-glass windows during the Anglo-Saxon period, managed to make Polly—who'd once smiled through an eight-hour-long celebrity chess tournament—glance longingly at the clock. Her attempts to steer the conversation toward anything remotely engaging were met with all the enthusiasm of a stalled car.

The second author, a lethargic-sounding woman with a nasal voice, talked in monotone about the ease of microwave cooking and the recipes she'd collected for almost instant meals. But she was as bland as a bowl of dried breadcrumbs.

By the time Polly hung up the phone, she'd endured a marathon of mind-numbing monologues. None of the authors had the spark, charisma, or, frankly, the ability to string together a sentence without inducing yawns. Elliot Davies had set the bar high—maybe too high for these others even to graze with a stepladder.

Polly sighed dramatically, tossing her notepad onto the coffee table with a flick of her wrist. "Well, that was a monumental snore," she muttered, rubbing her temples to massage away the lingering effects of a headache. "A history of stained glass and a dissertation on the miracle of meals in minutes does not an intriguing afternoon make."

Tiara looked up from her novel. "Tomorrow, Elliot Davies will make up for all that. If his charm on the phone is anything to go by, I'd say we're in for witty banter, intellectual flirtation, and maybe even some insight into a writer's soul. At the least, you'll be spared another riveting sermon on how microwaving frozen lasagna in plastic is a one-way ticket to chemical poisoning."

Polly couldn't help but smile, her earlier disappointment fading. Her resolve renewed, she stood up and exclaimed, "Let's make sure everything's perfect for tea. I want Elliot to walk out of here thinking Thistlethorne Lodge—and especially you—is nothing short of extraordinary."

The castle practically hummed in anticipation of the arrival of Elliot Davies. Even the sun, which had been hiding all morning, made a valiant effort to break through the dense blanket of clouds that hung over the property. Weak sunbeams streamed through the tall windows, casting a warm hue over the reception room. The crackling fire in the hearth added a comforting glow but did little to ease the nervous energy that buzzed between Polly, Tiara, Tim—and even Mr. Boots, who couldn't seem to get comfortable on the settee. Tiara even lit scented candles throughout the house—in case—God forbid—Loki the ghost dog decided to pay a fragrant visit.

They had each rehearsed their roles for the interview. Polly would ask questions to draw out details of Elliot's professional and personal life—without seeming too nosy. She'd been interviewed so many times herself, she knew every trick in the book. Her goal was to determine Elliot's suitability for the festival— and as a potential playmate for Tiara.

Tiara would serve as Polly's personal assistant—the position she actually held. However, today, her duties were more about observation than sucking up to the boss. She'd listen carefully, take notes, and gauge Elliot's body language, catching nuances Polly might miss in the heat of conversation.

Tim would stay in the background. His job was to ensure Polly felt secure with an unfamiliar person in the house. He had his mother's knack for reading people, and if anything seemed off about Elliot Davies, Tim would be the first to notice and take action.

As noon approached, Tiara stood near the window in the

reception room, her fingers absently toying with the velvet draperies as she gazed out at the courtyard. She was a woman who effortlessly commanded attention, not only for her striking appearance but for the quiet strength and intellect that radiated from within. She carried herself with the grace of someone who had learned to navigate the world with confidence and poise. But despite her best efforts to project calm this morning, she was a bundle of nerves beneath the polished surface.

Polly's composure was fraying, too. Her eyes darted to the clock on the mantel, each tick of the second hand making her pulse quicken. She adjusted her dress for what felt like the hundredth time, wondering if she'd overdressed or, worse, underdressed.

Tim, who had been nervously straightening picture frames on the walls, finally flopped into a wingback chair. "Why am I nervous?" he muttered. "It's not like I'm auditioning for the role of 'Charming Dinner Companion.' Though, honestly, I'd probably get the part."

Then ... At last ... The moment they'd all been waiting for finally arrived. "He's here!" Tiara said, moving away from the window. The plan was set, their roles were clear, and now it was time to put their carefully rehearsed performance to the test.

As Tim ushered Elliot Davies into the reception room, Polly flashed a radiant welcoming smile. *Understated sophistication*, she thought, admiring the man smiling back at her. He wore a classic, light-blue button-down shirt neatly tucked into a pair of well-fitted, dark khaki trousers. Elliot Davies was a man who knew how to make an impression without even trying.

As they settled into the cozy warmth of the room, Elara appeared with a silver tea service and Tiara's lemon drizzle cake on a rolling cart. Polly effortlessly guided the conversation, her questions flowing naturally as if she were merely catching up with an old friend. Soon, it was clear Elliot was everything they'd hoped he would be—charming, articulate, and sincere. His voice resonated in the room, adding a layer of richness to his words, making even the most mundane details seem intriguing. Of course, his English accent was captivating, too.

Polly began the interview with light, professional questions, gently exploring his background as a writer. Elliot spoke about his journey as an independent author, sharing the challenges he and many writers face in gaining recognition. He reflected on his university education in English literature and the responses from agents who said they admired his manuscripts but ultimately declined to represent him.

Tiara hung on Elliot's every word, pretending to be scribbling on her notepad. He spoke about his love for nature and how he found inspiration in the quiet moments of life, like watching a sunrise or tending to his small garden. When he said he volunteered at the local animal shelter, Tiara couldn't help but feel a pang of envy for the critters and the people who got to spend time with him on a regular basis. He seemed like the real deal—everything his bio had promised. And she couldn't take her eyes off the strands of dark chest hair peeking out from the V of his unbuttoned collar. She tried not to be obvious but wondered if Elliot could tell she was imagining his undressed body—and things she would like to do to it.

Elliot mentioned a small inheritance from his father, explaining it gave him the freedom—at least for about another year—to focus fully on his writing. "Some in my family and among my friends think this is a hobby because it costs more than it brings in," he said. "But I treat it like a job. I have a set schedule—early mornings, no excuses. I write every day, even when I don't feel inspired. For me, it's about showing up, whether the words flow easily or I'm wrangling them like wild horses."

Polly asked about his life outside of writing, and Elliot didn't hesitate to share. Then, with a hint of shyness that only made him more endearing, he revealed he was single.

"Writing is what fulfils me—it's what gives me purpose—but I've realized it can feel lonely without someone to share the journey. I hope to find someone who understands the rhythms of a creative life, who won't resent the solitude it demands. Someone who cherishes the simple joys, like curling up by the fireplace with a good book, savoring a quiet evening, and maybe sharing a bottle of wine."

Tiara fixed her eyes on Elliot with an intensity that spoke volumes about her desires. Polly, for her part, couldn't help but feel a fleeting pang of something. She wouldn't dare call it envy —curiosity, perhaps? Of course, her heart belonged to her darling Terrence, the steadfast editor of the *Abbots Clover Overview*. But there was *something* in Elliot's quiet charm that was hard for her to ignore.

Polly leaned back in the Chesterfield, and a satisfied smile crept onto her lips as the interview began to wind down. She could see potential in Elliot Davies—both as a speaker at the festival and as someone who had clearly made a positive impression on Tiara—and herself.

"Well, Elliot," Polly said, her tone warm and approving, "I have to say, this has been an enjoyable conversation. You've got the insight and charm to make an excellent addition to the Abbots Clover Literary Festival's speakers series."

Elliot smiled, his eyes flicking over to Tiara, who was seated opposite. "This means a lot. I'm truly honored to even be considered," he said, his voice full of genuine appreciation. "It's been terrific meeting both of you."

Polly nodded, her mind already made up. "FYI, I'm going to heartily recommend you to the selection committee. Frankly, I'd be shocked if they didn't feel the same way after I report what you've shared today." She flashed him a bright smile, the kind that always closed deals in Hollywood.

Elliot's gaze shifted back to Tiara, who met his eyes with a warm smile of her own. There was a subtle but unmistakable connection between them, something that had been building quietly throughout the interview.

Tiara, who had been relatively quiet, letting Polly do most of the talking, finally spoke up. "And it's been terrific meeting you, too, Elliot. It's not every day someone interesting, easy-going, and talented comes along. I'll be downloading your books to my Kindle right away." Her words carried a warmth that made Elliot's smile widen a bit more. Tiara couldn't resist adding, "This wraps things up for today, but please don't be a stranger. We'd love to have you back at Thistlethorne Lodge. Anytime. That's not lip service." *Lip service? You dummy! You sound like you're only interested in his lips, for crying out loud! Of course you are, but really?*

8

The dining room at Thistlethorne Lodge was bathed in the warm glow of candlelight. Adele's soulful voice drifted through the music system, adding a touch of charm to the evening. The aroma of Tiara's beef Wellington wafted from the kitchen as Polly and her team took their usual places at the table and made sounds of yummy expectation.

As they lifted their cutlery and were about to tuck in, Polly couldn't resist stirring the gossip pot. She'd waited all day for this moment and faced Tiara with a glint in her eye. "I propose a toast!" she announced, her tone dripping with monkey business. "To our brilliant chef ... the lady who couldn't stop drooling over a certain romance novelist whose initials are—*Elliot Davies!*"

Tim, who had sipped his wine, snorted into his glass. A few drops of wine splashed onto the table, but he was too busy chuckling to care. "You are wicked, Mother!" He gasped between fits of laughter.

Tiara groaned and instinctively raised a hand to her flushed cheeks, feeling the warmth spread across her skin. "Polly! That's totally not true! *Is it?* I didn't drool! *Did I?*" She looked to Tim for reassurance.

Polly wasn't done with her devilry. "And may she always keep her fainting couch nearby!"

"You're too much!" Tiara protested. "I was completely in control, and you know it! *Wasn't I?* Do you think he noticed? *I'd be mortified!*"

"Prepare for serious mortification, sweetums!" Polly quipped. "'It's not every day someone interesting, easy going, and talented comes along. I'll be downloading your books to my Kindle right away,'" she parroted Tiara. "I haven't seen a woman bat her eyelashes like that since Scarlett O'Hara caught sight of Rhett Butler for the first time! 'I'd like to give you lip service …?' You laid it on with a trowel, my dear!"

Tiara tried to maintain her composure, but laughter bubbled up, and she couldn't help but shake her head. "I didn't say that, and you know it! You're ridiculous." She rolled her eyes as she reached for her wine glass, though her smile betrayed that she wasn't entirely displeased with the teasing.

Tim followed his mother's lead and, with the slow, syrupy drawl of a Southern belle, said, "Darlin', I declare, you had that poor man tied up in knots tighter than a corset at a Sunday barbeque! Oh, Mr. Davies, you're such a big, strong, and handsome writer man with all them fancy words and clever ideas of yours. Why, my head's spinnin' with all this talk of plots and themes and metaphors! Would you be a dear and fetch me a mint julep before I simply swoon from all your intellectual stimulation?"

Tiara buried her face in her hands, her laughter muffled by her fingers. "Stop! Both of you! You're killing me!" She shook her head, her eyes bright with amusement. "You've had your fun. But for the record, I was not flirting—I was being friendly."

Polly winked, her Southern belle persona fading. "Of course. I get it. Just being friendly. I can't wait to see how friendly you get the next time you see Elliot Davies. That is, if you didn't scare him away." She raised her glass, a gleam of triumph in her eyes. "Cupid calls at Thistlethorne Lodge!"

Polly was about to add another playful jab when her phone, resting beside her place setting, suddenly blared with its lively ringtone. She glanced at the screen. "It's Rose," she said excitedly and swiped to answer. She tapped the speaker icon. "Rose! You've heard something?"

"Maybe ..." Rose's voice filled the room. There was a pause, and Polly began squirming in her seat. Her heart skipped a beat, and she leaned forward, gripping the table's edge. "Rose, tell me. I can take it."

Rose couldn't hold back a small chuckle, clearly enjoying the rare opportunity to keep Polly in suspense. "Well, I was about to leave the library when I noticed a new email ... from a certain PhD. A world-renowned literary manuscript expert."

Polly's eyes widened, and she practically leaped out of her chair. "Rose, stop teasing! Tell me everything. Right now!"

"He's been a fan of Abigail Townsend and her novel, *The Chains of Conscience*, since his days at university! He's intrigued by the possibility of finding her lost manuscript! I'll read you what he said:

"Dear Rose, blah, blah, blah, I would very much like to come to Abbots Clover to examine the manuscript in person—immediately. As you know, such work requires time, and I may need to stay in your village for a while. The British Library will not pay for accommodation if I'm engaged in a freelance assignment. Would it be possible for me and my assistant to stay at Thistlethorne Lodge during my visit? I understand this is an unusual request, but given the potential importance of the find, I believe it would be best if I were close at hand."

Rose finished reading and paused, waiting for Polly to respond—which took less than a fraction of a nanosecond.

"OMG! OMG!" Polly practically shrieked, bolting upright as though she'd been electrified. "He knows who Abigail Townsend is! He's a fan of *The Chains of Conscience!*" Her words tumbled out in a rush as her hands gestured wildly. "This is huge! We're talking about a bona fide expert who already loves Abigail's work!"

Rose got back to business, though amusement leaked from her voice. "So is it possible for him to stay with you at Thistlethorne? Sounds like he's taking this seriously."

"Are you kidding? We'll roll out the red carpet! Give him the best room in the castle ... monogrammed bath towels ... a rose in a silver bud vase on his breakfast tray! We'll make sure he's pampered like the King of Antiquarian Bookland! The answer is yes, yes, YES!"

Polly ended the call, and for a brief moment, the room was silent, as if everyone were holding their breath, waiting for the news to sink in. Then they erupted. "Can you believe it?" Polly exclaimed, her voice a mix of glee and disbelief. "Dr. Field-stone is coming here—to Thistlethorne! To look at the manuscript!"

Tiara lamented, "If it turns out *Vanity and Virtue* was written by Prudence Nobody Pembersnitch instead of semi-famous Abigail Townsend, we're stuck playing host to a stuffy old library guy. I'll give you five to one he looks like Albus Dumbledore and acts like cantankerous Dr. Kingfield from that old movie *The Paper Chase*," she said, shaking her head.

"Indiana Jones was a doctor. Archaeology," Tim smiled. "I'm holding out this doctor looks more like Harrison Ford. But only from *Raiders of the Lost Ark* or *Temple of Doom*. And maybe *Working Girl*. Oh, who am I kidding? Even if it were Indy from *Dial of Destiny*, I'd let him inspect my artifacts."

The next two days passed in a haze of neurotic anticipation for Polly and her team. Their excitement, laced with an undercurrent of anxiety, was contagious. Even Mr. Boots, usually indifferent to the comings and goings of the household, seemed more alert, following Polly around as if sensing the importance of the occasion.

Finally, the morning arrived. Rose was there too, and just past noon, the sound of gravel crunching under tires signaled Fieldstone's taxi was there. Polly smoothed down her dress. Tiara took a deep breath. And Tim opened another button on his shirt (in case their Dr. guest was indeed an Indiana Jones clone). As if they were in an old TV period drama like *Downton Abbey*, where the servants in a manor house gather to greet the returning lord, Polly and her brood moved to the front courtyard. There, stepping out of the black taxi, was Dr. Jonathan Fieldstone.

Forget a grizzled old Dumbledore, Fieldstone couldn't have been more than thirty-five years old! His lean body was dressed in a tweed blazer with elbow patches, a crisp white shirt, and dark trousers, he looked too young to be the erudite academic they were expecting. Just under six feet tall, he had a fresh, handsome face. His straight jet-black hair was longer than currently fashionable and gave him a slightly rakish look. He looked up at the house and stopped in his tracks. "Crikey!" he exclaimed. "You live in a real-life castle!" His gaze swept over the towering turrets and the ivy-covered walls.

Tim made a soft, guttural, growling sound of approval.

There was something incongruous about Dr. Fieldstone. For all his scholarly gravitas, there was a youthful, enthusiastic twinkle in his eye. He gave Rose the hug of an old friend and shook hands with Tim and Tiara.

Polly stepped forward. "Welcome to Thistlethorne Lodge. I hope you had an easy journey."

"Crikey! I can't believe I get to meet the famous Polly Pepper, too!" Fieldstone gushed, not caring a wit if he came off as the sycophant he was. "I have a bootleg tape of a horror flick you made, *Crawling Eyeballs II: The Vision Returns*. A misunderstood masterpiece of the genre, in my humble opinion. You were absolutely smashing in that role!"

Well, that did it. Polly instantly dissolved and fell head over heels in love. Forget about her panting for Terrence. Or even her affection for Elliot Davies. Here was Dr. Fieldstone, a man who could probably quote Shakespeare and Chaucer, confessing love for a rubbish film she'd made. "You have excellent taste, sweetums," she cooed. "The critics were beasts to me, but I still get fan mail from some who say it's as brilliant as *Killer Klowns from Outer Space*. Who am I to argue?"

As they entered the house and walked through the grand hallway, Dr. Fieldstone couldn't help but marvel at his surroundings. The antique furniture, ornate chandeliers, and artwork were like stepping back into old-world elegance. "There'll be plenty of time for us to talk later," Dr. Fieldstone said. "Can we please get immediately to the heart of my visit? I am nearly hyperventilating in anticipation."

Polly led the way, and Fieldstone smiled when he entered the library and found wall-to-wall celebrities staring at him from their frames. A closer inspection could wait, and Polly, with a sense of theatricality, moved to the bookcase beside the fireplace. She pressed the rosette carving, and the panel slowly swung open, revealing the secret room.

"Crikey!" Dr. Fieldstone said again.

"A priest hole," Rose explained with delight. Like most people, Fieldstone had only heard about such features in ancient houses but had never seen one in person.

Polly carefully retrieved the manuscript. The moment she placed it on the desk and began to unwrap it, Fieldstone's attempt at professional composure vanished. When the manuscript was fully revealed, he slipped on a pair of cotton gloves and slowly reached out for it. His fingertips gently grazed the aged pages as though he might frighten them away if he touched them too quickly. He finally looked up at the group, his voice hushed but filled with conviction. "This ... is extraordinary." His words were heavy with appreciation. "The paper, the ink, the handwriting—I'd say this manuscript is most likely ... authentic."

Time seemed to stand still. Polly felt her heart swell with triumph. Tim's eyes lit up as he let out an incredulous chuckle, while Tiara clasped her hands to her chest. Even Rose, usually the epitome of calm, broke into a rare, delighted grin, her eyes gleaming with satisfaction.

Dr. Fieldstone's thoughts were racing. "Of course, we'll need to conduct a thorough examination—material analysis, handwriting comparison, and so on. My assistant, Rachel, arrives on Monday. But everything about this feels right. It should be in a vault," he said, his tone tinged with concern. "A priest hole isn't the ideal place to keep it."

Rose nodded. "There's a safe in the library. And I've also set up the storage room as a makeshift lab to conduct your analysis. It's a more controlled environment than at Thistlethorne, and you'll have all the space you need."

9

Monday night's Lush Hour rolled around, and all Polly could say to Dr. Fieldstone and his assistant, Rachel Hawthorne, was, "You've had a whole day to slap your Good Housekeeping seal of approval on the manuscript. Just tell me how many zillions of smackers I'll get when Jeff Bezos takes it off my hands."

Dr. Fieldstone, seated in a wing chair with his second glass of champagne, took a deep breath, bracing himself to repeat—for what felt like the millionth time—that his authentication job could not be rushed. "Polly, I can't wave a magic wand and declare the manuscript is the real deal. That's not how it works in academia. My reputation isn't built on simply brushing off dusty old papers—I have to make sure those dusty old papers are genuine. When I put my name behind an authentication, I'm signing a sworn affidavit, under oath, standing on a stack of Bibles, cross my heart hope to die, stick a needle somewhere dumb and painful. There can't be any shadow of a doubt."

Bored by details, Polly groaned. "I don't understand why we can't sweep past the red tape and get to the part where I get richer and more famous than I already am."

Fieldstone couldn't conceal an eye roll. "I understand your frustration. But this isn't about simply verifying a signature or matching handwriting samples. The process is far more complex, especially with a potentially significant document."

He took another sip of champagne, gathering his thoughts. "First, there's the paper analysis. We have to confirm the material itself dates back to the right time period. That involves microscopic examination of the paper fibers. Then there's the ink—does it match what was commonly used in Abigail Townsend's era? And that's not even considering the stylistic analysis, where we compare the writing style, phrasing, and thematic elements. The stakes are incredibly high, and any mistake in authentication could have serious consequences. Not just for you, my career and reputation, but for the entire literary world."

Fieldstone's assistant, Rachel Hawthorne, seated beside him, nodded in agreement. "We can't just say it's authentic, Ms. Pepper. We have to prove it—to scholars, collectors, and the world. That's why we must be thorough."

Tiara nodded, her expression more empathetic than exasperated. "Think of it this way, Polly, the more thorough they are, the more valuable the manuscript will be in the long run. You know what they say, 'Patience isn't a virtue; it's an investment.' And if you can keep from pacing a hole in the floor, the returns could be substantial."

"She's right, Mom," Tim said. "The longer they take, the more airtight the authentication will be. And when it's all said and done, we're probably talking about a payday that'll be worth the wait. So let them dot every I and cross every T."

Polly's gaze ping-ponged between Tim and Tiara, and Dr. Fieldstone and Rachel. She knew they were right—of course—but that didn't make the acceptance any easier. "Fine," she relented, though her voice was tinged with the sound of someone making a monumental sacrifice. Lifting her glass in a mock toast, she quipped, "Just know that every day this drags on creates another line on my face. I'm billing you for the Botox!"

The stockroom of the Abbots Clover Library had been transformed into a laboratory for scholarly research. The room, previously a mundane storage space filled with dusty boxes and old audio-visual equipment, now housed one of the long reading tables from the library's main room. It was strewn with magnifying glasses, a microscope, a video spectral comparator, and various archival tools. Despite the careful arrangement of the workspace, the overhead lights were a constant source of anxiety for Fieldstone. He knew fluorescent bulbs emitted ultra-violet radiation—a potential disaster for delicate materials like *Vanity and Virtue's* centuries-old paper and ink. UV light could accelerate the fading of inks, make paper brittle, and cause irre-versible damage to the fragile manuscript, jeopardizing the authenticity he was trying to establish.

The library's volunteer staff had done their best to make the room suitable and safe, covering the windows with heavy curtains to block natural light and placing a few standing lamps around the table to provide softer, more controlled illumination. Still, the stockroom was far from the climate-controlled, and museum-quality spaces Fieldstone was used to.

Rachel Hawthorne was an eager assistant. A year out of university, she was determined to prove herself in the field of forensic document examination. With her youthful enthusiasm and a mind as sharp as the quill pens she admired, she'd quickly become indispensable to Dr. Fieldstone. Though she was still relatively new to the world of dusty manuscripts and scholarly debates, she carried herself with a quiet confidence that belied her inexperience and ambition. She wanted to learn everything Fieldstone could teach her—although she was in a hurry to do so.

Seated across from Fieldstone at the worktable, her brow furrowed in concentration, Rachel carefully compared the hand-writing in the manuscript to known samples from Abigail Townsend. Her attention to detail was precise. Every few minutes, she would pause, biting her lip in thought, before noting an observation on her iPad. Rachel's meticulous nature was evident in the way she handled each fragile page, her cotton-gloved hands moving with the care and respect of someone who understood the weight of history that rested in her hands.

Despite the less-than-ideal conditions, Rachel was completely absorbed in her work. She knew this was her chance to make a mark and show Dr. Fieldstone and the academic world she was more than an eager post-grad doctoral candidate. She was determined to prove she was a rising star in the world of antiquarian studies.

It was late Friday afternoon, and the room was filled with the quiet intensity of their work. Dr. Fieldstone and Rachel were lost in their meticulous examination, their focus unbroken by the ticking clock. Then, suddenly, a sharp knock on the door echoed through the room, shattering the stillness. Rachel blinked, momentarily disoriented as she was pulled from the world of Abigail Townsend's delicate script back to the present. She exchanged a quick glance with Dr. Fieldstone, who merely nodded, signaling her to handle the interruption. She rose from her chair and moved to the door, her mind still half-occupied with the work she'd been doing. When she opened it, she found Rose, her expression a mix of urgency and concern.

"Sorry to bother," Rose began, keeping her voice low. "There's a gentleman in the main reading room. He's heard about the manuscript—nothing stays secret for long in this village. He says his name is Arthur ... Arthur Townsend." She paused, letting the weight of the name sink in. "He claims he's a distant relative of Abigail Townsend."

Dr. Fieldstone's pen froze mid-note as he finally looked up from the manuscript, his usually composed expression darkening with suspicion. "A relative?" he repeated, his voice tinged with wariness. "Abigail Townsend's been dead for over two hundred years."

Rose nodded, and her eyes flickered nervously as she looked over her shoulder, scanning the main reading room. "The Townsend family still has a few branches scattered around the region."

Fieldstone's grip tightened on his pen, his knuckles whitening. "What does he want?"

"The manuscript," Rose whispered, her voice barely audible, as if saying it aloud would summon something—or someone—ominous. "He says it's his family's property and rightfully belongs to him."

Rubbing his temples, Fieldstone could feel the tendrils of a headache tightening around his skull. "That's ridiculous. Being distantly related to Abigail Townsend doesn't grant him ownership. There's no way he's getting anywhere near this manuscript."

Just then, Arthur Townsend appeared behind Rose in the doorway, his posture stiff and expression severe. "I'm here to reclaim what belongs to the Townsend family," he said curtly, his voice dripping with entitlement.

In his mid-fifties, Arthur Townsend exuded a presence that filled the room. Standing under six feet tall, with broad shoulders and a sculpted jawline, he had an aristocratic air. His chiseled features were set in a permanent state of mild disapproval, as though the world had continually failed to live up to his exacting standards. His eyes—deep-set and stormy gray—had a way of drilling into people, making them feel as though they were being judged for reasons they couldn't understand. There was an intensity to his gaze, and a simmering tension in his demeanor, the kind that suggested he could explode at any moment.

Dr. Fieldstone barely had time to process the man's appearance and audacity before Arthur's sharp eyes zeroed in on the worktable, where several pages of the manuscript were carefully laid out. His gaze narrowed, and his whole bearing shifted like a predator stalking prey. He took a step closer, his eyes locked on the yellowed pages as though they were the Rosetta Stone of literature. "Is that the manuscript?"

Dr. Fieldstone moved protectively closer to the manuscript, his pulse quickening as he watched the man's eyes gleam with something akin to greed.

Townsend's breathing grew heavier, his nostrils flaring as he practically salivated at the sight of the ancient document. "That ... belongs to the Townsend estate," Arthur said, his hand twitching as if he wanted to reach out and snatch the manuscript from the table. The reverence in his voice was overshadowed by a possessiveness that sent a shiver down Rachel's spine as she watched helplessly.

Dr. Fieldstone's voice cut through the tension, firm and unyielding. "Mr. Townsend, I must remind you this manuscript is under our care and supervision for authentication, and until that process is complete, it remains here. I understand your connection to Abigail Townsend, but you cannot claim ownership of something simply because of your lineage."

Townsend's eyes flickered with frustration, but he didn't back down. "You may be an expert in old books, Doctor, but this manuscript belongs to my family. And I intend to see it returned." He took another step forward, and Fieldstone instinctively moved to block his approach, his body language subtly defensive.

The atmosphere in the room grew dense with tension. Dr. Fieldstone was all too familiar with the thorny complications that could arise when old family legacies intersected with valuable artifacts. "This manuscript is potentially a significant piece of history, and its rightful place will be determined by thorough research and verified authenticity, not merely by family ties."

Arthur Townsend stepped closer, his gaze hardening as he squared his shoulders. His eyes darted between Fieldstone and the manuscript. "*Vanity and Virtue* was written by my ancestor. It's our family's legacy. We've been custodians of Abigail's memory for generations. We have a right to protect it and to ensure it's handled with the respect and dignity it deserves."

Dr. Fieldstone met Arthur Townsend's gaze. His tone, though controlled, carried a weight of authority that made it clear he wouldn't be bullied. "Respect and dignity are exactly what we're ensuring," he countered, his words measured yet firm. "This isn't about family heirlooms, Mr. Townsend. If this manuscript is genuine, it belongs to the world."

Townsend's eyes narrowed as he sized up Fieldstone, clearly displeased. "You may have your procedures, Doctor, but this manuscript wouldn't even exist without my family. We won't be sidelined."

"Mr. Townsend, I appreciate you want to claim this as your own, but there are factors you have to consider. For one, the manuscript was discovered in Thistlethorne Lodge, which legally places it in the current owner's possession—Ms. Polly Pepper's. Additionally, there is the matter of authentication."

Townsend's jaw tightened. "I don't need a lecture on legalities, Doctor. What I need is for the manuscript to be returned to my family. Surely, a man with your intelligence can recognize the significance of family inheritance."

Fieldstone nodded, his expression calm but firm. "Indeed, but we're dealing with a potentially valuable piece of literary history. The manuscript's provenance must be thoroughly established and authenticated before ownership can be considered."

Townsend's lip curled slightly. "Do you expect me to simply stand by and watch while my ancestor's work is dissected by strangers?"

Rose couldn't hold back any longer. "You don't have a choice. With due respect, Mr. Townsend, where have you been all these years? If this manuscript was so important to your family, why wasn't it safeguarded or even known about? It's easy to claim ownership now the manuscript's been found and could be worth a lot of money, but where was the concern for your legacy when it was gathering dust in an attic, forgotten by everyone— including the Townsends?"

Arthur Townsend's eyes flashed with anger, his voice cold with condescension. "The manuscript was lost to time—hidden away. But that doesn't diminish its significance to the Townsend family. We can't be held responsible for what was forgotten in history's shadow. Now that it's come to light, it's my duty to ensure it is returned. Its worth isn't purely monetary, Ms. Harding. This is about family and legacy—something that can't be measured in money."

Rose wasn't backing down. "I understand the importance of legacy, Mr. Townsend, but this manuscript may have historical significance beyond one family. If it is what we hope, it belongs to the public, where scholars, readers, and historians can access it. Your family's claim doesn't outweigh the cultural and literary value that could be shared with the world."

Townsend took a step closer. "That's where we differ. You see it as an artifact for scholars. I see a piece of my family's history that deserves to be returned. Even museums are doing that now —returning antiquities to their home countries. My family has lived in this area for centuries, and it's our responsibility to protect what's ours."

Fieldstone interjected, "Mr. Townsend, we're not dismissing your connection to Abigail Townsend or the importance of family legacy. However, the manuscript was discovered in Thistlethorne Lodge, and by law, possession is a significant factor in determining ownership. Until its authenticity is fully verified and its provenance established, the manuscript will remain under lock and key."

Townsend's eyes narrowed further as they shifted from Fieldstone to the tall steel safe against a side wall. His gaze lingered there, a calculating look crossing his features as he weighed his options. The muscles in his jaw tightened, and for a moment, a flicker of something darker crossed his expression—a mix of frustration and determination. "And what if I refuse to accept that?" His voice was low, almost a growl. "What if I insist on taking the manuscript with me today?"

The atmosphere in the room grew even tenser, the weight of Townsend's insinuated threat hanging in the air. His stance was firm, his eyes cold and resolute, as though he dared Fieldstone to try to stop him. There was no mistaking the underlying implication in his words—the manuscript was a prize he wasn't willing to let slip away easily.

Dr. Fieldstone didn't waver. "If you attempt to remove the manuscript or interfere in any way with our work, we'll call the police. I'm a member of the Royal Historical Society of London, and we have the authority—and obligation—to protect documents deemed of cultural importance. This isn't about who found it or to whom it once belonged—there are legal procedures in place for a reason. Any rash action could jeopardize your claim of ownership and the preservation of this potentially important piece of history."

Townsend's eyes flickered with frustration and defiance.

"And am I supposed to trust you're not stalling to keep it for yourselves? How do I know this so-called authentication process isn't a way to keep my family's legacy out of our hands?"

Fieldstone remained composed, though his voice carried a steely edge. "Because, Mr. Townsend, our only interest here is the truth. Authenticating a document like this is a delicate and time-consuming process that requires expertise, not haste. The truth will be revealed in time, and that truth, whatever it may be, will dictate the manuscript's rightful place. But until then, it remains under our care."

Townsend was mute, his frustration evident. His gaze returned to the pages on the table as he fought to keep his emotions in check. "I'll be watching you," he warned, his tone filled with quiet menace. "And I'll do whatever it takes to see this manuscript is returned to me. Mark my words. The Townsend family will reclaim what's rightfully ours. One way or another."

Arthur Townsend turned on his heel and strode out of the library, his footsteps echoing ominously through the main reading room. The tension in the supply room didn't break until they heard the heavy front door close with a definitive thud, and Townsend was gone from the building.

Rose let her breath out in a rush, the sound almost startling in the stillness. "Well, that was dramatic," she said, shaking her head and regaining her composure.

Dr. Fieldstone adjusted his glasses, his normally calm demeanor slightly rattled. "I've dealt with difficult heirs before, but Townsend ... This feels different." His voice trailed off as he exchanged a worried glance with Rachel.

"I think we need to be careful of that one," Rachel agreed quietly, her usual professionalism burnished with unease. "I don't trust him. He seemed ... desperate."

10

The annual Abbots Clover Village Literary Festival was just around the corner. A highlight of each spring, the weekend event transformed the village's cobblestone streets into a lively celebration of literature, food, and entertainment. Stalls would offer everything from classic fish and chips to gourmet meat pies and literary-themed treats: *Treasure Island rum balls*, *Peter Pan's Neverland fairy cakes*, and *To Kill a Mockingbird mocktails*. There was something for everyone.

Famous writers would mingle with wannabes, sharing stories and insights. There would be workshops for aspiring writers, ranging from creative writing sessions to tips on finding an agent and how to get published. Children would be captivated by storytelling periods, with tales of adventure and magic coming to life. The atmosphere was one of community and shared passion for book lovers and foodies alike.

But this year's festival was already shaping up to be notably different. Word had spread that Polly Pepper had unearthed a literary treasure in the attic of Thistlethorne Lodge—a manuscript supposedly written by the enigmatic Abigail

Townsend. Adding to the buzz, whispers of a feud between Polly and Arthur Townsend had heightened the intrigue.

The villagers were quick to take sides in the unfolding drama, each faction fueled by a mix of loyalty, skepticism, and self-interest. On one side were the "Old Guard," villagers who had deep roots in Abbots Clover, their families having lived here for generations. These folks supported Arthur Townsend, whom they might not have known personally but whose lineage stretched back centuries. They saw the manuscript as a rightful heirloom of the Townsend family and, by extension, a part of the village's heritage. To them, Polly Pepper was an outsider, a Hollywood interloper who had stumbled upon something that didn't belong to her—including her castle bequeathed by Alistair Drake.

On the other side were the "Newcomers," a smaller but equally vocal group who had moved to the village from London or Bristol in recent years, drawn here by the rural charm but unburdened by its history. They were more inclined to side with Polly Pepper, seeing her discovery as a stroke of luck. "Finders keepers," they argued. "Why should it go back to some family who didn't care enough to keep track of it in the first place?"

At Bound to Read, the village's popular bookshop and coffee hangout, the air was always heavy with the rich aroma of espresso and the sharper tang of gossip. This morning, writer Mary Radcliff, ostensibly there to pound out the next chapter of her latest potboiler, had her laptop open but untouched. Instead, she was shamelessly tuned in to the chatter around her. The usual laments about the miserable weather or Mrs. Lawrence's suspiciously frequent visits from Nigel the milkman on Tuesday and Thursday mornings had given way to something far juicier: whispers from the next table about the manuscript Polly Pepper had found.

"I heard it's worth millions," whispered octogenarian Lenora

Wainwright as she leaned in close to her friend Patty Dobbs, who was nursing a pot of Earl Grey. "She's that actress from America. Found the manuscript in her attic, buried under a pile of old clothes! Can you imagine? She should give it back!"

Mrs. Dobbs nodded vigorously. "They say it could be a long-lost novel by a famous writer! I never heard of her, but they say she lived around here at the same time as that other writer, Jane What's-her-name. I never read her books either, but I once saw a movie based on one of them starring that Emma Thompson actress. Imagine finding something written more than two hundred years ago! She never got it published. Poor dear. They're keeping her manuscript at the library and checking to see if it's fake."

Mary Radcliff, the self-published author of *Lust Among the Bluebells*, and a writer known for "borrowing" her plots from real-life village scandals, nearly choked on her black coffee as she overheard the conversation. She was supposed to be working on her new novel—which was little more than a rehash of the same tired tropes she'd recycled in her last book—but she'd run out of story ideas. The manuscript the old ladies were discussing immediately piqued her interest, and an idea began to form in her mind—one that could give her lackluster writing career the boost it desperately needed.

Mary's mind was racing. A long-lost manuscript? Unpublished? Written by a dead writer? This could be my big chance. She leaned back in her chair, pretending to stretch, but her ears were trained on the conversation at the next table. Who would know if someone just ... maybe ... used a bit of the story? After all, it wasn't like there was a petty author who could scream "copyright infringement."

The more Mary thought about it, the more the idea seemed not just feasible but brilliant. She could take the story, change all the character names and locations, throw in some steamy sex scenes to keep up with modern tastes—and publish it under her own name. *Voila!* No one would be the wiser.

Mary could even picture the cover: a shirtless stud pressed against the bare flesh of a raven-haired vixen with globe-like boobies. The title: *Surrender to the Storm*. No. *The Duke's Dark Desire*. Hmm. How about *The Temptress of the Moors*. It didn't matter. She'd come up with something suitably salacious later. It would be a big hit, and television streaming services would pay a fortune to make it into a series. Mary's heart pounded excitedly as she imagined the accolades, the interviews and, especially, the money. She could see it all so clearly: glowing reviews, the bestseller lists, interviews on YouTube, TikTok, and Facebook Live chat shows. Finally, the recognition she'd always wanted and felt she deserved. She needed to find a way to get her hands on that manuscript.

It's time to renew my library card.

Dressed in a deep burgundy blouse with a plunging neckline and black capri trousers that hugged her pear-shaped heinie— Mary Radcliff entered the Abbots Clover Library with a confident stride. Her heavy perfume was a mix of gardenias and something more cloying. *Patchouli?* She glanced around before heading directly for the lending desk, where Rose Harding and her volunteer assistants were cataloging newly returned books.

Rose sniffed the air, and without looking up, said, "I've explained before: we're not including *Lust Among the Bluebells* in the library's collection. Our budget is limited, and we have to prioritize books that are in high demand—or at least reviewed positively in legitimate sources." She stopped herself from adding, *And for heaven's sake, hire a decent copy editor!*

Mary stood before Rose, her lips glued into a saccharine

smile. She was tired of hearing this rejection of her book. "Rose," she purred, her voice dripping with faux sweetness, "I'm not here about *Lust Among the Bluebells*. Although I must say, it's a real shame you're not interested. The villagers would eat it up. I wrote it in only a month! Just flew out of me! It could be a big hit."

Rose raised an eyebrow, her expression unimpressed. She'd heard Mary's pitch too many times. "We don't have the shelf space."

Mary waved a manicured hand dismissively as if brushing aside a pesky fly. "Yes, yes, I know all about your 'shelf space.'" Her tone was somewhere between mocking and resigned. "But that's not why I'm here."

Rose was guardedly intrigued. Mary Radcliff never did anything without an ulterior motive, and the fact she wasn't here to push her book was, well, curious.

"You see," Mary continued, fluttering her eyelashes, "I've heard through the village grapevine that Polly Pepper found a handwritten book in her attic by someone named Amelia Thompson. Of course, as a writer myself, I can't help being fascinated by this. As a fellow creative, I'd love to ... I was wondering if ... maybe I could take a peek at *Varnish and Valor*. Love the title, by the way ..."

"*Vanity and Virtue*," Rose corrected. "And it's not by anyone named Amelia Thompson."

"Um. Right. Whatever." *Idiot! Varnish and Valor! Where the heck did that come from?!* "As I was saying, as a fellow writer, I'm dying to see what all the fuss is about."

Rose's eyes narrowed, her focus sharpening. "I'm afraid the manuscript is off-limits for public viewing, Mary. It's in the middle of a delicate authentication process by a representative from the Antiquarian Books Department at the British Library."

Mary's smile faltered briefly before she pressed on, determined not to be dismissed. She straightened her spine, her smile slipping into a pout of mock disappointment. "Oh, I understand, I do. But you see, I can't help feeling ... a connection ... to this piece of history. I mean, how often does someone have the dumb luck to stumble upon a lost, unpublished, unread manuscript by a famous writer nobody even remembers? It's too amazing, isn't it?"

"What exactly do you want, Mary?"

"I'm wondering if there's any chance I could pretty please take a wee look at it. Just for inspiration, you know? Not even to touch it—just a quick glance. As a writer, it would mean so much to feel that connection with another talented woman who lived and breathed words all those years ago right here in Abbots Clover."

Rose's expression hardened. "Mary, I appreciate your enthusiasm for local history, but that's simply not possible. The manuscript is extremely delicate."

Mary's smile tightened, a flicker of frustration crossing her face. "Come on, Rose. Be a sport. It's not like I'm asking to check it out of the library as if it were another title on the *Sunday Times* Bestseller's List, for pity's sake. You can be there with me the whole time—heck, I'll bring my own gloves if it'll make you feel better."

Rose didn't budge. "The answer is no, Mary. The manuscript is off-limits until the experts complete their work."

Mary's eyes flashed with irritation, but she quickly masked it with another saccharine smile. "Of course, Rose. I completely understand. I wouldn't want to interfere with something so important."

Rose gave her a curt nod, her suspicion deepening. "Good-bye, Mary."

Mary lingered, her gaze flickering to the door that led to the library's storage room. "Oh, I completely get it, Rose. But maybe an itsy-bitsy, teensy-weensy, sneaky-peeky? I'm sure I'd be inspired purely by osmosis. As a writer, it's important to stay inspired, and what could be more inspiring than seeing the lost work of a local literary legend? Plus, wouldn't it be great to have a local author's perspective on Amelia—er, Abigail's work? I mean, I could write a piece for the festival's website. Maybe it would even help generate more buzz for the library."

Rose's exasperation was obvious. "I appreciate your enthusiasm, Mary, but no one is allowed to see the manuscript. Even I haven't read it."

Good. The fewer people who know what it's about, the better. Mary's eyes darted around the room, searching for another angle. "If it is a long-lost masterpiece, wouldn't it be amazing to have a modern writer's take on it? I could write a companion piece. Like a 'now and then' comparison between my contemporary novels and that dead writer's old ones! I'm sure that would draw a lot of interest. And honestly, I wouldn't even need to touch it—I could look at a few pages, take some notes ..."

Rose shook her head. "If you're truly interested in Abigail Townsend, there are resources about her in the public collection. You're welcome to explore those."

Mary's face hardened for a split second before she quickly masked it with a tight-lipped smile. "Right. Of course. I understand," she said for the umpteenth time, her tone laced with thinly veiled frustration. "I guess I'll have to wait like everyone else."

When Rose didn't offer any further openings for debate, Mary finally turned on her heel and left, her mind already racing with alternative plans. Rose's refusal had only fueled her determination. *There's got to be a way to get my hands on that manuscript,* she thought, her frustration morphing into resolve as she left the library and walked down the cobbled street. *I need to be more ... creative.*

11

Polly, Tim, and Tiara glanced longingly at the grandfather clock in the main reception room at Thistlethorne, feeling the familiar itch of impatience as they realized there were still fifteen agonizing minutes to go before the official start of Lush Hour. *Never before six p.m.,* Polly reminded herself sternly. She had rules for cocktail time—standards, even. None of that tacky "it's 5:00 somewhere" nonsense for her. No, she had class. And restraint.

As she was biding her time, giving Mr. Boots a half-hearted belly rub and contemplating whether she should hold a séance to contact Abigail Townsend and get her to pinkie swear that the manuscript was indeed her own original work, the sound of the front entrance door creaking open and closing echoed through the hall.

A moment later, Dr. Fieldstone and his assistant, Rachel, appeared in the doorway of the reception room. "I'm glad you're all here ..." he said. His eyes flicked between Polly, Tim, and Tiara as though weighing the impact of his next words. He paused—long enough to draw everyone in. "I have something to tell you ..." His words hung in the air, thick with suspense. He exchanged a glance with Rachel, who was struggling to remain inscrutable, then turned back to the group.

Polly and Co. instinctively sat up straighter, their curiosity piqued by the gravity in Fieldstone's tone.

Taking a deep breath, Dr. Fieldstone finally broke the silence. "Okay. I just have to come out and say it. There's good news, and ... well, not-too-terrible not-good news." He cleared his throat to steady himself for what was coming next. "After meticulous examination, cross-referencing, and analysis, I'm confident in declaring the manuscript we've been studying is, without a shadow of a doubt ... drumroll ... the long-lost work of Abigail Townsend. It's genuine."

His words seemed to freeze in the air for a fraction of a second. The trio stared at him, wide-eyed, as if the magnitude of the revelation had momentarily knocked the wind from their lungs. Time itself seemed to stand still, like a pendulum halted mid-swing.

Then, in a burst of excitement, Polly leaped up. "I knew it!" She spun toward Tim and Tiara, her eyes blazing with vindication. "You never listen to me! Nobody ever listens to me!" The long-lost manuscript, believed to be a myth by some, was real. It would change everything.

Dr. Fieldstone paused to let the significance of his words sink in as they all leaned in closer, hanging on every word. "We began with the handwriting. Comparing the script to known samples of Abigail Townsend's, we found a match. Not only in the style, but in the subtle, unique quirks—certain flourishes, the way she looped her G's and crossed her T's—all of it lined up perfectly."

Standing beside him, Rachel nodded in agreement, her excitement barely contained. "We also analyzed the ink and paper," she said. "The materials are consistent with what was used in the nineteenth century, specifically in this region. The paper fibers and ink composition all point to that period."

"I also consulted with a specialist in forensic linguistics to study the language used in the manuscript," Fieldstone continued, his voice growing more animated as he recounted the process. "The vocabulary, the phrasing—everything is in line with Abigail Townsend's era and her style. But what truly sealed the deal for me was the content itself."

He paused again, glancing at Polly, who was almost dumbfounded. "The themes, the narrative structure, the character development—it's all quintessential Abigail Townsend. This manuscript isn't just a work of fiction; it seems to be a window into her thoughts. Her worldview. It's an extension of her only published novel, *The Chains of Conscience*, and it explores the same ideas of societal expectations, personal integrity, and the complexities of human relationships. *Vanity and Virtue* is, essentially, a continuation of that story."

Polly's heart raced as Dr. Fieldstone spoke. Perched on the edge of her seat, her hands clasped tightly in her lap, she could hardly contain her excitement. "It's real! It's really, real!" she exclaimed, the words tumbling out in a rush. All her doubts and impatience had been worth it for this moment of validation. She could practically see the headlines: *Polly Pepper Discovers Lost Literary Treasure!*

It was more thrilling than walking an opening-night red carpet. Now, like old-time movie star Hedy Lamarr, who had invented frequency-hopping technology during World War II, Polly would be known for more than her comedic chops. And the manuscript's sale would fund the badly needed repairs on the castle.

Fieldstone smiled warmly, his eyes sparkling with the thrill of discovery. "Yes, Polly. It's as real as it gets. This manuscript is a literary treasure, and its value—both historically and mone-tarily—is inestimable."

Tiara's face was also alight with the thrill of the authentica-tion. She was swept up in the infectious energy of the moment, eager to ride the wave of Polly's and Fieldstone's enthusiasm. But after a moment, and with a reluctant sigh, she said, "You said there was 'good news and not-too-terrible not-good news.'" The excitement from her voice moments before was now tinged with unease. For a brief, uneasy moment, she wondered if all the fun might be snatched away.

Dr. Fieldstone nodded thoughtfully, his brow furrowing slightly. "Hmm. Well, it's not terrible, not-good news, but ..." He hesitated, trying to find the right way to diminish the impact. "I'm afraid it's not a complete manuscript. It's missing pages."

Polly's heart gave a small lurch. "Missing pages?" Her mind raced. She knew there had been gaps in the story when she read it. "How crucial are those pages ... to the manuscript's value, I mean?"

Fieldstone glanced between Polly and Tiara. "It shouldn't affect its value to the literary world—this is still an important find. Scholars will undoubtedly be eager to study it. However, it could reduce the price if you were to sell it." His tone was cautious but reassuring, like someone explaining a jackpot prize had been slightly downgraded but was still life-changing.

Polly's face fell. The manuscript might remain valuable to scholars, but its price tag had taken a hit—and she needed every penny. Her ancient castle wasn't going to repair itself. The west tower leaned precariously, a strong gust of wind away from collapse. The roof above the larder leaked so badly it had earned the nickname Lake Thistlethorne. The heating system groaned like a medieval dragon, and the dungeon, though atmospheric for potential tourists, reeked of mildew and despair. Even the windows weren't spared—Polly had tried to romanticize the eerie whistling of the wind through the bowed, leaded glass as a lullaby, but it was more like a wail of despair. And then there was the electrical system—a relic of another century that seemed intent on burning the place down.

Polly's dreams of a financial windfall felt as deflated as her ancient boiler, which hadn't worked properly since steam engines were cutting-edge technology.

The room remained quiet as the weight of Fieldstone's words settled. It wasn't disastrous news, but it certainly put a damper on their excitement. The manuscript was still a treasure —just not quite as perfect as they'd hoped.

Polly's smile faltered. "Why can't things ever be exactly as they seem? Last year, I was offered Drew Barrymore's iconic role in a Netflix remake of *Scream*. I was over the moon! I mean, Drew Barrymore—*hello!*" She paused for effect. "And then," she continued, her voice dripping with melodrama, "I watched the original movie again. Drew's character gets murdered in the first few minutes! That's it. No more Drew. And obviously, by extension, no more Polly Pepper! One scene and I'm done for. Talk about false advertising! Naturally, I passed on role."

Polly crossed her arms, shaking her head in disbelief. "And now," she said, turning to Fieldstone with an almost accusatory look, "you're telling me *Vanity and Virtue* is missing pages? Seriously? First Drew, now this. What's next?"

Tim took a deep breath and plastered on a brighter expression. "Let's focus on the fact that we've got an authentic piece of history in our hands. Don't let anything ruin the moment—not even an incomplete manuscript."

Fieldstone glanced around the room, clearly aware of everyone's disappointment. "And with all the fuss Arthur Townsend is stirring up about his family's claim, it's probably best to keep this news from the public as long as possible. The last thing you need is for this to leak and give him more ammunition."

"That's 'what's next.'" Polly groaned. "It's like finding buried treasure and realizing it's all cursed gold you can't spend."

Tiara, who had been quietly following Dr. Fieldstone's explanation, leaned forward, her brow furrowed. "Dr. Fieldstone, something's been bugging me since we read the manuscript. The gold brooch—it feels like it's practically a character in the story. Do you have any idea what that's about? And then there's mysterious letter tucked between the pages, signed with the initials RL. Have you figured out who that might be?"

Fieldstone's eyes lit up, clearly impressed by Tiara's attention to the finer details. "Ah, the brooch and the letter," he mused, his tone taking on the enthusiasm of a teacher with a bright student. "Two intriguing elements of this discovery."

He adjusted his glasses, a small smile playing on his lips. "Abigail was brilliant at using symbolism in her work. She used inanimate objects to represent deeper themes. In this case, the brooch seems to symbolize both the promise and burden of love. I think it's a riddle tied to the main character Cathryn Slocum's —and, by extension, Abigail's—struggle between adhering to her father's and society's expectations and following her personal desires. It's a mystery that unfolds gradually, with each clue bringing the protagonist—and the reader—closer to understanding what it means to own one's identity—and destiny."

Tiara nodded, still curious. "Okay. What about the letter signed by RL? Who is that?"

Fieldstone's expression grew thoughtful. "The letter is one of the most fascinating aspects of your discovery. It's signed 'RL,' but it probably isn't the fictional Rupert Lancaster. And Abigail doesn't provide any real clues about who this person might be. But it's likely the person was someone significant to her— perhaps even a secret lover."

Fieldstone's expression grew even more thoughtful, a hint of something deeper flickering in his eyes. He seemed to be weighing his next words as if what he was about to reveal carried more weight than they might have anticipated. "Actually, there's more to the letter than the ambiguity of it being signed with initials," he said slowly, each word deliberately chosen. "I don't know as much as I'd like about Abigail's personal life, but Professor Richard Lockhart, the linguistics expert with whom I consulted, has spent his entire career studying all the British female writers of the eighteenth and nineteenth centuries. He's particularly entranced by Abigail Townsend."

Dr. Fieldstone chuckled as he tried to paint a picture of Professor Lockhart's fixation on the work and mystique of Abigail Townsend. "To him, she's a rock star. You think Elvis Presley's or Judy Garland's fans are maniacal? Lockhart makes a pilgrimage to Abigail's grave every year on her birthday. He owns a quill pen he believes belonged to her. He holds readings from *The Chains of Conscience* and places a first-edition copy of the book and an antique shawl on an empty chair that he imagines Abigail is sitting in. I knew he'd be the right man to add the final seal of approval to the manuscript. After some intense analysis, he believes this letter reveals something personal about Abigail's romantic life."

Polly, Tiara, and Tim exchanged glances, their interest piqued by the shift in Fieldstone's tone. They could sense whatever he was about to say was important. "Go on," Polly urged, leaning forward, her gaze fixed on Fieldstone as the suspense in the room grew.

"As I dug deeper into the manuscript and shared my findings with Professor Lockhart, we began to notice certain parallels between Abigail's life and the life of Cathryn Slocum, her protagonist in the novel. The more we discussed it, the more we became convinced Cathryn is, in fact, the alter ego of Abigail—a fictionalized version of herself."

Polly leaned forward, absorbing his words. "That makes

sense," she said, her voice hushed. "Writers, like actors, pour themselves into their characters. Sometimes you can't tell where fact becomes fiction."

"Exactly," Fieldstone agreed. "Cathryn's struggles, her desires, her conflicts—they all mirror what little we know of Abigail's own life. And then there's the letter signed by RL. At first, I thought it wasn't all that important. But the language in the letter is so charged with emotion, so raw and intimate, it suggests something far more personal. I now believe RL was an alias for Walter Langley. He was known to have been an intimate of Abigail's, someone who knew her secrets and perhaps even took advantage of her, as Rupert Lancaster does in the manuscript."

Rachel, who had been quietly listening, spoke up, her voice tinged with sympathy. "If Cathryn is Abigail's alter ego, then it makes sense RL was a real person in her life—a lover who betrayed her trust. The letter hints at a relationship filled with passion, but also one that left Abigail feeling manipulated."

Tiara's eyes widened. "So this manuscript isn't a work of fiction. It's Abigail's way of telling her story and processing her emotional pain."

Fieldstone nodded. "That's our suspicion. And if that's true, it adds another layer of significance to this manuscript. It's not just a lost novel—it's a window into the soul of a creative woman who lived centuries ago. A woman who faced struggles and heartbreaks in a society that offered few options to her."

The room fell silent again, everyone absorbing the gravity of what had been said. It wasn't just a manuscript they were dealing with anymore—it was the story of a woman who had been lost to time. Her voice, buried beneath the dust of history, was finally uncovered.

Tiara was the first to break the hush. "If this is Abigail's story

—her real story—then we're not just unveiling a manuscript. We're unveiling her life."

Dr. Fieldstone nodded, his expression thoughtful. "Exactly. That's why the authentication process had to be so thorough. We weren't just verifying the paper or ink; we were unraveling history, trying to honor the legacy of a woman who fought to be heard." He paused, letting the weight of his words sink in.

Polly's initial excitement deepened into something more profound. The magnitude of the manuscript's importance pressed on her—the responsibility of reviving Abigail's voice, of sharing her story with the world. *This isn't a relic,* Polly thought. *It's a testament to Abigail's defiance and determination to leave a mark on a world that tried to silence her.*

Fieldstone cleared his throat, bringing their focus back to him. "But," he said cautiously, "you need to proceed carefully. If Abigail's story contains truths the world wasn't ready for back then, it may still provoke strong reactions today. Especially from Arthur Townsend."

Polly's thoughts turned to Townsend, who had already gone to great lengths to defend his ancestor's legacy. What would he do now that the manuscript was authenticated? Would he see it as a threat? Worse, would he try to suppress it—or even steal it? Taking a deep breath, she steadied herself. Polly wasn't one to back down, but this challenge felt personal. Her jaw set in determination. "If Arthur Townsend—or anyone else—thinks they can silence Abigail's voice again, they'll have to go through me first."

Throughout the night and well into the next morning, Polly continued to be intrigued by the cryptic phrase in the letter: *The oak that stands alone guards its resting place.* When she'd finished her breakfast energy drink (aka Bloody Mary), and the weather app on her phone assured her rain wasn't expected for several hours (although it was usually wrong), she conscripted Tiara and Tim into taking an exploratory walk. "There's something that's been bugging me," she whined. "The riddle in the note by RL. 'The oak guards its resting place.' What the heck does that even mean?"

Curiosity flickered across Tiara's face. "You think there's something to that? Or are we about to chase another wild goose?"

"Well," Polly mused, leading the way into the cool air outside, "Fieldstone said Abigail used a lot of symbolism in her writing ..."

"But the note wasn't written by Abigail," Tiara reminded.

"Still, it has to mean something. 'The oak that stands alone guards its resting place.'"

Tim followed closely behind, surveying the estate grounds sprawling before them. "Problem is, I don't see any oaks at all—standing alone or otherwise," he said with a hint of skepticism. "We've got clusters of trees, but nothing screams 'solitary guardian' to me."

As they wandered farther across the property, Polly scanned the landscape. The ten-acre grounds were dotted with small groves, but nothing unusual caught her eye. "Maybe we're not looking in the right spot," she muttered. "There has to be something we're missing. They say sometimes the most obvious things are hiding in plain sight."

The deeper they ventured, the more Polly's frustration grew. She had expected the oak to leap out at them—something standing proudly by itself. But every tree seemed to be part of a grouping.

Tim kicked a stray stone. "Maybe we're interpreting the riddle wrong."

"Or maybe we're looking for the wrong thing," Tiara added. "What if the oak isn't literal? That's what symbolism in literature is all about ... giving objects or events deeper meaning."

Polly sighed, her voice tinged with impatience. "But what if it is literal? We have to keep looking."

Finally, after an hour, they found themselves near the far edge of the estate. Tiara sighed dramatically and leaned against a tree. "Okay, I give up. Maybe there's no oak. Maybe the riddle doesn't mean what we think it does. Or maybe someone chopped it down for firewood a hundred years ago."

Polly paused, hands on her hips, surveying the land before them. "Maybe it represents, I don't know, wisdom and knowledge. Or strength and endurance. Or protection and shelter," she suggested. "I don't know what to think anymore. I never understood symbolism even when Mrs. Espindle taught that in English class. Why can't writers say what they mean? A tree is a tree, for Pete's sake. Sometimes it's a big, tall thing that drops leaves everywhere and clogs the gutters on your house."

Tiara brushed a stray leaf from her jacket. "So we're calling it quits? Because I'm not exactly heartbroken about heading back inside. It's cold, and my feet are killing me."

With a collective sense of relief, the three turned and started back toward the house, the allure of the mystery temporarily dulled by the chilly air and their tired legs.

Polly looked at her watch and shook her head as they approached the house. "You know," she said thoughtfully, "maybe the answer isn't out here after all. Maybe we're looking in the wrong place. Maybe the oak we're looking for is a piece of furniture. Who knows. But I've got to get to the library and Rose's damn festival committee meeting."

12

The meeting room of the Abbots Clover Library was a snug, wood-paneled space that carried the scent of aged paper and polished oak. Bookshelves lined the walls, while a long rectangular table dominated the center of the room, surrounded by the festival's planning committee. The aroma of freshly brewed coffee, courtesy of a library volunteer, mingled with the quiet hum of focused activity.

At the head of the table, Rose presided with her signature authority, her color-coded notes meticulously arranged before her. Her sharp gaze swept across the room, ensuring the group's attention was fixed on the tasks at hand.

Seated around the table were Sarah Rogers, owner of the Bound to Read bookshop; Constable Jenkins, ready to outline festival logistics like traffic flow and security; Polly Pepper, who had appointed herself the festival's Hollywood glamour consultant; Elliot Davies, a self-published romance author Polly had invited to speak; and the heads of the subcommittees, each prepared to report on their progress.

Rose cleared her throat, drawing the room's attention. "Thank you all for coming," she began, her voice steady. "I know everyone's been working tirelessly to ensure our festival is its usual success. Today, we need to finalize a few things, including the lineup of speakers. Polly Pepper is in charge of introducing all the authors who are presenting programs. She's selected a self-published author who will give a lecture about this increasingly popular avenue for writers who are not traditionally published. I yield the floor to Ms. Pepper."

Polly smiled and straightened her posture, radiating confidence as she prepared to introduce Elliot Davies. "I'm happy to introduce a talented writer. A romance novelist. I'm certain readers of all stripes will find him interesting." Polly smiled warmly, concluding, "I'm confident Elliot will entertain and inspire everyone attending his lecture. He represents cutting-edge publication trends. I believe he'll elevate the festival with an inspiring program."

Polly leaned back, satisfied she had made her case. All eyes turned to Elliot, who was about to introduce himself, when Mrs. Tillman, an elderly committee member in charge of judging the homemade sausage rolls contest, leaned forward with a frown. "No offense, Ms. Pepper, nor to you, Mr. Davies," she began, her tone measured but pointed, "but shouldn't we be showcasing our own talent from right here in Abbots Clover? Mr. Davies is from a different village. Here, we have writers like Mary Radcliff. Her last book wasn't much good, but maybe the exposure would give her more confidence to write better. Wouldn't giving one of our own a platform be more appropriate?"

The room fell into a brief, uncomfortable silence, all eyes shifting between Polly, Mrs. Tillman, and Elliot Davies. Rose glanced at Polly, silently urging her to respond with care.

Polly's smile tightened a fraction. "I completely understand where you're coming from, Mrs. Tillman, and I agree we have talented writers here in Abbots Clover. But I think bringing in voices from outside the village is also important. Elliot doesn't live that far away ... just over in Shepperton Foal. That's practically our sister village. It's not more than twenty minutes from here. His perspective is unique. More than Mary Radcliff's. He also has a growing readership that could draw more people to the festival. It's about broadening our horizons while still celebrating talent."

Mrs. Tillman looked unconvinced, but another committee member, David Abernathy, chimed in before she could respond. "I think Polly's right. It's good to mix things up a bit. Besides, Mary Radcliff's books suck."

Uncomfortable giggles circulated around the table as Mr. Abernathy continued, "I tried to read her last one, *Lust Among the Bluebells*. I couldn't get past her opening paragraph: 'The field of bluebells stretched out like a big, blue carpet, the kind you'd find in a fancy hotel lobby, but outside and with flowers instead of nylon or wool. The sky was also blue, like the bluebells, so it was like being in a big, blue sandwich of blueness. Each bluebell was like a tiny, droopy umbrella, hanging down as if it were shy or maybe tired of being a flower. The sun was shining, but not too brightly, as if it didn't want to outshine the bluebells, which were the stars of the show. The breeze whispered through the field, making the bluebells sway back and forth, like they were doing a slow dance at a high school prom. It was all blue, quiet, and boring if you think about it too much.'"

Hysterical laughter ricocheted off the walls as Sarah doubled over, clutching her stomach, tears streaming down her cheeks. Constable Jenkins slapped the table with a booming laugh. Polly frantically dabbed at her mascara, trying to salvage what was left of it before it streaked down her face. Even Rose, ever composed, bit her lip to stifle an uncharacteristic cackle. The room was a chorus of wheezing gasps and hiccupped chuckles when Mr. Abernathy exclaimed, "I had to reread it three times to figure out what on earth she was talking about—and I memorized it!" That set off another wave of howling, with someone choking out, "A big blue sandwich of blueness!"

As the laughter subsided and the room returned to a semblance of order, Rose straightened her notes and cleared her throat, regaining her usual poise. "Well," she said with a wry smile, "I'm giving Elliot Davies my seal of approval for the speaker series. Now, let's move on." She seamlessly shifted the discussion to updates from the hospitality, logistics, budget, social media, and children's events committees. Though ready to adjourn the meeting, Rose hesitated—there was still one topic she needed to address.

"Before we wrap things up," Rose said, leaning forward, "there's something I wanted to say to the committee." She paused, making sure all eyes were on her. "It's about the manuscript Polly Pepper discovered in her attic. I've spoken to Dr. Fieldstone from the British Library, who has been authenticating it. Although he's not ready to make an official public announcement yet, he suggested to me—confidentially, of course—it is indeed an original work by Abigail Townsend. Therefore, I think we should have a public unveiling at the festival. With Polly Pepper doing the presentation, of course. The citizens of Abbots Clover deserve to be the first on the planet to see what has been hidden right here in our village for more than two hundred years."

Polly's eyes widened, a spark of excitement flickering in them. "Me? Unveil the manuscript?" *Who else!* she thought, imagining cameras flashing, her name in the headlines, and applause from the crowd as she stood center stage, beaming. But outwardly, she kept her expression cool, forcing herself to sit straighter, her hands folded demurely on the tabletop. With a measured, almost casual nod, she gave a slight shrug as if this was another event in her already glamorous life. "Well, certainly. I'd be honored," she said, her voice smooth, though she could barely contain her excitement. Inside, she was doing cartwheels, but she let only a faint smile express her pleasure.

Time to celebrate! Polly thought, a triumphant glow still tingling through her after the successful festival committee meeting. In true Polly Pepper fashion, she wasn't one to let a good moment pass without making it spectacular. Why end on a high note when there could be a crescendo—and fireworks? An impromptu farewell dinner party was the thing!

Dr. Fieldstone and Rachel had wrapped up their work in Abbots Clover and were set to return to London first thing Monday morning. What better way to send them off than with one of Polly's famously unforgettable soirées?

The reception room at Thistlethorne buzzed with a mix of familiar faces. Near the fireplace, Sarah, the lively owner of Bound to Read, was deep in conversation with Terrence Marks, the editor of the *Abbots Clover Overview*. Ever curious, Terrence was peppering Sarah with questions about the literary festival, already crafting his next headline. His interest in the festival's success had only grown with the village abuzz over Arthur Townsend's rumored threats of a lawsuit against Polly. While Terrence wasn't exactly a Pulitzer Prize-winning investigative journalist, he had a knack for spinning even the smallest tidbits into stories that felt essential.

Grayson Jenkins, the village constable and Tim's heartthrob, was perched on the Chesterfield near the crackling fireplace deep in conversation with Dr. Fieldstone and Rachel. From across the room, Tim watched Gray's dimpled smile and the way his eyes lit up—his own knight in shining armor, who, for the record, looked equally dashing whether breaking up a pub brawl or nerding out over an ancient manuscript.

Gray leaned forward, his brow furrowing in an adorably intense way that made Tim's heart stutter. "So, you're telling me you can tell if a manuscript is fake by sniffing the ink and squinting at the paper?" he asked, his voice tinged with the fascination he usually reserved for police investigations.

Dr. Fieldstone chuckled, clearly delighted to have an enthusiastic audience. "Not quite sniffing, Constable, though the smell of old parchment can be revealing. We analyze the ink composition, examine the paper fibers under magnification, and even study the quirks of the handwriting. Think of it as detective work, except the suspects are long dead and occasionally wrote in Latin to mess with us."

Gray chuckled, tilting his head thoughtfully. "So, it's like a murder mystery, but the victim's been dead for centuries and they're made of vellum."

Rachel smirked, sipping her wine. "A quiet victim, but yes, that's the gist."

Rose stood nearby, quietly sipping wine from her glass, her composed demeanor softened by the faintest flicker of pride. She wasn't one for frivolity or idle chitchat, but tonight she allowed herself this small indulgence. It was her suggestion, after all, that had brought Dr. Fieldstone to Thistlethorne—and, by extension, into Polly's orbit. She had every reason to feel quietly triumphant.

Elliot Davies, on the other hand, remained the outsider—for now. Polly had taken it upon herself to remedy that, weaving opportunities for him to slip naturally into their circle. It didn't hurt that Tiara's face practically glowed whenever Elliot entered a room. And Polly had certainly noticed how Elliot seemed to gravitate toward Tiara, always finding a reason to hover closer than strictly necessary.

The spark between them was unmistakable, faint but promising—like the first flicker of a match catching flame. Polly, ever the romantic (despite her protestations to the contrary), sipped her champagne with a satisfied smile. She'd seen enough budding romances to know when something special was taking root. All it needed was a nudge—and Polly was nothing if not an expert in delivering the perfect nudge at the right moment.

As the guests mingled and the wine flowed, Polly made her rounds, ensuring everyone felt comfortable and pleased to be there. But she also realized there was something bittersweet about the evening. Dr. Fieldstone and Rachel would clear out their makeshift lab at the library and their bedrooms at Thistlethorne over the weekend and return to London. Thistlethorne Lodge would fall back into its everyday rhythm, and the whirlwind of the past few weeks would become another memory.

As the evening wore on and the guests finished a sumptuous meal, Polly noticed a subtle shadow fall across Fieldstone's face. He had been relatively quiet throughout the night, and now, as they lingered over coffee and tea, she inquired about his reserved attitude.

"I'm fine ... it's just ... But I've been meaning to talk to you about the festival," Fieldstone said, his voice uncharacteristically solemn. "Polly, I know how excited you are about unveiling the manuscript, but I have serious reservations about doing that."

Fieldstone sighed, glancing at Rachel and Rose before continuing, "Arthur Townsend dropped by the library this morning. Actually, he barged in. He's become more aggressive. He'd heard through the ridiculously short village grapevine that the manuscript is authentic. He confronted me again. For a moment, I was afraid. He insisted again the manuscript be returned to his family. Thankfully, I'd locked it up in the safe. But he made fresh threats. I think showing off the manuscript at the festival could provoke him further. He'll think we're rubbing his nose in it. The manuscript may be a Pandora's box. Revealing it in a public setting might not be a good idea."

Polly met Dr. Fieldstone's eyes, her resolve wavering for the first time. His concern was valid, but her initial reaction was disappointment laced with indignation. How dare Arthur Townsend! She had discovered the manuscript, and now this entitled man wanted to snatch it away. But as Fieldstone's words settled, the gravity of the situation began to sink in.

Tiara, seated beside her, voiced the unease they all felt. "Do you think he'd try something antagonistic—or worse? It's a public literary festival, for crying out loud. What could he possibly do in front of everyone?"

Tim leaned forward, his tone serious. "Never underestimate people who feel backed into a corner—especially someone like Townsend, who thinks he's been wronged. And let's not forget the stakes. There's potentially a lot of money tied to the manuscript."

Polly's thoughts raced, darting between the grand unveiling she had envisioned—the crowds, the applause, her moment of triumph—and the nightmare of the chaos Townsend could unleash. She could see it now: the festival remembered not for celebrating literature, but for a public, ugly confrontation.

And yet, Polly Pepper was not one to back down. She had faced her share of challenges—both on the stage and off. This was about more than her own glory; it was about the legacy of Abigail Townsend and the team that had brought her voice back to life. Her gaze returned to Fieldstone. "Are you suggesting we hide it away? Pretend we didn't find it?"

Fieldstone shook his head, his expression grave. "I'm suggesting you think carefully about how you proceed. There has to be a way to honor Abigail Townsend's legacy without putting yourselves—or the manuscript—at risk."

Rachel, who had been quietly listening, spoke up. "Maybe

you could do a private unveiling for a select group—the village council, the mayor, and other dignitaries—before the festival. That might defuse any tensions before they escalate in front of a larger audience."

Polly's thoughts raced. A private unveiling? It felt like a cheat. She wanted applause, admiration, and her moment in the spotlight—a chance to remind everyone Polly Pepper was someone special. The idea of stepping back, of playing it safe, gnawed at her.

Still, the prospect of avoiding potential chaos weighed heavily. Could she set aside her love of the limelight for the greater good? Polly wrestled with the thought, torn between her unyielding desire for recognition and the growing realization that discretion might, for once, be the better choice. Finally, she drew a deep breath and nodded. "All right, let's think this through ..."

Elliot Davies, who had been quietly observing, leaned forward. "I might have an idea," he began, his voice cutting through the room's contemplative hush. He glanced around, meeting everyone's gazes with calm confidence. "What if we create something more unique than a public unveiling at the festival? Something that honors Abigail Townsend's legacy but without putting anyone or the manuscript at risk."

Polly raised an eyebrow, intrigued but cautious. "Such as?"

"I was thinking you could maybe do a staged reading of *Vanity and Virtue*."

Rose nodded slowly, seeing the merit in the idea. "That would reduce the risk of creating a spectacle that might provoke Townsend. It also allows us to not show the original manuscript while still sharing the idea of it with the village."

Tiara, whose admiration for Elliot was becoming increasingly difficult to hide, smiled warmly at him. "It's a great idea, Elliot. This is a way to focus on Abigail's legacy rather than the drama surrounding the manuscript. And it keeps Polly at the center of it all!"

All eyes turned to Polly, who was smiling and nodding in agreement. "By turning it into a reading, we avoid the potential chaos Townsend might bring." Her eyes sparkled with renewed energy. "Elliot, I love it. Abbots Clover's own off-off-Broadway recitation of *Vanity and Virtue*. Watch out, Meryl Streep—I'm coming for your crown!"

13

Monday evening rolled around after a day that had been anything but peaceful for the residents of Thistlethorne Lodge. They'd reluctantly waved goodbye to Dr. Fieldstone and Rachel in the morning. Then Star Lady seriously took to heart Elliot Davies's suggestion to perform a staged reading of *Vanity and Virtue*. But when she realized someone would have to type up the manuscript, she changed direction. In true Polly Pepper fashion, she hijacked the idea of a staged reading and turned it into her own one-woman tour de force. *Why share the spotlight when you can hog it all to yourself?* was her life-long motto.

"I've read thousands of scripts over the years. Writing a one-act play will be easy breezy," Polly declared with the naïve confidence of someone who believed mastering a word search puzzle qualified them to crack a spy code. Her past contributions to scripts mainly involved suggesting the occasional comma and insisting every scene needed more "star shine."

By the time she finally knocked off for the day and held her well-earned Lush Hour flute of champagne, Polly was utterly convinced she was on her way to penning a theatrical master-piece. With each scene she wrote, she envisioned herself commanding the stage with her dazzling presence—dramatic pauses, tearful soliloquies, and the occasional triumphant fist pump. "I'll be the talk of the festival!" she proclaimed. "And since no one's read the manuscript, they won't know if I fudge a few details."

Dinner was served. The washing-up completed. The evening wore on. And they all began preparing for bed. But something didn't seem right. At least not to Tim, who hadn't received Gray's nightly "sweet slumbers, my fuzzy-wuzzy honey bunny" call. Then his phone finally rang with Ed Sheeran's "Perfect," the personal ringtone Tim had assigned to Grayson.

But instead of the usual "how was your day, sexy ... I missed you ..." Gray's words tumbled out in an avalanche. "I need to talk to you ... and everyone ... It's urgent ... I'm coming over."

Tim's heart skipped a beat, and his mind raced with possibilities. There was a seriousness in Gray's voice that made his stomach churn with unease. "What's wrong?" But Gray had already hung up. Tim's heart pounded as he looked up from his phone, catching Polly's eye. "Gray's on his way over. He needs to talk to all of us. He's never come over this late just to say goodnight."

A few minutes later, Tiara stepped into the reception room, drying her hands on a dish towel and getting ready to say good-night. "What's going on?" she asked, glancing between Polly and Tim, both of whom looked unusually tense.

"Grayson's on his way over," Polly replied, her voice betraying a tremor despite her attempt to stay calm. "He says it's important. He wants to see all of us."

The words hung heavy in the air, thickening the silence. Before anyone could speak again, a sharp knock echoed from the front door, making all three of them flinch.

Tim shot a look at Polly and Tiara, then rushed to the foyer. The doorknocker thudded again, louder this time as if urging him to hurry. At the door, Grayson's eyes held a dark, haunted look. His face was ashen, his posture rigid. And he was still in uniform—though it was long past the time he'd usually changed into his "civvies," as he called his civilian clothes.

"Gray?" Tim's voice faltered. "What's up?"

Grayson didn't answer. He held Tim's gaze for a moment, his intensity cutting through the air like a blade. "Where are the others?" Without waiting for a response, he brushed past Tim and strode down the hallway. The reception room, so recently filled with music and laughter, now felt strangely empty. The fire crackled in the hearth, and the chandelier cast its golden glow, but the warmth of the room seemed hollow—overwhelmed by the icy tension Grayson brought with him.

Polly sat on the Chesterfield, absently stroking Mr. Boots. But the moment her eyes locked on Grayson's face, she froze. Her hand stopped mid-stroke, her heart thudding in her chest. She glanced at Tiara, whose wide eyes mirrored her own rising panic. "What is it?" Polly's voice cracked, the question trembling in the air.

Grayson stood at the center of the room, visibly weighed down by something dark. He opened his mouth, but no words came. He swallowed hard, his eyes flicking to Tim and Tiara before returning to Polly. His face, usually fun and expressive, had been stripped of emotion, leaving only a raw, hollow blankness. Gathering strength for what had to be said, he clenched his hands at his sides. "It's about Dr. Fieldstone ..." His voice was low and rough as if forcing the words out was physically painful. "I just came from the library. There was ... an incident. Dr. Fieldstone ..." He stopped again, his throat working around the words. "Dr. Fieldstone is dead. Rose found him. This evening."

The room seemed to inhale simultaneously, the revelation

landing like a physical blow. Polly's mouth parted in silent shock, her breath catching in her throat; Tiara gasped, one hand flying to her mouth as her eyes filled with sudden terror; and Tim felt the ground shift beneath him, his stomach plummeting.

Dead. The word reverberated in their ears, heavy and unyielding, like a stone dropped into a well.

Polly's eyes widened in shock. "What! How?" her voice trembled as the color drained from her face. The thought of that brilliant young scholar dead was impossible to grasp.

Tiara's face was ashen as she clutched a chair's armrest for support, her mind reeling from the news. "Details," she managed to say, her voice barely above a whisper.

Grayson looked down, his expression a mixture of sorrow and frustration. "We think he was ... *murdered*. Blunt force trauma to the head. The police from Bristol are treating it as a homicide."

Tim's legs felt weak beneath him as he sank into a chair, his head spinning. "Murdered? Why? Who ...?" He couldn't even finish the thought.

Grayson ran a hand through his hair, his voice tinged with anger. "And ... Abigail Townsend's manuscript ... it's missing from the safe. Well, except for one page Dr. Fieldstone was clutching in his hand. We don't have any concrete evidence yet, but if you ask me, the main suspect is Arthur Townsend. There's been bad blood between him and Fieldstone. Fieldstone told me Townsend had become increasingly aggressive lately, making threats ... and now this."

Polly's head whirled with a thousand questions, but one stood out. She looked at Grayson, her brow furrowed in confusion. "But ... Dr. Fieldstone went back to London this morning."

Grayson's expression tightened, clearly grappling with the same question. "We don't know what happened or why he was still here in Abbots Clover. When I talked to him at your dinner Friday, he told me he was expected back to work at the British Library Monday afternoon. He must have decided to stay behind for some reason."

Polly's mind raced as she tried to make sense of it all. "The taxi picked him and Rachel up here at nine o'clock this morning. They were taking the ten-twenty train to Paddington."

Pale and shaken, Tiara added, "If Arthur Townsend was behind this ... then why? What would killing Fieldstone accomplish? Oh, right. The manuscript."

Tim added, "Could there maybe have been something in the manuscript Arthur Townsend didn't want anyone else to know about? Or maybe Townsend might have thought since Fieldstone hadn't officially announced the authentication, it would be easier to claim the manuscript for himself."

Polly shook her head, feeling a deep, overwhelming sense of loss. "Fieldstone was a lovely man. He didn't deserve this. He was just doing his job. And now ..." She couldn't finish the thought, her voice breaking.

Grayson gently placed a hand on her shoulder, his voice soft but firm. "Polly, I know this is a shock. The police will find out what happened, but we need to be careful. Whoever did this—if it wasn't Arthur Townsend—they might not be done yet. We need to focus on keeping everyone safe."

The next morning's rain matched Polly's sorrow. The relentless drizzle blurred the world outside her window into a watercolor of gray. She'd encountered her fair share of murdered bodies over the years, some even belonging to people she knew fairly well. But the death of Dr. Fieldstone struck a chord she hadn't expected. They'd only been acquainted for three weeks, yet in that short time, he'd not only been her house guest, but also a kindred spirit. She'd come to appreciate his sharp academic mind and unexpected passion for old movies. His presence had brought a spark of intellectual excitement to Thistlethorne Lodge. Now, all of that was achingly absent.

With a heavy heart, Polly picked up the phone and tapped Rose's number. She needed to hear what had happened straight from the horse's mouth. The line rang twice before Rose's familiar voice answered, her tone flat and edged with sadness. "Polly. You've heard."

Polly hesitated, the words catching in her throat, before finally speaking. "Rose, what happened?"

"Polly, I don't know what to do. I—I'm trying to make sense of it, but I can't."

"Take a deep breath, Rose. I'm here. Start from the beginning. Tell me everything."

"The last time I saw Dr. Fieldstone alive was on Saturday afternoon when I ran into him at Bound to Read having a coffee. We talked about your dinner party, the upcoming festival, and how much he'd miss Abbots Clover. He reiterated he was going back to London first thing Monday morning. Then we said goodbye. Oh, and we talked briefly Monday, when I called to ask what he wanted me to do with a notebook he'd left in the supply room. He said it wasn't important, and I could mail it whenever."

Polly listened attentively, sensing there was more. "So it was a shock to find him still in the village."

"A shock?" Rose let out a dry, humorless laugh. "It wasn't that he never left the village—it's where I found him. The last time I'd been in there was before I opened the library. I had to retrieve some supplies. That's when I found his notebook. Everything looked completely normal otherwise. Nothing out of place that I noticed."

Polly could almost picture Rose's steady hands shaking as

she held the phone. "And what time did you find him last night?"

"Around seven. I was about to leave for the day. Then there was a sound. Something in the supply room. I went to check. It was that darn badger we've had problems with. He got in again through the open door. That's when I saw Dr. Fieldstone. Just lying there dead on the floor. And the safe—" She broke off as if struggling to make sense of the words before she said them. "It was open. And empty. The only thing I kept in there was Abigail Townsend's manuscript. And now ... it's gone."

Polly's mind raced, trying to connect the dots. "So everything seemed right the last time you were in the room. Then, before closing up, you found Dr. Fieldstone dead and the safe empty?"

"It doesn't add up, Polly. None of it does. How could everything change so drastically in only a few hours? And why would he be in the supply room of all places? He wasn't even supposed to be in Abbots Clover."

Polly could hear the frustration and confusion in Rose's voice, emotions that were rare in the typically composed librarian. "Rose, listen to me. We'll figure this out together. But for now ... do you want to come here? You don't have to go through this alone."

Rose sighed, a mix of relief and lingering anxiety. "I'm just ... I've never been so thrown off. I keep thinking I should've noticed something earlier but didn't." She paused, her mind clouded with thoughts. "There were only two people who knew the combination to the safe. Me and ... Dr. Fieldstone. I gave him the combination because he was often here when I wasn't available. Nobody, not even my volunteer assistants, knows the combination."

Polly nodded, trying to piece together all the information Rose was providing. "Do you have any idea who might have wanted to harm Dr. Fieldstone?"

Without missing a beat, Rose said, "Arthur Townsend, of course. He's been sniffing around that manuscript for weeks, acting like it's his right to own. Always asking questions, making threats," Rose said, her voice hardening. "I bet he did it. And the manuscript is gone. It's too much of a coincidence."

14

A bbots Clover was a village rooted in tradition and resilience, priding itself on weathering whatever the winds of change brought its way. Over the centuries, it had survived the Black Death, the turbulence of Henry VIII's reign, the Industrial Revolution, two world wars, and even a 21st-century pandemic. Through floods, economic downturns, and hardships, the village had always found a way to endure. Now, in the wake of Dr. Fieldstone's shocking murder, Polly and Rose knew they had to press on with the upcoming literary festival. Canceling it was unthinkable; the consequences would ripple far beyond the world of book lovers, impacting vendors and the entire community.

Librarian Rose Harding, normally the embodiment of the British "stiff upper lip" attitude, was now far from her usual unflappable self. In the wake of finding Dr. Fieldstone's body, her nerves were frayed. And with the festival so close, she found herself grappling with what seemed like an endless barrage of urgent tasks, each one more critical than the last. She'd master-minded this annual event for over two decades, but this year was different. Everything felt like it was teetering on the brink of chaos. Even her age weighed more heavily on her. The bound-less energy she'd once had was flagging with the strain of trying to hold everything together.

Desperate to lighten her load, Rose reluctantly turned to Polly for help. Polly, however, was drowning in her own sea of work—crumpled pages and discarded ideas for her one-woman play littered the table as she furiously wrote (and rewrote) her script for what she now called "*Vanity and Virtue: Confessions of a Scandalous Spinster*." She thought the new title was clever and added the right mix of intrigue and humor to make it appealing to modern audiences.

Rose arrived at Thistlethorne bearing a bribe: a dozen Bakewells from the Tasty Tart bakery. She hoped the sweet jam and almond pastries might soften Polly's mood before she asked for yet another favor. Now, sitting across from Polly and Tiara in the castle's kitchen, Rose didn't need to say a word—Polly could see the exhaustion written all over her face.

"You look dreadful," Polly said, with all the subtlety of a brick. "Not that I blame you. Finding dead bodies isn't anyone's idea of a good time—unless, of course, it's a husband who forgot your birthday or a boss who made you work overtime. So, any updates from the police? Any leads?"

Rose's expression darkened, the strain of the past few days evident in her tired eyes. "Nothing concrete. They've got theories, but nothing holds up. Arthur Townsend seems to have a rock-solid alibi, too. The whole village is buzzing with gossip, but none of it leads anywhere."

Polly nodded, her smile tinged with sympathy. She leaned in slightly, her voice softer. "If you need a shoulder ..."

Rose offered a grateful smile but clearly wanted to change the subject. She took a deep breath. "Actually, there is something I need to talk about with you, Polly. You once said you wanted to volunteer for the festival—even though we both know that was a ruse, I could use your help now."

Lies always come back to bite, Tiara thought, watching Polly prepare for whatever was coming next.

"I want you to moderate the author Q&As at the festival," Rose continued. "You're a natural onstage—and quick on your feet. You're exactly what we need right now, and I'm drowning in too many other tasks."

Polly blinked, caught off guard. "Rose, I'd love to help, but I'm up to my eyeballs. I'm rewriting and polishing my script, and I still haven't gotten into character. I've got a million things to do. I have zero time."

Rose crossed her arms, clearly unconvinced. "You thrive on a hectic schedule and being in front of an audience. It's what you do."

Polly sighed and waved her script in the air. "This is my magnum opus! I'm still writing it and learning the lines. If I don't get this right, I'll be laughed out of Abbots Clover. I can't worry about wrangling a bunch of eccentric writers. What if they're all arrogant Jonathan Franzen divos with sharp tongues and poison pens?"

Rose raised an eyebrow. "It takes a diva to know a divo."

Tiara sniggered. "If being a diva were an Olympic sport, Polly would have more gold than Michael Phelps."

Polly put the back of her hand to her forehead. "I haven't even selected my costume yet! Am I going full Regency era or something Chanel? And don't even get me started on the props. It's hard to find a good quill and ink set these days. Or a lace fan. Never mind a proper bonnet and shawl. One wrong prop, and the whole illusion shatters! My entire production could be ruined by a subpar parasol!"

Rose wasn't giving up easily. She leaned in, her voice softening but her determination clear. "You're telling me you can't spare an hour or two to sit onstage with an author and ask a few simple questions? It'll be easy-breezy. Writers are like actors—but with less charm and more neuroses. They absolutely live for attention —though they'll swear they're tortured introverts who hate the spotlight. Just toss 'em a few compliments, then sit back and enjoy the show. They'll ramble on until the cows come home—probably about how the way the cows come home inspires their work. Trust me, they'll bask in their own self-indulgent glory."

Polly raised an eyebrow. "What would I even ask?"

"Which of your characters is you?" Tiara suggested. "When did you first realize you were a misunderstood genius?"

"Exactly!" Rose said. "Or 'Tell us about your *process*.' Writers love that. If you throw in a line about how their work is 'revolutionary' or 'genre-defining,' they'll light up like a Christmas tree."

Polly leaned back, nodding her head. "The longer they talk about themselves, the less work I have to do? Okay. Maybe. D'ya think?"

Rose's expression softened as she handed Polly a neatly organized folder. "I knew I could count on you. Here's everything you'll need—background information on each of the authors, synopses of their latest books, and some sample questions. I've also included fact sheets about their quirks and personalities. Give 'em a call and discuss which topics they're most comfortable with."

Polly took the folder, glancing at the notes inside. "Psychological profiles?"

"Authors can be ... peculiar," Rose said. "Geraldine McIntosh, for example, has a passion for supernatural romance. Lionel Crumple writes about underworld crime. And then there's Penelope Greeves, who's spent her whole life researching Abbots Clover's history and scandals. She gets easily carried away, so be prepared to steer the conversation back on track." Rose smiled, her eyes twinkling with a hint of mischief. "A lot of flattery for all of them will go a long way. Just remember, keep it fun, lively, and, most importantly, moving. The last thing we need is a panel that drags on and loses the audience's attention."

With that, Rose left the castle, and Polly made her first call.

Geraldine McIntosh, the paranormal romance writer, was best known for writing love triangles between vampires, werewolves, and poltergeists. Polly dialed her number, and as the phone rang, she glanced at the accompanying fact sheet. "Honestly, if I wanted to read books about emotionally unavailable demons, I'd stick to Hollywood actors," she muttered. "At least they don't sparkle in the sunlight or turn into furballs every full moon. Well, most of them anyway."

After their initial introductions, Polly plowed forward with Geraldine. She asked about potential topics to discuss or avoid at the festival.

There was a brief pause on the other end before Geraldine's voice floated through, as velvety as one of her vampire heroes. "Hmm. Maybe ask what inspires me to create the perfect, sexy, undead lover. But better steer clear of asking why all my demonic forces are based on my ex-husband. I'd have to deny that—as part of my spousal maintenance agreement, you under-stand. Any resemblance between Frank and an incubus who seduces humans and drains their life force is purely coincidental —though it's easy to see why some might be confused."

Polly shook her head as she scribbled notes, stifling a giggle. "Would people be interested in how your characters manage to spark passion when they can barely find a pulse!"

Geraldine's tone grew grave. "I will not have you mock my art form. Although, between us, when you've been dead for a few centuries, it is sorta weird. But my readers don't care. Who needs a pulse when you've got centuries of pent-up desire? Though I'll admit, the whole 'no heartbeat' thing can be a bit of a buzzkill."

She was quiet for a long moment before continuing in a conspiratorial whisper, "Speaking of buzzkills ... I heard you were friends with Dr. Fieldstone, the guy who got murdered in the library. Now that's a whodunit even my vampires would sink their teeth into. What do you think about it? Who killed him?"

Polly's hand stilled, the pen hovering over her notebook. "Such a tragedy. But why are you asking me? I'm not the police."

"Yes. Tragedy," Geraldine agreed. "If I were writing Dr. Fieldstone's murder as a paranormal romance, I'd set it in a gothic manor house—not a library supply room, for crying out loud. So uninspired. I'd have Dr. Fieldstone found dead in a wine cellar. And I'd throw in an old manuscript page—clutched in his hand. A look of terror on his dead face would suggest an unspeakable horror before his death."

Polly froze. *A page from a manuscript clutched in his hand. Only Rose and the police knew that detail of Fieldstone's death. Would they have revealed that specific bit of information to anyone in the village? Doubtful.* A wave of unease washed over Polly. It also felt grossly inappropriate to be turning the tragic and real murder of Dr. Fieldstone into a plot twist for a romance novel.

"The suspects would be as shadowy as the manor itself," Geraldine continued. "Perhaps a vampire lord ... centuries old ... who holds the estate in his cold, unyielding grip. Or a werewolf driven mad by an unrequited obsession with scholars like Dr. Fieldstone. And you—yes, you—would be the fierce, strong-willed heroine who uncovers the truth. You are investigating this, aren't you? Your Wikipedia page says you've solved murder mysteries in Hollywood."

Polly felt a chill creeping up her spine, her unease deepening. "You certainly have a vivid imagination, Geraldine. But all this talk about vampire lords, ancient secrets, and scandalous love affairs ... it's fiction, right? I mean, you don't have any inside information on what happened to Fieldstone. Is there something you should tell the police?"

Geraldine let out a soft, throaty chuckle. "Oh my lord, no! You give me too much credit! That's the writer in me, always spinning tales and imagining the most dramatic scenarios. You know how we authors are." She paused for a moment as if carefully considering her next words. "But then again, small villages like Abbots Clover do tend to have their fair share of scandals, don't they?" Her tone was light, but there was an undercurrent of something Polly couldn't quite put her finger on. "I'd hate for reality to outshine my stories," Geraldine added, her tone lightening again. "Now, I've got to get back to my lonely antique dealer who accidentally awakens a centuries-old spirit she falls in love with—one who helps her understand why she's cursed to date werewolves. I'm on a deadline. These books don't write themselves!"

As Geraldine hung up, Polly couldn't help but wonder if the author's imagination was the only thing fueling her stories—or if something more sinister was lurking beneath the surface. Otherwise, why would she have suggested the page of a manuscript clutched in Dr. Fieldstone's dead hand? Fiction? Maybe. Maybe not.

Next on Polly's list was Lionel Crumple. According to Rose's notes, he was a reclusive author of dark, police procedural mysteries. They often left readers sleeping with the lights on—or not sleeping at all. The line clicked, and his voice came through, low and gravelly. "What?"

My, aren't we the perky one. "Lionel Crumple? Polly Pepper here." She injected as much brightness into her voice as possible, hoping to counterbalance the shadowy tone of his. "I'll be moderating your panel at the festival, and I thought I'd touch base to see what you'd like to discuss during the Q&A period. Anything you're particularly keen on revealing to readers?"

There was a pause, and Polly imagined Lionel sitting in a dimly lit room, his face half in shadow, staring at a taxidermized raven and animal heads. "I suppose ... you could ask about my *process* ..."

Polly barely stifled a laugh. That infamous "process"—otherwise known as rearranging desk clutter and convincing yourself that clipping your fingernails is absolutely essential before you can settle in to typing on your keyboard.

"Or perhaps ask how I channel my darkness to create stories that chill the soul."

Polly scribbled "channel darkness ... chill soul" on his bio and fact sheet page. "We can definitely delve into that abyss if you like. But what about contrast? Maybe we lighten the mood with something unexpected, like, 'What does the author of brooding mysteries do when he's not—brooding?' Or 'Do you ever write a happy ending just to see how that feels?'"

Lionel let out a low, humorless chuckle. "My work isn't about lifting moods," he said, his voice dripping with disdain. "It's about peeling back the layers of human depravity, exposing the darkness that lurks in every corner of the soul." Lionel's voice took on a cold edge. "If you're looking for sunshine and rainbows, I suggest you pick up a children's book. My work delves into the shadows, where light only comes from the flicker of a dying candle—and even that's just to make sure the bogeyman isn't under the bed."

Polly smirked, leaning into sarcasm. "Right. My notes say your series features a reclusive ex-detective who retreats to a small village in Scotland after a tragic case shatters his career and psyche. Charming."

There was a long silence on the other end, and Polly

wondered if she'd insulted the author. But then Lionel let out a subtle laugh—an unexpected sound that somehow managed to be both eerie and amused. "You think you're funny, Polly Pepper. Perhaps you should go on the stage and do stand-up."

"Yes, I have a talent to amuse," Polly said, channeling her inner Noël Coward, knowing Lionel didn't have a clue about her showbiz career. That made them Even Steven because she'd never read any of his books. "I'll leave the stage work to Judi, Maggie, and Audra. For now, I'm happy to volunteer for the festival. Let me know if there's anything you absolutely want to cover—besides the darkness within, of course."

There was another pause, this one longer and more unnerving, before Lionel spoke again, his voice lowered to a conspiratorial whisper. "There is something. You knew Dr. Fieldstone, didn't you? Rumors are swirling in the village about the investigation into his murder. A man like him, delving into old manuscripts—one that's gone missing, no less. What if he came across something hidden for two hundred years? Something someone would go to great lengths to keep hidden. Ever read my bestseller *The Mind's Dark Corner*? After the sudden death of her estranged father, a professor of antiquities, Evelyn Hart returns to her sleepy Scottish home village to settle his affairs. Among his personal effects, she finds an old manuscript, but it's missing pages. Her father's last scribbled note suggests the manuscript holds the key to an unsolved mystery. Does that sound familiar?"

Polly's breath caught for a moment, a chill creeping down her spine as Lionel's words hung in the air.

"I've heard whispers," Lionel continued, his tone still dark and ominous, "the manuscript Dr. Fieldstone was authenticating has mysteriously disappeared. And the police are struggling to find leads. Odd, isn't it? In a village as tight-knit as Abbots Clover, you'd expect someone to have noticed something

... unusual. But it's as if the murder happened in the shadows, completely unnoticed."

Polly tried to shake off the unease that was gnawing at her. "It is strange," she replied cautiously, her mind racing with questions. "But the police haven't shared much. How did you hear they're struggling to find leads?"

Lionel's chuckle was soft, almost like he was savoring a private joke. "You know how it is—nothing stays buried forever. But it's interesting, isn't it? The way things can be hidden in plain sight. Sometimes, the most ordinary places—like a library supply room—hold the darkest secrets."

Polly forced a chuckle, though her thoughts were anything but calm. "I suppose so. It's such a small village; someone would have seen something."

Lionel was silent for a beat, then let out an almost reflective, "Hmm. Yes. But I suppose whoever killed Fieldstone knew how to blend in. Sometimes inconspicuous people can go completely unnoticed, don't you think? Especially if they're used to working in the shadows or on the sidelines. But as you said, the police will figure it out ... eventually."

Polly's fingers tightened around the phone, her knuckles blanching as Lionel's words settled over her like a cold fog. His tone sent a shiver down her spine. The implications were clear —and the way he spoke of someone blending in and working in the shadows left her with an unsettled feeling. "Right," she agreed, her voice flat and devoid of its usual warmth. "I'm sure they will ... eventually," she added, her tone hollow. "Thanks for your insight, Lionel. Let's hope you're right about the police. See you at the festival."

As she ended the call, Polly set the phone down with more force than intended. She stared at it for a long moment, feeling perhaps Lionel knew more than he was letting on—and his parting words had carried a darkness she wasn't prepared to face.

With a heavy sigh, Polly tried to shake off the lingering unease. There was no time to dwell on ominous conversations. She had a job to do, and author Q&As were an important aspect of that. Steeling herself, she reached for another bio and fact sheet and tapped her phone with the next number—Penelope Greeves, the village's historian and connoisseur of all things offbeat.

If anyone could offer a distraction from Lionel's cryptic musings, it was Penelope. According to Rose's notes, a conversation with her might be like diving headfirst into a rabbit hole of Abbots Clover's most bizarre and embarrassing moments, and Polly was more than ready for a change of pace.

Penelope had recently self-published *A Scandalous History of Abbots Clover*, a tome so thick and comprehensive it could double as a doorstop for the village hall. Penelope's labor of love had been twenty-five years in the making. The book was a wild ride through the village's most ridiculous—and often mortifying —moments. She had chronicled everything from the infamous Turnip Famine of 1783 to the Magpie Mayhem of 1867, when a marauding flock of magpies inexplicably took over the town square and held it hostage for three days. She'd referenced it as Alfred Hitchcock's inspiration for his film *The Birds*. However, Polly knew "Hitch" (he'd told her so personally!) got the idea from the Daphne du Maurier short story of the same name.

Penelope didn't pull any punches regarding the village's more scandalous affairs. In fact, she'd written an entire chapter dedicated to the Duke of Droitwich—the looney tune who'd built Thistlethorne Lodge. Penelope's account of the duke was told with a seriousness that only made his ridiculousness all the more delicious.

Her book expanded on the legend Polly had heard: the duke

was an insufferable buffoon, utterly besotted with his "fur baby," Loki. His devotion to the dog was matched only by his disdain for human company—or basic decency. The dog had an astonishing ability to clear rooms with silent farts. Penelope, in her characteristic understatement, wrote: "Loki's presence at any gathering was less a social boon and more an olfactory assault, yet the duke defended his companion with the zeal of a man who had lost all sense of smell—and perhaps brain cells."

Penelope's book reserved its sharpest criticism not for the dog (who lived on a diet of indigestible animal organs) but for the duke himself. "The duke's devotion to Loki might have been touching," she'd concluded, "had it not been coupled with his utter disregard for the suffering of others. In a way, he was much like his dog, entirely unaware of the effect he had on those around him. The duke was believed to have suffered from lead poisoning—or syphilis—and truly believed Loki was his misunderstood child." Penelope had even uncovered letters from the duke boasting the dog had saved him from "tedious holidays with my in-laws."

"I'm so glad you called!" Penelope answered her phone with enthusiasm. "The village history is absolutely brimming with scandal and intrigue. I wouldn't mind a question about the stories I was forced to leave *out*." She giggled. "Did you know during the late 1700s, there was a massive scandal involving St. Clematis Church?"

"A church scandal? No way!" Polly feigned disbelief.

"Oh, yes! St. Clematis played a central role in a big village drama. It all started when Lord Tavistock was accused of embezzling funds from the church's coffers—a classic story, right? He was supposed to finance repairs to the church roof. But rumors started spreading he'd pocketed the money and even hid some of his jewels in secret places inside the church."

Polly leaned forward in her chair. "Wait. He hid jewels inside the church? Because it was a sacred space, and no one would think to rob it?"

"Exactly! After Lord Tavistock's sudden and mysterious death—some say it was from inhaling fumes from Loki while in an unventilated room—his family and the church became at odds. There were whispers that treasures were hidden, maybe in one of the old oak beams in the nave."

"So, were they never recovered?"

"No! And the rumors hung around for years. Some villagers believed during the church renovations, the workers found something valuable, but they were paid off by the vicar to keep it quiet. The whole affair was swept under the rug, and it became one of those hush-hush village stories no one ever discusses openly. I'm not allowed to, either. Vicar Aylsworth said I'd never be allowed inside again if I wrote about it in my book."

Polly was about to comment when Penelope's tone shifted slightly, turning almost somber. "By the way, have you heard any updates on Dr. Fieldstone's murder? The gossip says you were good friends. I'm collecting information for *A Scandalous History of Abbots Clover Part Two*. I can't help but wonder what he was doing in the library supply room. It's such a strange place to meet one's end, don't you think? I've heard the police are baffled. I wonder if the killer read my book and knew there was another murder in that supply room in 1820."

Polly perked up as Penelope continued her history lesson, her voice dropping almost to a whisper. "The murder in 1820 was one of the village's darker moments. It involved a librarian named Martin Pritchard. Women weren't allowed to be librarians in those days. Pritchard was known for his stern demeanor and obsession with building the new library's collections— much like our Rose Harding today. He was found strangled to death in the supply room where Dr. Fieldstone's body was discovered. The only clue was a page from a handwritten manuscript clutched in his hand. And they never found the manuscript."

Penelope paused for a moment, letting the weight of the story settle. "The parallels to Fieldstone's death are ... uncanny, don't you think? I can't help but wonder if the past has come back to haunt us. Maybe it's an attempt to keep secrets buried. Maybe Dr. Fieldstone uncovered inconvenient truths while authenticating Abigail Townsend's book."

Polly froze for a moment, processing Penelope's words. How did Penelope know the police were baffled by the missing manuscript? And why did she suggest the killer might know the village's history? The suggestion that Fieldstone might have unearthed something worth killing for sent a new wave of unease through her.

Polly finished the call, but Penelope's mention of Dr. Fieldstone's murder lingered in her thoughts. She couldn't shake the feeling that more secrets were hidden in Abbots Clover than she'd ever imagined.

Trying to push away that thought, Polly made her last call: to Elliot Davies, the romance novelist she'd personally selected for the festival—and maybe/hopefully for Tiara's heart, too. She was saving for last what she hoped would be the best call. The phone rang twice before Elliot picked up, his voice warm and friendly, as if he were a suave character in one of his stories and was about to sweep her off her feet with a sonnet.

"Polly, it's good to hear from you," Elliot began, but his voice changed, becoming serious. "May I say how deeply sorry I am about Dr. Fieldstone. I was absolutely shocked when I heard the news. I still can't believe it—especially after meeting him at your dinner the other night."

Polly paused, feeling a pang of sadness. "It's been a blow. It's hard to believe he's gone ... and in such a horrible way."

Elliot sighed. "I'll always remember how happy he seemed

when talking about his work. His passion was contagious. We had a long chat about historical texts and some of the other manuscripts he authenticated. I was looking forward to seeing him again. It's unimaginable that something like this could happen, especially in Abbots Clover."

"We have to keep going," Polly said. "The festival has to happen, not just for the village, but to honor Dr. Fieldstone. It's more important than ever that we make it a success."

"Absolutely," Elliot said, his voice resolute. "I'm here to help with whatever you need."

"Excellent. On to business then. Guess who your moderator is for the Q&A part of the festival?" She let a bit of brightness return to her voice. "None other than *moi!* So I thought I'd touch base and see what you'd like to talk about—and any burning questions you want me to throw your way."

There was a brief pause on the other end, and Polly could almost hear the surprise in his voice. "Polly Pepper, moderating *my* panel? This is amazing news," he replied. "I must admit, no one ever cares enough to ask about my work, let alone what I might want to discuss in a public forum."

Polly understood. "I have writer friends in America. They all say the same thing. Nobody cares about what they do. Everybody assumes writers are magical creatures whose characters spring to the page fully formed."

Elliot's laugh made Polly picture him leaning back in a leather armchair, swirling a glass of brandy. "People think writers sit down, let our fingers roam the keyboard, and voilà—a book is born. They can't fathom the discipline it takes ... the endless hours of work, the countless rewrites, or the existential panic over what shade of blue the main character's eyes should be. Ice blue? Sky blue? Aquamarine? Cornflower blue? Electric blue? Azure?"

"Do I go with 'smoldering sapphire' or 'brooding cerulean'?"

Polly laughed. "And let's not forget which shade best complements his tortured soul?"

"You've got it!" Elliot laughed. "And no one who isn't a writer ever thinks about the soul-crushing experience of trying to get an agent. Querying is like casting messages in bottles out to sea —except the bottles keep coming back with notes that say, 'Go away. Don't bother us.' Heck, my own mother always asks when I'll be getting a 'real' job. And my brother, bless his ignorant soul, brags about getting free downloads of my books—as if that's the same as supporting my work. He recently confessed he hasn't read any of my work. 'Maybe I'll skim one in the winter, when there's nothing else to do.' Where do these people come from?"

Elliot chuckled. "Thanks for talking to me about my work, Polly. You've made me feel understood for once! Maybe you should turn the panel into a group therapy session for writers."

Polly shifted into business mode. "At the festival, I'll ask you a few questions about your work, and then you'll have the floor all to yourself to talk about *Full-Service Provider* or anything else that pleases you. We're kicking off the weekend with a welcome reception on Friday, followed the next day by panels and talks on everything from paranormal romance to local history. It's going to be quite the literary whirlwind!"

15

With her lit festival phone calls completed, Polly sat in the library at Thistlethorne Lodge, absently stroking Mr. Boots. Her thoughts were as restless as the fire in the hearth. But no amount of warmth from the logs could chase away the chill that shrouded her. It had nothing to do with the drafty house or early spring air but everything to do with the unsettling conversations she'd had. The authors had asked subtle questions about the mystery of Dr. Fieldstone's murder and the missing manuscript.

Penelope's detailed recounting of the village's darker history was unsettling, but it was when she'd drawn parallels between Fieldstone's death and a murder from 1820 that Polly's heart had begun to race. Penelope had casually mentioned a manuscript had gone missing from the library the same night the librarian was murdered. Exactly as had happened this week. Was it another piece of village lore, one of many bizarre tales Penelope loved to recount? Or what if that missing manuscript was *Vanity and Virtue*—the same manuscript Polly had found in the attic? Was that possible? Polly was overwhelmed by the idea.

Her heart began to race, her mind connecting dots scattered

across centuries. What if *Vanity and Virtue* had been stolen all those years ago and hidden away—hidden right here at Thistlethorne Lodge? After all, this was the house where Abigail's friend and mentor, Walter Langley, had lived. What if the manuscript contained something so explosive, so scandalous for its time, someone had killed to get their hands on it in the nineteenth century—and again in the twenty-first century?

Polly's hands shook slightly as she set her teacup down. The fire crackled again, louder this time as if echoing the urgency in her thoughts. She took a deep breath, trying to steady herself against the growing unease in her chest.

Alone with her thoughts, Polly knew it was time to dig deeper and push through the fog of uncertainty surrounding Dr. Fieldstone's death. The police, though well-intended, were over-worked and stretched thin—as most law enforcement agencies are. Anyway, Polly knew she was better suited for this particular investigation on her own. She had solved murder cases before by relying on her sharp intuition and an uncanny ability to read people in ways the authorities couldn't—or wouldn't. Her acting career had been the perfect training ground for this work, requiring her to dissect every nuance of a character's behavior. She could sense when someone was hiding something, when a smile didn't ring true, or when a casual remark was anything but.

As she sat there, pondering her next move, it dawned on her if anyone could shed light on a motive for Dr. Fieldstone's murder, it would be his assistant, Rachel Hawthorne. Rachel had been by Fieldstone's side day in and day out, observing his meticulous process, hearing his muttered thoughts, even catching glimpses of his private life. Rachel might have noticed if something had unsettled Fieldstone in his final days.

Polly straightened in her chair, her resolve hardening. This was her stage now, and she was ready to play the role she knew best—the determined investigator, probing the shadows, piecing together a narrative that would reveal the truth.

Polly's thoughts raced as she reached for her phone. Scrolling through her Contacts, she found Rachel's number. She hesitated for a moment, staring at the name on the screen before tapping the Call icon. As the phone rang, each high-pitched trill stretched into the silence that had settled over Thistlethorne's library. Polly's thoughts swirled.

Finally, a tentative voice answered. "Hello?"

Polly straightened in her chair, her resolve hardening as she heard uncertainty in Rachel's voice. "It's Polly Pepper. I hope I'm not calling at a bad time, but I was wondering if we could talk. There are a few things I'd like to ask you about Dr. Fieldstone ... things that might help me better understand why this terrible thing happened to him."

Polly steered the conversation. "I know this is hard, but you were with Dr. Fieldstone every day while he was here in Abbots Clover. Did you ever notice anything ... unusual? Maybe something about the manuscript he was authenticating?"

The line went quiet for a moment, the weight of the question hanging heavily in the air. Polly could almost feel Rachel wrestling with her thoughts.

Rachel's voice returned, laced with the weight of what she was about to share. "Polly, I've gone over everything with Constable Jenkins in Abbots Clover and the detective inspector in Bristol. I didn't think there was anything more to add, but ... I've been replaying a lot in my mind, trying to make sense of it all." She hesitated, her words heavy with unspoken thoughts. "I even discussed Jonathan's private life—romantic or otherwise— but there wasn't much to tell. He dated occasionally, but nothing serious. His life was his work. And now that you mention the manuscript ... a few things stand out in a way they didn't before."

She paused, as if gathering her thoughts, the silence stretching between them. "I remember Jonathan staring at certain pages—sometimes for what felt like ages. It was very much like him to be absorbed in his work, but with those pages ... it was different. He seemed almost lost. No, stuck is more accurate. It was like he couldn't quite grasp something. I don't know. He seemed ... frustrated."

Polly sat up straighter, her pulse quickening. "What was on those pages, Rachel? Did he ever say what was bothering him?" Her voice was calm, but there was an urgency beneath the surface, a silent plea for information.

Rachel hesitated, the tension palpable through the phone. "He mentioned something. He called it a 'deception.' It got under his skin. Of course, there were the missing pages too ..."

"Right. I remember he said the manuscript wasn't fully intact, which could bring down the sale price from collectors."

"He seemed convinced those pages were important. He thought they would answer his questions about the 'deception' and a 'truth' that was being hidden. The pages were gone, and it drove him crazy."

Polly could feel the weight of the mystery pressing down on her, urging her to dig deeper. "Rachel," she said gently, "was there anyone else who might have wanted to cause harm to Jonathan? Anyone who might have had a reason to want to steal the manuscript?"

Rachel took a deep breath. "A couple of people came by while we were working on the project. You know about Arthur Townsend. He was scary." Rachel's voice dropped as she recalled a confrontation. "There was one time ... It all happened so fast. Arthur Townsend barged into the supply room the day Jonathan determined the manuscript was authentic. He didn't even bother to knock—pushed the door open like he owned the place. Rose wouldn't keep the door locked. Said there were fire safety rules for public buildings. But she was supposed to guard against anyone entering without permission."

Polly could picture the scene: the usually composed Fieldstone interrupted by the intrusion of a man who clearly believed the world revolved around him.

"Mr. Townsend didn't waste time with pleasantries. He got straight to the point. He demanded, again, the manuscript be handed over to him—claiming it was the rightful property of the Townsend family. Frankly, I thought he was a bit of a broken record. I mean, how many times had he said the same thing?"

Polly could almost hear the sneer in Townsend's voice, his privileged upbringing giving him the confidence to speak with authority.

"But Jonathan wasn't having any of it. He stood up to Mr. Townsend. Face-to-face. He told him the manuscript was not an heirloom to be locked away. It was a piece of history, a vital artifact belonging to the world. He said he was going to use his influence to have the British Library acquire it for their permanent collection."

Polly felt a surge of admiration for Dr. Fieldstone. She could see him standing there, his back straight, his presence commanding, his eyes blazing with conviction as he defended the manuscript against Townsend's demands. She could almost hear the steel in his voice, the unyielding determination must have resonated in the room.

"Mr. Townsend was pretty angry," Rachel went on, her tone hushed as if she feared him even now and he might overhear. "He stepped closer to Jonathan, his voice rising. 'You don't understand. I will not let you or anyone else take it away from us!'"

Polly's heart pounded in her chest as she listened. She could vividly picture the confrontation, as if she were standing in the room, watching the clash of wills. Fieldstone, with his commitment to preserving history, and Townsend, desperate to cling to a legacy he felt slipping through his fingers. The air must have been thick with raw emotion—and the potential for violence. It wasn't a disagreement over a document but a battle of ideologies, pride, and possession versus integrity and truth. Polly could almost feel the moment's intensity, the hairs on the back of her neck standing on end.

"Jonathan didn't get upset often," Rachel said, her voice trembling slightly, "but that day, he slammed his fist on the table so hard I jumped. He was furious. He said he wasn't going to let Townsend push him around and even threatened to call the police. Then he grabbed the manuscript, walked over to the safe, shoved it in, and slammed the door. He spun the combination lock, then turned around with this look on his face—like he was daring Townsend to do something about it. Honestly, I think he got a kick out of showing he was in charge."

Polly could almost see the glint in Dr. Fieldstone's eyes, a smirk of satisfaction as he secured the manuscript, knowing he had the upper hand. It was a power play, a clear message he wouldn't be intimidated no matter who stood before him. But as Rachel's words sank in, Polly couldn't help but wonder if that moment of defiance had sealed his fate. Had he pushed Townsend too far? Had the act of locking away the manuscript turned a heated argument into something far more menacing?

Rachel paused, her breath shaky as she remembered the scene. "Townsend stood there, glaring at Jonathan like he was trying to decide whether to fight or back down. He looked furious—like he could snap at any second. Then, without saying a word, he turned and stormed out, slamming the door so hard the walls shook. Jonathan muttered something under his breath —I couldn't catch it, but from the look on his face, I could tell Mr. Townsend had gotten to him."

Polly felt the weight of Rachel's words. Was Townsend desperate enough to kill Jonathan to reclaim his family's legacy?

"Oh, and did you know someone named Mary Radcliff showed up a couple of times?" Rachel continued. "She thought she was clever, but I saw right through her. She was after the manuscript, too. I heard she fancies herself a writer. First, she tried to charm Dr. Fieldstone, but he didn't fall for it. He knew her interest wasn't academic. Then she tried to guilt him, saying he was elitist for keeping the manuscript away from someone like her. I remember her saying something like, 'You're an outsider in our village. You may be a book expert, but this is our heritage. You can't keep that from us.'"

Rachel's voice grew quieter as she recounted the next part. "Jonathan told her it wasn't up for debate. He said the manuscript was more than a piece of history—it required careful handling—and told her to leave, or he'd make her leave. His voice had this edge to it, almost like a hiss. Mary stood there for a moment, glaring at him. I could see the anger in her eyes— she looked ready to say something, but instead, she stormed out. Honestly, the way she left ... I wouldn't be surprised if she was stewing over it for days. Maybe even looking for a way to get back at him."

Polly's heart pounded. Arthur Townsend and Mary Radcliff ... both had reasons for wanting the manuscript—and perhaps committing a murder to get it. She took a deep breath, her mind racing as she considered the possibilities, her voice steady but laced with a hint of uncertainty. "Rachel, I know this is a lot to process, but was there anyone else? Anyone who might have shown an extra interest in the manuscript? I know this might sound absurd, but ... what about ... Rose the librarian? Or any of her volunteer assistants?"

Rachel fell silent. She was clearly taken aback by the sugges-tion. "Rose? The other librarians?" she repeated, her voice laced with disbelief. "I never ... I mean, Rose is the most dedicated person I've ever met. I think she lives for her library. She was a friend of Jonathan's. He trusted her. He even let her read some of the pages we were working on. She was exceedingly interested ... but only because of its potential literary importance. I can't speak about her assistants, but ... Rose?"

Polly nodded, the weight of the question heavy between them. "I know it sounds far-fetched," she admitted, her tone softening. "Rose has always been loyal to the library and the village. But with everything that's happened, I can't rule anyone out—not even someone as trustworthy as her. If she knows something, anything, or if she were involved in some way—by accident or out of misguided loyalty—I need to find out."

Rachel was quiet for a few more moments, clearly struggling with the idea. "I just ... I can't picture Rose ... But then again, I never imagined any of this happening in the first place. But no. I think that's impossible. That's not the Rose I observed for the three weeks we were in her library."

"I had to ask," Polly admitted, her voice softening. "I can't help but question everyone's motives. But you're right—it's hard to picture Rose ..."

"While we're on the subject of covering bases, there was another visitor a couple of weeks ago," Rachel said. "But he was part of Dr. Fieldstone's authentication team. Professor Richard Lockhart, the linguistics expert. Jonathan invited him to consult on some of the language used in the book. They spent a few days poring over the manuscript together. Professor Lockhart was famous. Once. Famous to academics, I mean. He authenticated the Sherborne manuscript. That's a famous fourteenth-century text. It had initially been dismissed as a forgery. But Professor Lockhart changed that perception. He was one of the foremost experts in medieval literature when he was younger. He's out of fashion now."

Polly made a mental note: Professor Lockhart. "Were they close? Did they work together a lot?"

Rachel hesitated as if she were piecing together a puzzle in her mind. "They weren't buddy-buddy, if that's what you mean. But they were professional. I think there was a rivalry between them. You know, older professor on the way out and the talented rising star with a promising future. I could tell Professor Lockhart was sometimes irritated with Jonathan. And vice versa. There was one meeting where Professor Lockhart raised his voice at Jonathan. Lockhart's assistant, Monte, and I were asked to leave the room, so I don't know what they talked about. But Jonathan did say something weird later. He said, 'That's the thanks I get for being a sport. No good deed goes unpunished.'"

16

The clock struck precisely six o'clock as Polly came into the reception room with an extra bouncy bounce in her step. Her eyes sparkled, and she plopped down on the Chesterfield settee and reached for the flute of bubbly Tiara had placed on the side table. After a long, indulgent slug—letting the cool, effervescent champagne dance on her tongue—she breathed a tender "Ahh," utterly satisfied with the taste and tingle. "La-de-da, my little dumplings, this Star Lady's had an excruciatingly unnerving day. Oh, the things that came from the lips of the authors I spoke to!" Without missing a beat and blissfully disregarding any potential interruptions about anyone else's activities that day, she dove into the details of her phone conversations. She recounted every detail and suspicion, her excitement growing with each revelation.

When she came up for air, Polly wiggled her empty glass at Tiara, expecting a top-up. "I've done a lot of thinking about what they all said," she continued, her voice cutting through the sounds of a string quartet sawing Vivaldi on the music system. "You know the old proverb 'The best way to get to the truth is to listen to both sides.' *In vino veritas* and all that."

"'*In vino* ...'" Tiara looked askance at her boss. "What does wine have to do with ...? What've you got up your sleeve, missy?" Over their twenty-plus years of friendship, she knew when Polly was hatching a self-indulgent scheme.

"What makes you think ...?"

"Drop your little-lost-lamb act," Tiara cut in. "You don't fool me. When you're about to pull a Lucy Ricardo, your eyes narrow, and you glance around as if Little Red Riding Hood might show up and catch you eating grandma. Your voice drops. And the way you avoid direct eye contact? Subtle, but it's there. If you're thinking of inviting that werewolf lady for drinks or the guy who writes gory detective mysteries scary enough to send Stephen King checking under his bed, I won't be here to play along."

Polly pretended to be offended by Tiara's insinuation. "Gee whiz! Are you nuts? I'd never. Ye of little faith!" Biting her bottom lip, she said, "You know I only court the most interesting people. Those two authors are so dull and wrapped up in supernatural love shenanigans and graphic human meat grinder moments. Not my type at all."

She raised an eyebrow at Tiara, her eyes widening in disbelief as if she couldn't believe what she'd heard from her maid and confidante. Then (as Tiara had totally predicted), Polly dropped the other shoe. "Not to worry. Not the paranormal kook. Or Mr. Misery Bones." She waited a beat. "I'm inviting ... Arthur Townsend to dinner."

A collective gasp escaped from Tiara and Tim. Even Mr. Boots made a hissing sound.

"You're serious?" Tiara whined. "Yeah, he's got an alibi for where he was at the time of Fieldstone's murder, but in my book, he's still a prime suspect, for crying out loud. I think he's a homicidal maniac. You can't ask him over for a meal like he's some long-lost relative or a neighbor."

Tim leaned forward, his face a mix of concern and disbelief.

"You know you're insane, right. Inviting Townsend here is like waving a red cape in front of a bull. Daring him to charge. This isn't one of those cozy mysteries Tiara reads where everyone calmly gathers in the drawing room to witness the big reveal of who the killer is. This is real life. There's no guaranteed happy ending."

Polly remained unflappable and brimming with naïve enthusiasm. She waved away their concerns with a breezy smile. "Trust me. If Townsend's guilty of killing Dr. Fieldstone and stealing the manuscript, the best way to get him to slip up and reveal himself is to make him feel at home. We'll lull him into a false sense of security. Let him think he's got the upper hand. People tell me all sorts of secrets when they're relaxed and sipping a fine wine."

"A 'Murderous Malbec'?" Tiara groused. "What if he's more dangerous than you think? It's a huge risk."

Polly's expression softened, but her eyes remained sharp with conviction. "And that's precisely why we have to take a chance. Think about it. How else can we get close to him? We have to meet him socially. To take the lead and prove we're the bigger man. Maybe if he thinks we're a bunch of dumb, clueless, Hollywood wackadoodles... A dinner party is the perfect setting. It's intimate, it's disarming, and it's where I can work my magic."

Tim raised an eyebrow. "You're saying nothing disarms a possible murderer quite like Tiara's canapés and your sparkling conversation?" He paused, shaking his head. "Mom, this isn't an improv class where you can ad-lib your way out of trouble. The guy might bring something sharper than your wit to the table."

Polly leaned in, her voice lowering conspiratorially. "The magic of conversation. I've spent my entire career reading people, making actors reveal themselves without them even realizing it. The dinner table is another stage. And if Townsend is innocent, he might still reveal something that could help us find Jonathan's killer. Either way, we get closer to the truth. Win-win!"

Tiara was clearly troubled. "Polly, I get it—you've always been able to charm the pants off anyone. But this is different. Townsend isn't some idiot marketing exec at Disney you can easily outsmart. He's a man who might've killed someone and stolen a valuable manuscript. What if he realizes what you're doing? What if he gets suspicious or, worse, gets violent? I know you love the thrill of the chase, but this isn't a game."

Polly's smile softened, but there was a steely resolve behind it. "He won't try anything funny. Not with Terrence and Gray here. I'm inviting them, too. And maybe Sarah for good measure. To make it more of a boy, girl, boy, girl seating-arrangement thing. Or nearly. We'll all be watching like hawks." She paused, leaning in slightly, her voice firm. "Do you think Arthur Townsend would risk doing anything nefarious to me? *The* Polly Pepper. Trust me, if Townsend's going to let his guard down anywhere, it'll be at my table with a glass of wine in hand, something yummy cooked by Tiara, and surrounded by people who seem too Hollywood to be dangerous."

There was no point challenging Polly, and soon they were listening to her wax poetic about the upcoming lit festival and her one-woman show. She coaxed Tim and Tiara into being her captive audience for a preview of what she'd written thus far. She desperately needed a practice run-through—to see where she still needed to punch things up. Once the dinner plates were cleared away, they gathered in the reception room. Its high ceilings and ornate furnishings made it an ideal stand-in for the setting of a Regency-era drawing room. Polly had even created a makeshift stage area beside the grand piano. Now, standing there, the script she'd printed in hand, Polly could feel the weight of an opening night. Assuming a confident stance, she straightened her posture and cleared her throat. "Prepare to be dazzled."

Tim raised an eyebrow, already sensing the "dazzling" part might be up for debate. At the same time, Tiara leaned back, champagne glass in hand, amused by the evening's turn of events.

Polly took a deep breath. *Showtime.*

"Ahem, ladies and gentlemen ... tonight, for the first time on any stage anywhere on the planet, I will perform an abridged version of *Vanity and Virtue*, or, as I've re-subtitled it, *Corsets, Curtsies, and Catastrophes!* Written by *moi*, Polly Diva Pepper. This is based on an unpublished novel by Abigail Townsend, which I discovered in the attic at Thistlethorne Lodge. Sadly, the manuscript has gone missing, so this might be your only chance to hear *La* Townsend's tale."

Tim and Tiara exchanged amused glances. They were used to Polly's dramatic exhibitions, but tonight, she seemed especially animated, her energy practically bouncing off the walls.

Polly's voice dropped into a deep, serious tone as she glanced dramatically at her script. "Time and place: the scandal-ridden English society of yore. Although, let's be honest, centuries come and go, but somehow, the problems of the rich stay the same. Affairs of the heart—and body. Reputations shredded. People desperately vying for power and position. Sound familiar? We begin our tale with Lady Cathryn Slocum, a young woman in her early twenties, of formidable intelligence and beauty, who—against all societal expectations—dares to buck the rules with her wits—and a tightly laced corset. Nothing makes a woman more determined to avoid fainting at a ball than a corset that could strangle a horse!"

Tim giggled, trying to hold back a full-blown laugh, and Tiara rolled her eyes.

"Of course," Polly continued, flipping through her script, "Cathryn's beauty alone would have secured her many admirers, but her sharp tongue made her notorious. In fact, she had a talent for delivering cutting remarks sharp enough to trim the hedges in the duke's garden."

Polly turned another page in her script. "Cathryn Slocum's rivals are a gaggle of powdered and painted young ladies who vie for the attention of every eligible bachelor landowner within a hundred miles. But Cathryn is no mere wallflower. No! She's a master of intrigue, a woman of great—as the title suggests— *virtue!*"

Polly's eyes sparkled as she turned another page. "The battle lines are drawn, the social stakes have never been higher, and Cathryn is caught between two suitors—one, a dashing rake with a dubious reputation as dark as his raven hair, and the other, an elderly nobleman set on winning a fair virgin's hand, heart, and dowry."

Tim couldn't contain a snigger.

Polly stopped and turned to her audience. "Cathryn will play these men against each other with a wink and a well-placed compliment. She has the rake second-guessing his conniving ways and the rich, elderly landowner questioning Cathryn's virginal virtues. But, of course, she can't let on she's playing both sides. No, she must appear as pure as the driven snow. Even as she schemes beneath her demure exterior."

With a flourish, Polly stepped back, her hand clutching the script. "And so Cathryn dances her way through the treacherous halls of society, where every whisper could ruin her, and every glance might be her undoing. But she, like the corset that binds her, remains unyielding. Until—the corset snaps!"

This time, it was Tiara who burst out laughing, nearly spilling her champagne. "Heavens no! A metaphor if ever I heard one! Breaking free from societal constraints? Rebellion against repression? Maybe sexual liberation?"

Polly gave an exaggerated curtsy. "I hadn't thought of that but thank you. And please stop interrupting. You're not Groundlings in the pit at the Old Globe, talking back to the actors!" She returned to the script with a dramatic sigh. "But even as her corset snaps and the fabric of her carefully constructed life begins to unravel, our heroine remains as sharp as ever. As the corset gives way, so too does the rigid structure of society, and Cathryn seizes the moment to finally breathe."

Tim couldn't hold back. "So does she lead a revolution in her petticoats?"

Polly grinned, leaning in as if sharing a juicy secret. "Almost. But first, she must maneuver through the scandal of the century: Her suitors have been revealed to be corrupt—and find themselves at her mercy. She's about to bring the whole house of cards tumbling down while making it look like an innocent faux pas. End scene."

Polly beamed, closing the script with a flourish. "And that, my darlings, is where I leave you for now. The rest ... well, I'm obviously still writing it. You'll have to wait for the full production to find out what happens to our dear Cathryn. I'm not sure I even know yet! But I assure you, it'll be filled with twists, turns, and more sartorial snafus. Oh, and a happy ending, too."

With a final bow, Polly left the makeshift stage, her energy still crackling from the performance.

"Brava!" Tim exclaimed, raising his glass. "But it was nothing like I remember from Abigail's manuscript."

Tiara nodded in agreement, swirling her champagne thoughtfully. "Abigail's story was all about social propriety, the pitfalls of vanity, and the moral dilemmas of the upper class. Your version—well, let's say it has a lot more ... something else."

Polly returned to the Chesterfield and took another sip of bubbly to wet her dry mouth. "Bless Abigail's no-longer-beating heart, but her version was, shall we say, dull? All endless moralizing, tedious lectures on virtue, and characters as stiff as the corsets they wore. Too much frowning and finger-wagging. Theatre should be entertaining, above all else. I have to breathe some life into those fuddy-duddy characters—give them a touch of my flair to keep modern audiences from snoozing."

Tiara grinned, her earlier concern giving way to amusement. "So instead of a treatise on moral virtue, we get a scandalous spinster who dismantles society with nothing but a broken corset and witticisms?"

"Exactly!" Polly said, her eyes sparkling. "Abigail's story had bones. I simply dressed them in a new wardrobe that's a bit more ... realistic. After all, who wouldn't want to see a woman like Cathryn, armed with nothing but her intelligence and a sharp tongue, take down the patriarchy one suitor at a time? I've made her like Villanelle in *Killing Eve*—but without the sociopathic assassin tendencies."

"Only you, Mother, could take a literary novel and turn it into a comedic tour de force," Tim said, almost proudly.

Polly raised her glass in a toast to herself. "I'm simply paying homage to Abigail's work by bringing it into the twenty-first century. I'm sure she'd appreciate my efforts. We'd be best girlfriends if I lived way back then."

Tiara clinked her glass against Polly's. "Well, if tonight's performance is anything to go by, I'd say you're well on your way to a smashing success. Just don't forget us when you're taking your bows in the West End."

"Before I start planning my curtain call, there's a certain

dinner party that requires my attention ... and a guest list that needs finalizing. I shall see you both in the morning. I need to think about how to lure Abigail Townsend's distant relative into my trap."

17

Morning light reluctantly crept into the breakfast room, its weak glow doing little to clear the fog clinging to Polly's thoughts. Her red-rimmed eyes darted between her notebook—its pages crowded with half-baked schemes—and the Bloody Mary waiting at her place. The drink's sharp tang didn't offer much comfort, but she swallowed it anyway. She stifled a yawn, refusing to let exhaustion win. She'd spent the night trying—without much success—to concoct a way to lure Arthur Townsend to dine at Thistlethorne.

Across the table, Tim was jittery in his seat, his leg bouncing uncontrollably as he downed his second Red Bull. Tiara sat serenely sipping a cup of Earl Grey and scratching Mr. Boots behind the ears as he purred on her lap. And, from the kitchen came the sound of Elara humming—a cheerful, slightly off-key tune that grated on everyone's nerves.

"When I wasn't plotting ways to entice Townsend to my dinner party, I was having nightmares about him not showing up at all," Polly said, her voice weary as her fingers lazily stirred the pickled okra stem in her glass.

Tiara raised an eyebrow. "Entice? Is this a dinner or a seduction?" she teased, sipping her tea.

Polly picked up her notebook, its pages crowded with chaotic notes, half-baked ideas, and crossed-out sentences. She skimmed her scribbles, muttering, "I've tried every angle—flattery, mystery, you name it. I need a plan so irresistible he can't say no." Taking a sip of her Bloody Mary, she let the gears in her brain turn.

"I could appeal to his sense of legacy. From what Dr. Fieldstone said, Townsend's obsessed with his lineage. If I hint that I've found some letters in the attic—private correspondence from Abigail Townsend herself—he'd be desperate to know if they could elevate or tarnish the family name."

Polly's eyes lit up. "Or I could make it all about him. Men like Townsend love being the center of attention, especially when it's wrapped in flattery. I'll tell him I'm hosting an exclusive dinner —select, intimate—and he simply has to be there because he's a pillar of the community. He isn't, but who doesn't want to feel important?"

Tim leaned back in his chair, watching Polly with a half-amused, half-exasperated look. "You know, Mother, you could always try something with less ... subterfuge. Instead of playing the long game with 'private letters' or 'flattery,' why not be up front?"

Polly raised an eyebrow. "Up front? What's that supposed to mean?"

"Maybe skip the mind games and outright say, 'Oh, Mr. Townsend, cookie, sweetie, baby, do be a doll and tell me where you've stashed Abigail's manuscript. And by the way, I'm not terribly impressed with your alibi for the day of the murder.'" Tim leaned forward in his chair, taking another swig of Red Bull. "Although I realize being obvious has never been your strong suit."

Tiara, who had been quietly sipping her tea, set her cup down with a thoughtful clink. She looked at Polly, then at Tim, carefully choosing her words. "I think you're both wrong. Men like Townsend ... they love feeling indispensable. Important. In charge. If you challenge him directly, he'll just put up walls. But if you make it about you *needing* him—well, that's a completely different ball game. Appeal to his sense of superiority."

Polly made a face, and she set her Bloody Mary down. "You're not suggesting ... I am not stroking some man's ego, especially not Arthur Townsend's. The idea of making him feel *superior*—ugh! No way!" She shuddered theatrically. "What feminist, gender-equality advocate would I be if I played into that tired, old routine? I'd be no better than those vacuous little twits in corsets Abigail wrote about."

Tiara remained calm, her hands folded neatly around her teacup. "I understand. But you wouldn't be 'playing into' anything. You're not conceding to him. You're using *his* vanity to *your* advantage. It's a *strategy*, not a submission."

Tim chimed in with a sly grin. "Oh, I get it. It's like a chess game. You're making the move that makes him think he's winning, but really, you're setting him up for a checkmate."

Tiara leaned in slightly, her tone practical. "You could say something like, 'Mr. Townsend, I've come across a few historical details about the Townsend family that I find fascinating, and there's no one else in the village with the knowledge of your family to help me understand.'" She paused, smirking. "Men like Townsend love playing the savior. Give him a reason to feel like he's important, and he'll come to dinner not out of curiosity—but because he thinks you need him."

Tim sniggered, nodding in agreement. "That's brilliant! Flatter his ego, and he'll be here faster than you can set the table."

Tiara continued, her voice soft yet persuasive, "You're not

telling him he's better than you. You're making him think he's solving a problem only *he* can solve, which puts *you* in control. And let's be real—what's more fulfilling than outsmarting someone while they think they're in charge?"

The tiniest glint of mischief returned to Polly's eyes. "So you're saying ... I let him feel like the hero of this little marionette performance, but really, I'm the one pulling the strings?"

"Exactly!" Tiara said with a smile. "It's all smoke and mirrors. Let him feel clever, but you'll be the one guiding the conversation where it needs to go."

Tim, involuntarily tapping his Red Bull-fueled feet, grinned. "That's the Polly Pepper everyone knows and loves. Puller of strings."

Polly paced the length of the library, her phone in hand, occasionally glancing at it as though it might do the calling for her. The usual bravado that had carried her through a life of auditions and press junket interviews was absent as she stared at Arthur Townsend's number. She muttered under her breath, "Just make the call, Polly. It's not like you're asking Dracula over for a midnight snack." Taking a deep breath, she finally mustered the courage to tap the Call button. The phone rang once, twice ... by the third ring, her nerves had bubbled over, and as she was about to chicken out, a clipped voice answered.

"What?"

Polly was caught off guard by the sharpness. "Mr. Townsend? This is Polly Pepp—"

"I'm not surprised," Townsend snapped, cutting her off midsentence. His tone was cold and defensive. "If this is some roundabout way to accuse me of taking Abigail's manuscript, you can save your breath."

Polly froze for a second, the accusation hanging in the air. She hadn't expected such a hostile reception. Her mind raced, and she quickly shifted gears, opting for disarming charm rather than confrontation. "The manuscript? Good heavens, no!" she said, injecting a breezy laugh into her voice, though her heart was pounding. "You won't find me pointing fingers, Mr. Townsend. I've heard those ridiculous rumors flying around, and frankly, I think they're all silly nonsense. I'm calling with a far less dramatic request. In fact, I think you might rather enjoy it."

There was a brief pause on the other end, but Townsend's tone remained wary. "I doubt it."

Polly cleared her throat, summoning her most soothing and nonthreatening tone. "I'm inviting you to dinner here at Thistlethorne Lodge. Tomorrow. Friday. Nothing grand. Just a few friends in for nibbles."

Another pause ensued, but Polly could practically hear his suspicion crackling through the phone.

"Why on earth would I want to join you for dinner, especially now when everyone's circling me like vultures, whispering behind my back? I've nothing to say about Dr. Fieldstone's death —although it's a tragedy—or that damned manuscript. Which I didn't steal! But if I did, it belongs to me anyway!"

Polly bit her lip, her thoughts racing. Townsend was clearly on high alert, and if she wasn't careful, he'd hang up, and she'd lose her shot at getting him to dinner. *Change tactics, Polly. Fast.*

She softened her tone, allowing a hint of vulnerability to show. "I understand, Mr. Townsend. Truly, I do. Things are tense for everyone right now, including me. But this isn't about accusations, gossip, or lawsuits—it's about history. Your history. Abigail's history. I've always been fascinated by people's life stories, especially those of remarkable women like Abigail. She's practically a celebrity now, and no one knows more about her than you. I'd love your help in understanding her better."

Polly sensed she'd struck a chord. She gently pressed on. "You're a man of knowledge ... of legacy. There's no one else in the universe with better insight to help me understand Abigail's full story. It's a story only you can tell."

A long silence followed, and Polly's heart beat faster as she waited. Finally, Townsend expelled a sigh, though there was still guardedness in his voice. "And what exactly do you think I know?"

Polly's tone was light but with the right touch of curiosity. "Abigail's life—her legacy—is fascinating. Especially when it comes to how her story connects with the village." She paused, letting the intrigue simmer. "I'm hoping you can shed some light on a few of the more ... cryptic elements." She held her breath, hoping she'd found the right balance between curiosity and flattery.

Townsend finally relented, though his tone was still gruff and full of suspicion. "Fine. But only to set the record straight. If I get even the slightest whiff of an accusation ... of any kind ... I'm leaving immediately."

"Understood," Polly said adamantly, her smile widening as the call ended. "Thank you, Mr. Townsend. I look forward to tomorrow. Seven o'clock. And please call me Polly. May I call you ...?" But he'd hung up before she could finish her sentence.

18

F riday evening arrived far too quickly for Polly's liking. Yet, when Tim ushered Arthur Townsend into the reception room, she effortlessly transformed into the epitome of charm—a gracious hostess with a warm smile concealing the simmering dread beneath her composed exterior.

Arthur Townsend wasn't as tall or intimidating as Polly had imagined, but he carried himself with the air of someone who believed his opinion could bend the laws of physics. His dark eyes swept over the room, narrowing slightly as though the assembled guests were an unpleasant surprise he hadn't quite braced himself for. Polly felt his irritation prick the air like static electricity before he even opened his mouth, his thin-lipped expression broadcasting a silent but unmistakable *What fresh hell is this?*

Polly set her most dazzling smile and swept forward, her hand outstretched. "Mr. Townsend! Delighted!" she said with practiced warmth, as though she hadn't noticed how his eyes had narrowed when he spotted Constable Grayson Jenkins in the room.

His handshake was firm but cold. "I wasn't expecting ..." His gaze landed on Gray, his displeasure evident.

"Just our extended family, sweetums," Polly said, handing him a flute of champagne and introducing him to the others. "They're all part of the furniture here at Thistlethorne," she said with a disarming laugh. "Do you know Sarah Rogers from Bound to Read, our lovely village bookshop and coffee bar? And Terrence Marks, editor of the *Abbots Clover Overview*?"

Townsend's frown deepened, his jaw tightening, but before he could voice his displeasure, something soft and furry brushed against his ankle. He glanced down, and his hardened expression softened slightly as Mr. Boots wound his way around Townsend's legs, purring.

"Ah, Mr. Boots," Polly said with a knowing smile. "He has a knack for knowing exactly who needs a bit of affection." She watched as Townsend's initial irritation gave way, and he bent down to scratch behind the cat's ears.

"Charming," Townsend muttered, his voice gruff but noticeably warmer. "Clever creatures. Independent."

Polly seized the opportunity, her eyes twinkling. "I knew you'd be a cat person, Arthur. Intelligent company for an intelligent man."

Townsend straightened, but not before giving Mr. Boots one last pat. "Indeed," he said, his tone now less frosty, though the glances he continued to throw in Grayson's direction made it clear he wasn't thrilled with the police presence. *Is this some sort of trap?* he wondered.

As the group settled in, Polly felt her tension ease. The first act was going smoothly—Townsend was here, the stage was set, and Mr. Boots had, surprisingly, become a most effective co-conspirator in disarming the man. Now, she had to steer the evening through an iceberg-laden ocean and not spook

Townsend away. She took a deep breath and mentally prepared for the delicate dance that would unfold during dinner, knowing every moment would be crucial in uncovering the truth about the dual mystery: murder and the missing manuscript.

The dining room at Thistlethorne Lodge exuded elegance. The long mahogany table gleamed under the soft light of twin silver candelabras, their flickering flames casting a warm, golden hue across the polished wood. Waterford crystal glasses sparkled, while the Royal Doulton china and carefully arranged silverware reflected an air of sophistication. A Pinot Noir Polly had specifically chosen for its velvety flavors—and its ability to loosen lips—had been poured.

Tiara had outdone herself preparing the meal. The aroma of herb-crusted lamb filled the room, mingling with the delicate scent of rosemary and garlic, creamy dauphinoise potatoes, and buttered asparagus. The clinking of cutlery and the hum of conversation filled the air while the stereo speakers carried classical violin strings.

Polly's thoughts, however, were entirely focused on the man to her right: Arthur Townsend.

Townsend was a study in self-assurance. His earlier displeasure at finding Grayson and the others present had softened, thanks in no small part to Polly's charm—and the vino. There had been a subtle shift in his demeanor: the way his shoulders had relaxed slightly, the edge in his voice dulling with every sip. His fork now moved less rigidly, and his posture, while still formal, was no longer as tightly held.

Midway through the meal—as rehearsed—Polly seized the moment, her eyes darting briefly toward the clock before widening in mock alarm. "Oh, dear me! I've utterly failed in my hostess duties!" she exclaimed, her voice pitched high enough to command attention. She pressed a hand to her chest and let out a dramatic sigh. "How could I have forgotten the most pleasant of rituals? I neglected to officially welcome our guest of honor with a toast!" She raised her glass with a warm smile. "To Arthur Townsend. Our new friend ..." she cooed, holding his gaze as the others followed suit, their glasses rising in chorus.

Townsend's brow furrowed slightly, his glass held above the table as he eyed Polly with wariness.

"To Arthur ... and to the legacies we all inherit from our ancestors," Polly continued, her tone light but with an undercurrent of deeper meaning. "We're delighted to have you with us tonight, Arthur. And you promised to share some of your family's fascinating history. Do you mind? You alone hold all the secrets."

There it was—an interrogation wrapped in a compliment. Townsend's gaze shifted. He was tense, as if trying to discern Polly's intentions. "What would you like to know?"

His words were polite, but Polly could see discomfort in his eyes. He took a sip of wine, the alcohol further softening his expression. Slowly, his guard seemed to lower a notch. He shifted slightly in his seat. His smile, when it came, was thin, more an act of politeness than anything heartfelt.

Polly leaned in slightly, her eyes sparkling as she set a trap wrapped in the guise of flattery. "I, for one, am simply entranced by families with significant history like yours," she said, swirling the wine in her glass. "The Townsends have been here since—well, almost before the dinosaurs! Tell me if I'm wrong, but I imagine being the descendant of a famous person like Abigail comes with pride—and also unique pressures."

Tim didn't miss a beat. "Tell me about it." He suppressed a giggle, raising his glass to his mother. "Whenever someone finds out who I'm related to, it's always, 'Oh, I've heard Polly Pepper has a room at Pepper Plantation where confetti sifts from the ceiling whenever she enters. Is it true she wears a tiara to bed? Does she still have a pet peacock named Barbra Streisand?'"

Laughter filled the room, and Polly wagged a finger at Tim. "For the record, it's not a tiara—it's a crown. As for Barbra and the peacock—they're both majestic creatures. A diva-like bird deserves a diva's name!"

Townsend cracked a reluctant smile. Even Mr. Boots, who was wandering around underfoot in a futile search for scraps, meowed as if amused by her response. Townsend took another sip of wine, his eyes narrowing slightly as he set his glass down. "Indeed. It can be complicated to come from a famous family." He paused, weighing his words carefully. "People think of legacy as something glamorous and prestigious. But what they don't understand is that it comes with chains. Invisible ones, but heavy just the same."

Polly smiled softly, sensing Townsend was starting to become more relaxed. She remained quiet, letting him fill the silence.

He leaned back in his chair and continued, "You're constantly judged against people you've never met. People who lived their lives in a world so different from your own, yet ... their lives and decisions shape everything about your present. There's always pressure to live up to expectations, to maintain an image. People look at you and too often see your ancestors. And if you don't measure up, it's not just a personal failure, it's as if you've let down an entire legacy."

Townsend's tone grew harder, a touch of bitterness creeping in. "The public sees famous people in history books, and maybe grand estates handed down through generations. But they don't see the personal struggles. They forget even famous families are made up of flawed, fragile people. People who made mistakes. And those mistakes? They can haunt every generation that follows."

Polly raised an eyebrow, sensing something specific behind his words. She ventured carefully, "It sounds like some mistakes are still casting a shadow over your family."

Townsend exhaled, a weary expression playing at the edges of his lips. "My family was once powerful—respected. But the empire they built, it crumbled two hundred years before I was born. And now, instead of standing on the shoulders of giants, I'm left sifting through the ruins, trying to figure out what went wrong." His eyes darkened, and his voice dropped to a near whisper. "Trying to figure out if there's anything left to salvage."

Polly stayed quiet, giving him space. She could see it now— Townsend wasn't weighed down by his family's history. He was consumed by it.

"People expect you to live up to the legacies, the expectations," Townsend continued. "It is ... unfair. You start asking yourself if the legacy is even worth preserving. Maybe it's better to let it die away."

Polly nodded, feigning innocent curiosity as she continued, "I've been thinking about your Abigail. Very few women of her day were writers. Most expressed their creativity with fancy needlework or by becoming accomplished at playing piano. I see that all the time in TV period dramas. But Abigail was different ... ahead of her time. What made her so ... unique?"

Townsend set down his cutlery. "From what I know, Abigail was extraordinary in ways that astonished and unsettled people around her. She was born into privilege, but she didn't conform to the expectations of her family. Apparently, she had a sharp mind that refused to be dulled by superficial chatter at tea parties. She loved books. She wrote endlessly. She defied the notion that a woman's only worth was as a wife and bearer of babies. That was almost unheard of in her day."

From the other side of the table, Sarah spoke up, her soft voice cutting through the conversation and drawing every eye.

"From what I know of that time period—I studied British lit at uni—women like Abigail rarely escaped consequences for their independence. There's always a cost."

She set her fork down carefully, the faint clink punctuating the heavy silence that followed. "If Abigail defied social norms or challenged the power in her family, she would have paid for it. Women asserting themselves has never been easy. Not then—and not now."

"From what I know, Abigail was a woman of contradictions," Townsend continued. "Brilliant, yes. A visionary, maybe. But also, someone who caused trouble—for the family and for herself."

"Trouble?" Sarah repeated, her voice almost a scoff. "Usually, when a woman is identified as 'trouble,' it's because she doesn't do as she's told. What was it about Abigail that was so ... *troublesome?*"

Townsend's expression remained neutral for a moment, his eyes flickering with something unreadable. His fingers tightened slightly around the stem of his glass. Polly felt a surge of excitement, though she hid it behind a face that was the picture of patience. She'd learned long ago there was often a lot of power in keeping still and listening. It was a passive way of steering the conversation, especially with men like Townsend.

Finally, Townsend exhaled, almost resigned to revealing more than he wanted to. "I believe she challenged the authority of her father. He was an important and powerful man across this entire region. For one thing, she rejected his expectations for her future. And when you come from a family like the Townsends, that doesn't come without cost."

Polly arched a brow ever so slightly, her voice dropping into something softer, almost conspiratorial. "What expectations did she flout?" she asked, a hint of intrigue seeping through her well-maintained composure.

Townsend hesitated, but before he could speak, Polly leaned forward slightly, her tone shifting into something more personal. "I ask because, even today, expectations for women are only slightly kinder than they were decades or centuries ago. My mother, who was clever and bright, had dreams and goals. Grand ones. However, society had a narrow idea of what a woman's future could look like. When she was young—in the nineteen fifties—women were either housewives, teachers, or nurses. That was as far as most women were encouraged to go. Her ambitions didn't fit into those neat little boxes. She broke the mold because she joined the navy. She was still a nurse, but at least she held rank as a lieutenant."

Polly paused, her gaze drifting as memories of her mother surfaced. "She had talents—she was smart, could sing, tell stories, and write like nobody's business. But in those days, women like her didn't get to chase dreams. They were told to be good wives, devoted mothers, and to set aside their ambitions for the sake of the family. That's how it was back then. You fell in line. You got married. You had children, even if it wasn't what you wanted. She once told me she loved me but regretted having a family."

She paused, glancing down at her hands. "You know, people say life is long, but it's not. Not really. It's a collection of moments, and if you're not careful, they slip through your fingers. You look back one day and wonder where it all went. And the worst part? You realize *you* let it happen. And you're left wondering what could've been if only you'd dared to take control. That's the part that haunts me about my mother. She could have been more."

Townsend's composure faltered, his own grief reflected in Polly's words. "And your mother?" he asked softly. "Did she ever ... find her way back to herself?"

Polly's faint smile was bittersweet. "No. But she made sure I had the chance to live the life I wanted. She didn't want me to repeat her mistakes. And that's why I fight so hard. Every day. Because I'll be damned if I let her story be mine too." She returned to the heart of the conversation, her voice thoughtful yet sharp. "But Abigail ... I imagine she wasn't fighting against the usual societal pressures. It sounds like she was up against something bigger and more dangerous—her father." She tilted her head slightly, eyes locked on Townsend. "What was she up against, Arthur? What was she so determined to write about that bothered her father?"

Townsend hesitated, his lips pressed into a thin line as though he was considering how much of the story was safe to share. He gave a small, bitter laugh and shook his head. "I don't know. That was two centuries ago. Family records suggest one thing, and Abigail's diaries and letters quite another. All I know is Abigail wasn't content with being a silent, dutiful daughter or wife. She wanted more. So she made waves."

Tiara, seated across the table, chimed in, "She was a rebel. Sounds like she'd fit in nicely in today's world."

A few sounds of agreement rippled through the room, but Townsend didn't smile. His voice lowered, taking on a more serious tone. "All I know is in her first book, Abigail wrote about things that angered certain members of the Townsend family. Her father was mortified when it was published. But he felt it was best not to say anything publicly that would draw even more attention to it. The 'Streisand effect,' before there was a Streisand."

Townsend's fingers drummed the table as his gaze flicked to Polly. "He thought it was a vanity project that would fade quickly. He hadn't anticipated the book's popularity—or the demand for another. Abigail's writing brought into the open things that should have stayed behind the Townsends' closed doors."

Polly leaned forward, her brow furrowed. "What things?"

Townsend hesitated, his fingers grazing the rim of his glass. "The manuscript you found might have confirmed my theories and the family legend, especially details about how Abigail's father built the family fortune through unscrupulous means—cheating investors or maybe even the unpardonable ... what we now call 'the slave trade.' From what I know, he wasn't what anyone would consider an honorable man."

He sighed, his shoulders sagging. "Her father was sure there'd be more revelations in her second book. So, some people were quite pleased when the manuscript conveniently disappeared."

Polly's pulse quickened. "*Vanity and Virtue* disappeared in 1820! The same manuscript I found in the attic?"

Townsend nodded slowly, his expression grave. "Yes. And someone—the librarian—was murdered as a result. That's why I was so desperate to see it and made such a fuss with Dr. Fieldstone."

Tim's eyebrows shot up. "Are you suggesting Abigail's father orchestrated the disappearance?"

"I don't know," Townsend said, leaning back slightly. "But it's possible. Some believed Abigail discovered something so appalling about his business practices she was ready to tear down everything he had built—his empire, his legacy, all of it."

He paused, his dark eyes flicking toward Polly. "There's also the theory Abigail sympathized with revolutionary politics, maybe had anti-monarchist sentiments. That could have ruined the family's standing with the Crown, which would have been a disaster for a family desperate to maintain favor."

Townsend glanced at Polly, the weight of generations in his gaze. "Abigail, from what I've gathered, knew too much about something and was ready to expose it. And her father—well, he couldn't let that happen." Townsend paused, staring into his wine and swirling it around the glass. "According to family history, some important people were relieved when the manuscript was no longer an issue. They imagined it had been destroyed and were happy to let Abigail and her story fade away. But it's haunted me—this family mystery—ever since I was boy and first heard about it. I thought maybe if I could get my hands on the manuscript—which we thought was gone forever—I might understand her. Maybe even ... redeem her, in a way. But instead ..." He trailed off, his jaw tightening as a flicker of regret flashed across his face.

Polly watched him carefully, her silence drawing him out. She could see it now—the weight of frustration in his soul.

Finally, Townsend spoke again, his voice quieter than before. "It's not about the manuscript—and now it's lost a second time. It's about understanding what happened to my ancestors. They were once among the most powerful in this part of England. Stonecroft Hall—that manor in the next village—was theirs. They were respected. And then, suddenly ... it was all gone. The money. The influence. It just ... vanished. And no one in my family ever talked about it or explained how or why it happened. I would have made a terrific lord, baron, or marquess." He chuckled for the first time evening. "Your American writer, Dorothy Parker, said it best: 'I don't know much about being a millionaire, but I bet I'd be darling at it.'"

Everyone around the table laughed. Who wouldn't like to have a lot of money and prestige?

Polly's curiosity sharpened. She leaned in slightly, her eyes narrowing. "How could a family like yours lose everything? And so quickly?"

Townsend shook his head, frustration lacing his words. "That's what I've been trying to figure out my whole life. It's like there's this mysterious gap in our history—a missing chapter. No one ever explained it to me. I asked my father and grandfather, but they always brushed it off. 'Bad investments and extravagant spending,' they'd say. But I never completely believed that. The Townsends were wealthy; they were smart. People don't lose fortunes overnight. Something happened. Something no one ever talked about."

Polly watched Townsend, her thoughts churning. She sensed the depth of his bitterness—the need for closure. "And you think Abigail's manuscript holds the key to discovering what happened?"

Townsend's eyes flickered with something between hope and desperation. "I don't know," he admitted, "but it's possible. Abigail questioned everything—especially the way my great-great-great and too many more 'greats' to count uncle ran the family business. There were rumors she'd found something out, something that could explain why it all fell apart. And if she wrote it down in that manuscript ... if *Vanity and Virtue* holds the answer ..."

His voice trailed off. Shaking his head, he said, "I thought if I could read it, I might finally understand what happened. Why our family went from being at the top of the social food chain to outright impoverishment. I want to understand who we were and why we lost everything. I've spent years trying to piece it together, but without the manuscript, I'm missing the final puzzle piece."

Polly's gaze softened slightly. She could sense the depth of Townsend's frustration—the way it gnawed at him. Then something struck her. She realized Townsend wasn't after the manuscript for pride or a return to wealth. He wanted answers —to make sense of his family's history and maybe, somehow, restore a part of their lost dignity. "And that's why you acted out as you did towards Dr. Fieldstone," she said. "You thought the manuscript might give you the answers your family never could."

Townsend nodded, his shoulders sagging. "Exactly. But I was too ... aggressive. I went about it the wrong way because I wanted it so badly. I wanted to understand my past. If I'd been more patient, maybe Fieldstone would have let me see the manuscript, even read it. Now ..." His voice faltered. "Now he's dead, and the manuscript is gone. It's too late."

A heavy silence settled over the table. Polly watched Townsend for a long moment, sensing the quiet devastation in his words. He was a man chasing shadows, haunted by the ghosts of a family legacy he might never understand. As Polly listened to him, something shifted in her mind. She had been so certain Townsend's eagerness to get his hands on *Vanity and Virtue* was rooted in greed or something darker. But now, watching him and listening to him explain his motives, she realized she had been wrong. There was no malice or greed in his words, only curiosity and a genuine interest in Abigail Townsend and his family's story. He hadn't been trying to keep secrets buried—he had been searching to unbury them. A sense of guilt pricked her, realizing her suspicions had been off target. But with that realization came another unsettling thought. If Townsend wasn't the one behind the missing manuscript or Fieldstone's death, then a murderer was still at large.

Polly could see how uncomfortable Townsend was and wanted to smooth things over. She drew the conversation to a close. Looking at her beau, Terrence, who had been silently observing from his end of the table, she said, "Speaking of legacies, how's the restoration work on St. Clematis going? I hear you're writing a story about it for the paper. They've apparently uncovered interesting artifacts."

Terrence caught on quickly and smoothly shifted the conversation away from the subject of the missing manuscript and the murder of Dr. Fieldstone and toward current events in the village. He launched into a detailed story about an unexpected discovery of chalices, crosses, and candlesticks, long hidden away in the church's underground chambers.

When the meal ended and Townsend had departed (he practically dashed away), Polly and her other guests assembled in the reception room for coffee and brandy. The flickering light from the crackling fire cast long shadows, and Polly and Terrence settled onto the worn leather of the Chesterfield settee, its creases soft with age. As the others found places in the room, a low murmur of conversation filled the space, along with soft notes from Ella Fitzgerald keeping time with the gentle ticking of the grandfather clock. The air still held the lingering scent of roast lamb, mingling with the smokiness of burning wood.

Tiara looked at Polly and grumbled, "Way to go, you. Setting poor Mr. Townsend up to confess to crimes he didn't commit. For shame."

"He'll get over it," Polly sighed, her shoulders finally relaxing as the tension from the evening began to ebb. "At least now, I'm pretty sure he didn't steal the manuscript or kill Dr. Fieldstone. That seems obvious."

"Does it?" Terrence asked, nursing his brandy and leaning forward with furrowed brows. "I'm not so sure. When you first brought up the missing manuscript, I could practically see steam coming out of his ears."

Polly gave a soft chuckle. "Because his pride is hurt. He doesn't want to be accused of being a greedy heir. He cares about the Townsend's legacy and their reputation. If there's any connection to the missing manuscript or the murder of Dr. Fieldstone, I don't think it's because he was involved. He seemed genuinely ... exhausted by it all."

Tiara, her arms crossed, and skepticism etched into her

expression, raised an eyebrow. "So, you're saying he's misunderstood?" Her tone carried a blend of doubt and sarcasm, as though challenging Polly's sympathetic assessment. She was less willing to let him off the hook. Her words hung in the air like a quiet dare, urging Polly to consider whether she might be excusing Townsend's actions too easily.

Polly swirled her drink, her eyes distant as she replayed the evening's conversation in her mind. "He's probably guilty of something. Maybe he would have grabbed the manuscript if he could have gotten away with it. But look, I've spent a lifetime reading people—creating characters based on my observations. I've acted opposite some of the most difficult stars in Hollywood, and I've learned to sniff out an inauthentic performance. Townsend wasn't performing tonight. Frankly, I don't think he's clever enough. He was too raw, too emotional. He was angry, yes, but it felt more like ... frustration. Like he's at the end of his rope. After all, he knows he was initially a prime suspect. He probably feels resentful. Like Robert Wagner when everyone suggested he killed Natalie Wood."

Grayson tilted his head, his expression thoughtful. "The police in Bristol are still keeping a close watch on Townsend, and I've been told to do the same. If he didn't take the manuscript—and I'm not convinced he didn't—and didn't kill Fieldstone ... I'm at a loss. We're out of suspects."

Watch this space, Polly thought before taking a long breath and setting her glass down on the side table. "We've been so focused on Townsend as the prime suspect maybe we've missed something—someone—right under our noses. We need to explore other suspects. Tonight, I was reading him the way I'd read an audience. My instincts—at least about audiences—are usually spot on."

Polly felt a strange sense of relief as she glanced toward the door where Arthur Townsend had left only a few minutes before. She admired how prickly proud he was of his heritage. Yes, he was arrogant—but there didn't seem to be any malevolence. At least not the kind that would lead to murder. She smiled as her thoughts were already spinning and moving toward the next step in unraveling the mystery of the missing manuscript and the murder of Dr. Fieldstone.

19

The next morning, Polly stood before the full-length mirror in her bedroom, holding her latest script of *Vanity and Virtue* and reciting lines for the millionth time. "I will not be silenced!" She spoke in the bold voice she'd created for Abigail Townsend, elongating her vowels and dropping her R's and T's. She sounded more like an American Southern belle than a British aristocrat. Her voice was steady and confident, but her mind drifted elsewhere. She paused mid-monologue, tilting her head as she glanced down at her hips. *Do I look fat?* She tugged at her blouse, trying to smooth it down. She sighed. *It's the lighting. Or the pasta. I haven't been to the gym since I left America, and I'm going onstage looking like a freakin' sausage.*

With an exaggerated roll of her eyes, she forced herself to refocus. *Your lines, Polly! Learn your lines!* She drew in a breath and tried again. "I will not be silenced!" But once more, her eyes narrowed at her reflection. *Does this character even sound believable?* she wondered, knowing Abigail Townsend had been a force of nature in her day. A trailblazer. Polly was struggling to embody the character's essence. She was creating Abigail pretty much from scratch, with only fragments of history and legend to guide her. "I'm supposed to channel a woman who stood up to her family and society ... and maybe even the monarch himself. Do I sound like someone bold enough to tear down an empire?"

Polly felt the weight of responsibility. She wanted to do justice to Abigail—especially now that she knew how obsessed Arthur Townsend was with his ancestor's legacy. The last thing she wanted was to reduce Abigail to a caricature. Yet each time she spoke her dialogue, something felt ... off. *Too safe?* Abigail hadn't played it safe in life—and neither had Polly Pepper.

Polly straightened up and tried again. "I will not be silenced!" she exclaimed, gesturing dramatically in front of the mirror. She froze, watching her reflection. *Too over the top?* "Abigail would've demonstrated how powerful she was without histrionics. No doubt she was cool. Controlled. Not some coat-hanger-waving Faye Dunaway lunatic type in *Mommie Dearest*."

She dropped her arms and took a long breath, stepping closer to the mirror and eyeing herself critically. *Do I even look the part?* She examined her face—*Too tired around the eyes?* She knew her workload, late nights, and restless thoughts about Dr. Fieldstone's murder weren't helping. She brushed a loose strand of hair behind her ear and shifted her posture, standing taller, more authoritatively.

Her eyes moved over her reflection, searching for a spark that would bring Abigail to life. She tried to imagine the nineteenth-century woman—challenging her formidable father, writing words that maybe even destroyed her family's fortune. *Why is it so daunting to embody her strength and defiance?* Polly recited another line, softer this time, more measured: "I am more than what they see. I am more than what they allow me to be."

She paused, the words sinking in. *Yes, that's better. You sound like a woman who's sick and tired of playing games where other people made all the rules. Sounds vaguely like me.* Her eyes flickered back to the mirror, and she couldn't help but catch the way her blouse creased awkwardly around her stomach again. She sighed, feeling the familiar tug of vanity. But this time, she let it go. "Would Abigail have cared about her appearance?"

With a quiet nod to herself, Polly turned the page of the script and went back to work. But soon, she stopped again. There was more than her upcoming performance gnawing at her. She stared into the mirror, but this time, instead of seeing herself, she saw Dr. Fieldstone. His lifeless body lying on the library's supply room floor flashed vividly in her mind.

Who else could have engineered the theft of Vanity and Virtue from the safe? Polly shook her head, trying to picture any of the volunteer library staff committing a literary crime—or, heaven forbid, a mortal sin. It was impossible to visualize. But then ... who else had the opportunity? And maybe—a motive?

She sighed and tried to recite the next line from memory. "I am more than what they allow me to be." Her voice faltered. "I am more ...!" The line gave her pause. Assistants—especially clever ones—often ended up doing their boss's work, she thought, while being dissuaded from stepping into the spotlight themselves. A boss, particularly an insecure one, wouldn't want their subordinate outshining them. That was true in business offices ... probably true in research labs, too. Polly picked up the script again and tried to focus. "I am more than what they see. I am more than what they allow me to be."

The words slipped through her mind like sand through her fingers, replaced by thoughts of Rachel Hawthorne. Could Rachel be more than she seemed? Polly frowned. She's smart. Probably ambitious. Polly had seen that type before. Young, eager to make a name for themselves. A person who wouldn't hesitate to seize an opportunity if it meant propelling their career forward. In showbiz, Polly thought with a wry smile, that type had a name: *Eve Harrington.*

Rachel had played the part well—harmless, wide-eyed, soft-spoken. A diligent assistant, grateful for every scrap of attention Dr. Fieldstone tossed her way. She'd linger at the edge of conversations, eyes bright with curiosity. To most, she probably seemed like an academic-in-the-making, content to learn, to stay in the background, and do her job. But now Polly wasn't so sure. Was there something more behind those innocent eyes—a hunger that had gone unnoticed?

Rachel now seemed suspicious to Polly. Each time she replayed their past interactions, she thought she recognized subtle manipulations. She'd built herself up to be indispensable to Dr. Fieldstone. Could Rachel have been wearing a mask of wide-eyed admiration, but beneath it was a woman driven by aspiration, willing to lie, deceive, and manipulate for a fast-track rise in the academic world?

Polly knew Rachel had been Fieldstone's assistant for about a year. But was there something too eager in her demeanor? Was there more than youthful excitement about working with such a prominent man and the opportunity to study rare documents with him? In the aftermath of Dr. Fieldstone's murder and the manuscript's disappearance, eagerness seemed maybe more like ... determination?

"I will not be silenced," Polly muttered to the mirror, half-heartedly delivering the line as her mind looped back to Rachel. Could Rachel have killed Fieldstone and stolen the manuscript? The thought sent a shiver down her spine. Polly leaned closer to the mirror, searching her reflection as though it might hold the answer. What if Fieldstone had refused to share the authentication credit with her? Did academia work way—cutthroat, like Hollywood? Probably.

And what if Rachel had seen the manuscript as her ticket

out of his shadow? What if she thought her contributions deserved equal recognition, but Fieldstone had refused to budge? Polly paced the bedroom, running her fingers through her hair, the scenario building momentum in her mind. It wasn't hard to picture any assistant, overlooked and frustrated, deciding to take matters into her own hands. Stealing *Vanity and Virtue*—a long-lost manuscript that could cement Rachel's career—was a bold move, but ambition demanded boldness.

But what if Fieldstone had caught her? Polly froze mid-step, the possibility chilling her. What if Rachel, cornered and desperate, had acted impulsively? Could she have silenced him before he could expose her?

Polly's stomach churned. "No," she whispered, brushing the thought aside. That was too extreme. Rachel might be driven, but murder? Even so, the coincidences pressed down on her: Fieldstone's murder. The missing manuscript. They were connected.

She turned back to the mirror and caught her own reflection, paler now under the weight of her suspicions. *You're overthinking this,* she told herself, shaking her head. Her gaze dropped to the script in her hand. She squared her shoulders and tried the next line again. "We must seize opportunities when they are presented!" The words came out sharper than she'd intended, almost accusatory. Was it the character speaking —or her imagining Rachel's thoughts, laced with ambition and resolve to take whatever opportunities arose?

Polly sighed, casting the script onto her bed with a frustrated huff. It was no use trying to focus on the play when her mind was replaying conversations, analyzing subtle glances and nervous tics. She sank down onto the edge of the bed. It was time for another, more in-depth conversation with Rachel. But this wasn't a conversation she could have over the phone. She needed to see her in person. Her body language would reveal as much as her words. But how could she coax her from London? Rachel was surely busy with her career at the British Library. And then a thought occurred to her. There was no other way to dig beneath that carefully constructed exterior without bringing her back to the scene of it all. Polly picked up her phone and tapped her fingers against the screen. Opening a blank email, she wrote what she hoped was a heartfelt invitation. The perfect bait:

Subject: Honoring Dr. Fieldstone

Dear Rachel,

I've been thinking about Dr. Fieldstone and feel we haven't truly honored him. The way things have been handled seems so cold and clinical. Would you join me at Thistlethorne on Saturday evening for a small gathering to celebrate his life and work? It'll be a relaxed evening—cocktails, hors d'oeuvres, and a buffet dinner—a few friends sharing stories and memories. You were such an important part of his life, and it would mean a lot to have you here. It's a bit of a journey from London, but of course, you'd stay the night. I hope you'll consider it—it feels like the send-off he deserves.

Polly paused before hitting Send. Was it the right balance of warmth and professionalism? Enough to make Rachel feel wanted and needed, but not enough to make her suspicious? She hovered her finger over the Send button, then tapped it quickly before she could overthink it. The email shot into the digital ether.

A small, satisfied smile crept across Polly's lips as she set the phone down. Rachel should have no legitimate reason to reject the invitation. She owed it to Fieldstone—or at least, Polly wanted to believe that.

The answer came sooner than Polly expected. Less than an hour later, a ping from her phone broke her concentration. Polly's eyes scanned the screen, her smile growing as she read:

Dear Polly,

Thank you for thinking of me. I've been struggling too, and I agree we haven't honored him properly. I'd be happy to join the gathering—it will be good to connect with others who cared about him and his work. Let me know the details, and I'll arrange the journey. You're two-hours from London, but for Dr. Fieldstone, it's worth it. You might also consider inviting Professor Richard Lockhart.

Best regards.

The late afternoon sun had long dipped behind the trees when Tim dropped Polly off at the Fox & Hare. Her standing Wednesday early evening dinner date with Terrence was the one constant in her week, the one thing she allowed herself to anticipate with something like giddiness. God, she needed this diversion tonight.

As Polly stepped into the pub, a wave of cozy warmth wrapped around her. The crackling fire cast golden flickers across the stone hearth, and the air was thick with the rich scent of wood smoke, mingling with the savory aroma of roasting meat and the earthy tang of ale. She paused for a moment, letting the ambiance settle over her, but it was the thought of seeing Terrence that set her heart stirring.

Her eyes adjusted to the dim light, the murmur of quiet conversations and bursts of laughter weaving a comforting backdrop.

And then she saw him. Terrence was at their usual corner table, his silhouette illuminated by the soft glow of the fire. He looked up as she approached, his eyes locking on to hers, and his smile—warm, effortless, and sincere—spread across his face. It was the smile that could make the rest of the world fall away, and for Polly, it did.

Two glasses of red wine sat on the table, their usual order placed by Natalie, the server, before Polly even arrived. "Rain-soaked but still radiant," Terrence said as she draped her coat over the back of her chair. His voice, with its low, velvety cadence, sent a shiver of pleasure through her. She pretended not to notice it.

Despite the comfort of the pub—the crackle of the fire, the scent of shepherd's pie, and Terrence's familiar presence—Polly felt a knot of tension in her chest, her thoughts still buzzing with the day's worries. She picked up her wine glass, letting the stem twirl between her fingers as she searched for the calm she hoped his company would bring.

"Long day?" Terrence asked, his tone gentle but probing, as though he could sense her inner turmoil.

Polly nodded, meeting his eyes for a beat too long before looking away. "The usual," she replied, forcing a smile. But even as her voice brushed the surface of casualness, her thoughts strayed to the way he leaned forward slightly when he spoke to her, the way he seemed to truly listen. If only he knew how much that mattered.

Even as she let herself breathe in the comfort of Terrence's presence, she couldn't dismiss the weight of her upcoming performance at the literary festival. Or the authors' interviews and Q&A sessions. Or her thoughts about grilling Rachel Hawthorne at the memorial. Of course, Dr. Fieldstone—his murder and the missing manuscript—were uppermost in Polly's thoughts. *You're here to relax,* she reminded herself. Let the wine and your darling Terrence do the rest.

They made small talk at first, as they always did, a polite dance around the real issues clouded Polly's mind. The weather, for one (which was always a variation on wet). "It's strange, though," Terrence mused, his tone casual, "for some reason, it's usually nice the weekend of the festival. Never fails. Every year, it's almost like Abbots Clover has a deal with the weather gods."

He leaned back in his chair, watching her closely, his brow creased with concern. He wasn't fooled by Polly's attempts to seem unfazed. There was a weight pressing down on her tonight. "You seem a little ... disconnected," he said, his voice gentle, though his words carried an edge of observation that made Polly glance up.

Their eyes met, and Polly saw his concern. It made her feel both understood and a bit too exposed.

He gave her a small, knowing smile. "I can tell you've got too much on your plate."

Polly sighed, swirling the wine in her glass, watching the burgundy liquid spin like her thoughts. "Maybe a little."

Terrence rested his forearms on the table, leaning in slightly. "Between your one-woman show, the authors' interviews, the murder ..." He paused, his smile warm but laced with concern. "Am I leaving anything out?"

Polly let out a soft laugh. "It's a three-ring circus, that's for sure. I thought juggling it all would be thrilling—energizing, even—but ..." She trailed off, the tension of the last few days was catching up with her, and for the first time, she let the exhaustion seep through her carefully constructed façade. "This should be a walk in the park compared to my schedule when I was on TV every week."

Terrence raised an eyebrow, leaning back in his chair. His expression softened. He crossed his arms as if mulling something over. "You know, you don't have to be Polly Pepper: Superwoman. The festival's a big deal, sure, but you're not obligated to carry so much of it on your shoulders. Not everything has to be absolutely perfect."

Polly chuckled softly, taking a sip of her wine. "In the old days, I'd be lucky to grab a sandwich between rehearsals, story meetings, costume fittings, press engagements, and interviews. My phone was constantly ringing, producers breathing down my neck, fans waiting outside the studio to catch a glimpse of me. I once did a twelve-hour shoot, then had to fly to New York for a press junket and back again to Hollywood for the Emmy broadcast. I won, so it was worth it. I'm a pro," Polly said with a wink, though her eyes softened at the memory. "The truth is, I barely had time to breathe. Every minute was spoken for. Running around trying to juggle so many things for this festival ... it's nothing compared to managing a TV production every week. I'm out of practice."

Terrence chuckled softly, his eyes warm. "You're a force of nature. But even hurricanes need to slow down to regain strength. Just ... don't forget to take care of yourself. This may be easier than your TV days, but you're still doing a lot." He leaned forward, resting his hand lightly on hers.

Polly glanced at their hands, feeling the warmth of his touch seep through the fatigue that clouded her mind. She smiled, appreciating his presence more than she could express, but as usual, she shrugged it off with a playful glint in her eye. "Oh, and the chef has added one more teensy-weensy little morsel to my plate."

Terrence raised an eyebrow.

She hesitated for a second, wondering how much to share. "I'm organizing a little ... memorial. Dr. Fieldstone didn't have any proper send-off. Nothing fancy, something at Thistlethorne to honor him and his work. You'll be there, of course." Polly sipped her wine to avoid saying more. "It's a way to bring some closure. The festival will be over soon; after that, I'll have all the time in the world—for us. I promise." That was precisely what she wanted more than anything: *us*.

Terrence smiled back, though it wasn't quite convincing. "Okay," he said quietly. "I trust you to know what you're doing. I can hang in there and play second fiddle. Or third. For now."

In the next moment, as Natalie, came to their table to take their meal orders, Polly glanced across the room, and her smile faltered. She caught sight of Mary Radcliff sweeping through the pub door, her eyes searching, then locking on Polly like a heat-seeking missile.

Polly's stomach tightened.

"Don't look now ..." she began softly, trying to keep the growing tension out of her voice. But it was too late, Terrence had followed her gaze and turned in time to see Mary marching toward them, her heels clicking sharply against the worn slate floor.

"What now?" he muttered, his voice low. "She looks like she's ready to throw a punch."

"Polly Pepper," Mary barked, her voice tight and shaking with barely controlled anger. Her hand gripped her umbrella like a truncheon she was eager to use. "It's Wednesday, so I knew I'd find you here. I've heard rumors," she said, spitting the words out as if they tasted foul. She didn't waste time on pleasantries. "Word around Abbots Clover is you think I'm behind the theft of Abigail Townsend's manuscript ... and maybe something worse. People are talking."

Terrence, uncomfortable at the sudden confrontation, shifted in his seat. "Mary, I think you're—"

"No, no, it's okay," Polly interrupted softly, keeping her gaze on Mary. "I'm usually the subject of gossip, so you have my sympathy. But trust me, I've never once uttered your name in public. Not once!" She raised an eyebrow, feeling the familiar tug of annoyance. *You're too boring for conversation.*

"Oh, cut the act, Polly Pepper," Mary snapped. "Don't play coy with me. I know how things work in this village better than you do. You start asking questions, poking around, and suddenly my name is popping up in all the wrong places."

Polly leaned back in her chair, her hands resting on the table. "So I'm the curious type. Maybe even nosey. I admit that. But only because there are so many unanswered questions about the murder and the missing manuscript. If people are jumping to conclusions, that's not something I can control. For the record," she added, her tone softening slightly, "I haven't publicly accused anyone of anything."

"No?" Mary's bitter laugh rang through the pub, sharp and unnatural. "Then why are people whispering, wondering if I'm involved? I'm a writer, not some petty thief."

Polly suppressed the urge to remind Mary of the blatant plagiarism she had been accused of in her last novel, *Lust Among the Bluebells*, but she held her tongue. Instead, she let the silence stretch between them, the weight of Mary's protest hanging heavy in the air.

"You should be looking at Arthur Townsend," Mary deflected.

"I've already interrog—spoken with Mr. Townsend," Polly replied coolly. "And with everything that's happened in the village, it's only natural people are suspicious of everyone else. Someone's dead, and the manuscript the victim was authenticating is missing."

"And you think I'm guilty." Mary's eyes flashed, the anger sharp and unmistakable. As Polly studied her, she thought she caught something else—something beneath the anger. Was it fear? Or something she couldn't quite name?

Polly remained silent for a moment, watching Mary's flushed face and the way her fingers fidgeted with the umbrella. She let the tension hang in the air, her mind working quickly. There was something Mary wasn't saying. Polly decided to press further. "I'm a wee bit curious," she said, her tone still casual though her eyes were sharp, "why did you go to the library to see Dr. Fieldstone? I've never thought of you as one for academic pursuits."

Mary blinked, caught off guard by the question. For a second, her mouth opened and closed without a sound, her brain scrambling for an answer. Her cheeks flushed an even deeper shade of red. "Oh, well, you know ... research," she blurted out. "For my book."

Polly raised an eyebrow. "Research?"

Mary nodded quickly. "Yes. For a new novel. I'm setting my next book in the Regency period. I'd heard Dr. Fieldstone was an expert, and I wanted his advice." She let out a nervous chuckle, though her hand tightened again around the umbrella as if she were about to snap it in two.

Polly tilted her head, her eyes narrowing slightly. "Interesting. What, exactly, were you researching? Because Dr. Fieldstone's expertise in that period was limited to literature. Not ballroom etiquette. Not the language of fans. Or the importance of one leaving their calling card."

Mary's gaze flickered toward the door, her discomfort growing by the second. "Oh, just ... general stuff. Historical accuracy, things like that. I didn't stay long. He was busy, and we only talked for a few minutes."

"Historical accuracy?" Polly echoed, her skepticism thinly veiled.

Mary's eyes widened slightly, and she hesitated a fraction too long before stammering, "Yes, well ... it was ... you know, for a future project. I work on more than one book at a time." She offered Polly a tight, brittle smile.

Polly leaned back in her chair, crossing her arms. "So you happened to drop by, happened to see the manuscript, and happened to leave right after that?" Her voice was soft, but there was a quiet challenge behind her words.

Mary's grip on the umbrella tightened even more, and she shifted uncomfortably, clearly sensing she was cornered. "I don't know why this is such a big deal, Polly. I was there for a quick visit."

"Convenient." Polly could practically see the cracks forming in Mary's façade.

Mary's face tightened. "I don't have to explain myself to you," she said, her voice sharp and defensive. "I know what you're insinuating, and I had nothing to do with the missing manuscript. Or anything else."

Polly didn't flinch or react to the anger in Mary's voice. She simply watched as Mary clutched her umbrella even tighter.

"I wanted to make sure you weren't dragging my name through the mud," Mary added, her tone clipped. "I have nothing to hide."

Polly offered a thin smile. "Of course."

Mary's eyes flashed again, frustration and something close to panic behind them. Without another word, she turned on her heel and strode out of the pub, her head held high but her steps too quick, as if she couldn't wait to escape.

Polly watched her go, her mind racing. She picked up her wine glass and swirled the liquid absently. "Perhaps the lady doth protest too much," she murmured, thinking of Mary's overly defensive tone. The excuses hadn't quite added up, and there was something about the way she'd clutched her umbrella —tight, almost protective—that felt ... off. Polly's eyes narrowed. Mary Radcliff was hiding something. And Polly intended to find out what.

20

A s the next morning dragged over Polly's bed, she stirred and caressed one of her warm pillows. She pretended it was Terrence. Boy was she stupid not going home with him after dinner last night. She regretted it. Now, she had to use her imagination to feel the heat radiating from his body and to feel his skin next to hers. *You're an idiot*, she berated herself as she regained full consciousness. *Don't screw this up. Don't think for one second you'll ever find another man as ideal for you as Terrence Marks! You'd better find more time to spend with him ... or he'll find someone who will.*

Polly took a deep breath and resolved that, as soon as the literary festival was over—whether or not she found Dr. Fieldstone's killer—she would be more sensible about not jeopardizing her future happiness. No more entangling herself in amateur theatrics, volunteering for things she barely cared about, or playing amateur detective. Especially since that didn't pay one red cent—and she needed big bucks to repair her thousand-year-old castle.

With Tim and Tiara both darting about the village doing who-knew-what, and Elara having her day off, Polly decided to indulge herself. She stayed wrapped in her pink, PP-mono-grammed silk bathrobe, feeling every bit the pampered recluse. She mixed her breakfast energy drink (cranberry juice with a splash of gin) and retreated to her bedroom suite, playscript in hand.

She plopped onto the chaise lounge and stared at the latest version of the show she'd rewritten for the fifth time. Her eyes scanned the familiar lines, but they still fell flat. The dialogue had all the charm of soggy cornflakes left in the bowl too long. The words stared back at her, lifeless. "How am I supposed to summon Abigail Townsend's spirit?"

Polly sighed and stood, pacing before the mirror. She read the lines aloud, but Abigail wasn't cooperating. The words sounded hollow, the rhythm off, the cadence forced. Her own reflection furrowed its brow at her. "This isn't Abigail. This is me in a bathrobe pretending to be clever."

She shook her head and took another sip of her drink. As an actress, she knew when a script wasn't working. She'd spent years living inside screenplays—and song lyrics—knowing when the dialogue or words weren't connecting with an audience. Now she stared into the mirror, hoping for inspiration or at least some clarity. But all she saw in the reflection was a woman overwhelmed by too many commitments. She sighed and ran a hand through her unbrushed hair. She let her script fall limply to her side, the pages crinkling in defeat.

She paced the floor, her steps sharp and uneven. "Murder! Manuscript! Memorial service!" Her voice rose with each word, the chaos in her head spilling out. She threw her free hand up in exasperation, nearly knocking over her drink. "How on earth am I supposed to channel a two-hundred-year-old feminist fire-brand when my own life is falling apart faster than a poorly written third act?"

She paused mid-stride, glancing at one of the dusty old

portraits on the wall, her voice dropping into a sarcastic mutter. "If Abigail Townsend has any pointers, now would be a great time to share."

Then, as Polly picked up her drink, eager for its calming effect to kick in, a chill swept through the room. The lights flickered momentarily, and a faint, silver mist curled at the edges of her vision. She froze, her heart thudding. Mr. Boots was snoozing under the duvet, and Polly was otherwise alone in the house—or so she thought.

She set her glass down carefully, her nerves tingling with apprehension. A shiver ran up her spine. This is England, she thought, trying to rationalize the situation. Old houses. Drafts. Probably nothing ... But even as she tried to dismiss the feeling, the mist thickened, swirling into a shape—humanlike, but otherworldly. It floated in front of her, its edges shimmering and faintly translucent. Polly blinked hard.

"Oh, for heaven's sake," she muttered under her breath. "Not this. Please don't bring the damn flatulent dog. I don't have my gas mask handy!"

It wasn't her first brush with the strange and unexplained within her castle. After dealing with Loki, the farting ghost dog, and the unsettling whispers that drifted through the halls on stormy nights, the idea of encountering a full-blown specter wasn't entirely far-fetched. Still, it sent a chill down her spine.

The figure seemed to force itself into focus. Its dark hair was swept back in a chignon, and its clothing, though indistinct, resembled the style of the women in the portraits lining the castle walls. The faint outline of lace at its throat hinted at another time, another fashion trend.

"Really?" Polly muttered, her voice wry but tinged with unease. "If you're here to add to my drama, congratulations—you've succeeded."

The ghost tilted its head slightly, its expression unreadable but oddly amused. "You're focusing too much on anger," it seemed to say, its voice coming from everywhere and nowhere all at once. "I was defiant, but I wasn't stomping around declaring my independence every five seconds."

Polly's brow furrowed. Her skepticism flickered. "Oh, terrific. A ghost giving me stage direction," she said, though her tone betrayed a growing curiosity. She studied the figure more closely, her initial fear ebbing into a strange fascination. "Who are you?" Polly asked, her voice softer now, as if speaking louder might break the delicate balance of the moment. "Did you used to be ... Abigail Townsend?"

"I still am." The figure seemed to nod, though its features remained frustratingly indistinct. "It's not all wrong," the image said, the voice softening. "But sometimes, virtue doesn't shout. Maybe it whispers."

Polly's chest tightened as realization washed over her. "You're telling me how to play you."

The ghost floated closer, its expression unreadable. "The truth didn't die with me. It was merely hidden. Find the manuscript—again—and you'll find the killer. I can't see into your future for guidance. I can only revisit my past. But this might help: the oak that stands alone guards its resting place."

Polly's mind reeled. "The riddle. From the letter tucked into *Vanity and Virtue*."

The ghost's form wavered, its edges dissolving like mist meeting sunlight. "Find the manuscript ... Don't let anything— or anyone—distract you. And if you find the gold brooch my beloved hid for safekeeping, leave it somewhere I can find it ... should I ever return."

Polly shivered as the room grew colder. Her eyes fixed on the ghost, which seemed to glow before fading completely. A faint whisper lingered, almost wistful. "You still have your life ... live it fully."

The riddle played on repeat in Polly's mind as the specter vanished: *The oak that stands alone guards its resting place.* She frowned, trying to piece together its meaning. The challenge gnawed at her.

If concentrating on her script had been grueling before Abigail's visitation, now it was downright impossible. The lines on the page blurred together, meaningless words mocked Polly's attempts to focus. She tossed the script aside with a huff, rubbing her temples as if that could somehow clear the fog of confusion. However, she remembered Abigail's ghost almost demanding, "Don't let anything—or anyone—distract you from what must be done."

Polly stood in front of the mirror for a long moment, staring at her reflection, trying to make sense of everything. Then she recalled the specter's other cryptic words: "Find the manuscript, and you'll find the killer." She snorted, rolling her eyes. "Duh!" she muttered, throwing her hands in the air. "That's no help at all!" She could practically hear Abigail's ghostly voice, detached, as if solving a murder were as easy as locating a misplaced pair of socks.

Polly leaned closer to the mirror, her frustration bubbling over. "Find the manuscript," she mimicked, her tone dripping with sarcasm. "Of course. I'll waltz right into the killer's lair, kindly ask for the manuscript, and then solve everything! Brilliant!" She groaned, slumping back onto the chaise, pressing her palms against her eyes as if she could block out the absurdity of it all.

The cold presence of the ghost, the cryptic clues, the whole "go solve this murder" vibe—it was all too much. Polly didn't sign up for this. She wanted her normal, everyday TV star life back: the stage, the applause, her biggest worry being which party invitation to accept.

"You know, Abigail," she grumbled, waving a hand at the

empty air like she was scolding an invisible stagehand, "more detail wouldn't have killed you. 'Find the manuscript,' she says. Oh sure, let me check Lost and Found. There it is, right next to Amelia Earhart's luggage."

She picked up the script again, her eyes lingering on the title: *Vanity and Virtue*. Funny how those two words seemed to echo in every corner of her life right now. It wasn't a title anymore; it was starting to feel like the theme of this entire ordeal, the backdrop against which everything was playing out.

Vanity—that was everywhere. Arthur Townsend, for instance. His pride all but consumed him, driving his relentless determination to uncover the truth about his family's legacy. At the dinner party, he'd practically vibrated with fanaticism, obsessed with why the once-powerful Townsends had faded into insignificance. And Mary Radcliff—what about her? All dramatic bluster at the pub. Was she defending her honor against malicious gossip, or was she covering her tracks? Tracks that might lead straight to Abigail Townsend's manuscript?

Polly sighed, the weight of her own thoughts pressing down. Vanity is everywhere, she admitted to herself. She wasn't blind to her own vanity. How could she be? She'd spent her entire career thriving in the spotlight, reveling in the chance to be at the center of any swirling drama. She wasn't immune to self-admiration—she knew that much.

But virtue? That was different. It wasn't lost on her that a part of her genuinely wanted to honor Abigail's life, to give voice to a woman who had been silenced for centuries. And then there was Dr. Jonathan Fieldstone. His virtuous voice had been silenced too—this time violently. Polly felt a deep responsibility to uncover the truth about his murder. She wanted justice, yes, but she couldn't help wondering: Was this about virtue, or was her vanity pulling the strings?

Was she doing this for the right reasons? Was she solving the mystery for Fieldstone—or was she trying to prove something to herself? To everyone? To show she could pull off the impossible by not only staging a one-woman show but also unmasking a killer, reclaiming the manuscript, and selling it for enough dough to guarantee her castle wouldn't collapse from lack of maintenance.

She shook her head, feeling the weight of the dilemma. *Vanity and Virtue.* These weren't abstract concepts in some forgotten manuscript. They were the forces at play all around her—and in her own life, too. And that was why the title resonated so deeply with her.

And then her phone rang.

Polly frowned and picked it up from the dressing table. She looked at the screen: Arthur Townsend. *It's about time the wanker thanked me. That dinner was days ago!* she thought, rolling her eyes. With a resigned sigh, she swiped to answer. "Arthur," she practically squealed, "I was wondering when we'd chat again." *Where are your manners, mister?*

Arthur Townsend's voice was polite, but there was a noticeable edge. "First, I want to thank you for inviting me to your evening. It was ... special."

Polly smiled faintly, though she intuited a dual purpose for the call.

"But I also wanted to say ..."

Here it comes.

He paused, the silence hanging a beat too long. "I've heard a rumor—"

This village is full of those!

"—you're doing a one-woman show for the literary festival. Based on Abigail's manuscript."

Polly's grip on her phone tightened slightly. "An abridged stage adaptation of *Vanity and Virtue.*"

Arthur's voice sharpened. "Why? How? You haven't studied the manuscript. There's no way you can do justice to it."

Polly bristled, though she kept her voice measured. "Arthur, I remember the story. The gist of it, at least. The basics."

"The gist? The basics? You can't possibly—"

Polly cut him off with a snort. "Arthur, it's not *Gone with the Wind*. It's a two-hundred-year-old novel about a woman stuck between bad suitors and tight corsets, for crying out loud. I think I can handle that. I've played more complicated characters than Cathryn Slocum—no offense—so let's not pretend this is some insurmountable artistic mountain."

"You read the manuscript once—"

That's once more than you!

"—so you're writing a play based on *impressions*. Without thoroughly studying and analyzing the story, you'll miss the depth and subtext that made her work significant in the first place. You'll reduce her to a shadow."

Polly pressed her lips together, trying not to bristle. "Hardly a shadow. I'm not trying to recreate the novel word for word. I'm honoring her memory."

"You can't honor something you don't fully understand, Polly. Without exploring her work in-depth, how can you be sure you'll capture the real Abigail Townsend? She deserves more than a quick glance back at her life."

"A glance?" Polly shot back "The point is to remind the world who Abigail Townsend was and what she stood for. The world should remember her—whether or not *Vanity and Virtue* ever resurfaces."

"With all respect, you're trivializing her work." Townsend's voice grew colder. "Abigail deserves more than an adaptation based on fragments of what you remember. That manuscript was a significant part of her life—and my family's legacy. I think you're doing this as some vanity project."

Polly's eyebrows rose. *Vanity project? Yeah. Maybe. Partly.* "I know what Abigail's work represents. I think she was the Helen Reddy 'I am woman, hear me roar' of her day. I know the weight of this. This is about shining a light on her legacy. If I don't do it, who will?"

"Maybe it's better left alone until the manuscript is found," Arthur said, his tone firm. "That way, her true voice can be heard fully, not pieced together by recollections."

Polly sat on the edge of her chaise, irritation bubbling up. "And what if the manuscript is never found? What then? Abigail's story dies? No, Arthur. We can't let that happen. I may not have access to her manuscript and every word she wrote, but I know her spirit." *Literally.*

Townsend sighed, and Polly could almost see him pinching the bridge of his nose. "If you go out there and present something half-formed, it risks tarnishing her name. I can't allow that."

Polly straightened her shoulders, her own frustration rising. "I'm not tarnishing anything, Arthur. And I'm not asking your permission. I'm keeping her memory alive, showing the world she was more than a historical footnote."

There was a pause, longer this time, and when Arthur spoke again, his voice had softened a fraction. "You think you understand her better than I do? I grew up with stories about Abigail. She's been a part of my life for as long as I can remember."

"Stories," Polly said gently. "Second-hand tales passed down through generations. But I know her through her own words. I know her not as some distant relative but as a real woman. Complicated. Brilliant."

Polly pressed on. "This isn't about family pride, Arthur. It's about bringing her back to life—if only for one hour during the festival—so people can get a glimpse of who she was. So they can hear her voice again even if it's through mine. If we wait for the manuscript to magically turn up, we could be waiting another two hundred years. I'll be old by then. And in the meantime, Abigail's story fades even more."

"You're putting a lot of trust in your talent, Polly," Townsend said quietly. "And I still don't think that's enough. Obviously, I can't stop you from doing this. But please remember my family's reputation—and Abigail's. They mean more to me than you realize. I hope you know what you're doing."

The line went dead before Polly could respond, leaving her staring at her phone, her reflection faintly visible in the darkened screen. *Of course I don't know what I'm doing,* she thought, her stomach knotting. That was what made this so terrifying— the sheer audacity of attempting to juggle a murder investigation, a missing manuscript, and a one-woman show without completely unraveling.

Polly set the phone aside and closed her eyes, allowing herself a moment of stillness. Abigail's ghost, Arthur's ire, and the weight of *Vanity and Virtue* swirled in her mind. There was so much at stake—for all of them. She took a deep breath, squared her shoulders, and opened her laptop. The words to the play weren't going to write themselves.

21

Polly slumped back in her chair in the library, fingers aching from hours of typing on her laptop, her eyes heavy from staring at the screen. She'd been at this since morning, and the afternoon sun had long surrendered to the chilly twilight. From downstairs came the faint sound of Tim and Tiara laughing in the main reception room, their voices carefree and light. Polly barely paid attention. Her mind was locked in a relentless cycle of revisions to her playscript. Abigail's words were beating like a drum in her head: "Don't let anything—or anyone—distract you from what must be done."

She glanced at the latest draft on the laptop screen, the cursor blinking in silent mockery. Despite all her efforts, it still felt inadequate—like Abigail's voice had slipped through her fingers yet again. Polly rubbed her temples, exhaustion and frustration colliding in a familiar way.

For the briefest moment, she considered abandoning the whole project, shutting the laptop, and joining the others downstairs. But Polly was not one to surrender when work became hard. She'd spent another day grinding through dialogue and scenes that felt both brilliant and terrible at the same time. Was this version any better than the last? She didn't know anymore. She was too close to it. She needed an audience. But now, it was Lush Hour—time for champagne and, hopefully, a receptive audience for her latest version of the play.

Downstairs, the house had come alive with the sound of clinking glasses and soft music. Polly could smell the comforting scent from the fireplace. With a deep breath, she grabbed freshly printed pages of the new script, shuffled them neatly, and headed downstairs. She entered the room to find her chums lounging comfortably and listening to Celine Dion. Tim was sprawled out on the Chesterfield settee, a glass of red wine in hand, while Tiara sat cross-legged on a wingback chair, scrolling through her BBC newsfeed.

"Well, if it isn't Lady Shakespeare!" Tim called out, raising his glass. "How's the masterpiece coming along?"

Polly forced a smile, her fingers tightening around the edges of the script as if it might escape her grasp. "Actually, you're about to find out," she declared, her tone dripping with theatrical confidence. She strode across the room with purpose, stopping before them like an actor about to deliver an important monologue. "I've rewritten it—again," she announced, her voice carrying the weight of a playwright unveiling their magnum opus. "And now, sweetums, you shall bear witness to ... whatever it is." She paused, raising a hand as though silencing an imaginary audience. "Right after my first glass of champers. Priorities, after all."

Tim and Tiara exchanged a glance, hoping the latest version of the play would be an improvement over the last. "Bring it on," Tiara said, handing her a flute of bubbly.

Polly took a long swallow, then inhaled deeply, her heart pounding. She set the glass down and flipped to the opening scene. This was it. The culmination of hours of relentless focus, fighting off every distraction, and pushing herself harder than she had in weeks. She was exhausted, but there was a feeling of fulfilment, too.

She cleared her throat, and the room quieted.

"I will not be silenced! I am no one's daughter to command, no one's wife to control. I am Abigail Townsend—my own woman!" Polly declared, her voice rising with theatrical intensity as her arms swept wide, her eyes blazing. She could feel the fire in the words, the righteous defiance she imagined Abigail must have carried. As the syllables reverberated in the air, a rush of adrenaline surged through her. But a crack formed in her confidence, spreading like a hairline fracture. The conviction in her voice faltered slightly, curling inward with doubt. A nagging unease twisted in her chest, pulling her out of the moment. She still didn't truly feel it.

She wanted to believe she was Abigail Townsend—a force of nature pushing back against control and expectation. But the fire she was trying to ignite felt dampened. The words hung in the air, heavy with potential, but they didn't land the way she'd imagined. The truth was, Polly wasn't entirely sure who Abigail was anymore—or what she truly stood for. And uncertainty gnawed at her, driving her insecurity. She finished with an exaggerated bow, holding the pose, waiting for applause.

Silence.

Not a clap. Not even a polite "meow" from Mr. Boots, who merely stretched lazily and tucked his head under his paw. Polly straightened, blinking into the silence, her breath still coming in quick bursts as she waited. Where was the murmur of approval? Even a raised eyebrow? The stillness pressed in on her. She brushed off an imaginary stray hair from her dress and forced a tight smile. "Well," she said dryly, "there's always room for improvement."

Tim was the first to speak, though the hesitation in his voice was telling. "I mean ... it's good," he said, drawing out the last word as though it could somehow cushion whatever critique was coming next. "But ..."

"But?" Polly's eyes narrowed.

Tiara leaned forward, her voice soft but firm. "Polly, you're ... you're giving it your all, I can tell. But I don't think you've found her yet. Abigail, I mean. It's like ..." She paused, searching for the right words. "It's like you're fighting to capture her spirit, but something's missing. She's not coming through."

Polly felt a flicker of frustration rise in her chest. "Not coming through? I'm giving the character defiance and anger. That's who Abigail was. A woman raging against the world."

Tiara shook her head gently. "Maybe that's part of her, sure. But I think Abigail's voice would be ... less bombastic ... maybe. She was trying to be understood. But I think you're focusing on one side of her—her defiance—when there had to be more. More layers. At least that's what I remember from the manuscript you read."

Polly's grip tightened around the script. She knew Tiara was right. No matter how many drafts she wrote or how fiercely she delivered the lines, it still felt like she was wearing a costume instead of living in Abigail's skin. She understood Abigail was more than her rebellion, but she couldn't seem to find the woman beneath the surface.

Tim chimed in. "Look, Mom, you're a powerhouse up there. There's no question. But it's like maybe you're trying too hard. The grand gestures, the drama—it's all very ... you know, Polly Pepper-*ish*. Maybe Abigail's voice isn't about how loud you can be, but what she's saying. Maybe it's simpler than you think."

Polly's chest tightened. "Simpler," she muttered as if the word itself were incomprehensible.

Tiara spoke again, her tone softer now. "You've written some great lines, and I think Abigail's voice is still somewhere in there, waiting to come through. You've got to stop trying so hard to be her, and maybe ..."

Polly looked down at the script in her hands, the pages crinkled from holding them so tightly. "As a matter of fact, I have listened to her. She appeared this morning in my bedroom. No, I didn't imagine it. She was nice." Polly described the visitation and said she'd rewritten the script based on Abigail's own direction. "But now that you mention it, she told me to tone it down. She said something like, 'Virtue doesn't shout. Sometimes it whispers.'"

"There you go!" Tiara said. "Straight from the phantom's mouth—or ectoplasm."

Polly stared at the script. "I don't know how to fix it, and the festival's in a week! I can't rewrite it again. I can't dig any deeper."

"Maybe it's time to bring in help," Tiara suggested, her tone casual but encouraging. "Hire a writer. A real writer."

Polly arched a brow. "In case you haven't noticed, we're about six thousand miles east of Hollywood. Heck, we're not even anywhere near London! I assure you there are no script doctors in Abbots Clover, England."

Tiara gave a small, knowing smile, as if she had anticipated Polly's resistance and already had a plan. She leaned back on the Chesterfield, crossing her arms. "You're right—we're not exactly rubbing elbows with Arthur Miller or Lin-Manuel Miranda. But maybe you don't need a professional scriptwriter. Sometimes, the best stories come from the heart, not the pen of a Pulitzer Prize winner."

Polly stared at her, a flicker of curiosity passing over her face.

"Maybe we need someone who knows how to write a good story, someone with another pair of creative eyes who can polish it up a little."

Polly's eyebrows arched. "Oh, let me guess. You're going to suggest someone local—someone who writes for the *Abbots*

Clover Overview. Terrence Marks. Or worse—Mary Radcliff. If she gets her hands on it, *Vanity and Virtue* will end up retitled *Between a Duke and His Hard Place* and have a picture on the cover of a half-naked guy clutching a swooning damsel."

Tiara rolled her eyes, a playful grin tugging at the corners of her lips. "I like where you're going with that, but I was thinking someone like ... maybe ... Elliot Davies."

Polly blinked, surprised.

Tiara nodded. "He's a real writer. Sure, his stories are provocative, like Mary's, but let's not pretend *Vanity and Virtue* doesn't have a few romance tropes in there, too."

"Elliot Davies writes stories," Tim agreed. "And whether you like it or not, *Vanity and Virtue* could use a bit of romance-novel flair. He might help give it more punch."

Polly pursed her lips, considering the suggestion, though skepticism hung in the air. "Elliot Davies. The man whose characters can't go two chapters without ripping off their clothes and jumping into the sack."

Tiara laughed softly, her smile conspiratorial. "You've already done the heavy lifting, Polly. But there's no harm in getting help to bring it to life."

Polly glanced down at the script in her lap, her fingers absently smoothing the pages. "You think Elliot could help?"

"It's worth a try." Tiara nodded. "And look, you're running out of time. You've been working your tail off, and there's no harm in bringing in a pro to make sure it's as good as it can be. Plus, it was his idea for you to do a show based on Abigail's manuscript in the first place. It's sorta his fault you're in this bind."

Polly let out a slow breath, the weight of the deadline pressing down on her. "All right," she said, finally giving a small nod. "I'll call and see if he's interested. But if he tries to add a steamy love triangle, it's over. I'm all by myself up there on stage. That would look weird."

The call turned out to be unexpectedly lively. Elliot had been thrilled by the idea and promised to be at Thistlethorne first thing in the morning to start work. Polly hung up, staring at the phone for a moment. She couldn't shake the feeling she'd invited chaos into her already precarious production. Still, a tiny part of her was relieved. If anyone could turn her fraying script into something wonderful, maybe it was Elliot Davies. As long as he kept the characters fully clothed.

Elliot arrived at Thistlethorne with a messenger bag stuffed with red pens, highlighters, and a laptop. After Polly enthusiastically walked him through her vision for the script, he retreated to the library, setting up shop like a student cramming for finals. Now, the house was quiet except for the occasional dramatic outburst from behind the closed library door.

Polly paused outside the room, straining to hear him.

"Oh dear," came Elliot's voice, followed by a low chuckle.

Polly rolled her eyes. Over the past few hours, she'd peeked in several times, each time finding him hunched over the partner's desk, glasses sliding down his nose, utterly absorbed. He scribbled furiously in the margins, occasionally shaking his head or squinting at the pages. Finally, unable to take the suspense, Polly knocked lightly on the door before stepping inside with a tray balanced on one hand: two mugs of tea and slices of Tiara's lemon drizzle cake.

Elliot looked up as she entered, flashing a wide grin that suggested he was far too pleased with himself. He leaned back in the chair, stretching his arms over his head with an audible sigh of satisfaction.

"Thoughts?" Polly asked, setting the tray down and bracing herself for his critique.

"Interesting," he said, nodding in agreement with himself.

"Interesting?" Polly raised an eyebrow, unsure whether that was a compliment or a critique in disguise.

"Let's call it a diamond in the rough—heavy on the rough. But with lots of potential." He gestured to the script. "It's obvious you've poured your heart into this, Polly. I can feel your passion for Abigail's story. That comes through, which is the most important thing."

Polly sat down across from him, crossing her arms. "But ...?"

Elliot leaned forward, resting his elbows on the desk. "But ... the structure's a bit all over the place. I think you're trying to do too much. It's only a one-hour play. You've got these grand, sweeping monologues where the Cathryn Slocum character fights against society. Suddenly, she's in a heated argument with her father, then jumping to a romance with RL—you need to give him a name, by the way—without letting the audience have any time to breathe."

Polly frowned, feeling a twinge of defensiveness. "It's a one-woman show. I have to be everyone. Abigail was fighting on multiple fronts. She was up against society, her family, and trying to find her own place in the world."

"I get that," Elliot said, nodding sympathetically. "But the problem is, in its current form, the emotional highs are happening so often they lose their impact. There's no build-up to make the climactic moments hit harder." He picked up the script again, flipping to a page marked with underlines. "Take this section, for example. You've got Abigail delivering this powerful speech about female autonomy and independence, which is great. But a few minutes later, she's back at it again, shouting about the same thing in slightly different words. You need to space it out. Give the audience time to digest one battle before launching into the next."

Polly pouted. "Less is more?"

"Exactly. Then when you do deliver those big moments, they'll hit so much harder." He flipped a few more pages, then stopped at another passage. "You've got some terrific lines here, but there are places where Abigail comes off a bit too … modern."

Polly narrowed her eyes.

"She's a woman ahead of her time, no doubt. But some of the language feels a bit too … twenty-first century. Like this line where she says, 'I'm done with all these men and their stupid rules.'" Elliot looked up at Polly, raising an eyebrow. "That sounds more like something someone would say today after a bad date, not Abigail Townsend fighting against the patriarchy of her time."

Polly nodded despite her disappointment.

Elliot leaned back again, his demeanor softening. "Look, your connection to Abigail is obvious. And I can feel the fire in your writing. But you need to let the audience experience her struggles without feeling like they're getting hit over the head every time she opens her mouth."

Polly sighed, resting her chin on her hand. "Who knew storytelling could be so hard."

Elliot smiled. "But I think I can help. Let me take this home and give it a go. I'll have another draft ASAP."

22

Tiara, with her pre-memorial to-do list in hand, wandered into the music room, where Tim was sifting through CDs and scribbling song titles for the event. She glanced at his notes. "'Poor Unfortunate Souls'? Really?" She raised an eyebrow. "'I'm Still Here,' 'Shake It Off.' Dr. Fieldstone liked Broadway and pop music but maybe go for something poignant. Something hopeful. 'Bring Him Home,' maybe, or 'Memory.' But 'Spirit in the Sky'? 'Defying Gravity'? A bit too on the nose, don't you think?" She smirked. *And I think your brain's lost its Wi-Fi connection.*

"Sad ballads are so last century," Tim explained. Though he was now second-guessing his selection of "Hit the Road Jack." "The whole atmosphere will be a downer if the tunes are too heavy. A total drag."

"Memorials are designed to be a total drag," Tiara huffed. "When it's my turn to pluck the celestial harp, I expect a symphony of sobbing. Maybe even some fainting. None of that 'Always Look on the Bright Side of Life' nonsense, please." Tiara looked at her list of chores and placed a checkmark next to MUSIC. "Have at it." But she prayed his choices wouldn't include "Stayin' Alive," or heaven forbid, "Another One Bites the Dust." With guests arriving in only a matter of hours, she had more urgent things to worry about.

By seven o'clock, the soft hum of reverential conversation permeated the main reception room at Thistlethorne Lodge. Candles flickered on every available surface, giving the room a surreal glow. Guests milled about, sipping wine and admiring the artwork in the old house. Everyone exchanged polite smiles and fond memories of Dr. Jonathan Fieldstone.

But despite the genial conversation, sadness was everywhere. No matter how hard the guests tried to focus on the positive aspects of Fieldstone's life and legacy, the darker reason for them being there refused to dissipate. The visitors weren't just honoring the life and career of an amazing man, they were there to reckon with the grim fact of how he died. *Murder.*

Polly glided through the room, champagne flute in hand, pausing here and there to exchange pleasantries with her guests. Near the fireplace, she caught sight of Professor Richard Lockhart engrossed in conversation with another guest. He stood with the posture that suggested he was used to holding court, even if his audience wasn't always paying attention.

In his mid-sixties, Lockhart's silver hair, combed into what might once have been a rakishly charming style, now merely emphasized the expanse of his forehead. Deep lines carved into his angular face and a sharp nose gave him a distinctly hawkish appearance. His pale blue eyes, slightly clouded beneath unruly brows, darted between his companion and the room, as if constantly taking stock of his surroundings. He wore a tweed jacket that had seen better days, with a pocket watch chain draped across his vest—a faint nod to bygone importance.

Polly noticed an antique gold lapel pin—ostentatious against his otherwise subdued attire, as if he'd attempted to inject a touch of flair into the ordinary. His expression was polite but detached with a shadow of weariness.

"You've done a lovely job with the memorial, Polly," he said quietly. "Jonathan would've appreciated the effort."

Polly tilted her head, studying him for a moment. "I sincerely hope so. He deserved nothing less. I know you two worked closely together. This must be ... especially difficult for you."

Lockhart's lips twitched into what might have been a smile, though it vanished almost instantly. He took a sip of wine, his gaze drifting past Polly to the cluster of guests across the room. "The academic world is poorer without him. That much is certain."

"Well," Polly said, forcing a lighter tone, "we can at least give him a send-off worthy of his accomplishments. He earned that much."

Lockhart gave a slight nod, his focus already elsewhere. Polly lingered a moment longer before moving on, making her way to the center of the reception room. When she determined her guests had all been sufficiently marinated with wine and plates of Tiara's home-cooked food, she cleared her throat and called for their attention.

Tim muted the stereo.

Tiara tapped her glass with a spoon.

The attendees stopped and turned toward their hostess.

Polly, a flute of champagne in hand, surveyed the small crowd, sizing up her audience. She cleared her throat again, then, like a stand-up comic determined to make an impression, she plowed ahead.

"When I think about Jonathan Fieldstone, PhD, the first thing that comes to mind—aside from the fact he rocked tweed like a country squire—is how dedicated he was to his profession. You've heard the term 'married to his work'? I mean, I think the man was having a love affair with eighteenth-century ink! Ever notice he incessantly talked about it like most people talk about fine wine?" She mimicked his voice. "'See this blot here? Definitely 1774. A good year for parchment.'"

The crowd, taken aback by Polly's unexpected irreverence, broke into cautious laughter. She grinned slightly and raised her glass higher. "I swear, Jonathan Fieldstone had more passion for faded ink than most people have for their actual lovers. The man literally *dated* historical documents."

It took a second for her audience to get the joke, but then their laughter swelled, and Polly clearly owned the room like the star performer she was. "But Jonathan was surprisingly funny, too. Not wet-your-pants ha-ha funny like me, but I mean funny for a stodgy academic." She paused, throwing a playful look around the room, her eyes gleaming with mischief. "No offense to all the stodgy academics here." More peals of laughter. "But come on—let's be real. When your idea of a thrilling weekend is spending it with a two-hundred-year-old manuscript, the bar for humor is set somewhere between footnotes and bibliographies."

Footnotes and bibliographies! The academics totally got it. They ate it up! The crowd laughed heartily; a few people were shaking their heads, amazed by her topical workplace humor. Even Tim and Tiara were impressed. When did she have time to write this comedy bit? Or was it off-the-cuff?

Polly, amping up the energy even more, continued, "Now, our dear Jonathan—he had a way of making you laugh over the most unexpected things. I mean, who else could get you to double over while explaining the intricacies of parchment degradation? The guy definitely had talent. He could break down the difference between goat-skin vellum and calfskin like nobody else. 'Ah, Polly, look at the texture!' Did I need to know that? He thought everyone did."

The laughter swelled again, and Polly threw her hands up in

feigned defeat. "And let's not even start on the times he tried to make ancient handwriting sexy. Have you ever seen seventeenth-century cursive? It's more like a Rorschach test for historians."

The crowd was howling, and Polly felt she was headlining in Vegas again. Her grin stretched wider, and she took another sip of champagne before delivering the next line, deadpan. "I once asked him, 'Jonathan, how do you manage to stay so enthusiastic about manuscripts after spending hours, days, weeks staring at faded ink and yellowing pages?' He looked me straight in the eye —dead serious—and said, 'Polly, if you can't tell the difference between eighteenth-century ink and nineteenth-century ink, are you even living?'"

The laughter crescendoed, the guests picturing Jonathan and his dedication to his profession as a document historian.

"Jonathan could take the dullest, dustiest old document— something that looked like it hadn't seen daylight since the actual Dark Ages—and suddenly, it was the sexiest thing in the world to him. He saw things the rest of us would miss. The beauty in paper fibers and watermarks ... every smudge on a document. Was that from ink or eighteenth-century spilled tea?"

Polly's voice softened again, a touch of sincerity and respect creeping in. "Jonathan saw stories hidden between the lines in handwritten documents. And that's one of the many reasons why we loved him. He cared enough to search through the details to find the truth."

Polly paused, taking a deep breath, her smile softening but still playful. "So here's to Dr. Jonathan Fieldstone—a man who could look at an old document and turn it into a mystery worthy of Sherlock Holmes. He brought the past to life, one dusty page and quill stroke at a time. Bless you, dear man. Here's to Jonathan."

"To Jonathan," everyone agreed softly.

Polly took a sip of her drink, the champagne fizzing softly over her tongue. She lowered her glass and glanced around the room. She caught Rachel's eye and noticed how her hand trembled slightly as she held her wine glass. Polly continued, her tone lightening slightly, "Obviously, some of you knew Jonathan far better than I. So if anyone would like to share a memory or say a few words about him, I'm sure it would mean a great deal to all of us."

For a moment, no one moved. Then Rose Harding stepped forward. Clearing her throat, she offered Polly a small nod. "I met Jonathan Fieldstone at an antiquarian book convention in London a few years ago. We got on instantly. When I invited him to Abbots Clover to examine the Abigail Townsend manuscript, he came at once. No hesitation. He was intense—in the best possible way. He became completely engrossed in the work but was never too busy to stop and share a bit of what he'd uncovered with me. I was enormously fond of him."

Polly divided her attention between Rose's testimonial and keeping her eye on her other guests—particularly Rachel Hawthorne. Rachel's body language made her stand out from all the others. She seemed overly anxious. It was obvious to Polly she didn't want to be there—but then, who did? As much as the evening was about celebrating Jonathan, Polly was on the lookout for signs of subterfuge in Rachel.

When Rose finished her tribute, polite applause rippled through the room. Polly's gaze swept over her guests, and she noted Rachel was inching toward the door to the hallway. Was she ducking out? Polly quickly seized the moment. "I know Jonathan's work brought him close to all of you, but there's one person who was by his side more than anyone else—Rachel Hawthorne."

Drats! Almost free, Rachel thought and stopped in her tracks.

She was visibly uncomfortable, her shoulders tensing at the mention of her name.

Polly could sense trepidation radiating from Rachel, but she pressed on. "Rachel, would you care to share a few words? I know it would mean a lot to all of us to hear about your time working with Jonathan."

Rachel's eyes widened slightly, and she shifted in her spot, her wine glass trembling ever so slightly in her hand. "Oh, I-I'm not much of a public speaker," she stammered, glancing nervously at the room full of expectant faces. "I wouldn't know what to say."

Polly tilted her head, her smile never wavering. "Just speak from your heart, dear. You knew Jonathan better than most of us."

Rachel hesitated, her gaze landing on the door as though she was seriously considering bolting. But after an uncomfortable moment, she set her wine glass on a nearby table and stepped forward. She cleared her throat, her voice shaky. "Well ... Jonathan —I mean, Dr. Fieldstone—was, um ... he was a wonderful mentor to me. He was ... um, working with him ... was a great honor. I learned everything from him." She paused, her eyes scanning the room, clearly uncomfortable under the weight of everyone's gaze. "About our work, he always said, 'If you can't prove it, it's just a story.' In other words, you have to find hard evidence to authenticate a document. Regardless of what other experts might say."

A soft ripple of agreement wafted through the crowd, and Polly noticed Rachel's eyes darted nervously toward Professor Lockhart, the linguistics expert standing near the fireplace. He seemed to offer a supportive nod and reassurance.

Taking a deep breath, Rachel continued, "Dr. Fieldstone and I spent a lot of time in libraries and institutions all over the country. We pored over old documents and manuscripts, trying to piece together their true history. He had a way of making the past feel alive, you know? And he was never afraid to challenge others who thought they knew better than he did. But he was never arrogant about it." Again, Rachel seemed to glance at Professor Lockhart, who nodded in agreement.

Rachel hesitated again, her voice trembling slightly, but she forced a smile. "Jonathan had a joke ..." She looked at Polly. "I'm not a comedienne like you, Ms. Pepper, but he said—whenever we'd come across something suspect—especially if someone seemed in a hurry for his conclusions—he'd say, 'Authenticating documents is like online dating—sometimes what looks promising at first turns out to be a phony.'" The joke landed, and Rachel's eyes once more sought out Professor Lockhart for confirmation.

Polly watched Rachel, taking in every emotional nuance, every nervous tic. There was something about the way she was holding herself that didn't seem completely genuine. *What are you hiding, Rachel?* she wondered with growing expectation. In Polly's life experience, the small details always gave people's secrets away: a shifting gaze, fidgeting hands. She could almost feel secrets simmering beneath the surface of Rachel's speech.

"But, um ... in all seriousness," Rachel continued, "Jonathan's dedication to uncovering the authenticity of a document was inspiring. I'll miss him a lot. Thank you."

Polly led the applause and gave Rachel a hug. "Thank you, dear," she said with genuine warmth. "Jonathan taught you well. I know he was proud of you. His work will live on through you."

Rachel nodded quickly, eager to retreat from the spotlight. She slipped back into the crowd, searching for her wine glass, then took a large gulp to steady her nerves.

After several other heartfelt testimonials from colleagues, the room returned to its low murmur of conversation. Polly kept track of Rachel, who had stopped briefly to speak to Professor

Lockhart and accept praise from several other guests. She had moved toward the edge of the gathering, looking as though she longed to escape the house. But as an overnight guest, she couldn't go far.

Polly's plans for the evening were going well. Now it was time to put the next phase into action. She took a slow, deliberate sip of her champagne, the bubbles fizzing faintly as her gaze swept the room and found Rachel, who stood examining a fox hunt painting. Polly glided over, her heels clicking softly on the hardwood floor. "Lovely speech, dear," she said, her voice sincere. She let the words hang between them, waiting for Rachel's response—which didn't come. "Jonathan would have appreciated the joke about fake documents and online dating. Your timing was excellent."

"He deserved more from me," Rachel said, her voice low, almost hollow.

Polly's eyebrows lifted slightly. The air between them felt heavier now. "Rachel, your testimonial was lovely. One of the best of the evening. It was heartfelt. People recognized that. I certainly did. Jonathan would have, too."

Rachel shook her head, her expression crumbling. "I don't mean the testimonial ..." she whispered, her voice barely audible. "I did okay with that. I mean he deserved more from me when he was alive. Jonathan was never cross with me—even when maybe he should have been. He gave me credit when credit was due. He encouraged me. And I turned around and ... on his last day, I ..."

Polly's eyes widened. A chill swept through her. She had always experienced Rachel and Dr. Fieldstone as an ideal team: professional, respectful, and perhaps even fond of each other in a careful, workplace way. What was Rachel saying?

"I was selfish. Inconsiderate," Rachel confessed, her voice cracking. "We'd worked together for a year, and I told him I wanted a promotion. I deserved it. I thought he should be recommending me for other positions. After we authenticated the Townsend manuscript, I thought it was time." She bit her lip, her face contorted with the weight of the memory. "But he said I wasn't ready to move up yet. Although I totally was. He brought up a couple of things—little things, really—he said there were errors with some past projects we'd worked on. I didn't think they were even errors. Just ... maybe not his way of doing things. That didn't make them wrong."

Polly felt a knot form in her stomach. She could sense where this was heading. She'd seen it many times before—bright, talented people propelled by ambition—not realizing how much more they had to learn before they could move forward. Ignoring the guidance of those with more experience.

"I was looking for better opportunities," Rachel continued, her voice rising, more insistent now, as though she was still arguing the point. "I'd worked hard. He knew that. He even told me he appreciated how conscientious I was. So why wouldn't he help me take the next step?"

Maybe because you're a self-absorbed little twit who doesn't know how to listen to someone who knows more than you. Polly tilted her head, choosing her next words carefully. "There's nothing wrong with wanting more, Rachel. We all reach a point where we feel we've outgrown our roles. I felt that after being on television for a decade. But it's how we handle that frustration that defines us. Some people dig in, work twice as hard ..." She let her words trail off, hoping Rachel would fill the gap.

"I was already working as hard as I could! Other people said so," Rachel snapped, her voice laced with annoyance. Her face flushed, her composure fraying. "I was doing a lot." She took a deep breath, forcing herself to remain calm. When she spoke again, her voice was low, resigned. "So I had no choice. I did what I had to do ..."

OMG! Please, please, please let this be a confession! A perfect way to end Jonathan Fieldstone's memorial evening! We can wrap the investigation up tonight! The room seemed to tilt slightly, and for a moment, Polly felt a surge of excitement. Was this going where she hoped it was going?

"I quit my job," Rachel said. "I told Jonathan I was going to work with Professor Lockhart at the Dunham Library."

Polly blinked, her mouth opening slightly, but no words came out. Of all the things Rachel could have said, this was nowhere on her mental bingo card.

Rachel's voice was flat, devoid of her earlier emotion. "Professor Lockhart and I had gotten to know each other when he was assisting Jonathan with the manuscript. We had dinner at the pub one night. He made me feel smart. At first, I thought maybe he was coming on to me—even though he's my father's age. And I thought he was, um ... He said nice things. That I was talented, and he was sacking his assistant, Monte, and I'd be an ideal replacement. He thought I was wasting my time with Jonathan Fieldstone, and he could help me. We could maybe help each other. He said he could fast-track me to head of Medieval Manuscripts at Dunham. The starting pay was basic, but there would be better opportunities down the road."

Polly raised an eyebrow. *It's astonishing how easily some people trade loyalty for flattery. A few compliments from Lockhart and Rachel was ready to jump ship. Ambition is a dangerous thing when mixed with insecurity,* she thought.

"I mostly wanted Jonathan to see that someone else recognized my value. I didn't want to hurt him. But ... I did. I told him about my decision on the way to the train. That's why he wasn't with me when I went back to London. He said he needed time alone to think about what I said. I thought he was maybe making some calls and deciding what he could do to keep me and make me happier in my job. Maybe he'd talk to the head of the department and get him to at least give me a small raise or a promise I'd be considered for any future openings for more prestigious jobs. If I'd only waited one more day before quitting, he wouldn't have been at the village library. He wouldn't have been—murdered."

The air seemed to thicken. Polly stared at Rachel for a moment, her mind scrambling to process what she had heard. She felt a strange mix of shock, disbelief, and beneath it all, a sense of disappointment in Rachel—and in the lack of a murder confession. *So that's why Jonathan wasn't on the train with her,* Polly thought. *There goes my theory of some dark plot by Rachel to steal the manuscript and murder her boss, all shot to hell.*

Polly studied Rachel's face, taking in the layers of guilt and sorrow. "It's not your fault Jonathan is dead. What you did was unprofessional and disrespectful to someone who had treated you well. But you didn't set his murder in motion."

Rachel looked up, tears welling in her eyes. "But I-I—"

"No," Polly cut in gently but decisively. "You insulted him but that doesn't make you an accessory to his death." She hesitated. "Someone else. It's on them."

Rachel's eyes shimmered with unshed tears. "And now Dr. Fieldstone's gone. And if I hadn't emailed my resignation to the entire chain of command at the library—to show I meant business—my mistake could have died with him. Maybe I would even have been promoted into his job. His death left an opening."

Good grief! You're still thinking about your career and your blind ambition!

Rachel blotted her eyes with a cocktail napkin, her voice barely above a whisper. "I guess I wanted to force his hand to meet my demands. Like I was holding him hostage for a ransom or something. Plus, Jonathan was right about the online dating analogy. You could substitute Professor Lockhart for dubious documents. I screwed up royally. His assistant, Monte, was lucky he got sacked."

"When do you start? The new job, I mean," Polly asked, trying to understand how inconsiderate Rachel had been to leave Dr. Fieldstone high and dry.

"I've started. I've been on the job since the day after I left Abbots Clover and got back to London," Rachel said. "I didn't even have a break. I shouldn't have rushed into it, but frankly, I expected Jonathan to call me back. Yeah, I have my own office now. But it's more a converted closet. It's up in one of the eaves of this old building in Croydon. Not exactly Oxford. And it's always freezing. I'm basically an assistant again. And Professor Lockhart ... I don't think he's even a real professor. At least not anymore. He made a name for himself a long time ago when he was young, but from what I've seen, he's not well regarded. I'm sure Jonathan was being nice, and he took pity on him when he invited him to assist with the Townsend manuscript."

A voice behind Polly suddenly said, "My ears are burning." She turned to find Professor Lockhart, his coat and umbrella draped over his arm. He nodded curtly to Rachel.

Polly forced a polite smile. "Professor Lockhart. A little ice on those ears, and you'll be fine," she said, pretending she didn't understand his reference to ears burning from gossip. "Thank you for joining us this evening. I'm sure Dr. Fieldstone would have appreciated it."

"I wouldn't have missed it," he said. "Jonathan was important to me. I was delighted to be in a position to authenticate the Townsend manuscript for him. I'm off now. Taxi's waiting. The last train back to London. Sorry we didn't have an opportunity to spend more time with each other, but please accept my deepest condolences. I'll surely see your one-woman show at the festival. Yes, I've heard all about it. I wouldn't miss anything having to do with dear Abby, er, Abigail." With another nod to Rachel, Professor Lockhart turned and left the room.

The grandfather clock struck 10:00, its chime heavy and deliberate, as guests began to follow the professor's lead and made their way toward the door. Polly, Tim, and Tiara stood by the entryway, forming a goodbye line. Their smiles, though genuine, were starting to fray at the edges. It had been a long day, but with a grace acquired over years of being hosts, they thanked each guest by name and ensured coats were retrieved from the hall tree and no umbrellas were forgotten. By 10:30 (with a stray scarf and a pair of reading glasses left behind), the house had settled, and overnight guest Rachel Hawthorne retreated to her room upstairs.

"And then there were none ..." Polly mused as she slipped off her heels and reclined on the Chesterfield. She put her feet up on Tim's lap for massaging and accepted a fresh flute of champagne from Tiara.

"You did an amazing job," Tim said. "I think people were grateful for the opportunity to mourn Jonathan together. I heard a lot of nice things about him. He was well-liked. If nothing else, the gathering brought some comfort and support."

"No, I mean 'and then there were none' suspects," Polly moaned. "I was banking on ..." She looked around in case Rachel—who'd said she was going to bed, but you never know—was within listening distance. She lowered her voice to a whisper. "I was sure I could wheedle a confession from Rachel. I got one. But it doubled as an alibi. Not what I'd hoped for. Drats!"

Mr. Boots slinked into the room, his tail flicking lazily behind him, his nose twitching as he took in the lingering scents: perfume, wine ... *Is that chicken zucchini casserole? My favorite!* His whiskers quivered as he sniffed the edges of a chair, investigating the unfamiliar scent left by a guest. Satisfied with his inspection, he gave a contented stretch, then jumped onto the Chesterfield and settled by Polly's side—where he was immediately bestowed lazy scratches behind his ears.

Polly lounged on the Chesterfield, staring blankly at the portrait of the dour duke frowning down from above the fireplace and dividing her attention between kitty cat belly rubs and sipping her champagne. Tim had tapped Classical Violin Solos on Spotify, but Polly was oblivious to the lush sounds. Her thoughts were crowded with the names and faces of Arthur Townsend, Mary Radcliff, Rachel Hawthorne, Rose Harding, and the lit festival authors she'd interviewed over the phone. She had initially turned each of them into potential suspects in the murder of Jonathan Fieldstone. But everything had unraveled when she started to tug on the threads of their motives and alibis. They were no longer potential murder suspects. She had exhausted her list one by one and ended up back at the same maddening place: Nowhereville.

Polly closed her eyes for a moment. There had to be something she was missing in her investigation, some crucial detail she'd overlooked. But what was it? Had her judgment been clouded by what she wanted to believe rather than what the evidence told her? *If you can't prove it, it's a story*, she heard Rachel's quotation from Dr. Fieldstone repeating in her head. Yes, each suspect had seemed plausible initially—but maybe that was it. Maybe she had been chasing the wrong leads because they had fit too easily into her Hollywood-style murder mystery scenario.

But time was running out. She'd given herself a deadline. After the literary festival was over—her murder investigation would be over, too. She'd promised herself it was time to investigate something else: a serious romantic relationship with Terrence Marks.

23

"He couldn't have written anything of value in only two days!" Polly scoffed when Tiara said Elliot Davies had called and was delivering a new draft of the play before lunchtime. "For Pete's sake, it took me longer to decide on a title. And don't call it *his* play. It's *my* play. He's merely adding a professional touch. Patching up a few bits and bobs here and there. He said that's all it needed because I gave it 'good bones.'"

"So you're saying Elliot can't get to your level of creative genius in forty-eight hours?" Tiara teased. "Probably had to use duct tape on those 'bones.'"

"Nothing of any lasting value could come in such a short amount of time," Polly continued dismissively. "Real writing involves lots of layers. You write something. Hate it. Toss it out. Write it again. Hate it again. Maybe less hate after the fifth time. Then stare at it for days, wondering if there's anything salvageable. Only then, after a ridiculous amount of self-doubt, do you produce something maybe remotely passable. At least that's what someone said in the *New York Times* after they won the National Book Award."

Tiara couldn't contain a scowl. "Or maybe Elliot's a pro and knows what he's doing. He maybe doesn't need to suffer for his art."

Polly huffed. "I'm not getting too excited. Even if he did pull off a minor miracle, I'll still need to *Polly Pepper* it."

"As a matter of fact, I think he's written something amazing —maybe brilliant," Tiara said. "And if by 'patching up a few bits and bobs' you mean he's fully fleshed out Cathryn Slocum's backstory and internal conflicts, smoothed over her speeches to move the plot forward, and given it an emotional climax—then yeah, I'd say he's patched it up."

Polly's eyes narrowed with the suspicion of a security guard watching a shopper linger too long in front of the jewelry case. "What's up with you today?" she harrumphed. "You're awfully defensive. And how do you know what Elliot's done to the play? Unless ..."

A light dawned. Polly folded her arms across her chest. "Oh, it's all starting to make sense," she said, nodding and scrunching up her face. "You've been acting different the past few days. You talk on your phone more than usual. You slip away whenever there's a message ping. Tim saw you wandering around the courtyard yesterday, looking all aimless and daydreamy. Lots of giggling coming from your room late at night, too—while I'm trying to concentrate on imagining Terrence sneaking into my room without his shirt on. And you're eating less."

Tiara shrugged. "Maybe I'm on a diet. And I go outside for fresh air because you suck up all the oxygen in this place. You're not the only one with a lot of stuff on her mind, missy."

Polly raised an eyebrow and stared at Tiara. "By 'stuff on your mind,' you wouldn't mean ... I don't know ... maybe there's an adorable romance-novelist-turned-playwright in the picture? Hmm ...?"

Tiara rolled her eyes in mock exasperation, but a smile was

already betraying her. "Maybe ..." She waited a beat. "He is pretty adorable, isn't he? You know I like 'em skinny and hairy and all ruddy complexiony. And that Ringo Starr accent of his. Don't get me started!"

Polly clutched her chest like she'd been mortally wounded. "Why haven't we discussed this? I'm supposed to be your bestie! For twenty years, we've told each other every disgusting little thing about the men we date. I mean, I was totally open with you about how Terrence eats his cereal with a fork so he can 'save all the milk for last'! And how he smiles at himself in the mirror every time he passes one—every single time. And don't even get me started on how he insists he's not afraid of spiders, but he practically runs a marathon to get away when he sees one."

Polly continued and pressed a hand dramatically to her forehead. "I should've been the first to know you and Elliot are ... what are you? But no, here I am, finding out by pure accident from someone who's become a stranger to me! I'll bet the village grapevine has all the inside poop. Does Tim know? He's always been your favorite. Have you and Elliot ... ya know ... wink, wink?"

"Wink, wink? What are you, twelve years old?" Tiara scoffed. "We haven't carved our initials into a tree or planned a romantic getaway to Tuscany—if that's what your 'wink, wink' euphemism means." She leaned in, lowering her voice. "Although, if/when we ... 'wink, wink' ... you'll be the *last* to know!"

Polly threw her hands up in mock outrage. "Unbelievable. So you're daydreaming about Tuscany—and 'wink, wink'—with Mr. Literary Hero, while I'm relegated to the sidelines all alone, worrying about finding Jonathan Fieldstone's murderer and the missing manuscript and exposing my soul on a stage at a village literary festival. I feel abandoned and betrayed."

"Don't take it personally," Tiara said with a shrug. "You know I never talk about potentially life-changing *anything* until it's fully baked and out of the oven. I don't want to jinx it. And Elliot is far from a done deal. He happened to call last night and read his new draft to me. He got rid of all the boring parts."

Polly gasped in mock horror.

Tiara's grin widened. "Mr. Boots snored through your last read-through, remember? But Elliot's made Cathryn's character feel real. Her motivations are clearer. The pacing flows more naturally. I think it's solid. You're gonna love it. Audiences will, too."

Polly couldn't help but crack a smile. "Can't wait to see what Romeo's done to my baby—oh, and the *play*, too," she added with a knowing smirk, her innuendo landing squarely between them. Beneath the teasing, Polly was genuinely happy to see her friend looking so radiant and, dare she say it, *smitten*. Tiara, usually so level-headed and no-nonsense, was letting herself be swept up in something as unpredictable as romance. It might not be a "done deal" yet, but it was definitely heading in that direction. And for once, Tiara seemed willing to enjoy the ride.

Then, as if on cue, the iron knocker echoed from the entryway door down the hall, breaking their playful exchange.

"It's Mr. 'Skinny and hairy and all ruddy complexiony with a Ringo Starr accent,'" Polly teased as Tiara stood to answer the door. "And don't think you're off the hook," she called out. "This conversation is far from over."

Moments later, Elliot was smiling in the doorway, holding fresh copies of the revised script in his hands. The trio settled into the library, and Polly dove headfirst into reading the new version aloud—and making suggestions for "improvements." They'd entered a creative flow, tweaking, refining, and occasionally throwing crumpled papers in the air in frustration. They argued over the smallest details—whether anyone would have said "darn" in the 1700s to mean anything other than mending a sock, whether Cathryn's father's backstory needed more bite, and if the last scene should end with Cathryn slamming the door or simply walking out. And by the time the light outside had faded to dusk, they were nearly satisfied with their work. Cathryn Slocum had been transformed. She was no longer a flat, one-dimensional character mired in dialogue. She was a fierce, dynamic heroine who overcame her father's oppression.

Polly leaned back in her chair, script in hand, and sighed contentedly. "Cathryn's finally alive."

"You and Abigail Townsend gave her life." Elliot smiled, trying to be generous. "I just gave her CPR."

Tiara nudged Polly. "See? Brilliant. Right?"

"Pretty darned impressive, mister," Polly agreed with a twinkle in her eyes. "But don't go thinking you're the next Eugene O'Neill or August Wilson yet. I still have a few notes."

They agreed Cathryn's final act of rebellion needed work. The ending was almost, but not exactly, right. Elliot had written a satisfactory conclusion, but Polly's theatrical instincts knew there should still be at least one more punch.

Polly tapped her pen against the script. "I remember Abigail's manuscript saying Cathryn did something bold at the end. She threw her suitor's engagement ring at her father's feet. But that's too predictable and melodramatic. There must be something else she could do to show her defiance and independence."

Elliot furrowed his brows. "That crossed my mind too. Maybe there needs to be something symbolic at the end. She's breaking free from her father's control. Maybe she needs something that represents her evolution. Like ... like the glass unicorn in *The Glass Menagerie*. When Laura breaks the unicorn, it symbolizes she's breaking free from her domineering mother. Or maybe something like the red windbreaker James Dean wore in *Rebel Without a Cause*. The jacket symbolizes his rebellion against his parents and society."

Tiara, who had been scribbling notes, looked up. "What about the gold oak leaf brooch in the story? Remember? Cathryn's father wears it as a symbol of his status and authority. Maybe we could use that in some way?"

Polly sat up straighter in her chair, intrigued. There had always been something about the brooch that fascinated her. "What if ... Cathryn takes the gold brooch from her father—and wears it herself? Like she's not only rejecting him but claiming his power. She's not walking away; she's turning the tables!"

Elliot's eyes widened as if the idea had clicked into place. "So the brooch becomes more than an object—it's a symbol of her father's control. She's not just saying, 'I'm free,' she's saying, 'I'm in charge now.'" Elliot's enthusiasm grew as the concept took hold. "It could be like the crown in *Macbeth*! Macbeth obsesses about it because it represents not just power—but his whole identity. The brooch could have the same significance for Cathryn's father. When she takes it away from him, he's stripped of everything. He's powerless. Like Samson without his hair."

Polly leaned back in her chair, a storm of thoughts swirling in her head as Elliot waxed lyrical about the brooch as a metaphor, his enthusiasm filling the room. Then Tiara's voice cut through the chatter, her idea snapping Polly's attention back to the moment.

"Maybe, after their final confrontation, Cathryn pretends to embrace her father in an act of devotion and surreptitiously unpins the brooch from his coat and fixes it to her dress. The final image would be Polly standing alone onstage, victorious—the pin in spotlight as the room goes dark."

"Brilliant!" Elliot interjected. "But in order for that ending to work, I think we need to explain the significance of the brooch to the audience. We mention it a lot in passing, but it has to have some deeper meaning. Maybe like in *The Necklace*, it's a symbol of status and wealth, but turns out to be fake."

Tiara made a quizzical face and teased, "I like your literary references. And maybe that's what happened to the Townsend family's fortune. The reason they went broke was because their wealth was all an illusion. Or something like that."

Polly's heart skipped a beat. "An illusion." Tiara had tossed out the comment casually, but it struck Polly like a bolt of lightning. Her mind raced, unearthing an old memory of *The Necklace,* the classic story about a woman who borrows an extravagant necklace, loses it, and spends her life repaying its cost—only to discover it was a worthless imitation all along. Could the Townsend empire have been built on something as hollow?

The conversation around her blurred into background noise as Polly's thoughts took flight. Was the Townsend family's wealth an illusion? It was a tantalizing idea—and it would explain so much.

She leaned back in her chair, her fingers tapping absently on the script in her lap. Her mind replayed fragments of her conversations with Arthur Townsend and his obsessive quest for the truth behind his family's downfall. The legend laid the blame squarely on Abigail—her supposed defiance had allegedly disgraced the family name and sealed their fate. But what if the real story was something entirely different?

What if the family's wealth had never existed at all? The idea buzzed in her head, gathering momentum. Maybe Abigail had uncovered the truth, and the brooch—a glittering symbol of the family's wealth and status—was the only tangible piece of their legacy. What if it was all a façade? Abigail could have been made the scapegoat, her rebellion a convenient excuse for the family's collapse, covering up something far more humiliating: the Townsend fortune was nothing more than an elaborate mirage.

Elliot's voice filtered into Polly's awareness, his words about the brooch pulling at something deep in her memory. It felt like trying to remember a dream, the details just out of reach, fuzzy but insistent. Polly frowned, her thoughts churning. Could there be something there—a connection she hadn't yet seen?

The oak leaf brooch.

In an instant, Polly could see it with perfect clarity: a circular brooch, about the size of a half dollar, its golden surface softened by the passage of centuries. While time had dulled its shine, the craftsmanship remained exquisite. At its center, two oak leaves intertwined in a graceful embrace, their tips meeting at the top while their slender stems crossed delicately at the base. The finely etched veins of the leaves were still striking, as if nature itself had been dipped in gold. Polly's fingers twitched in her lap. She could almost feel the brooch in her hand, its texture cool and slightly roughened by age.

Polly tried to refocus on tweaking the play, but she was distracted. She told herself what she visualized was impossible because she'd never seen the brooch in real life. Or had she? Of course, she'd seen the sketch on Abigail's manuscript. And Abigail described it pretty clearly in *Vanity and Virtue*. So maybe it just seemed real to her. Polly closed her eyes, reaching back into her memory, flipping through images like scanning video footage.

Then it hit her like a sudden blow: the memorial!

Polly's thoughts leaped back to Jonathan Fieldstone's memorial evening here at Thistlethorne. She'd been distracted that night while mourning Jonathan and playing hostess. But now her memory sharpened. She remembered spotting a decorative pin on someone's dress. No. Maybe it was on a coat? A jacket lapel! Yes! On Professor Richard Lockhart's lapel!

The realization crashed into Polly like a tsunami, knocking the air from her lungs. Suddenly, the memory surged to the surface, vivid and undeniable: Professor Lockhart at the reception, a wine glass casually held in one hand, making polite conversation with the other guests. She'd only briefly spoken to him; her attention had been focused on Rachel Hawthorne. But now, her mind's eye zoomed in with startling clarity—his old tweed jacket, worn and frayed like an artifact from a bygone era of academia. There had been something pinned to it. Not a patriotic flag pin. Not a university crest or an alumni badge.

It was ... the brooch. The oak leaf brooch, or at least *an* oak leaf brooch.

At the time, Polly had dismissed the Professor's pin as a quaint, almost frumpy accessory—something vintage an aging professor might have picked up at an estate sale. She hadn't thought twice about it. But now, the details screamed at her. If she'd recognized the pin for what it truly was and connected it to Abigail Townsend ... but she hadn't.

Her heart pounded, anxiety building as the pieces began to fall into place. Lockhart, as an ardent admirer of Abigail's work, would almost certainly have recognized her brooch. He might have read about it in Abigail's manuscript—the one he'd examined with Dr. Fieldstone.

Could he have had a replica made? Polly knew all too well how peculiar some fans could be. Admiration often morphed into something far stranger—a twisted sense of ownership over the celebrities they idolized. Her own career had provided plenty of unsettling encounters, but none quite like the man who had tattooed all her TV comedy-sketch characters—Mildred Picklechurch, Bendy Wendy, and the rest—across his body. He had stripped down at a fan convention to proudly display his ink, declaring himself the number one Polly Pepper fan on the planet.

So no, it wouldn't be entirely surprising if Lockhart had commissioned a replica of Abigail's brooch. But the thought didn't sit right with Polly. Something gnawed at her—a subtle, relentless feeling she couldn't shake. Fans like Lockhart, especially academics, didn't care about replicas. Authenticity was everything. Her stomach tightened as the realization struck: Lockhart wouldn't have settled for a copy. If he believed the brooch was the key to understanding Abigail's life—her influence, her power—he might have gone to great lengths to get his hands on the real one.

Elliot's voice jolted her back to the present. "What do you think, Polly? Should the brooch symbolize something deeper—maybe a long-buried family secret? When Cathryn takes the brooch, it's like she's defying her father in real time, dethroning him in front of everyone. That could be powerful."

Polly nodded absently, barely registering his words. Her thoughts were still spinning, trying to land on solid ground. The brooch. Lockhart. Abigail. What did they all mean collectively? She couldn't focus on the script anymore, not when this new puzzle was unraveling in her mind. Her pulse quickened, panic rising.

"Polly?" Elliot's voice broke through the fog again. "You still with us?"

She blinked, forcing a smile. "Sorry. Yes. I'm here. Just thinking about how perfect the ending is now," she managed, though her voice felt distant, disconnected from her racing thoughts.

Elliot beamed, his enthusiasm oblivious to the storm building in Polly's head. "Tiara's idea about the brooch—it's gonna make the ending iconic. I knew this lady was amazing." He took a long appreciative look at her.

Polly glanced between them, watching as Tiara, uncharacteristically flustered, tucked a strand of hair behind her ear, her lips curling into a shy smile. The room hummed with their energy, but Polly felt none of it. The weight of a new theory was suffocating, and the pressure to figure out the connection between Lockhart and the brooch grew more unbearable by the second. She needed to find out more. Now!

"I'll be back," Polly muttered, standing and excusing herself from the room. Neither Elliot nor Tiara seemed to notice her abrupt departure—they were too wrapped up in their creative banter, brainstorming the perfect dramatic ending to the story.

But Polly's own story was unfolding rapidly, and she couldn't ignore it. As she stepped into the hallway, her mind raced with questions that demanded answers, the weight of the brooch now heavy on her thoughts.

24

That evening, for the first time ever in the entire recorded history of civilization—or at least in the meticulously curated world of Polly Pepper—she was absent from the six p.m. Lush Hour ritual.

Yes, dear readers, you may alert the media.

It was practically a breach of natural law: Like a British pub without ale or an English summer without rain. Even Mr. Boots seemed baffled by the anomaly, prowling the halls of Thistlethorne in search of the leader of the pack. When he finally found her, Polly was seated at her makeup vanity, dividing her attention between memorizing lines from the newly revised script and tapping out the same text to Rachel every fifteen minutes: "Pls call re Prof L. Urgent." Two hours had passed, and Polly was starting to wonder if she was being ghosted.

"Sorry, sweetums," she cooed when Mr. Boots meowed for attention. She gave him a quick pat on the head before picking up the script again, her focus already drifting back to her preoccupation.

Just as she was about to send yet another agitated SOS, her phone rang. Rachel's name was finally on the screen, and Polly reacted so quickly she nearly knocked over a bottle of Shalimar. "About time!" she said, unable to keep the exasperation out of her voice.

Rachel sounded breathless and flustered. "Really? Eight messages? Some of us have to work for a living. I'm still in the office." She was as irritated as Polly. "Lockhart kept me late. I couldn't risk calling while he was here. He only just left."

Polly didn't have the time or patience for fun facts. "I want you to think back to Jonathan's memorial here. Do you remember the pin Professor Lockhart wore on his lapel that night?"

"*That* night?" Rachel scoffed, dismissing the singularity of one specific evening. "He wears that thing *all* the time. Never lets it out of his sight. It's like a good-luck charm. Like Taylor Swift's 13 ring. Am I too old to be a Swifty?"

Polly wasn't amused. "Do you know where he got it? The brooch? Is it, like, a family heirloom or something?"

"His girlfriend gave it to him."

Polly raised an eyebrow, and she nearly knocked over the Shalimar again. "His *girlfriend*?" she repeated, her voice dripping with disbelief. "I thought he was...'"

Rachel chuckled, clearly enjoying Polly's reaction. "He is. 'Girlfriend' is what I call Abigail Townsend because he has an obsessive crush on her."

Polly blinked, her brain catching up with Rachel's joke. "As in the dead-for-more-than-two-hundred-years Abigail Townsend? *She* gave it to him?"

"He seems to think so. He's like my crazy aunt who collects everything royal family: the commemorative cups, plates, and tea towels. With Lockhart, it's Abigail Townsend. His hobby—if you can call it that—is tracking down anything associated with her: letters, diaries ... Heck, he has a tooth he claims belonged to her. *A tooth!* Framed, no less, in his office. I've discussed this with my psychologist sister." She says there's a term for his behavior. She calls him a 'necrophiliac fan,' someone with an intensely emotional or mental investment in the life—and death—of a celebrity. Lockhart says Abigail left him clues in her diaries and letters about where to find the brooch. He thinks she's communicating with him through her writings."

The news should have been at least slightly disturbing to Polly. But it wasn't. She was merely intrigued. "It can't be the same brooch mentioned in her manuscript, can it?"

"He says it is. Said he spent all his life searching for it. Used his access to special collections at major libraries to dig through all sorts of archives searching for clues about where to find it."

Polly's thoughts were racing. If the brooch did belong to Abigail, it was more than a collector's item. It would be a genuine piece of history. Like Jane Austen's topaz cross necklace. "Was it in a private collection?" she asked. "How did he afford to buy it on a professor's salary?"

Rachel hesitated, and Polly could practically hear the gears turning in her head, debating whether to reveal what she knew. But the pause was fleeting. "You know, we academics are supposed to stick together, protect each other's reputations, keep each other's secrets, all that collegial nonsense ..." She sighed again as if sweeping away the idea of professional loyalty. "But honestly, I'm so over him. And this job. I understand why he's had a revolving door of assistants. He's been an absolute pill ever since I started working here. Belittling me. Barking orders like I'm some clueless grad student who doesn't know what end of a hypothesis to start with. It's like he gets some sick pleasure from reminding me I'll never be as good as Jonathan Fieldstone."

Polly realized Rachel didn't care about keeping anyone's

secrets. She had no qualms about throwing a colleague under the bus if it suited her and wasn't about to pretend otherwise. The unspoken rule of protecting a colleague's professional dignity was clearly one Rachel felt was optional, especially when it came to someone she resented. It wasn't any wonder she'd so easily up and left her job with Jonathan Fieldstone. Polly's eyes narrowed as she leaned forward on her vanity, ignoring Mr. Boots grazing her ankle. "Tell Aunt Polly everything. What else do you know about the brooch and how Lockhart came to own it?"

Rachel let out a bitter chuckle. "Right. So Lockhart told me he'd read a letter from Abigail Townsend's cousin mentioning an heirloom brooch Abigail's father believed gave him some special power over others. Professor Lockhart was obsessed with that legend. He tracked down a family journal that referenced the brooch disappearing before the Townsend family went broke."

Polly's pulse quickened, her mind racing to connect the dots. She leaned forward, gripping her phone tightly, willing Rachel to continue. "Is it even ethical for someone like Lockhart to use academic privileges like that? I mean, to get access to special collections for something that's more a personal quest than scholarly research?"

"It's a gray area. Technically, you're supposed to have legitimate academic reasons for accessing restricted materials. But Lockhart ... well, he knows how to play the system. He charmed antiquarians, librarians, historians, and anyone who might give him a lead. He said he was the only person alive who ever believed the brooch existed and was therefore the only one looking for it."

Polly felt a chill crawl down her spine. *The only person alive ...?*

Rachel continued, her tone more relaxed now, relieved to finally tell someone what had been on her mind. "Yeah. Lockhart wasn't exactly playing by the rules, but he wasn't breaking them either—not technically. He used Jonathan's position at the British Library to get access to restricted collections. I think that's how they met. Lockhart had to provide justification for viewing the Townsend collection, and he knew how to talk his way in. Jonathan told me he knew Lockhart's research wasn't exactly scholarly, but he went along with it—out of professional courtesy."

"Professional courtesy?" Polly muttered. She could practically see Lockhart weaving his way into Jonathan's life, using his charm to get what he wanted.

There was a long, unsettling silence on the line. Polly could almost hear Rachel's hesitation, feel the tension radiating through the phone like she was weighing every word before speaking.

When Rachel finally spoke again, her tone had shifted—cautious, almost conspiratorial. "But then ... things got weird. Jonathan started noticing how obsessed the professor was with anything connected to Abigail Townsend. I mean, it wasn't professional admiration—it was like Lockhart was fixated on her. Consumed. Like my father is about that old-time singer Karen Carpenter. Lockhart would bring up Abigail at every chance, like her ghost was haunting his thoughts. That's like my father, too. And then, when he caught wind of the manuscript you'd found ..." Rachel paused, her voice dropping lower, the tension growing. "Word traveled fast. The world of historical manuscripts is a small tightly knit universe."

Polly felt a cold prick of unease crawl up her spine, sensing what was coming even before Rachel said it:

"Jonathan told me when Lockhart learned Jonathan would

be authenticating the manuscript, it was like ... like Lockhart became manic—desperate. I was in the office when he called and begged Jonathan to let him assist with the project. And Jonathan—well, you know how he was. Always the nice guy. Eventually, he caved and let Lockhart in." Rachel's voice cracked, the bitterness palpable now. "But ... I know he regretted it. I think he realized too late he'd let someone—too close."

Polly frowned, her thoughts swirling. "That's not how Lockhart made it sound when we talked at the memorial. He acted like it was the other way around. Like he was responsible for authenticating the manuscript." Her voice sharpened with suspicion.

"Exactly. That's Lockhart's game. He always makes himself sound more important, like the mastermind behind every-thing. It's exhausting, really. Jonathan said it was an open secret Lockhart had taken undue credit for authenticating the Sherborne manuscript that made him known way back in the day."

Polly felt stirrings of doubt coil in her stomach. "But Jonathan said Lockhart's knowledge of Abigail Townsend was invaluable—like he knew things no one else would."

Rachel's laugh was sharp and bitter. "That's what Lockhart wanted him to think. Sure, he's obsessed with Abigail Townsend, but half of what he says is embellished, cobbled together from gossip and speculation. Jonathan only let him on the project because Lockhart badgered him. It wasn't about helping Jonathan—it was about making himself look like the expert, like the irreplaceable key to solving the mystery. He always needs to be in the spotlight, even if it means muscling his way in."

The pieces shifted uncomfortably in Polly's thoughts, and the image of Professor Lockhart she'd had started to fall apart. Was this whole thing more about Lockhart's ego and finding the brooch than authenticating the manuscript? That now seemed obvious.

But it was what Rachel revealed next that made Polly sit up straighter, her pulse quickening. "So Professor Lockhart came down to Abbots Clover for a few days. At first, he was thrilled to be there and to see the manuscript—like a kid in a candy store, practically hyperventilating with excitement. He couldn't believe his luck, getting so close to something his girlfriend had written. Paper she'd touched two hundred years ago. He kept saying he was thrilled to be one of the first in centuries to see it. He was ... consumed."

Polly's brow furrowed. "And then?" she prompted, sensing there was more—the other shoe about to drop.

Rachel's voice lowered as if she was now realizing the significance. "Something shifted. I didn't register it until right now. He didn't exactly lose interest in the manuscript, but something else took over. I think I remember the exact moment. It was right after he came across the letter, the one tucked between the pages of the manuscript."

"The one signed with someone's initials. RL, wasn't it?" Polly said. "Why would that make him lose interest in the manuscript —if that's what it did? I mean, it was just ... a love letter. Or something like that. I remember it was signed 'Yours in devotion.' A little cryptic but nothing earth-shattering, right?"

Rachel hesitated, the pause hanging in the air. "Polly, he studied that letter like it was the key to all the mysteries of life. He seemed totally mesmerized by it. I didn't think much about it at the time. I figured he was doing his job, being immersed in his work and being thorough, you know? But now ..." Her voice trailed off as if she were seeing something that had been hidden in plain sight. "He left the project the next day. Without even saying goodbye.

"Even his assistant, Monte, didn't know he'd left. Then again,

Professor Lockhart treated him like rubbish, so Monte was probably relieved to have a day away from his boss—especially after receiving the email saying his services were no longer required. Oh, and now that I think about it, when Lockhart was here in Abbots Clover, I don't recall ever seeing him wear the brooch as he does now. I don't know if it means anything, but it crossed my mind."

"Maybe he doesn't travel with the brooch because it's valuable—although, he did wear it to the memorial. Maybe he left the project because he'd had enough and thought he couldn't contribute anything more."

Rachel let out a slow breath. "One minute, he couldn't get enough of the manuscript, and the next, he's packing up and leaving? I think that's weird."

Polly's fingers tightened around her phone, her thoughts darting back to the first day, to the exact moment she'd glanced at the letter that had been pressed into the manuscript. What had Lockhart seen in the missive that changed everything for him? The note had seemed innocent enough to Polly—a vague expression of loyalty and devotion. But there was also the riddle: *The oak that stands alone ...* Did that mean something to Lockhart? "Rachel, what exactly did Lockhart do with the letter?" Polly asked, her voice dropping, eyes narrowing. She could feel the adrenaline starting to pulse in her veins.

Rachel hesitated again, her tone wavering with uncertainty. "He didn't try to take it, if that's what you mean. And Jonathan wouldn't allow anyone to photograph the pages. He was worried if photos ended up on someone's phone or camera, they could be leaked—or worse, if the device was stolen or lost. So Professor Lockhart transcribed the letter into his laptop. Word for word. Character by character. At the time, I thought he was being meticulous, but now ... something about it feels off."

Polly's stomach twisted. The letter had seemed like a

curiosity when she first read it, a small side note in the grand mystery of the manuscript. But now it felt like it was holding something far more important.

Polly's mind raced. It seemed Lockhart wasn't just another academic trying to get his name on a project that would prove valuable to the literary world. He was a fan consumed by Abigail Townsend's life and mystique. His obsession with the brooch, the letters, and the manuscript all fit together, making Polly uncomfortable because she knew the lengths to which fans sometimes go for their celebrity gods. "And Jonathan didn't see the danger in letting Lockhart have access to Abigail's work?" Polly pressed, feeling a mix of frustration and dread.

"I think eventually he did." Rachel sighed. "He told me Lockhart was acting strange—as if he knew something no one else did. But then he packed up and left. Happily, we never saw him again. Well, until I went to work for him. I'm an idiot."

Polly's blood ran cold. The realization crashed over her. Lockhart had manipulated Jonathan—and others—far more cunningly than she had imagined. Rachel had said how charming he could be when he wanted something and how easily he could manipulate people's good intentions to his advantage. And now, Polly recalled the disturbing detail Rachel had shared in passing—how Lockhart had even manipulated her, making her believe her career would flourish if she left Jonathan Fieldstone and worked for him.

Polly's pulse quickened, and the words spilled out before she could stop them. "Rachel ... did Lockhart ever have access to the safe in the library?"

There was a pause, long and suffocating. Then Rachel exhaled shakily, the weight of her confession sinking in. "Jonathan ... Rose gave him the combination, which he wrote down on a slip of paper and tucked into his notebook. I never looked at it, but I was responsible for keeping the notebook safe.

I remember I left Lockhart and his assistant, Monte, alone in the supply room one afternoon—only for a few minutes, when I went to the bathroom. Jonathan was out running an errand, and the notebook was right there on the table with the manuscript. I didn't think ... I never imagined ... The professor was holding it when I got back."

Polly's mind raced, pieces snapping together in a way that made her stomach ache. "You're saying Lockhart might have seen the combination? That he could've had access to the safe?" Her voice was rising now, the sense of impending disaster growing with each word.

Rachel's breath hitched. "I don't know for sure, Polly. I didn't even think about it at the time. But now ... I can't be sure. After the manuscript went missing ... and Jonathan was killed ... I tried to convince myself it wasn't possible. But yeah ... it is possible. I feel terrible. I never imagined ... I ..." Her voice faltered, the words catching in her throat. She was unraveling under the weight of her own guilt.

Polly clenched her jaw, struggling to keep her emotions in check. "Rachel, listen to me. It's not your fault. Professor Lockhart knew exactly what he was doing. From the start, he's been playing a game, manipulating everyone around him. He used your trust against you, like he did with Jonathan." She could feel the pulse of dread building, the dark web of Lockhart's lies stretching wider than she'd ever anticipated. "We don't have time for self-blame. We need to figure out a lot of stuff —and figure it out fast."

Rachel's silence was heavy, filled with remorse, but Polly could hear the shift in her breath, a quiet resolve settling in. "You're right," Rachel whispered, though her voice still trembled. "How can I help? I'll do whatever I can."

Polly nodded, her mind already racing with questions. Why did Lockhart leave the project so soon after coming aboard? Was there something about the letter signed by RL that caused him to abandon the authentication process before it was completed? Did he understand the riddle? If Lockhart had access to the safe, he was now a prime suspect in the theft of the manuscript—and the murder of Jonathan Fieldstone.

One thing was clear—Lockhart was an overzealous fan. That made him dangerous.

25

P olly couldn't miss Lush Hour altogether—that would be sacrilegious. The universe might retaliate with some apocalyptic tempest. Even with thousands of questions about Professor Lockhart swirling in her head, she'd only postponed the evening ritual, not abandoned it completely. And it was relocated to the cozy warmth of the kitchen, where Tim, Tiara, and Mr. Boots waited, their faces expectant. A hastily thrown-together meal of bubble and squeak sat steaming in the center of the table, filling the air with the comforting scent of fried potatoes and cabbage.

Polly swept into the kitchen with the air of someone late to a gala in their honor. "Apologies, sweetums," she trilled, lifting the flute of champagne Tiara had set at her place. "You know how I feel about punctuality, but I have a divine excuse." Her frazzled energy matched the sly grin she flashed as she raised her glass in a silent toast. "I've been on *el phono* with Rachel Hawthorne. She spilled a whole pot of tea. Just dumped it right out. Let's say, if this were *Clue*, I'd be holding the winning solution."

Tiara gave her a sideways glance. "Professor Plum in the library with the wrench?"

"Almost," Polly said, knocking back her drink and setting the glass down for a top-up. "Turns out our esteemed linguistics expert has been on a lifelong treasure hunt for anything remotely connected to Abigail Townsend—letters, diaries, *teeth*. Don't ask." She shuddered, then leaned in conspiratorially. "Abigail's gold brooch, the one she wrote about in her book, was his crown jewel. His Golden Fleece. His rainbow's end. He used his academic contacts—and Jonathan Fieldstone—to track it down. Lockhart begged to join the manuscript authentication team because he hoped it might hold one last clue to finding the brooch."

Tim's fork hovered in midair. "He should've gone after the Heart of the Ocean necklace instead. Probably more valuable."

Polly gave him an indulgent smile. "You do know that isn't real, right? Entirely made up for the movie."

"Then what did Kate Winslet throw overboard in *Titanic*?"

Polly sighed but pressed on. "Anyway, when Lockhart found out about *Vanity and Virtue*, he went absolutely cuckoo with envy. He'd spent years researching Abigail, and he knew the manuscript—if it existed—might hold the key to finding the brooch."

Tim tapped his fingers on the table, a slow grin spreading across his face. "So that's why Lockhart was desperate to get involved in the authentication process."

"Exactly," Polly said, her voice adamant. "He needed to be part of the team; otherwise, he might never find the brooch. The manuscript was surely the very last item belonging to Abigail that would ever be discovered. That's why he begged Jonathan to let him help authenticate the manuscript."

Tiara's eyes widened. "So, getting to read the manuscript wasn't even his primary goal?"

Polly couldn't deny it any longer—too much evidence pointed directly to Professor Lockhart. His motive was glaring: a lifelong obsession with collecting anything linked to Abigail Townsend. He'd had access to everything he needed, all while hiding behind the respectable façade of academia. The man clearly knew how to operate in the shadows.

"He's obsessed," Polly said. "He had motive and opportunity. And now, I'd wager he has blood on his hands." She paused, wondering how, after two hundred years, he had discovered where to find the brooch. Rachel had described Lockhart's keen interest in the letter signed by RL. That he'd been mesmerized by it. Polly realized the letter must have contained a clue leading to the brooch. But what was it?

She sat still for a long moment, her thoughts darting back to the riddle—the one that had gnawed at her since the beginning. *The oak that stands alone guards its resting place.* The words echoed in her brain, nagging. Relentless. She couldn't shake the feeling that the answer was right in front of her, just out of reach.

Polly's pulse quickened. There had to be something she was missing. "Back to that cryptic letter signed by RL," she said. "I'm thinking out loud ... but what if the 'oak' in the riddle isn't a literal tree. You know writers are always thinking up clever metaphors." Her mind whirred, desperate to latch on to the thread of a connection. It was as though the truth was teasing her, dancing beyond the edge of her understanding.

Tiara nodded in understanding, her brow furrowed in thought. She could feel the room crackling with tension. "Didn't I previously suggest that 'oak' might be symbolic?" she said, her voice tentative, as though afraid to shatter the delicate thread of thought Polly was clinging to. "It could mean something else that's as strong as an oak ... something as enduring."

"Like those ancient stone boundary walls everywhere around here," Tim suggested. "Or the Fox & Hare pub. Or the water mill over by the River Elderwynd. They're a good four hundred years old."

Polly froze, her breath catching in her throat. The room seemed to close in around her, and her heart began pounding so hard she thought everyone could hear it.

Something strong. Something enduring. The words grew louder in Polly's head. And then, like a flash of lightning on a dark night, it hit her. Polly's breath left her in a rush. The church! St. Clematis! The oak that stands alone. The church had been standing there for centuries. Strong. Enduring. The realization slammed into her, and for a moment, she felt the air had been sucked from the room. When it came, her voice was barely a whisper, almost afraid to give life to the idea she'd conceived. "St. Clematis," she said, the words trembling on her tongue.

The others stared at her, wide-eyed, their understanding mirroring her own. The revelation hung like a thick, oppressive fog wrapping itself around them. And then, like another jolt, something else hit her. "Rose Harding said Abigail Townsend was a woman of deep religious convictions ... The church was a sanctuary for her. It was a sacred place where she could pray her secrets and problems to God. St. Clematis wasn't just a symbol of strength and piety; it was the perfect hiding place and would have been untouchable in Abigail's time. In those days no one would dare violate or rob a church. The sanctity of the space would have made it one of the safest places to hide something precious."

Polly continued, "I spoke to an author in the village who's written a history of Abbots Clover. She told me about a scandal a couple of hundred years ago involving St. Clematis and a Lord Tavistock. There were whispers he'd hidden some of his wealth inside the church. Gold, jewels. What if the 'oak' is St. Clematis, standing alone, guarding Abigail's brooch?" She looked at the others, eyes wide with realization. "And Lockhart figured it out."

Tiara's eyes widened, her smirk broadening. "I didn't think you were sharp, missy," she teased. "Don't make me change my opinion now."

Polly paused, her brow furrowing as a thought formed. "Wait a minute ... Terrence mentioned he's writing an article about the restoration of St. Clematis and the artifacts they found." A sly smile crept onto her face. She looked at the clock on the wall. "Is it too late to call him? Never mind. He'll be happy to hear from me."

And then, from under the table, a soft, deliberate meow was heard. Mr. Boots, his head slightly tilted, seemed to understand the importance of what had been brought to light. Or he was demanding scraps of bubble and squeak. It was hard to tell.

26

Terrence was indeed happy to hear from Polly. He always was. "If you're looking for something strong and enduring, look no further than me." He chuckled, but Polly didn't respond with her usual lascivious friskiness. The silence on her end stretched, making the weight of her urgency clear. "Right, um, St. Clematis—of course," he continued. "You definitely don't have to look any further than that old church to find something strong and enduring. It's been there longer than anything else in the village. Centuries of wars, and all sorts of storms. St. Clematis isn't large or imposing, but it's solid and dependable—like a quiet guardian watching over the village. It'll be standing long after we're all gone."

Polly gripped the phone tighter as the pressure in her chest grew with every passing second. "Terrence, I need to know, was there anything especially curious you came across while writing the article? Did the restoration people find anything interesting? Hidden rooms, old documents ... anything that might have been buried or overlooked for a couple of hundred years?" Her words spilled out hurriedly, a torrent of questions fueled by wild theories racing through her mind.

"Well," he began cautiously, his tone thoughtful, "when the workers were excavating beneath the old crypt, they did uncover a few things. Mostly old brasses and coins, you know, the typical finds in an old place like St. Clematis. And there was a silver chalice—beautifully engraved, possibly medieval—but that's about it."

Polly's heart sank. "Terrence, I'm looking for something that could have been deliberately concealed. Or maybe a secret hiding place."

Terrence hesitated, and Polly's pulse raced, her imagination conjuring up all the possibilities of what might be waiting beneath the ancient stones of St. Clematis. Secrets buried for centuries.

"Well," Terrence began slowly, "they did find what was probably an old storeroom. It looked like it had been walled up a long time ago. But all they uncovered in there were a couple of pieces of old furniture. That sort of thing."

Polly's heart sank a little. She remained quiet, waiting, willing him to continue.

"There was this pretty amazing old altar, too," Terrence said. "You could tell it'd been there for centuries. The woodwork was incredible—beautiful intricate carvings. I think even the restoration team and the vicar were impressed."

Polly's pulse quickened. An old altar. She could practically picture it now—a grand piece standing in the heart of St. Clematis. Her voice betrayed the excitement rising inside her. "Terrence, that sounds like exactly the place someone could hide something—something valuable. Anything in the carvings that could be more than decoration?"

There was a pause on the line as Terrence considered it. "The carvings were so intricate. Lots of religious symbols. Flowers and vines. That sort of craftsmanship doesn't exist anymore."

Polly's imagination raced. If Abigail Townsend, or anyone, had needed to hide something important, the church altar would have been the ideal place. A sacred space no one would dare disturb ... and hiding in plain sight.

Polly's mind whirred with possibilities. "Terrence, I have to see it," she said, her voice laced with urgency.

Terrence paused. "Polly, the restoration is finished, and the chambers are restricted. We'd need Vicar Aylsworth's permission to go down there. Don't forget, he doesn't even like you. Maybe you shouldn't have suggested he killed your last housekeeper."

"Hasn't he gotten over that silliness?" Polly rolled her eyes. "He needs to put on his big boy cassock—or whatever saintly robes vicars wear when they mean business—and grant me access to that altar!"

Terrence's voice hesitated. "I get it, Polly, believe me. But even with my connections, sneaking you in there wouldn't be easy."

Polly sighed, feeling the weight of disappointment settle in.

Then Terrence's voice brightened with a sudden idea. "Wait. My article. It's almost ready for publication, but I could tell the vicar I need to confirm a few last-minute details before it goes to print. He knows how important this piece is for the village's history. He's quoted quite a bit, and his ego demands feeding. If I suggest I need to see the crypt one more time to check a few facts, he'll probably agree. And if I happen to bring along a 'guest' ..."

Polly's heart leaped. "You think that'll work?"

"I'll call him first thing in the morning. He's been cooperative so far, and I doubt he'll refuse with the article so close to publication. I'll make it sound urgent—which it is. And maybe he won't want to be in the same room as you, so he'll leave us to ourselves."

Polly could barely contain her excitement. "Terrence, you're brilliant. I love you!" The words slipped out, unfiltered and raw, propelled by an adrenaline rush. It took a heartbeat to realize what she'd said—the L-word—spoken without a second's thought. She froze, her mind racing. Neither of them had been brave enough to speak honestly about their feelings for each other. There had always been too much fear—of rejection, of stepping into something unknown. But there it was, out in the open, hanging between them.

And yet, amid her panic, there was a strange sense of relief. A part of her knew it was about time. This thing between them had been simmering for so long, and it wouldn't stay hidden forever.

The silence stretched, Terrence's breathing barely audible on the other end of the line. Polly held her breath, waiting for a response, her heart pounding.

Finally, Terrence let out a soft chuckle, the sound warm and familiar. "Polly ..." He paused, his tone shifting to something softer, more intimate. "... I do too."

Polly exhaled, the tension in her chest easing. She could almost picture his expression—a mix of humor and something deeper, more meaningful. Before she could say anything else, he added lightly, "Just promise me you won't try sneaking into the vestry or making off with the church silver. I'd rather not be writing your name in the *Abbots Clover Overview's* Police Blotter."

Tomorrow finally arrived, and Polly followed Terrence down narrow stone steps, into St. Clematis's subterranean chamber, each footfall echoing softly in the cool, musty air. The dim beam of Terrence's phone flashlight illuminated the rough-hewn walls, their surfaces worn smooth by centuries of dampness and time. The air was heavy with the scent of mildew and the faint, lingering hint of incense—a smell that felt ancient, steeped in centuries of whispered prayers and solemn rituals.

At the bottom of the steps, the passage opened into a low, vaulted chamber, the ceiling curving gently above them. Polly's breath caught in her throat as she took it in. The room was modest in size, the stone walls darkened with age and lined with small alcoves. Rusted iron sconces were set into the walls, empty now but once used to hold candles that must have bathed the space in a reverent glow.

And then, at the far end of the chamber stood the altar, a relic from another century.

Polly's eyes widened as she approached it, the soft light catching the delicate details of the ancient wood. The altar was a masterpiece of craftsmanship, carved from rich, dark oak that seemed to absorb the light. The carvings were intricate and finely detailed—interwoven vines and flowers framing scenes of saints and angels, their faces serene and ethereal, almost lifelike. Tiny birds and animals were hidden among the foliage. The center of the altar was dominated by an ornate panel depicting *The Last Supper* with astonishing realism. Each of the figures were carved with such precision their expressions seemed to shift with the changing light.

Polly instinctively reached out, her fingers brushing the edge of the wood. Its surface, untouched for centuries, seemed to glow with an otherworldly smoothness, as though preserving the reverence of those who last knelt before it. "This is incredible," she whispered, more to herself than to Terrence. Her eyes darted over the intricate carvings, searching for something—any sign of a hidden compartment or clue. "How old is it?"

"Late medieval, they think," Terrence replied quietly, his voice echoing softly in the still air. "It's been down here for centuries, likely to protect it from when Henry the Eighth and

Cromwell ran around destroying monasteries and plundering churches. It's amazing what one finds during a restoration project."

Polly ran her fingers lightly over the wood, tracing the lines of a carved vine. The craftsmanship was astounding, but her mind was racing with thoughts of what—if anything—might be hidden within it.

Terrence raised an eyebrow, watching her with amusement and curiosity. "Just promise me you won't pull on anything that looks like it's been holding the thing together for five hundred years," he said with a grin. "I'd rather not be the one explaining to the vicar why the altar collapsed."

Polly admired the intricate craftsmanship, but her mind was thinking of the priest hole concealed beside the library fireplace at Thistlethorne Lodge. She recalled how the rose carving, cleverly disguised as a decorative detail, had served as the latch to reveal the hidden space.

Biting her lip, Polly scanned the altar with intent. If something were hidden here, there would have to be a trigger—subtle and almost invisible, like the rosette. "There has to be something," she murmured, her fingers trailing over the carvings. She tapped lightly in places, listening for a hollow sound, her focus unwavering as she methodically tested the surface.

But after twenty minutes, the altar remained stubbornly silent. Polly was feeling the weight of disappointment, her determination giving way to frustration. Maybe there was nothing here after all. Maybe this wasn't where Abigail Townsend's lover had hidden her brooch. It now seemed likely that no one, not even Professor Lockhart, had ever discovered anything hidden here. She took a deep breath, preparing herself to admit defeat.

And then her fingers brushed against something—a small, raised knot in the wood, so discreetly carved into a cluster of acorns she almost missed it. Her breath caught. "Acorns!" *Acorns are oak trees in the making!*

Polly's pulse quickened. She pressed lightly, testing its give. Nothing happened. With more pressure, she tried again and felt the knot shift slightly beneath her fingers. Her heart leaped. This was it—her rosette! But it wasn't a rose this time. It was an acorn, almost hidden within the swirling patterns of oak leaves and vines. With one last push, there was a faint creak, followed by a soft groan of ancient wood reluctantly yielding. A hidden drawer popped open a fraction, as if the altar itself were exhaling a long-held secret. Polly's breath hitched, excitement flooding her senses. Had she found it?

"Terrence," she whispered, her eyes fixed on the hidden drawer, "I've got something!" Polly carefully pulled it open and peered inside. At first, it seemed empty. But then, a faint glint caught the flashlight's beam from Terrence's phone. Reaching in, her heart thudded with anticipation. In the corner was a ring. Polly's fingers carefully retrieved it. The cool metal felt heavy and significant. She turned to Terrence, her eyes wide with urgency. "Shine the light over here," she whispered.

Terrence raised his phone, illuminating the ring in a soft beam. The light revealed an engraved crest on its face, and Polly leaned closer to inspect the details. The design was ornate—a shield adorned with three crowns and an open book. Beneath the shield was an inscription. "Looks like a motto," Polly murmured, her brow furrowing as she tried to decipher the details. "What does it mean?"

Terrence looked closer, scrutinizing the ring with curiosity. He tilted his head, studying the design before his eyes widened slightly. "I know this seal," he said, his voice tinged with reverence. "It's Oxford University's emblem. An open book symbolizing the pursuit of knowledge. Three crowns. The inscription

..." He leaned in, squinting slightly. *"Dominus Illuminatio Mea'*—'The Lord is my light.' That's Oxford's motto."

A chill ran down Polly's spine. This ring wasn't a random trinket; it was a symbol of Professor Lockhart's identity as a scholar. She stared at the emblem, her mind racing. How did it get here? What was it doing in this secret drawer? "It's an offering," she said suddenly, the realization hitting her like a bolt of lightning. Her voice grew firmer as the pieces fell into place. "An expression of his devotion to Abigail Townsend. He left his ring behind in exchange for her brooch. I feel sure of it."

Terrence tilted his head, his expression skeptical but intrigued. "Why would he do that?"

Polly nodded, a scene playing in her mind. She could almost see Lockhart kneeling before the altar, his university ring placed carefully inside the hidden drawer, a solemn offering in exchange for Abigail's brooch. The brooch, cradled in his trembling hands, seemed to radiate the reverence—and madness—that burned in his eyes. To him, this was a ritual, a sacred trade. An act of devotion to the long-dead writer who had consumed his thoughts.

But how had Lockhart gained access to this concealed chamber in the church? Polly wondered. Then she recalled his reputation for worming his way into exclusive spaces, be it academic archives or locked library vaults. The man had an uncanny ability to charm, persuade, and, when necessary, deceive. She imagined Lockhart arriving at St. Clematis, armed with his scholarly credentials and a carefully curated air of academic authority. He would've spun a convincing tale, something about needing to study the altar's carvings as part of his ongoing research into ecclesiastical art of the medieval period, or something like that. Polly could almost hear him now, his voice dripping with gravitas as he buttered up the vicar. It was exactly the thing Lockhart excelled at.

Polly's lips pressed into a thin line. "That's how he did it," she murmured. Terrence looked up, startled, but she didn't elaborate. Instead, she turned the ring over in her hand, studying its engraved crest.

Pulling her phone from her jacket pocket, Polly quickly snapped photos of the ring, the drawer, and the altar. Then, carefully, she set the ring back in its nest and pushed the box into its hiding niche. "This is all the evidence we need," she said reverently.

27

The weather gods upheld their annual pact with the Abbots Clover Literary Festival, blessing the village with perfect skies. Soft sunshine streamed across the green, dappling ancient trees and lilac bushes with warmth. The air was rich with the mingled scents of blooming wisteria and freshly turned fields. A trio of musicians played lively tunes near the war memorial, their familiar melodies carried on the breeze. Vendors smiled from their stalls, their tables heaped with books, or hand-knitted scarves, artisan cheeses, and jars of homemade jams. Children darted through the crowd, playing tag.

Rachel Hawthorne wandered through the crowd, too, meandering absently between tables of paperbacks and hardcovers. She had come to the festival reluctantly, dragged here at Professor Lockhart's insistence. Her thoughts were elsewhere when a familiar figure caught her eye—a man standing near the ancient stocks and pillory—relics from a time when public shaming was a common form of punishment in England. It was Monte Addington, Professor Lockhart's former assistant.

Rachel paused mid-step, her breath catching in surprise. Monte was slender, wearing an unremarkable shirt and dark trousers that made him blend in with everyone else. *Nice of him to support the festival,* she thought. Weaving through the clusters of festival-goers, she edged closer to him. "Monte?" she called with a smile in her voice.

He turned slowly, a faint smile curved his lips, but his eyes remained distant. "Rachel," he said lightly, his head bobbing, "come to cheer on Polly Pepper as the reincarnated Abigail Townsend?"

Rachel forced a laugh. "Something like that. Lockhart insisted. By the way, he's here somewhere, lurking about, so be wary."

"Like I'm supposed to be afraid of him? Probably the other way around. He can't do anything more to hurt me."

Rachel ignored the rebuke and tried to make small talk. "Polly's show should be interesting. I've gotten to know her a bit. She's fascinating. But I didn't expect you to be here."

Monte tilted his head slightly. "The unemployed have all the time in the world for fun and games—and festivals. It's one of the silver linings of getting sacked."

Rachel flushed. "Monte, I-I'm sorry. I never meant to take your job. Lockhart just—"

Monte raised a hand, cutting her off. "No worries. I should have seen it coming. He's predictable. Only cares about one thing: Abigail Townsend. Losing my job gave me something I didn't have before. Perspective."

"That's a good way to look at it." Rachel nodded, glad Monty had developed some deep philosophical wisdom as a result of losing his job. "Frankly, you're better off not working for him. He's impossible—demands loyalty but gives none in return."

Monte's smile faded momentarily as he caught sight of Polly Pepper in the distance, wending her way through the crowd toward the library. "True enough," he said, returning his attention to Rachel. "Being cast aside changes you. Makes you stronger, I think. Certainly gives you ideas. Ideas you didn't realize you were capable of entertaining."

"Ideas?" Rachel sensed something simmering beneath the surface of Monte's words. "Like career path ideas?"

He chuckled, a strange look passing over his face. "Like 'balancing the scales' ideas. Like 'making someone pay for their crimes against humanity' ideas."

Rachel felt a shiver run down her spine but tried to keep her expression neutral. "'Balancing the scales'?"

Monte's smile widened slightly, his eyes almost twinkled. "You figure out what would destroy someone more than they destroyed you. Something they'd never see coming. You take away what they cherish most. Maybe something they've spent their entire life chasing, and you force them to watch as everything they've worked for disappears right in front of their eyes."

Rachel frowned, her unease deepening. There was something disturbing about Monte's tone, as though this wasn't a hypothetical scenario. Her mind whirred, connecting fragments of his words. *Something they spent their entire life chasing* ... Rachel forced a smile. "I suppose anyone who feels betrayed has similar thoughts," she said, trying to keep her tone light.

Monte's smile faded, replaced by a contemplative look. "Sure. Some people. But not everyone has the opportunity to even the score." His voice dropped lower, his gaze sharpening as he spoke. "It's funny, really. Sometimes exactly what you need falls right into your lap. Almost like fate gives you the chance to set things right."

Rachel's pulse quickened. Was it her imagination, or was Monte maybe talking about squaring it up with Professor Lockhart? Did he come to the festival to confront Lockhart? What else could it be? She forced herself to nod, hoping he would mistake her silence for understanding.

Monte's tone shifted, and his smile took on an edge. He

seemed to be enjoying talking, as if he were somehow unburdening himself. "You know," he continued, leaning closer, "when you work side by side with someone, day in and day out, you pick up on their patterns and weaknesses. You learn to see their Achilles' Heel."

"Achilles' Heel?" Rachel repeated. She wanted more information but didn't want to sound too inquisitive. She couldn't shake an ominous feeling.

Monte's eyes seemed to darken. He leaned in slightly, lowering his voice to a murmur. "It's funny. When you're dismissed so insensitively, you realize we're all replaceable. Disposable even." He paused, eyes narrowing as if recalling every slight ever made against him. "And that treatment ... well, it changes you."

Rachel felt a prickle of unease as his words sank in. She was almost afraid to ask but pressed him. "Changes you? How?"

Monte chuckled softly. "You start seeing people for who they are. Their weaknesses, their desires ... what drives them. It's fascinating, really. Professor Lockhart, for example—"

There it was! A specific reference to Lockhart.

"—he wants everyone to think he's driven by a noble quest for academic or historical truths." Monte's eyes met hers, holding her gaze with an intensity that made her skin crawl. "I know better. By now, you probably do, too. I know what he truly craves, and it's not the truth—it's possession."

Rachel blinked, trying to understand. "Possession?" She was pretty sure she knew what he meant. "Abigail Townsend?" she said tentatively.

"To Lockhart, she's not just a historical figure; she's his passion. But I suppose you've already seen that side of him."

Rachel's heart quickened, and she tried to mask her growing dread. "I've ... heard stories," she replied carefully.

Monte's grin widened slightly as if amused by her cautious

response. "A man like him—he doesn't let rules or regulations stand in the way of his goals. He removes the barriers. When you're obsessed with something, the lines between right and wrong, good and bad, blur, and what seems unthinkable becomes justifiable. If someone else has what you want ..." He let the sentence trail off as if the rest was too obvious to state.

Rachel felt a chill run through her, her mind racing to connect the dots. "And you ... you know all of this because ...?"

Monte's eyes held that faraway look again, a shadow of something dark and contemplative lurking behind his words. He seemed almost lost in thought until Rachel's voice broke the silence. "So ... are you saying Lockhart would go to extremes to get his hands on anything related to Abigail Townsend? Maybe her manuscript?"

Monte's expression hardened, and a brief flicker of annoyance appeared in his eyes. His voice was laced with irritation. "You're not following me, Rachel. You think Lockhart would steal that manuscript? Forget it. That would mean he murdered Dr. Fieldstone, too, because there isn't one crime without the other. But Lockhart's not bold enough to get his hands dirty."

Rachel felt her face flush, sensing she had misinterpreted. "Well, I just ... from what you seemed to be saying, I almost ..." she stammered, feeling foolish under Monte's scrutinizing gaze.

Monte ran a hand through his hair in frustration. "I thought you were sharper, Rachel. But maybe I'm glad you're not." He shook his head slowly. "Believe me, the professor doesn't have the guts—or the brains—to do something like that."

Rachel opened her mouth to respond, but Monte wasn't finished. He leaned forward, his eyes narrowing with exasperation. "Lockhart's a coward," he continued, barely whispering. "He's a spineless collector of other people's achievements. He thrives on manipulating others to do his dirty work while he basks in the glory. The man would sooner bribe, beg, or weasel his way into getting what he wants than take matters into his own hands. You think he's capable of ... murder?"

Rachel blinked, caught off guard by the intensity of his response. "That was a terrible thing for me to think. I'm sorry. But if it wasn't Lockhart ..." she began, her voice trailing off as her mind raced.

Monte rolled his eyes, letting out a short, mirthless laugh. "Let me clarify. Lockhart may be obsessive, but he's not a risk-taker. The man is a relic hunter, not a killer. And if he had the manuscript, he'd be parading it around like a trophy. The way he does with Abigail Townsend's brooch—which he spent years searching for and only found because that handwritten letter in the manuscript gave him the answer to its whereabouts."

"You know this for sure?" Rachel asked, her voice edged with unease.

Monte's smile darkened. "I know a lot of things for sure about Lockhart. Assistants always do. Bosses are stupid if they think we're blind. We see everything—every scheme, every lie, every weakness. And some of us," he said, his tone sharpening, "keep a record. Not because we're spiteful. Not at first, anyway. But in case we need it someday. And let me tell you, Lockhart gave me plenty to work with. And what better way to destroy him than to take the one thing he could never truly own? He'll never own Abigail Townsend's *Vanity and Virtue*. Someone has made sure of that."

Rachel felt a creeping sense of dread. "Then ... if Lockhart didn't steal the manuscript ..." she began, her voice faltering. The realization left Rachel terrified, her mind whirling with what she had learned.

Monte's eyes flashed with something dark, his smile tightening. He didn't confirm her thoughts outright, but the way he tilted his head, his silence spoke volumes. "Let's say, if you know someone's weakness, it's surprisingly easy to make them suffer."

Rachel's pulse quickened, and her stomach turned as she grasped what Monte was implying. She turned away abruptly, the festival's cheerful atmosphere feeling jarringly distant, as though it belonged to another world entirely—a world where people didn't steal priceless manuscripts or murder someone because of vindictive obsessions.

28

As Polly walked with Tim and Tiara through the crowded street en route to the village library, she felt like a condemned prisoner being led to the gallows. Her heart pounded furiously, and there was a relentless drumbeat in her chest. *Why on earth did I agree to this? Dumb! Dumb! Dumb!*

The library's stone façade came into view, its arched entrance draped in ivy and a banner proclaiming MEET THE AUTHORS. As she reminded herself to breathe, Polly thought of the authors' questions she'd written and rehearsed. "Just get through this," she muttered, clutching her notes. "One question, one moment at a time."

The weight of all she needed to accomplish this day: the Q&As, her performance of *Vanity and Virtue*, the accusation of murder she would level toward Professor Lockhart—pressed down on her. Polly arrived at the library entrance, pausing for a moment to collect herself. She took a deep breath, squared her shoulders, and reached for the door handle. She needed to project confidence, even if she was faking it.

Just as her fingers touched the cool steel, she heard someone call her name. "Polly!" The voice was urgent, almost breathless. She turned to see Rachel Hawthorne hurrying toward her, weaving her way through the crowd. Something in Rachel's expression stopped Polly short. There was a look of alarm in her eyes.

Rachel took a second to catch her breath. "Polly," she began, lowering her voice, "I think ... I think you might be wrong about Professor Lockhart."

Polly glanced nervously at the library door, her responsibilities looming on the other side. But Rachel's words anchored her in place.

"I ran into Monte Addington. Professor Lockhart's former assistant? The one who was fired, and I took his place? Remember?" Rachel hesitated, her brow furrowing as she chose her words carefully. "He said some strange things. About being sacked by Lockhart ... about revenge—destroying someone who destroyed him—and taking away the things they cherished most. And then he said Lockhart was a spineless coward who wouldn't have the guts or the brains to steal the manuscript ... or kill Jonathan Fieldstone."

Rachel's voice dropped, almost as if she were afraid to say it aloud. "But the way Monte said it—it was weird, Polly. Like he wanted me to connect the dots but didn't want to say it outright. He kept talking about revenge, about taking away what Lockhart valued most, and I couldn't help but wonder ..."

She paused, her unease palpable. "Maybe it wasn't Professor Lockhart. As much as I dislike him, murder and theft don't fit his profile. He's arrogant, yes, but he's meticulous—too careful and academic to risk his reputation on something so reckless. Monte, on the other hand ... he's different. Being fired devastated him—left him bitter and humiliated. If Monte thought stealing the manuscript would get back at Lockhart or prove his own worth, it adds up. And as for Jonathan ... maybe Monte didn't plan to kill him. Maybe it happened because Jonathan got in the way."

Polly's eyes narrowed. "So this Monte person is a disgruntled ex-assistant skulking around the festival, spouting bitter philosophies like some rejected Shakespearean villain? Rachel, people who rant about revenge are usually all talk. They want someone to listen to how unfair the world has treated them. It's cheap therapy, that's all. It doesn't mean they're out there committing theft or ... murder."

Rachel hesitated. "Maybe. But Polly, Monte said if Lockhart had the manuscript, he's the type to be showing it off somehow, like he does Abigail's brooch. And her tooth, for crying out loud. Monte said some crazy things. His veiled threats suggest he's capable of revenge, and his anger gives him motive. He even talked about knowing Lockhart's 'weaknesses' and how to hurt him."

Polly crossed her arms, frowning as Rachel's words sank in. "Hurt him how? Revenge against Lockhart is one thing, but ... stealing the manuscript? Murder ...?"

Rachel pressed on. "Monte said something about 'balancing the scales'—which I took to mean revenge—and making someone 'watch everything they've chased disappear.' Like maybe the manuscript. And his dismissal of Lockhart as incapable of murder ..."

Polly's stomach twisted. Some of Rachel's reasoning made sense, but she shoved those arguments aside. "I don't know," she said, trying to reassure herself. Monte had never been on her radar as a suspect. Why would he be? He was Lockhart's assistant, barely noticeable during his brief time in the library. When Lockhart left, Monte did too. He was far removed from the chaos surrounding the investigation—wasn't he?

Polly clenched her jaw, her thoughts spinning in circles. Professor Lockhart was the perfect suspect—arrogant, obsessive, and entirely self-serving. Everything about him screamed guilty. The idea of shifting her suspicion to Monte felt like undoing all the careful logic she'd pieced together. It didn't make sense. No, it had to be Lockhart. Straightening her spine, Polly clung to her conclusion like a lifeline. "I've figured it all out," she said, her voice firm. "Every single sign points to Professor Lockhart. His obsession with Abigail Townsend drives everything he does. He wants to own her legacy, every piece of it."

But even as she spoke, doubt wormed its way in. Rachel's recounting of Monte's veiled threats and shadowy presence at the festival were not easy to dismiss. She unfolded her arms. "Rachel, I need to go."

"Just think about it, Polly. Monte might seem like a nobody, but sometimes those are the people capable of doing the unthinkable."

Polly nodded stiffly. She wasn't ready to let go of her conclusions about Lockhart, but Rachel's words lingered like a splinter under her skin. She took a steadying breath and turned toward the library door, bracing herself. She couldn't afford to be wrong —not now. She took one last steadying breath, turned to the library door, and pulled it open. "Showtime," she whispered. She could hear the low murmur of the audience, a gentle hum of conversation that only exaggerated her nerves.

At the front of the room was a small stage, a raised platform where story hour was usually held for children. It had been dressed up with a backdrop of deep red velvet curtains, their edges slightly worn but lending an air of charm to the setting. Two simple metal folding chairs sat side by side, angled slightly towards each other. And a single hand-held microphone rested on a table between them.

Polly's palms were clammy, and she consciously tried not to wipe them on her dress lest she appear even more frazzled than she felt. She stepped onto the platform, feeling the boards creak slightly beneath her feet. For a split second, she considered bolting—running out of the building and hiding behind the largest tree in the village green.

Polly Pepper! Get a grip. She scolded herself silently, taking another shaky breath. She scanned the audience, offering what she hoped was a warm, confident smile. Villagers and visitors filled the rows of mismatched chairs arranged to face the platform, their faces a sea of polite expectation. Her mind raced as she tried to organize her thoughts. But her carefully rehearsed lines were a jumbled mess.

Stay calm. Don't panic. Smile. "Good afternoon, everyone," she began, her voice a touch too high and breathy. She cleared her throat and forced a brighter tone. "Thank you all for joining us today. We have a wonderful lineup of authors, and I'm so pleased to welcome them to Abbots Clover and our wonderful annual literary festival."

Polly's voice steadied as she continued her introduction. The audience settled in, eyes focused on her, eager for the first author to be introduced. She adjusted her stance, feeling the edges of her anxiety blur as she invited Geraldine Macintosh to the stage. As Geraldine took her seat, Polly tried to ignore the beads of sweat forming at the nape of her neck. She could feel her heart still racing, a stubborn reminder of how much was riding on today.

Polly stole a quick glance at the audience, catching sight of familiar faces: Rose, Sarah, Terrence, Tim, and Tiara—each expecting her to pull this off without a hitch. She forced herself to focus, knowing that letting her nerves win wasn't an option.

"Geraldine," Polly managed, her voice steady, as she glanced at a note card, "your latest book, *Passion of the Phantom*, has been described as a 'heart-wrenching tale of love between a centuries-old ghost and a modern-day pastry chef.' And you include recipes, too! That's hopping on the culinary mystery bandwagon, isn't it? But quite original for a paranormal romance. What inspired this ... unique pairing?"

As Geraldine launched into a rehearsed explanation about her inspiration for her novel, Polly allowed herself a fleeting moment to recall what Rachel had told her about Professor Lockhart's assistant, Monte. Monte, of all people! Rachel's words wouldn't stop echoing in her head. Something about Monte "balancing the scales, exacting revenge against his former boss, making someone watch everything they've chased disappear." Maybe meaning Abigail's manuscript? And Monte's dismissal of Lockhart as incapable of murder, the implication being ...

Polly forced herself to nod politely at Geraldine's animated discourse, but her thoughts were miles away. Had she gotten the mystery wrong all along? No, she couldn't have. Professor Lockhart was guilty as sin; every clue reinforced that. The professor's obsession had driven him to murder. But Monte's presence at the festival and his remarks to Rachel hinted at something different—a vendetta born out of resentment and the desire to best his former employer.

Monte had been the professor's right hand, privy to Lockhart's secrets and ambitions. He'd been sacked. And now, maybe Monte had found a way to seize control of the narrative, to claim the one thing of Abigail's that Lockhart could never own: the manuscript.

Polly's fingers tightened imperceptibly around her notecards. If Monte had stolen Abigail's manuscript, maybe it was an act of rebellion, a way to assert his independence from the man who had cast him aside. But the implications went further than that. Dr. Fieldstone had been murdered, and if Monte had been the one to take the manuscript, it was possible he had gone a step further to protect his prize. *Find the manuscript, and you'll find the killer.*

A fresh wave of doubt washed over Polly. She glanced at the

audience, their faces attentive, and forced a small smile to keep up appearances. *Stay focused, Polly*, she told herself. But the certainty of Lockhart's guilt she'd felt only a short while ago was slipping away.

"—and that's why I always recommend adding a dash of cinnamon to spectral shortbread!" Geraldine finished with a flourish, her eyes twinkling with delight.

Polly blinked, catching only the last bit of Geraldine's talk. "Thank you, Geraldine," she said, her voice steady, though her thoughts were anything but. "It sounds so good, I'd half expect Julia Child to appear in my kitchen, wielding a rolling pin and demanding more butter."

The audience applauded, but Polly barely registered the sound. Her mind buzzed, trying to fit the jagged pieces of the mystery into a coherent picture. As the next author was invited to the stage, Polly straightened in her chair, nodding and smiling in all the right places. But behind her polite demeanor, her thoughts churned relentlessly. The plan she'd concocted earlier replayed in her mind, each step designed to corner Professor Lockhart.

It was bold, perhaps too bold. One misstep and she could tip her hand too soon, giving him the chance to cover his tracks—or worse, to slip away altogether. But if she executed it perfectly, she could draw Lockhart out and force him to react in front of everyone. Timing would be crucial. She needed the right moment to set her trap.

As the last interview wrapped up, Polly realized the program had gone way over schedule, and it was nearly time for her big event in the marquee that had been erected in Bart Jamison's cow field. She'd prepared all she could for the performance, and now it was time to hustle clear across the village to her stage in the tent and change into her costume.

29

With Tim and Tiara in tow, Polly arrived at the marquee to find a sold-out audience. She glanced around the tent, taking in the faces of villagers and visitors, all eagerly waiting for the main event. Exhaling slowly, the butterflies in her stomach felt more like a murder of mischievous crows. Her eyes narrowed when she spotted Professor Lockhart seated squarely in the center of the front row. She placed a steadying hand on Tim's arm and leaned in, her voice barely above a whisper. "Make sure Gray is standing by," she said. "There might be a ... development."

Tiara's smile was encouraging. "Polly," she said, her voice gentle, "you're going to be brilliant. You've practiced this a million times and have the chops to pull it off. Just ... take a breath and remember who *you* are up there."

Polly closed her eyes briefly, letting Tiara's words sink in. She knew who she was: a woman who, like Abigail Townsend, had faced down fears and doubts more times than she could count. A woman now embodying the spirit of a strong, like-minded woman who had lived two hundred years ago. "Bless you," Polly whispered, gripping Tiara's hand.

Tim glanced towards the stage, then back at Polly. "Okay," he said firmly, "you've got this. But we'll be here if you need us."

Polly nodded, taking a deep breath. "Showtime," she murmured, steeling her nerves for what would come. She stood center stage, the spotlight pooling around her like a halo, and adjusted her dress—a sweeping, period-appropriate gown that billowed slightly with her movement. Over her shoulders, a delicate shawl, styled as Abigail Townsend might have worn it, completed the transformation. The tent theater became silent, the audience in intense anticipation.

Without introduction, Polly took a steadying breath and raised her chin. She let the onlookers' energy settle over her, drawing her into the moment. Then, with a slightly haughty tone, she began to speak, slipping seamlessly into Abigail's persona. "It is an odd thing, is it not?" she said, her voice steady and resonant, carrying a hint of indignation. "To be pursued in death as you were in life—as if one's spirit could be captured and claimed by those with idle ambitions."

Polly felt the audience leaning into her words, their collective anticipation almost tangible in the charged air. The faint rustle of movement had stilled, replaced by a quiet intensity that told her they were fully with her, hanging on every line. She, too, was slipping deeper into Abigail's mindset, the lines blurring between past and present, reality and fiction. This wasn't a performance—it was something electric, a rare harmony between actor and audience. Polly had rehearsed this monologue a dozen times, but today, something felt profoundly different. A current ran through her words and body, a visceral energy she had only experienced a handful of times in her career.

"Legacy, they call it," Polly continued, her voice moving through the stillness. "A noble cause, they claim. But where is the nobility in theft? In prying secrets from the bones of the dead." She paused, the weight of her words hanging in the air.

"And yet, there are those who believe themselves justified, as if the mere possession of a relic could bind them to a person in the past."

A chill ran down Polly's spine, and she shivered involuntarily. Ever since she first held Abigail Townsend's manuscript, she had felt a deep connection to the writer—a shared kinship with her independence and tenacity. But today, that connection felt stronger, almost visceral, as if Abigail's presence lingered in the room, watching from beyond the veil of time. Polly's breath quickened, and she tried to steady herself, her chest tightening with a strange sense of foreboding. Something's different, she thought, the realization brushing against her mind like a shadow she couldn't quite catch.

She pressed on, driven by an inexplicable urgency, as if someone were guiding her, pushing her forward. "It is a cruel fate," she continued, her voice faltering slightly, "to be hunted even in death ... one's legacy twisted and contorted by the whims of those who wish to claim ownership of you." Her eyes scanned the audience, searching their faces as if seeking answers. And then, as she spoke the next line, something within her shifted—a sudden, almost overwhelming sense of clarity.

"They believe they can steal from me and possess what is not theirs. But I shall not be bound by their chains nor let them deceive those who seek the truth." A strange sensation washed over Polly, a feeling almost like an embrace—a soft, ethereal presence, as if Abigail's spirit had intertwined with her own. Polly couldn't even blink; her vision blurred momentarily as the world seemed to sway around her. The audience faded into the background, and all she could hear was the rhythmic pounding of her own heartbeat. It was as if Abigail's voice was whispering in her ear, urging her forward, guiding her thoughts and the dialogue she didn't recall rehearsing.

"Like my father, another man is not to be believed," Polly

declared, her voice low and almost reverent, each word landing with deliberate force. It felt like Abigail's spirit had taken hold of her voice and was steering her performance. "This man covets what is not his, and he would take what belongs to me."

A murmur rippled through the audience, but Polly barely noticed. Her thoughts were racing, puzzle pieces rearranging in her mind. Lockhart had stolen Abigail's brooch—of that, she was certain. The physical evidence proved it. But as her gaze swept the room, her mind snagged on something Rachel had said earlier: Lockhart would flaunt the manuscript if he had it, as he did with the brooch and other bits of Abigail's legacy. That wasn't the behavior of someone who'd need to kill to cover his tracks. The realization struck her like a flash of lightning: Lockhart hadn't taken the manuscript, nor had he taken Jonathan Fieldstone's life. Someone else had.

"Desperation breeds many things," Polly continued, her voice growing more insistent. "Weakness, yes. Obsession, certainly. Murder?" Polly's mind flashed back to an incident from years ago, during her days as the star of her hit TV show. There had been a junior writer, Ian Fuches, who had seemed promising at first—eager, talented, and brimming with ideas. But Ian's ambition had outpaced his patience, and his behavior had grown erratic when Polly rejected his increasingly far-fetched comedy sketch plotlines. She'd had to let him go.

Standing on the stage now, Polly felt that familiar chill creep up her spine. Ian's bitterness had driven him to attempt to sabotage and smear Polly's good name, but he hadn't had the opportunity to do anything worse. Monte, on the other hand ... Had he found a way to get even with Professor Lockhart?

It all somehow seemed to make sense now to Polly. She took a deep, shuddering breath, the lines between reality and performance blurring in her mind. Polly glanced at the audience, her heart pounding furiously, but there was a strange sense of calm beneath the storm. It was as if Abigail's presence had given her the strength to face the truth, no matter how unsettling it might be.

"I shall not be bound by the lies of the living," Polly said, her voice resonant with a finality that sent a shiver down her spine. "For the truth shall rise." Her voice seemed to linger in the air, heavy with the weight of Abigail's presence. For a moment, she felt utterly connected to the woman whose words she was speaking, as if Abigail herself had come to finish what she could not in life. Her voice resonated in the silence, and the audience seemed to be holding a collective breath, waiting for her next line.

Then, Professor Lockhart abruptly shot to his feet, his voice booming across the tent. "That's not how Abigail Townsend talks!" He huffed loudly, storming toward the exit, but paused mid-stride to turn back toward the stage. "A travesty, Miss Polly Pepper!" he bellowed, his face flushed with indignation. "I know Abigail Townsend better than anyone alive or who has ever lived, and what you're presenting is pure fiction—fantasy spun for your amusement and ego!"

Polly met his gaze, her face impassive. She'd faced her share of hecklers and unruly audiences throughout the years and could usually handle them light-heartedly. "Some things are not as fictional as they appear, Professor," she replied calmly, her voice carrying through the hushed audience.

She could feel every eye on her. But she wasn't finished yet—not by a long shot. Before Lockhart could respond, there was a sudden movement near the front of the audience. Rachel Hawthorne, her face pale but determined, rose from her seat. She moved toward the front row and hesitated momentarily, as if weighing her thoughts. Then she turned to Polly, her voice trembling slightly. "You're not *playing* Abigail right now, are you, Polly? She's here. You know the truth."

Polly took a breath, her resolve hardening. "I know *a* truth," she said. The words held a weight that sent a ripple of tension through the audience. "I know Abigail. She has spoken to us exactly as she would have in life."

Rachel swallowed hard, glancing at Professor Lockhart before turning back to Polly. "Let Abigail speak."

Before Polly could respond, another figure emerged from the shadows—Monte Addington. He stepped forward, his face a mask of indifference. But something dark lurked in his eyes, a flicker of anger and hostility.

"This is quite the show you're putting on, Miss Pepper," Monte said, his voice thick with sarcasm. "A theater is supposed to be a place where stories come to life, and we escape reality. So kudos for staying on theme. But if you expect us to believe the spirit of Abigail Townsend decided to make a guest appearance today, you might need to add 'medium' to your résumé along-side 'funny lady.'"

Polly met his gaze. She took a deep breath, feeling a strange calm settle over her. "This wasn't a performance. I know who took Abigail Townsend's manuscript—and Dr. Fieldstone's life."

A collective gasp rippled through the audience, followed by silence. All eyes were fixed on Polly. The weight of her words hung in the air, drawing everyone to the edge of their seats. Even the rustling of the tent fabric seemed to pause, as though the entire world was holding its breath.

Monte shifted uneasily, his composure beginning to crack. "You're absurd," he muttered, but his voice had no conviction—only a rising sense of panic.

Polly pressed on, her gaze unwavering as she locked eyes with Monte. "You were Professor Lockhart's assistant," she said, her voice steady but cutting, making sure the audience under-stood his connection to the professor. "You had access to all his research, his secrets, his ambitions. You knew Abigail

Townsend almost as intimately as he did—absorbing every detail through him. But then he sacked you, stripped you of your position, your pride, and your purpose. All he left you with was indignation, bitterness, and a burning desire for revenge."

Monte's face paled, his façade starting to fracture under the weight of her words. His jaw was clenched so tightly the muscle in his temple twitched. His eyes sought out Rachel Hawthorne, and he glared at her.

Polly continued, her voice gaining strength with each word. "You knew about the manuscript and where it was kept because you were there at the library—if only for a few days. The combination to the safe was in Dr. Fieldstone's notebook, which Rachel inadvertently left out while away for a few minutes one afternoon. You had access to it. I believe you stole the manuscript—not out of scholarly ambition but out of a desire to obtain something the Professor coveted but could never own. To show him the one he cast aside was more cunning, resourceful, and ruthless than he could ever be."

A murmur rippled through the audience like an electric current, and Polly saw Monte's face go even paler as the implications sank in. "But there's more," Polly said, her voice lowering ominously. "Dr. Fieldstone returned to the library the afternoon he died to collect that notebook—which he'd accidentally left behind. When he walked in, he saw you taking the manuscript, didn't he? And in that split second, you had a choice—to flee or to silence him. It could have been Rose the librarian who'd walked in, if she'd been so unlucky."

Monte's eyes darted around the tent, searching frantically for a way out, but there was nowhere to go.

Polly took a step forward on the stage, her voice sharp. "You chose to kill him," she said, the words ringing out like a verdict in a courtroom. "You took Dr. Fieldstone's life so you could keep hold of the manuscript and boast about it to Professor Lockhart."

Monte's lips parted as if to protest, but no words came out. He swallowed hard, his Adam's apple bobbing. The audience collectively held their breath, waiting for what he would say next. Monte's composure cracked further. His pale face flushed, and his eyes darted wildly, landing briefly on the tent's exit. He took a halting step backward, then forward again, like a cornered animal searching for escape.

The tension in the room thickened, and Polly, still center stage, noticed the shift in his demeanor. *He's going to do something.*

Before she could react, Monte lunged toward the stage, his movements frantic, his face contorted with a mix of anger and fear. Gasps erupted from the audience as he stormed the stage.

Polly instinctively stepped back, but her billowing dress caught on the edge of the prop table, sending a cascade of books clattering to the floor.

"Stop this!" Monte hissed, his voice hoarse with rage. "You don't know what you're talking about!"

Polly's heart raced, her mind scrambling for what to do next.

Monte took another step forward, his hands clenching into fists, and for a moment, Polly wondered if he would strike her— or worse.

"Monte, stand down! Now!" Constable Grayson Jenkins's voice rang out, sharp and unyielding, slicing through the chaos like a whip. "Take one more step, and you'll regret it."

Monte froze, his head snapping toward the voice. The uniformed constable, accompanied by two other officers, advanced with speed, his hand hovering near the Taser clipped to his belt. Monte's eyes darted between Grayson and the exit again, but the presence of the officers—and the collective attention of the audience—rooted him in place.

"Monte Addington, I am arresting you on suspicion of the murder of Dr. Jonathan Fieldstone and the theft of property," Grayson shouted. "You do not have to say anything, but it may harm your defense if you do not mention when questioned something you later rely on in court. Anything you do say may be given in evidence."

As the officers moved in to take him into custody, Monte's face crumpled, the defiance draining away. He didn't argue or struggle. He did as he was instructed to do, as he always had while working for Professor Lockhart and probably every other job he'd ever held. He stared at Polly with a momentary look that resembled resignation, as if he had been expecting this moment all along.

As the officers escorted Monte to the exit, Professor Lockhart approached the stage, his smugness barely concealed. He clapped his hands together, his face alight with exaggerated admiration. "Miss Polly Pepper, what an extraordinary performance!" he gushed, his voice oozing with oily enthusiasm. "I apologize for my earlier outburst. Your brilliance knows no bounds! I was skeptical, but you've achieved what no one else could have: uncovering the truth behind Dr. Fieldstone's tragic murder. Remarkable, simply remarkable."

He paused, bowing his head in a theatrical display of deference, his tone dipping into near reverence. "I don't know how any of us can ever thank you. And may I dare to hope your extraordinary powers of deduction might also uncover the fate of Abigail Townsend's manuscript?" His lips curved into a self-satisfied smile, his shoulders relaxing as though a great weight had been lifted. He straightened his jacket, absently touching his lapel.

Polly turned her gaze to him, a small, knowing smile playing at the corners of her lips. "Thank you, Professor Lockhart," she began smoothly, her tone almost indulgent, "I appreciate your praise. And yes, I'm quite hopeful about the manuscript's return. It will undoubtedly be among Monte Addington's possessions."

Lockhart gave a small, approving nod, clearly savoring what he thought was a shared moment of triumph.

Polly paused, letting the silence stretch, her eyes narrowing slightly. Lockhart's smile faltered, for a moment, as though he'd caught the faintest whiff of danger. Then her voice took on a sharper edge, cutting through his smugness. "But there's something else we need to address. You've spent your life pursuing Abigail's legacy, Professor, chasing her every word, every artifact. You allowed your obsession to consume you."

Lockhart blinked, his self-assured mask slipping ever so slightly. "I ... I don't quite follow," he stammered, his fingers fidgeting with his lapel.

Polly stepped closer to the edge of the stage, her gaze locking on to his with laser-like precision. "You're a thief, Professor, like Monte Addington. You stole Abigail's brooch—the one you so brazenly display on your lapel right now—from its resting place in St. Clematis. A sanctuary, might I remind you, you defiled with your greed."

Professor Lockhart's face blanched as his hand involuntarily reached for his lapel again. He took a quick look at the brooch, then quickly regained his composure. A bitter laugh escaped his lips. "You're nuts, lady. What are you even talking about?" His voice dripped with indignation. "On what proof do you base this ludicrous assertion?"

Polly met his gaze without flinching. "It isn't ludicrous, Professor," she replied calmly. Reaching into a pocket in her dress, she retrieved her cell phone. She held it up for the audience to see. "I deal in facts, Professor. Just as you, as an academic, were trained to do. "This," Polly continued, her voice steady and resolute, "is a photograph of your signet ring ..."

Lockhart instantly looked down at his ring finger.

"You know exactly where it is: resting in the secret drawer in the altar in St. Clematis where Abigail's brooch—the one you're wearing—was hidden for over two hundred years. A signet ring bearing the seal of your alma mater. Oxford University. I suspect you imagined your ring was an exchange for Abigail's gold brooch. Or perhaps you were exchanging gifts with your beloved."

A ripple of murmurs spread through the audience as they leaned forward, eyes straining to see what was on Polly's phone screen.

Lockhart's eyes widened, and his breath caught in his throat as he recognized the ring. His face turned ashen. "That's ... You can't believe ... How did you ...? You can't prove that's mine," he stammered, his voice barely above a whisper.

Polly cut him off, her tone sharp and unyielding. "Perhaps the inscription inside— 'Congratulations Richard'—was a reference to Richard Attenborough. Or Richard Branson. Or Richard Gere." She paused, her gaze piercing. "And that wee acorn beside it? A fascinating embellishment.

"I think you wanted to honor Abigail Townsend. To leave something you cherished to someone you loved," Polly continued, her voice steady. "Or maybe it was your way of proving your devotion to her legacy. Either way, it was a foolish mistake, Professor. You left behind your own provable token of guilt. Of course, you never believed your ring would ever be found. After all, you were the first in two hundred years to figure out the riddle of the oak tree." And you thought it would be another two hundred years—if ever—before anyone else solved it."

Lockhart's expression faltered. He opened his mouth to respond, hesitated, and then with a trembling voice said, "You don't understand. Abigail ... Abigail is my soulmate." He paused, his pale eyes locking onto Polly's. "She wasn't just a literary figure. She isn't. We know each other intimately. Across time. Across lives. She speaks to me."

Polly blinked, her brow furrowing as she tried to process Lockhart's words. "You sound as if you're lovers," she said, disbelief thickening her voice.

Lockhart's gaze burned with intensity. "More profound than that," he said, his tone low but unwavering, as if daring Polly—or anyone in the tent—to challenge him. "I have proof—definitive proof. The initials on the note hidden in the manuscript: 'RL.' That's me. Richard Lockhart! The moment I saw that, I realized I'd written it ... in eighteen twenty."

A gasp rippled through the audience, followed by murmurs that grew louder with each passing second. Polly felt the air in the tent grow heavier, the collective skepticism almost tangible. She glanced at the faces staring at Lockhart—some wide-eyed, others narrowing in suspicion, a few shaking their heads in outright disbelief.

Polly turned back to Lockhart, her lips parting as she tried to form a response. Her mind raced, torn between dismissing his claim outright and probing further into his delusion. *Could he truly believe this?* she thought, a chill running down her spine. "That's ... quite an assertion," she said finally, her voice carefully measured. "You're saying you—Richard Lockhart—somehow wrote that note in Abigail Townsend's time? Two hundred years ago?"

Lockhart lifted his chin, his expression resolute. "Yes," he said, the conviction in his voice sending another wave of unease through the crowd.

Polly's stomach tightened. She had dealt with her fair share of eccentrics over the years, but this? The weight of his delusion —or arrogance—made her chest tighten. She couldn't tell whether he was spinning a wild fabrication or fully believed his words, and that uncertainty only deepened the unease in the room.

"It's true," Lockhart continued. "Abigail wanted me to have her brooch. She left clues. A trail of breadcrumbs leading directly to it. I've spent years poring over her letters, her diaries —each one pulling me closer to her and what she wanted me to find. She meant for me to have it, to protect it for her. Don't you see? It's all connected. The manuscript, the brooch, the riddle— it was all meant to bring her back to me."

Polly nodded, trying to comprehend Lockhart's fantasy. In a way, she could almost understand his adoration for Abigail. She herself felt a deep connection to Dolores Gray, a singer/actress she'd never met or seen on stage and only heard on the cast recording of an old Broadway musical, *Destry Rides Again*. "Your obsession consumes you. What would Abigail think of the lengths you've gone to? And the people you've hurt along the way?"

Lockhart shrugged. He lowered his head, his voice barely above a whisper. "I was doing it for her. For us."

Grayson now approached him, handcuffs glinting in the tent's half-light. Lockhart didn't resist as his wrists were secured, his shoulders sagging in defeat, the life he had built around his obsession was collapsing like a sandcastle under a relentless tide.

Polly watched as Monte and Professor Lockhart were led away, her heart heavy with the knowledge of what had transpired. The past had been unearthed but at a great cost. The weight of it all settled over her, exhaustion threatening to pull her under.

The audience stirred, the initial shock giving way to a low hum of whispered conversation and questions. Polly took a deep breath before addressing them again. "Ladies and gentlemen," she said, her voice weary but resolute, "the past is never truly gone, I guess—it lingers in the shadows, waiting for someone to bring it into the light again."

She paused, her eyes scanning the audience, meeting the gazes of those who had witnessed the unraveling of long-buried secrets. The air was thick with the weight of revelation. Then the audience erupted into applause—not the usual polite clapping, but a solemn, respectful acknowledgment of the truth Polly had brought to light.

The energy in the tent was electric. Polly stood there, her heart pounding furiously, the exhaustion of the day and the past few weeks threatening to overwhelm her. But beneath the fatigue, there was a sense of fulfillment. A truth had been uncovered, and those responsible for the murder of Jonathan Fieldstone and the theft of Abigail Townsend's manuscript and her gold brooch would face their reckoning.

The applause began to fade, and the audience waited, almost holding their breath in anticipation of what might happen next.

For a fleeting moment, Polly considered stepping off the stage. But then she remembered why she was there in the first place: why they had all gathered in this tent on a rare sunny afternoon at the literary festival. She took a deep breath and straightened her shoulders. "Ladies and gentlemen," she said, her voice carrying a new strength, "you came here to see and hear a story about love, loss, ambition, and betrayal. And while we've uncovered the final chapter of one tale, the story you came for still needs to be told. Hell, I didn't cram myself into this damn corset to leave you all hanging."

Laughter erupted, and the audience began to chant, "Show ... must ... go ... on! Show ... must ... go ... on!"

Polly felt the tension in the room dissolve, a collective exhale from the audience seemed to breathe life into her. Her gaze fell to another table, where the prop version of *Vanity and Virtue* lay.

With deliberate care, she picked it up, cradling it against her chest as if it were Abigail's spirit itself.

The audience leaned in, spellbound, their faces a sea of rapt attention. Polly felt the familiar, electric rush of adrenaline coursing through her veins, the one that came only when she was fully immersed in a performance. This wasn't a role—it was a bridge, a way to breathe life into words that had waited centuries to be heard.

Polly's earlier exhaustion melted away as she stood taller, embodying Abigail's defiance and courage. Abigail Townsend, who had fought to carve out her place in a world that sought to silence her, felt vividly present in this moment. As Polly looked into the sea of faces before her, she knew with unwavering certainty the stage was where she belonged—it was where Abigail's voice could finally be heard again, echoing across the centuries.

"The world did not understand the weight of my secrets," she said, her head held high, "but secrets, like shadows, are only hidden until there is light, when the darkness can no longer protect them ..."

EPILOGUE

Abbots Clover's annual literary festival had been a triumph unlike any in its storied history. Attendance had soared to record-breaking numbers. Visitors came from neighboring villages and as far away as Bristol and London. Vendors reported unprecedented sales. The Fox & Hare pub had run out of ale. And Bound to Read sold more copies of *Shadows at Midnight* in two days than in the previous six months.

Every corner of the village was still buzzing with chatter about Polly Pepper's theatrical performance, her daring accusations, and the arrests of Professor Lockhart and Monte Addington. Not to mention the recovery of Abigail Townsend's *Vanity and Virtue* manuscript.

Now, with the festival concluded, a different celebration was underway at Thistlethorne Lodge.

Polly sat on the Chesterfield in the reception room, her legs tucked beneath her, a flute of champagne in hand. Beside her, Mr. Boots lounged with regal nonchalance, lazily flicking his tail as if to say, *Sure, lady, you cracked the case, but who led you to the manuscript in the first place?* Polly smirked at that thought before letting her gaze drift around the room. The familiar faces of her inner circle came into focus—tired yet content, their shared trials of the past few weeks seeming to have drawn them even closer together.

For a long while, no one spoke. Only the sounds from the crackling fire and Billie Holiday's sultry voice over the stereo speakers filled the air. Tim finally broke the silence. Swirling his champagne with mock casualness, he said, "So, Mom, what's the plan? Have you had enough of chasing sociopathic killers for a while?"

Polly smiled faintly, her fingers idly stroking Mr. Boots's fur. She took a sip of champagne, letting the moment stretch long enough for everyone to lean in, anticipating her response. "I've been thinking about that," she finally said, her tone contemplative. "I'm definitely taking time off from drama. No more stodgy academics with obsessive delusions about two-hundred-year-dead authors. No more assistants with inferiority complexes wreaking revenge on their bosses. I want to take it easy—with Terrence." She reached for his hand and gave it a gentle squeeze. After a pause, giving weight to her next words, she said, "And ... I've decided to relinquish my claim to the manuscript."

The room erupted in a chorus of shock. Heads snapped toward her, and their collective gasp seemed to suck all the air out of the room.

"What?" Tiara's voice cut through the stunned silence, her wine glass tipping dangerously. "After all you've gone through? Have you lost your marbles? You need the money from selling the manuscript to fix up this crumbling pile. I hope you have some miracle crowdfunding plan!"

Polly held up a hand. "Some things are bigger than money. Although I never in a million trillion years thought I'd ever say *that!*" She took another sip of champagne before continuing, "I've come to realize *Vanity and Virtue* belongs to Abbots Clover. It's part of the village's cultural legacy. It could be displayed in the library and draw tourists—and prevent Arthur Townsend from getting his mitts on it for whatever self-serving plans he's hatching."

Rose's eyes shone with gratitude. "Polly, that's ... incredibly generous. Now, everyone will be able to see it. That's what Jonathan hoped for. And me, too. He'd be proud of you. I am."

Sarah, perched on the arm of a wingback chair, raised her glass. "Think of all the people queuing to see it, like the Domesday Book or the Treaty of Versailles. And it's in the public domain, so I can sell copies in the bookshop. Most importantly, Abigail Townsend will be remembered—and published again."

Elliot leaned back in his chair, fingers intertwined with Tiara's and thoughtfully swirled the last sip of his drink. "Polly," he began, his voice carrying a note of intrigue, "you know, there's still a way for you to turn *Vanity and Virtue* into a money source. Give your one-woman show another run."

Polly tilted her head, arching a skeptical brow. "Another run? Elliot, I've barely recovered from the first one. It's exhausting being Abigail Townsend reincarnate."

"I'm serious," he said. "Your performance was terrific. You were Abigail Townsend, and the audience loved every second of it. Imagine taking the show on the road—tours across England. Maybe even America. Abigail's story deserves a bigger stage—and so do you. We'd have to expanded it by more than an hour, but there's plenty of material."

Tiara beamed, giving Elliot's hand an affectionate squeeze. "I knew I fell for a genius. A tour would be amazing, Polly—think of the repairs it could fund! And, naturally," she added with a mock-serious glance at Elliot, "you'll need to give this brilliant man an 'adapted by' credit. Polly Pepper might be the star, but you're not stealing *all* the thunder."

The room buzzed with animated agreement as everyone envisioned packed theatres and glowing reviews. As the laughter and chatter swirled, Polly leaned closer to Terrence. "I do have one regret from the past few weeks," she said softly.

He raised an eyebrow. "Not catching Monte sooner? Giving up the manuscript in an act of selflessness? Not absconding with the oak leaf brooch?"

She shook her head. "That I didn't realize sooner how important it is to make time for the people who matter. I've been so caught up in the murder and the missing manuscript I nearly overlooked the main character standing right in front of me."

Terrence's grin softened as he leaned closer, the teasing edge in his voice giving way to tenderness. "You've always followed your instincts, Polly, and they've never let you down. Whatever you decide, I'm with you—every step of the way." He kissed her gently, the warmth in his touch carrying quiet reassurance. "No regrets, Polly. Not now, not ever."

Polly and Terrence's kiss didn't go unnoticed. Emboldened, Elliot turned to Tiara, his hand brushing hers as their eyes met. With a spark of unspoken understanding, he leaned in, their lips meeting in a kiss that lingered with promises and possibilities.

When they finally pulled apart, Tiara tilted her head, a playful smile curving her lips. "So, this is what it's like living in one of your romance novels," she murmured, her voice teasing but her eyes glowing with affection.

Elliot chuckled, his voice low and warm. "This is going to be my first bestseller."

Tiara let out a soft laugh, her cheeks warm with passion as she leaned closer to him. "Only if you write a happy ending," she whispered, her tone half-serious.

Elliot's grin widened. "With you, Tiara, there's no other kind."

Across the room, Tim grinned at Grayson, giving him a playful nudge. "Well, it looks like everyone's in the mood for public displays of affection tonight." Before Grayson could comment, Tim pulled him into a kiss, their amorous giggles breaking through the intimate hush of the room.

Sarah raised her glass, her smile wry as she glanced around the room. "Well, it's clearly couples' night, and here I am, stuck in a love triangle with Rose and Mr. Boots. Let's be honest, though—Mr. Boots is the only one with real prospects. Cats don't need dating apps, they stare at you, and you're theirs." She sighed, then added with mock wistfulness, "Maybe I should start practicing my purr."

Mr. Boots flicked his tail in agreement, letting out a soft meow that said, *Maybe I'm just not as picky as you are.*

Terrence leaned forward and raised his glass to the group. "To mysteries solved and surviving a literary festival where Polly Pepper somehow didn't accuse half the village of murder."

The group laughed in agreement, their glasses raised as they toasted again. Even Mr. Boots let out a soft, approving meow as if to say, *I knew I'd solve this mystery—you're welcome.*

The laughter carried on, filling the room with warmth and camaraderie. Outside, the stars scattered across the English night sky as Thistlethorne Lodge stood resilient, its stories safe for another day—and another book.

ALSO BY RICHARD TYLER JORDAN

<u>Polly Pepper Cozy Mystery Series</u>

Murder and a Missing Manuscript

Shadows at Midnight

A Corpse in the Castle

Remains to be Scene

Final Curtain

A Talent for Murder

Set Sail for Murder

<u>LGBTQ+ Titles</u>

Strangers in the Night

Overnight Sensation

Gay Blades

One Night Stand

Breakfast at Timothy's

ABOUT THE AUTHOR

RICHARD TYLER JORDAN began his career in Hollywood, spending 30 years as a senior publicist at the Walt Disney Studios, where he worked on marketing campaigns for more than 500 feature films. He later turned to writing novels and is the author of the Polly Pepper cozy mystery series, including *Murder and a Missing Manuscript*, *Shadows at Midnight*, and *A Corpse in the Castle* and several more. He is also the author of the novels *Breakfast at Timothy's*, *Overnight Sensation*, *Strangers in the Night*, *Gay Blades*, and *One Night Stand*, among others. He also wrote the non-fiction book *But Darling, I'm Your Auntie Mame!* Jordan is an American expat writer living in a 500-year-old stone cottage in England. For more information about him, visit www.RichardTylerJordan.com.